SPARK AWAKENING

THE PROGENITOR SAGA

KATE CORCINO

I0615962

This is a work of fiction. Names, characters, places and incidents are either the product of the author's imagination or are used fictitiously. Any resemblance to actual persons, living or dead, business establishments, events, or locales is entirely coincidental.

Spark Awakening: The Progenitor Saga
COPYRIGHT © 2016 by Kate Corcino

No part of this book may be reproduced, copied, stored, scanned, transmitted or distributed in any form or by any means, including but not limited to mechanical, printed, or electronic form, without prior written permission of the author. Please do not participate in or encourage piracy of copyrighted materials in violation of the author's rights.
Contact Information: www.katecorcino.com

First paperback edition September 2016
All Rights Reserved.

Publishing History
First Edition, September, 2016
Print ISBN: 978-0-9907328-4-6

Published in the United States of America

For my parents,
who lit the spark of my creativity
and nurtured the flame.

And for my sibs...
John, who never guessed hand-me-down copies of SF/F and late-night D&D and Traveller games would grow into this;
Tim, because enthusiasm, listening, and time (yes, you are the niece & nephew whisperer) are a gift I can never repay;
and
Jenn, whose bravery and sense of adventure as she travels the world inspire me and my characters (yep, even the ones you don't like!).

I love you all.

SPARK AWAKENING

THE PROGENITOR SAGA

KATE CORCINO

ONE

Alex

Chips of stone fell to earth like spattering raindrops following the boom of his gun. In spite of the miss, the sound made him happy. No, not the sound. The woman lining up her next shot made him happy.

These moments fell on Alex's heart like a soft rain. They renewed him. They encouraged tender, soft things long hidden to unfurl and grow. They scared the shit out of him, not that he'd ever let it show.

He stood to the side and traced the line of Lena's body, her arms still extended and palms curled around his gun. More and more often this summer, he'd found himself watching her, committing some part of her—of them together—to memory. He wanted more of it all—more time, more them, more her.

She took a long, shaky breath that became a sound somewhere between uneasy and laughter. When she spoke, her raised voice echoed in the canyon. He guessed her ears still rang.

"I did not expect to be able to see fire coming out the top of it."

"Gunpowder and Dust," Alex reminded her. He chuckled, and his warm breath puffed back from her skin as he leaned in to kiss the back of her neck. "Remind me again why I'm out here in the sun teaching you to fire a gun instead of back in the cabin playing find my favorite freckle?"

"I don't know why you're out here." She carefully sighted

down the barrel like he'd taught her. "But I'm out here because I believe in reciprocity. I teach. You teach." She slid her index finger from along the side of the gun and curled it so just the pad of her finger touched the trigger.

Damn, the woman learned fast.

The boom as his gun went off cracked against the canyon wall a half mile away and echoed back to them. Lena missed again, but her second shot landed closer. She turned her head to him with a cheeky grin. "Well, reciprocity, and because Thomas said I couldn't."

He snorted, believing her. She turned back to sight again. This time, she fired several shots in a row, took a breather, and finished the mag. Her last few shots caused bark to fly up and scatter from the big deadfall he'd leaned against a pair of boulders.

She sighed in satisfaction and looked back. "So why are you out here in the sun teaching me?"

"Because you asked." He flashed her a quick smirk and winked. "And because Thomas said I shouldn't."

"Clearly we both have issues with authority." She laughed, then her face became pensive. "What's his problem with me? Ever since we all got back, things have been…"

Alex shook his head. "It's not you."

Lena snorted. Alex couldn't blame her for doubting. Thomas had made a series of decisions without her that summer—starting with the decision at the Conclave to place the blame for a missing shipment of girls on her shoulders. Once they'd returned, she'd finally confessed that she'd overheard Fort Nevada men plotting to take her out. Alex had been raring to go hunt them down. Thomas had played it cool. He'd thought perhaps she was overreacting or having an emotional response to the decisions they'd made without her at Conclave.

That was bullshit. Thomas's responsibilities overwhelmed him, but he wouldn't delegate anything kicking his ass at this point. And the man couldn't or wouldn't see that all that frustration got dumped on Lena's shoulders.

"It's not you. We've reached critical mass at this

point…stretched thin and on the cusp of achieving what we've dreamed of. But we've also got new problems, new players. I think it's got him rattled. It's a lot to manage."

"He's just…dismissed all of my concerns. You were there. You were mad, too."

Thomas had told her he'd been working on finding the threat against her, but they'd found nothing, and they needed the men investigating elsewhere. If she could find more evidence, he'd draw them back again. It wasn't fair. And as Alex had expressed then, it wasn't smart, either.

Alex smiled down at her and stepped around to take the gun with one hand and stroke her cheek with the other. "He's overextended. It's not you."

A frown fluttered across her face, but his fingers on her skin had the desired effect. She smiled, willing to be soothed.

He dipped his head down and left a trail of soft kisses across her lips. "This is our last day out here…by ourselves…and I leave in the morning for six months. Maybe we should head back to the cabin. I can think of ways to make these last hours more memorable."

"How memorable?"

Instead of answering, he pulled her tight against him in a one-armed embrace and stole her breath with a long, deep kiss. When he pulled back, he was satisfied to see the heated, dreamy look in her eyes that he craved.

The rolling crack of a rockfall came from behind them. Alex spun, releasing the mag, and removing a spare from his belt to smack it into the gun. He raised the weapon.

They waited, but only the slither of earth settling back into place sounded off to the left. His eyes scanned for movement.

Lena laughed at Alex's automatic response. "It's just an animal—a cougar or a wild dog."

"Make me feel better." He pointed with his chin, eyes narrowed. "Check."

Still laughing, Lena focused her attention on the other side of the rocky canyon wall. She abruptly stopped laughing.

"It's a man." She automatically lowered her voice to a tense whisper. "Moving away and heading toward the red rock and pines up the other side of the canyon."

Alex nodded, grabbed the empty magazine from the ground, and ran to the wall that separated them from whomever had been watching a moment before. He refused to lose him. That meant sacrificing subtlety for speed.

He ignored the rocks that slid down behind him and crested the wall minutes later. Lena moved behind him and to his right. She silently pointed, indicating their prey moved away from what was left of the gravel road into rougher country of tumbled boulders and steep canyons. Alex didn't worry about losing the man. He had an advantage. He had Lena.

He cut across on the descent. At the bottom, Alex gestured her down the middle of the canyon with him, intent on pulling ahead.

They ran down the canyon. When he judged they might be ahead of their watcher, he glanced back at Lena to confirm.

Her eyes became faraway as she reached for the Dust. Her brows drew down. A moment passed before she shook her head.

"He's gone." She swallowed and made a slow circle. Alex knew she reached, asking the Dust to show her where the man hid. "It's not possible. But he's really gone."

"Gone?"

She raised one arm in the air. "How could he be gone somewhere I can't see him?"

"He can't be. He's not gone. He's hiding."

"Alex, he can't hide from the Dust."

"Unless he's using the Dust."

She stared at him. "How? I've never even..." She looked around, and a new fear rose in her eyes. "We need to go back."

"Lena—"

"We need to go back! If there's someone out here stalking me, and he can do that—the girls are in danger, too."

"We don't know that he was stalking you."

She tilted her head at him in disbelief.

He closed his eyes, acknowledging the truth. Between the Council and the hidden conspiracy at Fort Nevada, odds were someone stalked her. They needed to head in. He scanned the canyon around them one more time.

"You're right. We've got to get back. You've got to get to the girls, and I've got to report this to Thom and get a message to D—to Councilor Three."

She gave him a sharp look. "To D—Councilor Three?"

"I was going to say 'Dumbass'," he lied. "The man likes to think he can plan for himself." The second half wasn't a lie. Lena's brother Dan had definite ideas about how to lead Zone Three. Unfortunately, he was put in place by Alex. And Alex expected Dan to toe the line.

Part of toeing the line meant keeping his mouth shut and not trying to reach out to Lena. Alex planned to tell her the truth. He just wanted them stable enough to weather the deception first.

Alex couldn't believe he'd been so distracted by the Dust-hidden watcher that he'd almost slipped. He could see from Lena's face that she knew he'd held something back. Her eyes had clouded over, and she stepped away from him, her body a little more stiff.

"Let's head back then," was all she said. She turned away and started up the path to the cabin and the little electric vehicle that would return them to Fort Nevada. Their weekend interlude was over.

Alex swallowed. He couldn't keep lying to her. You didn't lie to someone you wanted to build a life with.

Not unless you know the truth might make her walk away for good.

Alex couldn't risk that.

They drove back in silence. Alex imagined Lena thought about the watcher from the canyon and her girls. Perhaps she wondered what Alex was hiding. Alex's mind kept working over the watcher. It helped him not deal with his fear of losing her.

Once they arrived, they hoisted their small bags onto their shoulders and marched through the halls. They'd reach the intersection where they'd part ways soon, her to head off to her classrooms where she'd find the girls, and him up to report to Thom. Alex sighed heavily. Morning would come too soon, and with it, his trip to the east. He'd worked hard to have everything prepped in advance of his departure so he'd have this time with Lena. Uncertainty and fear spoiled all of the precious stolen moments.

He cursed the unknown man from the canyon and reached out to gently take her arm and pull her back to him. "We still have time tonight for a proper goodbye."

She looked past him, over his shoulder. He waited in silence until she finally turned her gaze to him. Anxiety pulsed there.

"And you'll tell me what Thom says. All of it?"

He nodded. Before he could reassure her, someone called his name from down the hall.

A haggard, travel-worm man stood at the end of the hall. Dust and stains covered his patched uniform. Even his sandy hair curled and stuck out at odd angles.

"Patrick?"

His old friend's face split into a wide smile. They met halfway down the hall.

Alex slapped his friend on the shoulder. "What are you doing here? You look like you've been traveling rough."

Patrick nodded. "I have, for weeks. I'm about to go up and report in to Thomas. My cover was blown. I barely—" He stopped, looking over Alex's shoulder.

Alex turned. Lena had trailed him down the hall, curious. He gestured her over. "This is Patrick. He's one of the Originals." He referred to the original band of dorm mates who'd banded together as wards to form the core of the founders of the revolution under Alex and Thomas. "This is Lena."

Patrick dipped his head at her. "The infamous Lena, huh?"

Lena gave the man a small smile and flicked her gaze between the men. "You said your cover was blown?"

Alex knew her visible concern went deeper than just the movement or an agent's safety. She wasn't looking forward to his trip. He'd make a circuit through the badlands of Texas and to the southern Zone Two, then north to Zone One, and across to the very dangerous Zone Six before heading home again while dodging winter weather. But Alex wasn't using a cover for this trip, so there was no danger of being "blown". Instead, he risked traveling into hostile territory as himself, the man whom many suspected was involved in revolution. Reactions to him and to his access would tell him a great deal about where people stood. In a new identity, he'd lose that access and add the risk that someone who knew him would recognize him. Then he'd run the risk of arrest.

Patrick looked at Alex to gauge how openly he could speak, and at Alex's slight nod, he answered, "It was. And I had a persistent little bastard trailing me back, too. I managed to slip him about a day out. Though he probably figured I was heading for the school. There's not much else out here."

"You were being followed by a single man?"

"As far as I can tell, just one, yeah."

Alex cocked his head at Lena. "You see? It's entirely possible the man in the canyons had nothing to do with you or the girls at all."

"Entirely possible?" she answered, voice tart. "It's also possible the Council decided to move against me after you and Thomas made me the poster girl for the movement. It's also possible it was one of the internal conspirators. I'm not interested in possible. I want answers."

Thanks to decisions Thomas made at the end of the Conclave two months before, the Council knew of Lena and the girls they'd all saved. Thomas had taken it upon himself to create a figurehead for the movement they were calling Spark Rising. All he wanted was a charismatic woman for Sparks to rally to as they moved forward. Alex and Ace, Lena's friend and a Dragonfly House trader, had stolen the latest shipment of powered girls meant for Council prison camps. Thomas planted a taunting note he'd signed with Lena's name. If Alex had been the one to find it, he'd have destroyed it. But he'd been busy hiding the girls, and by the time it had gone up the Security chain of command, he'd had no choice but to present it to the Council.

They'd stolen the six five-year-old girls, smuggling them

back to Lena and safety. Instead of allowing the theft to be a mystery, Thomas had handed the responsibility to Lena. He wanted to build her legend, he'd told Alex. On the heels of the attack on Councilor Three's caravan, it made her even more dangerous. The Council wanted Lena now. Warrants had been issued for her. Those warrants put her, and by extension her girls, at risk.

She must have been thinking much the same, because her brows drew down as he watched.

Alex settled his hand on the side of her face. He traced over her brow with his thumb, smoothing the anger from it.

"One way or another, I will get you answers. And even though we came back early, I'm hoping we can talk more tonight." He gave her a lopsided smile. "We can reserve tonight for us alone?"

Lena narrowed her eyes, playing with Alex. "I don't know," she said. "I'll have to see if I can clear my schedule."

His snort became a laugh. "Good idea. Do that."

She stuck her tongue out at him.

He took it as an invitation, swooping his head down for a quick kiss that left her breathless. From her gusty sigh as he pulled away, he figured she wanted more time for the two of them, too—and not time spent arguing with each other or Thomas.

"Go report, then," she managed. "Both of you."

Alex glanced over at Patrick. He eyed Alex and Lena, brows raised high.

"It was nice to meet you," she told Patrick as she turned away down the hall to the classrooms she'd taken over.

"Likewise." Amusement tinged his voice.

She looked back as she turned the corner at the hallway intersection. "Real answers," she called back to Alex. "I'm tired of being put off. By both of you."

Alex saluted her, and she disappeared around the corner. He turned back to find Patrick grinning at Alex, hands on hips and still laughing. "Well…that's…a development. Were you planning to share with the rest of us?"

Alex gave him a sharp look. “Excuse me?”

“The news. Not the woman. Although with the corona around that one, I have to imagine—”

Alex shoved his laughing friend ahead down the hall. “Don’t,” he growled. He glanced over his shoulder where she’d disappeared, then took a deep breath to center himself. His focus needed to be on Patrick’s blown cover and getting more answers out of an increasingly cagey Thomas. He had the afternoon to make it happen.

The weight of the truth hanging over his head grew every day, and it hung by an ever-thinner thread. He had to give her something. Perhaps smaller truths along the way would make the eventual crash when she discovered the truth of his deception about her brother easier to bear? Perhaps they’d even make it forgivable?

TWO

Lena

"I did it!" Marissa squealed. She went still, her mouth frozen in a wide smile. A moment later, she blinked, and her face became mobile again. She beamed up at the little boy on Lena's lap. He'd stopped whimpering with pain. Now, he inspected his arm. It wasn't broken anymore. Marissa had healed it.

Lena gave the little girl a smile rooted deep in her heart's softest parts. Marissa worked so hard, and she was always so enthusiastic. "You did. And all by yourself this time."

Marissa stopped laughing. Something in her smile became secretive. The slight turn of her head? The way she avoided Lena's gaze?

"Thank you." The boy, Ruben, was suitably impressed. He squirmed, and Lena allowed him to slide off her lap. He turned to face her. "Do you think I could learn that?"

The question was more than a little wistful. When Lena had returned from her mission with Alex three months before, she'd made a plan for teaching. In addition to the girls, she'd wanted to focus on younger wards from the Ward School. But when Thomas returned from the Conclave, he'd put her to work on "Their Shared Vision." Unfortunately, the only vision Lena and Thomas shared was Lena teaching.

Thomas insisted she start with older students. They'd be in the world sooner, he told her, and older students could help teach other wards what they mastered. Accelerated access was practical.

Thomas was all about practical.

Lena scowled, and the little boy stepped back, eyes widening. She forced herself to smooth the frown away, shoving her hair behind her ears. "I wish you could, but I have to teach the students chosen by the Councilor."

The boy's face fell.

"I'll tell you what." Lena leaned forward in her seat. "You go find Agent Lee and tell him that Lena said he's to tutor you in healing. He's as good as I am."

"Really?" The boy's brown eyes widened further.

"Really. Now get back to your class on the obstacle course."

He nodded and took off, weaving through the desks in Lena's classroom and then out the door.

Lena sat back and watched Marissa again. The soft happiness she'd lost somewhere in the canyons that morning returned. Fear came with it. Lena could feel the fragility of it. If she looked at the joy too long, if she tried to hold on to it, it would collapse. She knew where the fear came from. This place and the people in it were her greatest comfort and the source of her deepest anxiety and anger.

Marissa looked up, her faraway look fading.

"You okay?" The lesson itself wouldn't have overtaxed Marissa. But wherever she went in her head when her eyes clouded over… the prison memories the girls carried within them weren't happy ones. Lena did her best to help the girls push the past far away.

The little girl flashed a grin and nodded, though something of the clouds remained in her eyes. "Yep."

Some things shouldn't be pushed away to memory. Some things were too precious.

Lena kept her voice as gentle as possible. "Were you thinking about Jubilee?"

Marissa blinked back quick tears at her lost match's name.

Lena wished for the thousandth time since they'd returned that Thomas's men had found some trace of the girl when they went back to the prison area. Jubilee was gone. The Council had managed to spirit her away. Lena couldn't even promise Marissa they'd find Jubilee someday. They wouldn't stop trying, no. But the odds of them succeeding…

Lena opened her arms to Marissa instead. The girl leaned in, snuggling her face into Lena's chest.

"Sometimes," the little girl whispered, "she's right here with me. Then she's gone, and it hurts all over again."

Lena stroked Marissa's long, dark hair away from her face. "I know. I feel like that about my mom." She sighed and leaned back to look into Marissa's face. "It's okay to miss her. It's okay to cry about it, too."

"Lena? Hey, Lena?" A husky little voice came from the doorway behind Lena.

She turned to see a small boy with too-wise eyes that always regarded her with suspicion. "Leo. Hey, Leo."

The girls would have laughed at her mimicry if it had been one of them. Four-year-old Leo stared at her. His expression told her he was not amused.

She sighed. "Yes, Leo?"

"Rose wants to know if you're coming up to the garden. She says you're late."

She'd sent a four-year-old to find Lena?

"I decided to come look for you."

No. She hadn't sent him. But she'd be looking for him now.

"Leo. You can't just go off wherever you want."

"Why not? Agents train here. Like Alex. It's the safest place in the whole world." He blinked at her.

She took a breath and smiled at Marissa. "Leo's right. We're late."

Marissa nodded and hopped down. She skipped over to Leo, her tears already forgotten. Lena wished she could dismiss her own doubts and fears as easily.

She watched as they ranged ahead. Marissa chattered, and Leo watched her with wide eyes. Every so often, he glanced back at Lena over his shoulder. Lena knew his glances checked she remained at a respectable distance and weren't to comfort himself that she was back there.

Leo had come back from the Conclave with Alex. He'd been orphaned in the attack on Councilor Three's caravan. Lena supposed Alex felt responsible for the boy, though he'd explained that Leo had attached himself to Alex. He admired the persistent little boy. He had tried to take Leo to the Zone Three orphanage after they'd returned, but the boy ran away and came to find him at the Council building.

Three times.

Alex told her something about Leo reminded him of Lena. She had to wonder if there was more than a little about Leo that reminded Alex of himself.

Rose and the older girls waited upstairs in the sunlight of the private garden. When the three of them appeared, Rose raised her brow at the boy. "Figured that's where you took off to, impatient child."

He gave her an unrepentant smile and ran off into the garden, calling out, "I'm hiding. And you all have to find me!"

He loved the games of hide and seek. He never had to seek. Lena and Rose made the girls hide from each other in the garden. The finder could use her eyes, but they got more points if they used the Dust to find each other by heat, or heartbeat, or vibration. It was wonderful exercise in using the Dust to do more, to be more than the boys of the Ward School could.

Lena and Rose called the girls to them, went over the rules again, then sent all but Phoebe running through the winding paths between tall grass, flowering bushes, and gnarled desert trees.

Phoebe waited with them, her back turned as she counted to fifty. "Ready or not, here I come," she called out in a sing-song voice for the smaller girls' benefit. She marched down the main path.

Rose peeled away and took the far path. Lena could feel her reaching for the Dust as she prepared to keep an eye on the girls and their use of their Spark. Lena stepped back into the shade offered by a trio of desert willows, intending to make her way around the garden's opposite side. Before she could turn, though, Phoebe's dodging movement caught her eye. Phoebe curved wide on the path to avoid two men leaving the garden.

She skirted a guardian and a senior ward. They both glanced back after the tall, curvy seventeen-year-old with the wild head of tight curls. The senior ward spoke as they watched her disappear around a curve in the path. Lena didn't hear the first part of his comment, but a shift in the desert breeze brought her the rest. "—wait until next Spring."

Lena's stomach twisted. Next Spring? Was it coincidence he watched one of her girls as he referred to Spring? The two men she'd overheard months before plotting to rid themselves of her to gain access to the girls had planned to move in the Spring.

The young guardian laughed and glanced back, too. "Be patient. It's coming."

Lena swallowed back fear and fury and stepped out from the shade of the gnarled desert trees and into their path.

When they turned back to continue and found her planted in front of them, they both started. The senior ward paled and stepped back. The guardian kept his cool.

"What's coming, Guardian?" She wouldn't get much from his carefully-trained, neutral face. He was an agent, after all. She tilted her head to look at the student. "What will be happening next Spring?"

His mouth opened, but no sound came out.

The guardian reached out to the young man's shoulder to push his student around Lena and forward. "He's eager for the oldest of them to come of age," he explained frankly. "Can you blame him? Everyone sees the example of your relationship with Agent Reyes."

He left before she could find her voice, urging his student out of the garden. Lena stared after them, nausea roiling her stomach.

She crossed her arms over her chest and turned, looking around at the few guardians sitting at the tables in the early fall sunshine. As she faced the gardens, she could hear little girl shrieks as well as Phoebe calling out.

The guardian's explanation made perfect sense on the surface. Except she knew it was a lie. She knew what someone—some*ones*—had in store for her this Spring. She'd overheard the plot just before she'd left with Alex to go and claim her vengeance on Councilor Three. And after what had happened that morning…

Thomas dismissed her concerns.

He wouldn't now. He needed to know it was still ongoing. It was time for him to step up to keep *her* wards safe.

Lena used the Dust to help her find Rose. "I have to go talk to Thomas." Lena could hear the tension in her own voice. "Can you keep them together until lunch?"

The afternoon meal was less than an hour away. No one would move against her or her girls with so many others around. Rose would keep them safe until then. Her Neo-Barb match was as eager to protect them, and as fierce as Lena in her own wild way.

Rose frowned. "What's going on?"

"I don't know. I just—I overheard something again, and I need to talk to Thom about it."

"Another threat?"

"Possibly."

Rose stared at her.

"Probably," Lena amended.

"We should leave this place," Rose told her, repeating the secret desire she and Lena had shared many evenings. "We both know places far away where no one could find us while we train them to keep themselves safe. They shouldn't be exposed to all this other—" Rose waved her hand, indicating the school's male energy.

Lena swallowed. Thomas believed the only way for the girls to heal their experiences from the Council prison was to come to understand that men in general weren't a threat. On a certain level, Lena agreed.

Except she didn't think he understood that as long as there was a threat to them here none of them would have the confidence to truly heal. Being on constant alert, waiting for the next attempt on them, was debilitating.

Lena inhaled a long, shaky breath and nodded. "We'll talk later."

Rose nodded once, angry again. She made no secret of her distaste for the rules imposed by Thomas and the guardians.

Lena turned away and left, focused on moving through the

halls and straight to Thomas's office. She hoped Alex and Patrick would still be there. Alex took the threats more seriously, as they were directly against Lena. He'd kept the pressure on Thomas to find the men she'd heard and dig deeper into a possible conspiracy here under their noses.

When she reached Thomas's office, the anteroom was empty. She crossed to the door and reached for the knob, but paused when she heard a deep, surprised voice from within—and it didn't belong to Alex. It didn't seem to fit her brief experience of Patrick's voice, either.

"Even Alex?"

"Yes, even Alex." Thomas's answering voice was heavy. He sounded tired and upset. "It has to be unexpected, regardless of the cost, or this'll never work."

Unexpected? Cost? The same sense of unease she'd felt in the garden curled in her chest again.

There was a beat of silence. Lena held her breath.

The stranger spoke again. "You made the decision, and the logic is sound. You've committed us. Don't torture yourself."

Her breath slipped back out. *This is* Thomas. *He weighs every decision. Calm down.*

Lena wanted to hear more, but voices from behind her warned her of Thomas's assistant's return with another man. She lifted her hand, tapped two knocks, and opened the door. She swept her gaze to Thomas first. He sat behind his desk, leaned forward over files and papers.

In the seconds before his face registered surprise at the intrusion, she read a mix of fury, disappointment, and disgust. At himself? Or at the man talking to him?

On the heels of the flash of surprise, Thomas pasted on his usual formal neutrality. She darted a look at the other man in the room, a man of middle height and nondescript looks. He looked back, face bland. She couldn't even tell his age. He was utterly forgettable. The perfect agent.

She turned back to Thomas. "I'm sorry, I don't mean to interrupt. Carl—" She pointed over her shoulder to indicate his assistant and imply that her entry had been okayed. The men entered the entry area behind Lena and the door. "And there's someone else here, too."

"Theo." Thomas gave her a small, tight smile and waved her in. "I was expecting him."

She glanced back and gestured for the newcomer to follow her into the office. While his height and the prettiness of his features and light brown eyes reminded her of her best friend Ace, he was leaner and his movements more graceful.

"Lena, meet Theo." Thomas then indicated the man already in the room with him. "And this is West. This is Lena, gentlemen."

Lena looked at each of them again. "More of your Originals?"

Thomas's face registered a blip of surprise again. "Yes. I take it you met Patrick?"

She nodded. "Alex introduced us, yes."

"He and Alex are working on his report, going over…events. They've all come in to report and help with our next steps." He smiled, another tight expression.

Lena had a feeling she wore the same expression. Did she dare hope those 'next steps' included taking the threat against her seriously? Things hadn't been the same between them since he'd returned from Conclave. Lena had never been very good at pretending not to care about being disrespected.

But I promised Alex I'd try harder

"Did you need something?" he prompted her.

She glanced at the other two men.

"They're Originals, Lena. There's little they don't already know." Thomas leaned back, clasping his hands over his flat stomach.

She took a breath. "Alex told you about our watcher in the canyon?" At his nod, she continued. "Just now, I was up in the garden with the girls, working on an exercise. I saw a guardian and a senior ward watching. They said something alarming—about waiting for Spring—And the guardian told him to be patient. It was coming."

"What was coming?" Thomas gave her his whole attention.

They all did.

"He referenced Spring, Thomas. The same time of year others have plans for me." If he tried to pretend he didn't know what she thought the guardian meant, there was no point in her being here at all. In fact, there was no point in either she or the girls she was sworn to protect remaining here. "What do you think?"

"It's more important what *you* think, and why. Were these men threatening? Did you confront them? Can you identify them?"

She shook her head. "No, of course not. If they'd been threatening I would have handled it right then. And I did confront them. I stepped out and asked what he meant. They gave me a bullshit answer about the wards being eager for the girls to come of age." She was not pleased by the accepting nod Thomas made. "And no, I didn't know them—though I'm sure I can keep an eye out for the guardian. He was young, and there aren't that many of you under fifty."

She'd been avoiding the guardians as much as she was able. It made identifying them that much harder.

Thomas sighed. "Lena, how can you be sure it was a bullshit answer?"

"Because I was there. Because it came right after someone tracked me down—"

"Someone was tracking *Patrick.* This sounds pretty innocuous to me. This is a school filled with young men—"

Theo made a snorting noise. Thomas flipped his gaze to the man behind her.

"It sounds like someone trying to sound innocuous to me." Theo crossed his arms over his chest.

Thomas gave the agent a long look. "Okay. Well, then after lunch, you can go see Lena and get descriptions, then start an investigation to make sure this latest incident is not just Lena being sensitive to implied threats."

The way he said the words "latest incident" had her grinding her teeth. It wasn't her being sensitive, whatever the hell that meant. She knew what she'd seen and heard; she knew what she'd overheard in the halls months before when two men scheduled her demise for Spring.

Thomas rubbed his eyes and shook his head. His glance moved to West behind her, and then back to Lena again. "Is that all? Or was there something else?"

"Is that all? Is it not enough?" Her heart beat loud and fast.

"Please don't start accusing me of not taking you seriously again. I've just assigned someone—and someone very good—to investigate. That's what you wanted, and it'll be the *second* investigation on these threats. If there's a plot, and if these men are a part of it—"

"*If* there's a plot?" Lena stared at him. She turned her head to look at the men behind her. They watched her, one with an odd, detached expression and the other with something approaching sympathy.

She swallowed.

If there's a plot. That's perfect. One of the two men who had welcomed her into the fold, who had sworn to treat her as an equal, had dismissed everything that kept her up nights. He'd implied that she was wrong, or overreacting, or lying.

Thomas was content to root out the plot against her at his leisure and to demand Lena trust him to handle it without explanation of what he was doing, or when, or to whom. He expected her to trust him but wouldn't discuss how he'd decided to out her during the Conclave without discussing it with her first. She hadn't been presented as a marauding ghost, a possibility to haunt the Council. He had started the whispers using her name, her history, and her plans for the girls.

They'd told the Council about her dream of a school.

She looked at Thomas. She knew anger and disappointment were written on her face.

I made a promise to the man who does care.

She closed her eyes and took a deep breath. When she opened them again, she didn't meet his pale eyes. It was important to keep her cool. It mattered to Alex. He mattered to her.

I promised to try harder.

"Thank you," she managed through stiff lips. She looked

back at Theo. “I’ll expect you after lunch then?”

He nodded. “Yes, ma’am.”

She did smile at that as she turned to leave. Ma’am. Yeah, right.

THREE

Alex

Alex didn't regret the PDA. The only witness had been one of the men he trusted most in the world. Besides, it had been a quick kiss.

Quick but thorough. He couldn't help the smug thought.

It was worth the harassment he was no doubt about to receive. He glanced over his shoulder, and Patrick leaned back in the conference room chair, arms crossed, watching Alex. His head moved in tiny, knowing nods.

Yeah. Patrick wasn't going to let it go.

Alex finished pouring his drink—they called it coffee, even though it wasn't. His grimace as he turned around was both for the make-do beverage and the details of Patrick's escape from Zone Six they'd just covered.

Patrick had made it to Zone Three on his own. From what he'd already shared with Alex, it was a harrowing journey. He was tired and still pissed over his blown cover, even after weeks of travel and being hunted. After spending the morning hashing out his report and the details he'd been obsessing over for weeks, Patrick was ready for a little distraction. Even if it was at Alex's expense.

Especially if it was at Alex's expense.

Alex sighed. "Let's get it over with."

Patrick laughed. "You brought it on yourself."

Alex raised his brows.

"You broke a solemn vow between brothers." Patrick dipped his head and shook it, but his voice was joking. "For a redhead, admittedly. But still…"

"Uh huh."

"How's Thomas taking it? Is she the source of the tension I felt when I checked in upstairs?"

Alex frowned. "I don't know. Thomas is—" The frown turned into a grimace.

"So he's pissed?"

"Don't know. He's something. He's distanced himself since Conclave. I have no idea if it's stress as we head toward the finish line or if it's Lena. I have a hard time believing he has an issue with my relationship."

Patrick arched a brow. "Except—all joking aside—we did make a promise. No real relationships. Nothing long-term, no distractions. The revolution would be our—"

"We were kids," Alex scoffed.

"Hey, I'm not giving you shit about it. I like my women tall and soft, but give me a sassy redhead that glows like a sunset over the Rockies, and I'd be making the same grab for a little bit of normal you are." Patrick grinned. "I just want to know how much of an issue it is."

"It shouldn't be an issue at all. She's as committed as we are. Maybe more."

"So then what's Thomas's problem?"

Alex shrugged. "It's been tense, but I don't think it's the relationship. I think it's—" He paused, thinking about it. What was it? The relationship between Thom and Lena was definitely strained. "I think she can feel the secrets and half-truths. She blames Thomas."

Patrick leaned in. "Thomas likes his secrets and half-truths."

"We all do. It's how we do what we do. But we don't lie to each other. He's been lying to her. So have I." Alex shook his head. "It's no way to build a relationship, not even a working relationship."

"So tell her the truth. You can't be keeping that much from her."

Alex grimaced again. "Tell her about the trails of other girls you've tracked? About the prison locations we suspect? About her *brother*?" He shook his head. "I'm not ready to go down that road. She'll either want to leave to go track them down herself, or she'll want to leave period because she's pissed that I used her family without telling her."

"She hasn't asked about Daniel at all? Lucky break, but…hmm. Are you sure she doesn't know?"

"She hasn't asked because her family…let's say there's a history of disconnect, even before she went off to live on her own. She believes he betrayed her, so she's put him out of mind to preserve her mental health. I'm not looking forward to having to tell her the truth."

"You're going to tell her? I thought you said—"

"I owe her the truth, but it'll have to wait 'til I get back. I want to be around to make sure she doesn't disappear. Even if it means loud voices. And possibly explosions."

"Not shy about letting you know when you've fucked up, huh? No reverence for the mystery that is Alejandro Reyes." Patrick laughed again. "I like her already."

"Good. 'Cause I want you to be the one to run interference between her and Thom."

Patrick's laugh died. "Nuh, nuh. I'm heading back out—"

Alex shook his head. "You had a major position in a sensitive zone. And you were just blown, Patrick." Alex held his friend's stubborn gaze and tapped the notes he'd been scrawling as his friend talked this morning. "They, whoever this mystery kid in black reports to, had all of your activities. They knew you. We can't risk you going back out now."

"But…babysitting?" Patrick rolled his eyes.

"Please, for the love all that's holy, don't *ever* let her hear you say that. You *will* live to regret it." Alex rubbed his eyes and laughed ruefully. "And no, not babysitting. Be a liaison. Help her by being a layer between her and Thomas."

"Dust, Alex. Is it that bad?"

Alex swallowed. "Yeah. It is. She's trying, for me. He…I can't get through to him how close he is to blowing it."

Patrick blew out a breath and nodded. "Okay. So what do you get to be doing again while I'm liaisoning?"

"I'll be traveling rough for a little more than a month—"

"Done it."

"Then joining Lena's best friend, Ace Coffey, the newest Platinum Pin Holder of the Dragonfly House, on his trade caravan across three zones. He's providing means and access."

"A representative of Dragonfly House?" Patrick stared at him, mouth open.

Alex grinned. It was a coup. Lena's contacts were convenient. "Yep."

"Oh, you poor bastard. I feel so sorry for you." Patrick wadded up a sliver of paper he'd been toying with and threw it at Alex. He shook his head in disgust. "Dragonfly House. Receptions and fine wine and all the intrigue you can shake a stick at."

"Yep."

"I hate you."

Alex laughed. "Be a good boy for the next six months, and we'll see what we can set up for you when I get back. That means keep my woman safe."

"Your woman. Now I really hate you."

FOUR

Jubilee

She hid whenever the old man's friend came into the room. She'd dart behind the old man's legs or under the table. She peered up at them from underneath it now.

"Look at her," the old man said. His big hands, covered in brown spots and patches, rubbed the edge of his chair. "Have you ever seen such a delightful child?" He tilted his head to look at her. He liked it when she hid under there. She was only permitted to sit on the floor, and he preferred that she stay at his feet. If she forgot herself and scooted away too far, he'd yank her back by her hair.

But Jubilee was smart. She'd learned what made him yank. He was almost nice now.

Not like his friend with the very white hair and yellow skin. He had mean eyes. Jubilee shivered when he looked at her.

"She's a monster," he said now to the old man. "Sparks like her are practically feral. Not an appropriate pet. One day she'll turn on you. You should put her down now and spare yourself the trouble later."

"She's my monster," the old man said. His voice was sharp. "And she has a place and a purpose."

"Like your grandson did?"

The two old men stared at each other. The silence grew. Jubilee shrank back further under the table. All she could see of them now were their feet. The tops of the old man's stockings sagged down over his skinny white legs in front of her. His legs disappeared into the shiny red robe tied tight around his thin body. His friend wore slippers like a girl's. They were dark blue, almost purple, with silver swirls of threads. The tips of the toes were shiny, pointed metal.

Jubilee knew those points hurt. She rubbed her side, up under her left arm. He'd told the old man it was an accident, but Jubilee knew better. He liked to kick.

She waited for them to whisper and hiss at each other like snakes. They always did that before the old man's friend left. And then the man would be angry for the rest of the afternoon. If he was too angry to work with her, she wouldn't get her treats. He might even send her back to her cage early. No treats. No dinner.

She wished his friend would leave already.

Jubilee slid all the way back under the table until her back caught against the leg on the opposite end. She risked her hair getting pulled now, but she wanted away from those metal toes. Jubilee curled into herself, pulling her legs up to her chest and rocking forward and back on her bottom.

She wished Marissa was here with her. She closed her eyes, rocking, rocking, and reached out for Marissa. No matter how far apart they'd been carried, Jubilee could feel her. She was focused again, learning something new. Jubilee would rather sneak into Marissa's mind and see what she was doing than listen to the old men hissing at each other. She could feel her eyes flutter beneath her lids, and her rocking stilled.

Marissa was practicing again, on a boy in the room with them. Lena had brought him in. His arm was broken. Were they fixing him? Jubilee reached with her mind to see through Marissa's eyes, to feel with Marissa's hands. They were fixing him, the Dust moving to burst in bright spots over the break, knitting it together again. She felt a pulse of shared excitement. Marissa, aware of her. *Do you see*?

Jubilee opened her eyes. *I see*. Her lips curved up. She reached her hand around again to hover over the sore spot under her left arm. Eyes open, her vision blurred out as she moved the Dust beneath her skin. When she was done, she pressed her fingertips against the spot. Hard. Harder. Her smile widened. Her first try, and she'd done it.

The door on the wall near the table opened to let in a brief burst of voices. It closed again, and the room was hushed once more, but for the sound of footsteps approaching. Jubilee didn't recognize the feet or the low, dusty boots.

"Councilor." Jubilee listened to the young man's voice. "The eastern patrol found two men returning from the attack this summer." The young man stopped.

Jubilee didn't need to see the old man's face to know why. He hated it when things didn't go as planned. That summer, nothing had gone as planned—not the attack on a caravan, not the Council Meet itself. The old man had lost things dear to him. He had been very unhappy for a very long time.

"Continue." Yes, he was angry.

Jubilee's excited smile of moments ago faded. She was hungry. She wanted her treats. She wanted her dinner.

The messenger man cleared his throat. "There were two men, sir, both gravely wounded. One didn't make it back, but the other—is your grandson! He's here, sir. He's alive."

The room fell so quiet that Jubilee could hear the blood pounding in her ears. She waited, holding her breath, although she didn't know why.

"And he was the only survivor?"

"Yes, sir. There was another with him, but they had an encounter with a bear at some point before the patrol found them. He died of infection before the guard could get them back here to safety."

"And my grandson is wounded how?"

"Broken bones, sir, healed badly. From a beating taken in battle, or wounds from the journey home over the mountains in the months since. Wounds from being slashed by the bear, festering, but not gangrenous yet."

"And his report?" The old man's voice was calm now. He knew the answer. He'd known it since the Meet had gone so wrong two months before. "Did he achieve my objective?"

"He did not, sir."

Another moment of silence. "I see. Anything else?"

"Councilor, sir, he *was* hurt in the attack. He fought...." The messenger's voice drifted away. "He says he has information for you, sir. Only for you."

Jubilee thought she could hear the man swallow, even tucked away as she was deep under the table.

"Is that so? I'll speak to my wayward grandson myself shortly. He'll still be alive?"

"Yes, sir, barring some sudden change, he will, sir."

"Good. Instruct them not to dose him with anything for his pain until then. I want his mind sharp when I question him. He can have some relief if he pleases me."

The old man's friend made a noise at that, somewhere between a growl and a laugh. His pointy metal-toed foot swung out as he crossed his legs and began swinging his foot.

"You may go."

Jubilee swallowed. His voice had not sounded like this except for once, the first night she was brought to him from the prison. She shivered. The quiet voice was worse than the angry voice.

"Yes, sir." The young messenger turned and left the room.

Jubilee wished she could go with him. Her body moved forward a tiny bit as the door opened and revealed the flash of light and voices from outside.

The old man's friend spoke into the silence that fell after the door closed. "We shouldn't have moved on Three. Other than Six, he was our one firm ally. And what that attack cost us—"

"Will be recouped ten-fold." The old man's voice remained quiet, but there was a sound in it that she hadn't heard before, like an animal right before it starts to snarl. "Two will soon be ours whether she believes or not, and I have another in my pocket." There was a small tinkling sound as the old man stirred the tea in front of him. "The death of Three is a loss of charisma only, and one I had already planned for. The man was a brilliant speaker, but his appetites were tiresome. I hand-picked his successor."

"Who was not named Councilor this summer," his friend reminded him. "We lost Azcon to the Spark brother of that...girl."

"We'll be fine. It takes many cogs to run the machinery of a zone, and a Councilor is but the largest. Azcon is still ours."

"It needs to be. If we lose one half of our pincer, how will we squeeze the LDS?"

"I'm not certain we'll have to. They agree it is time for wider stability. I'm confident we can convince them it's time to solidify alliances here so we can begin to reach abroad again. And it won't be a stretch to convince them the girls are monstrosities. If we can, then we will have the west."

"Except for Five, of course, in Canev."

"Canev itself is strategically unimportant, locked between desert and dead zones. I'm shocked it's managed to survive this long. And Five will soon no longer be an issue. I have been courting a guardian high in the leadership there at the Ward School. He's hungry for power. If we give him the school, he'll dispose of Five and we can install another at Canev at next year's Meet."

The old man's friend gasped, and his foot dropped to the floor. "Give those Spark animals the Ward School?" He sounded like he was choking.

"Temporarily," the old man barked back. "Remember, they're already running it, they just think they're so clever that we don't know. We'll take it back when the rest of our pieces are in place and bring the Sparks back in line."

"Soon, I hope. I'm not happy with the irregularities at the school."

"Soon. Allow me time to work, Marcus." The old man sipped noisily.

His friend slid down a little in his seat, and his legs stretched out under the table. Jubilee leaned away again. "Be careful who you work with. If you surround yourself with the unholy, you will be corrupted."

"That's why I have you, Marcus." The old man's voice drifted toward normal again. Perhaps if Jubilee showed him her new trick, he would be in the mood to indulge her?

She ignored them now as she slunk out from under the table and skirted its edge, crawling on hands and knees and keeping an eye on those metal toes. She made her way to the end of the table where the old man sat and sidled up to the side of his chair. To show he was aware of her, he dropped his hand down from the table and stroked her head. His friend hated when the old man touched her. He'd leave soon.

As if she'd ordered him herself, the old man's friend rose from his seat. Jubilee glanced up at him through her lashes. His lip was curled in a snarl as he looked down at her. She ducked her head down.

"Marcus," the old man said, his voice mild, "leave her be."

Marcus murmured something that Jubilee could not hear, but it sounded like a song. Another prayer. The men chanted them together often. She hated it, because she had to go in her cage then, and the old man sometimes forgot to get her out again.

He bowed his head now, agreeing with whatever his friend had sung. Marcus rested his hand upon the old man's head and then took his leave. He didn't look back at Jubilee again.

Jubilee waited for the old man to raise his head. His lips were moving, but there were no words that she could hear. When he lifted his eyes and his face, he looked tired. Worried. Jubilee raised her hand, expecting the cuff that would come if he wasn't in the mood to indulge her. She touched his knee, the barest weight from her small hand pressing down, and waited for him to notice her.

He finished his tea before acknowledging her. When he did, his eyes flicked down, and he smiled. "Such a good girl," he told her. "So obedient."

Jubilee felt a smile spread across her face. "I have a new trick," she breathed. She couldn't wait to show him. "But I need the man."

The old man frowned. "What man?"

"The broken man? From the bear?"

He shouldn't be frowning. Her heart beat a little faster. His brows rose, pulling the frown from his face. "You need *my grandson*?"

She nodded again, quick and firm.

His grey eyes searched her face. He nodded, much the same as she had, once, in a hard jerk. "All right then. Let's be off. I'd like to see what you've come up with."

The old man stood, and Jubilee darted back and away so she wouldn't be in his way. He pulled his robe tighter around his middle and adjusted the belt, and then led the way to a side door behind him. Jubilee rose to her feet. She walked past him at the deliberate pace he preferred, keeping her head down and her eyes downcast. He snapped the door shut behind them and then continued down the dim hallway.

It was a long hall, lit at irregular intervals by sconces holding oil lamps. The hall ran the length of the old man's personal rooms and connected all of them so that he could avoid the main hallway to the front. She thought he preferred it back here, in the dark, where no one could see him. He paced ahead of her, not looking back, trusting that she would follow.

She had tried to run away once when she'd been brought to him from the prison after the other girls had escaped. He'd instructed them to remove the collar. That night as he'd walked to dinner, with her pacing beside him, an outside door had opened. She'd seen dark skies and starlight and smelled the air fresh from rain. Without thinking, she ran for the door, to the world outside. She hadn't made it very far. She never made the mistake again.

Jubilee's shoulders hunched in at the memory. She would be a good and obedient little monster. She would learn whatever tricks he wanted. She would never try to escape again, so long as he kept her inside, away from the Scary Boys.

The old man paused outside a door, waiting for her. He opened the door and ushered her ahead of him. As soon as she had crossed the threshold from hallway to inner room, she dropped to her knees.

Jubilee wrinkled her nose. It smelled in this room. With bare wood floors and plain furniture, it wasn't as nice as the old man's rooms, either. A bed stood close to the fireplace on the opposite wall. In the bed rested a pale man with bandages wrapped across his chest, spots of fluid spreading up through the wrappings from the wounds beneath them.

The wall beside the bed was hidden behind young men. The Scary Boys who had been lounging against it when Jubilee and the old man entered stood now, straight and wary, watching the old man. Jubilee stayed back, by the door. Chills chased up her back, making her neck crawl.

These Scary Boys looked the same as those she'd been given to that first night. They all looked the same. Dark hair cut short with a fringe of bangs, pale skin. They were all different heights, different ages, but none of them was more than ten years older than Jubilee. They were big kids. They were the old man's Scary Boys. She tried not to look at them. They liked it too much. Her gaze jumped up, though, and met that of the taller boy.

His eyes were pale and focused directly on her. She remembered those eyes. It was the meanest of the Scary Boys, the one who'd hurt her most. He was here. He knew she was scared of him, and he liked it. He smiled at her. Her stomach twisted and dropped. Jubilee whimpered.

The old man snapped his fingers for her attention. She flushed and dropped lower to the floor in embarrassment. Jubilee crawled across the room to him where he stood near the broken man, her stomach almost dragging on the floor. When she reached him, she knelt at his feet beside the bed.

"Show me this trick, then." He didn't sound impatient. He never sounded impatient, but she knew he was. In a few short months, she had learned to read his moods.

Jubilee turned to the man on the bed. Her gaze started to move upward, toward his face, but she snapped it back to his chest. She didn't need to see his eyes. Standing on tip toe, she reached her small hands across him to the edge of the bandages draped across his wounds and peeled them back. The smell in the room became thicker now—like growing things, but wrong somehow. Jubilee held her breath as she set the wraps with their long wet patches to the side, on the man's sheet-covered belly.

She stared down at his wounds. Four deep cuts slashed from one side of his chest to the other. The wounds oozed, the edges dark red and puckered as they spread like petals. Instead of the sweet smell of flowers, though, these petals released the stink of flesh starting to rot. Jubilee glanced over her shoulder at the old man. He watched her, three of his fingers tapping against his chin. He nodded at her, giving her permission to begin.

She took a deep breath and reached across the man again. She placed her small hands to either side of the longest of the tears and focused. Her breath slid out, long and easy, like Marissa's had. She reached for the Dust, found them, awake and waiting. She showed them what she wanted, told them. *No more stink. No more yuck. Just pink and healthy and right*. She watched them with her mind instead of her blurred vision. They worked.

When she blinked her eyes and used them to see again, all four of the scratches had closed. The old man's hand was tight on her shoulder. He leaned in over her and pressed his fingers against the skin that moments before had been torn and infected. It was whole and healthy. She had done it.

The young man himself had lifted his head and stared down at his chest in disbelief. "No. That can't—she shouldn't be able to—you brought one of them into our house?"

The old man's gaze rose to his. The old man frowned.

"This is very good, Jubilee. A very good trick. We'll have to insure you get plenty of practice with your new skill." He leaned back away from the young man and rapped her on the head. "But we don't reward those who have failed us."

She turned her head to look at him. Was he angry? He wasn't looking at her. His stare bored into the young man.

"Undo it, Jubilee. Return him to how he was."

"What? Grandfather, please—"

Jubilee blinked. Her stomach twisted again. "I don't know how," she whispered.

"Figure it out." His voice was hard.

Jubilee took a deep breath. She could feel tears welling in her eyes, and her chin quivered. She took another ragged breath and nodded her head. "Okay." Her voice was very small. "I don't think I can make the smelly part come back." In a rush, before the old man could decide she had messed up, before he could look at the Scary Boys and tell them they could have her again, she added, "But I can make it hurt more?"

A smile fluttered over the old man's face. He nodded, clearly feeling generous. "That will be fine. Do that."

"*Grandfather*—"

Jubilee turned back. The young man shook his head in small movements, his eyes full of fear. He reminded her…of her. After another ragged breath to push the tears from her throat, Jubilee focused on his chest again. She looked beneath his skin, deep inside his new-knit flesh, and spoke to the Dust again. She showed it what she wanted.

She came back to herself slowly this time, as the Dust still worked. Her awareness of the skin before her grew as it split open again, but from the inside this time. As the skin separated, popping open with wet, tearing sounds, small eruptions of blood flared and flowed across the man's chest. A shrieking wail ebbed and flowed like the bright blood across skin.

There was a popping sound behind her, too, but different. The old man snapped his fingers at the Scary Boys. Two of them rushed forward, one hurrying around behind Jubilee and the old man. They each took one of the young man's arms, pinning him to the bed as the four jagged tears across his chest spread like red fissures.

After a moment, it was done. The stink of infection had faded, but new smells cropped up in its place—bowels emptied beneath the bed sheets and a metallic tang that filled Jubilee's nose. The old man leaned forward, inspecting her work again. Jubilee held her breath.

When he turned to her again, he wore the broadest, most lovely smile Jubilee remembered ever seeing. She had pleased him. She had pleased him very much. She could feel an answering smile spread across her face.

"This is very good, Jubilee. Very, very good." The man patted her head, a caress over her hair and ears.

Relief flowed through her.

He looked away then, to meet the glazed eyes of the young man in the bed. "You, however, have some explaining to do. Shall we begin, Lucas?"

Jubilee watched, avid, as the old man leaned in again. She felt someone watching her and glanced past the old man to the Scary Boy across the bed, holding onto one arm and shoulder. His eyes seemed paler with the white ring around them. He stared at her, and he wasn't smiling anymore. Jubilee met his eyes without blinking, and the boy, almost a man, swallowed. She watched his throat move. He was afraid, she realized.

He was afraid of her.

Jubilee smiled.

FIVE

Lena

Energy slapped at her, rough, unconscious, and overwhelmingly male. For a moment, Lena was sucked back into a memory of standing before the massed wards and guardians at Fort Nevada a few months before. Remembered anger ignited within her chest like a flame that had been quieted but never extinguished. She stopped in the doorway to the cafeteria. Boys and young men swerved to move around her.

They knew better than to make an off-the-cuff remark, but it didn't stop the curious looks. Lena searched the big room beyond, looking for Rose and their wards. She saw Marissa first, standing beside Leo still, but somehow very much apart. The little girl stared off into space, a small smile on her face. Marissa's happiness seemed to have an edge of—was it wistfulness? Almost sadness?

It was. Lena had built up enough of that over these last tumultuous months to recognize it, even when it was hidden behind a sparkling smile. Or in Lena's case, hidden behind enough frustration to power a relo-city. Had she thought things would be easier once she returned to Fort Nevada to build a school for her own students? Had she been fool enough to think they'd be easier still once Alex and Thomas returned from Conclave?

She turned her head and searched the cafeteria for them. Neither was anywhere in the room. She wasn't surprised. Both men had a habit of working through meals, and Thomas had dismissed her and settled in to work with his agents. Alex would leave for his three-zone sweep in the morning, and probably had plenty of last-minute details to handle.

She stepped over to the table, waving her arm to get Marissa's attention. Rose saw her and tapped the dreamy little girl on the shoulder to send her over. The other students at their shared table already stood in their places behind their chairs. Across the room, Rose took her own place, solemn-faced Leo beside her. The rest of the girls wove through the room to their own tables. There were twelve of them now: the six original rescues—Marissa, Hania, Charity, and Constance, and Phoebe and Marin—plus the six little five- and six-year-old girls Alex and Ace had stolen at the close of the Conclave.

Ace, newly promoted to Director of his trade house, no longer merely collected information for others to use. He listened to the gathered whispered secrets of his own network. He'd heard of a Council shipment of girls from the eastern zones to Zone Four and had taken the information to Alex. The two men had worked together to steal and smuggle them out in Ace's returning goods.

If the appearance of Alex with six little girls hadn't shocked her, the story of how they'd come to be with him would have. She knew Ace was brilliant. She'd had no idea he'd ever trust Alex enough to work with him. So much had happened at the Conclave.

So much had happened since the Conclave.

Was that why Leo preferred Rose to her? Calm Rose kept her head, even when she was determined to be done with it all. Lena struggled every day to stay steady. She usually failed. What child would want to be around someone who was so angry all the time?

I'm trying. I am trying.

What she and Alex had built between them was worth the effort of getting along with Thomas and the other guardians. Alex might be occasionally high-handed and infuriating, but he made her feel alive like no one else. That was worth protecting.

She looked around the room. All of the girls were in their places. Since she'd declared herself, and Rose in her absence, as guardians, the girls were considered wards and required to dine at the formal mid-day lunch with the boys and young men.

Thomas had said it was a small concession. Alex tried to explain it away as a way for the girls to practice shielding themselves from the heavy weight of the male energy in small time periods. It was a way for her and Rose, and Alex and Thomas, too, to observe interactions with the girls and with Lena herself to try to flush out the few participants in the plot she struggled so hard to get Thomas to act upon.

She tolerated the requirement because each guardian headed a table of their own. They sat with wards of different levels—from the newest six-year-olds to those twenty-year-olds nearing senior ward status. One-on-one exposure to the other guardians was minimal.

In spite of the enforced exposure to the concentrated male energy, all of the girls looked healthier. It wasn't merely added weight due to the regular meals but also the smiles and the laughter. Even Hania, the saddest after the loss of her match, Lydie, in the rescue from the prison, wore a small smile. She tried to make her way out of her self-imposed shell. Lena couldn't wait to get them settled somewhere more permanent, without the constant energy bombardment. It *would* happen.

Of course, taking the girls away from the fort's protections was one of many ideas Thomas was set against. It was a source of constant friction between Lena and Alex as he applied pressure to get her to cooperate and she chafed against his friend's restrictions.

The noise in the room died as boys and men took their own places. By the time the second bell sounded, the room was silent.

"You may be seated," Lena told the students at her table, using the formal phrasing the guardians insisted upon. The phrase was echoed around the room.

The students at her table sat. She had nine of them, ranging in age from Marissa's six years to the young man facing her who would be taking his Junior exams next summer. Lena had never cared for him. All too often when Marc's gaze came to rest upon Marissa, Lena saw the same weighing, avaricious expression she found in the eyes of certain guardians.

Lena's stomach turned. Marissa was the youngest of the original group of girls they'd rescued. That certain men of power saw her only as a tool, even as a receptacle, left Lena awash in surges of furious fire and ice.

She watched Marc as the others at the table began the daily ritual of sharing their morning activities while eating lunch. He pretended to be attentive to the boys, but his focus returned again and again to the small girl seated at Lena's right.

She'd had enough. She settled her fork beside her plate and leaned in, face set and stare boring into Marc. It wasn't long before he felt the force of her glare. The moment his gaze turned to hers and he realized he'd been caught, shock flared across his face, and he dropped his gaze to his plate. Before Lena could feel any satisfaction, though, he raised his head and met Lena's glower. A defiant smirk lifted his lips.

Warmth from the slow spread of an enraged flush spread up the skin of her chest and over her neck and face. Only a junior ward who thought he could act with impunity would meet her eyes with such insolent defiance. Was he involved with those plotting against her? Like the senior ward and young guardian in the garden up on the surface?

Thomas dismissed their behavior as innocuous. Now this idiot smirked at her as if she should be afraid of him.

Thomas wants proof? I'll give him proof.

The ward's smile turned into a wet gasp. She watched, face impassive, as he paled, and a cold sweat beaded on his upper lip. His hands clutched his lower stomach. He swallowed spasmodically.

"Marc?" Lena managed to make her voice sound concerned. "Are you okay?"

Eight pairs of eyes swiveled to Marc.

He couldn't even shake his head. Of course, he couldn't. His gut twisted as if Lena had reached her hands inside of him to squeeze and knot his entrails. His mouth hung open, and he was white with shock.

Lena rose from her place at the head of the table and circled to him. "The rest of you go ahead and finish eating. I'll be back as soon as I've delivered Marc to the infirmary."

Clever boy fought it enough to manage a shake of his head. He knew he was in trouble. Did he know it was too late?

Lena lifted him from his chair, slipping an arm around him. The Dust moved his legs for her, firing energy into his nerves and muscles.

"It's okay, Erwin," Lena told the Fort historian who rose in concern from his seat at the table next to hers. "I'm taking him to the infirmary. We'll be fine. Keep an eye on my wards for me until I get back, will you?"

The man nodded, his lion's mane of hair making him look even more fierce as he swept his gaze over her remaining students.

"I'll be right back, Marissa," she whispered to the wide-eyed. "I've just got to take care of Marc." She gave the little girl a tight smile to reassure her.

It was true enough. She would take care of Marc, assuming he cooperated. With Thomas in his office and Alex busy prepping for departure somewhere else in the Fort, Lena was free to make sure the ward cooperated.

Lena led him from the cafeteria. Once they were in the hall, her hand tightened on Marc's shoulder, and she all but dragged him along to find an empty classroom on the way to the infirmary. She'd only need to use it for a few minutes.

Focused on dragging Marc away, she almost didn't hear the shout behind her.

"Lena!" Jackson loped up the hall from the other direction. He shifted course from the cafeteria to Lena.

"Hi, Jackson," she called out cheerily. "Can't stop." She turned and kept Marc moving.

"Did I miss my chance to slip in and grab some food? Are they already seated?" He came closer and saw Marc's sweating, agonized face in profile. His wide smile faltered. "Lena? What's going on?"

"Marc got sick. I'm helping him to the infirmary." That much was true. She flashed him a quick smile and turned away again, throwing back over her shoulder, "If you're starving, go keep

Marissa company and have my lunch. Believe me, you'd be doing me a favor. I can grab something after."

"Nah," he answered, almost close enough to reach out for Marc now, "no need for that. Let me help you—"

"No!" Smile gone, she rounded on Jackson. "I'm handling this, Jackson." She held his gaze with hers and lowered her voice. "Go eat. Or go plan an exit for me, because I'll be taking the girls sooner rather than later. Marc is mine to handle." She left the words "as I see fit" unspoken. He'd understand. He was already drawing back from her as he realized what she meant and what was really going on. He just didn't know why.

Jackson's face hardened. "No, Lena. Not again."

Not again? Well, of course Jackson would assume she meant to torture and kill the young man. Never mind that she'd been on her best behavior for the last two months. As far as Jackson was concerned, she was a danger to everyone, including herself. But Marc wasn't Councilor Three. He hadn't hurt her family. He had information she needed to keep herself and those she loved safe. As long as he cooperated, she had no intention of killing him. The coldness of Jackson's voice told her he wouldn't likely believe her.

They hadn't spoken of what happened that night on Councilor Three's train car, though Jackson had tried several times. Lena refused every time. She didn't need a reminder of his face, of his words, once he'd realized how dark she was inside. She refused to answer now, too.

She dragged Marc away down the hall, the Dust moving his legs so his weight wasn't more than her slight frame could handle. Jackson paced behind her. She turned the corner, found a dark, empty classroom, and opened the door. She shoved Marc's collapsing body inside.

Before the young ward hit the floor, she rounded on Jackson.

He was ready for her. He reached and grabbed her arms, forcing her back into the room as he used his foot to catch the door and slam it behind them.

"You are *not* doing this again." His voice was tight and furious.

"Who do you think you are?!"

"The only one who seems to give a damn about what you're doing to yourself."

"For Dust's sake, Jackson!" Lena rolled her eyes and pushed him away, using the Dust to shock his hands from her when he wouldn't let go.

Jackson shook them, backing away. Lena returned her attention to Marc on the floor. The young man's eyes were white around the edges and rolled toward Jackson behind her as she approached. Lena sat cross-legged beside him. Using a delicate touch, she put her fingers on the side of his chin and tilted his head toward her. He needed to pay attention to the one person who'd matter the most in his life in the next few minutes—her.

She leaned in. "You've either been collaborating, or you know of the plot against myself and my girls. Tell me what you know."

"He's a junior ward. He doesn't know anything!"

"Tell me what you know. Tell me now."

Marc swallowed. His head tilted back and twisted from side to side.

Lena didn't hesitate. She told the Dust where to move, what she needed to make the twisting pain in Marc's gut became agony. Always eager to please, the Dust flashed through him to comply.

Marc arched off the floor, no longer panting. He didn't moan. The pain froze his breath in his lungs. His fingers twitched toward his belly, but he couldn't even manage to move his arms to curl them over his abdomen.

"This is insane, Lena. Stop it!"

Lena gave it a few more moments before she told the Dust to ease back. Marc's back collapsed to the floor. His breath gasped out, little hiccups of pain and fear. She leaned in over him, making sure he could see her face above his.

"The next time it won't just be twisting, Marc. You'll be bleeding out. You have ten seconds to compose yourself and start talking."

He blinked at her. His lips twisted, then compressed. "Not

telling…anything.”

“Nine…eight…seven….”

“I won’t let you do this.” Jackson’s voice drew closer.

“Five…four….”

“You’re so obsessed I’m not even sure you know what’s real anymore! Alex should have handled this months ago. You have to stop!”

She felt him looming over her. Intellectually, she knew Jackson didn’t want to hurt her. But his own obsession with keeping her safe, even from her own nature, and his inability to see her for what she was made him a danger right now. She whipped her head around. There were tears in Jackson’s eyes. His fisted hand was raised, shaking.

“Stop interfering.”

Jackson’s feet left the ground with the force of her push. He stumbled back against the table, his weight sliding it back across the floor. The Dust held him there, immobile.

Lena turned back to Marc. “And zero.” His body didn’t arch this time. He twitched. A soft keening leaked from his throat. She let it go on—actual tearing inside this time—until the smell of his voided colon hit her. She glanced down. A puddle of urine spread from beneath him.

She crawled up to his head, looming over him from behind as she slipped her hands around his cheeks to hold his head in place. She eased off again.

“I can fix that, Marc. Jackson can fix it, and he actually wants to. But I won’t allow it unless you tell me the truth. If you don’t, I’m going to start on your brain next. There’s no recovery from that. Not ever.”

“Lena, please stop—”

“Okay!” Marc’s gasp cut off Jackson. “They’re guardians. And agents. Former students. About a third of the seniors. It’s true. They’re recruiting us.”

“No.” Jackson’s denial was flat. “He’s only saying that because of the pain. It can't be that widespread. Thomas and Alex would know. I’d *know*.”

“You’d know?” Lena couldn’t help the small laugh that

escaped her. "Jackson, you'd be the last person to realize the people around you are plotting. All you want to see is goodness. You've handicapped yourself." She turned back to the young man on the floor. "Tell me something useful. Tell me something I don't already know, or I'll start again."

Marc moaned and gasped. He tried to shake his head, but she held it fast. He took a quick series of breaths and then groaned out, "They moved it up. We were going to take you out this Spring, but they moved it up. To take advantage of Agent Dynamo being gone."

Agent Dynamo? *Alex.* He would leave in the morning. He'd be gone six months, give or take a couple of weeks.

That's what the guardian meant this morning when he said 'it's coming'. They planned to strike at her in the next six months.

Lena's breath caught. She leaned back and looked over to Jackson, immobile but for the shock and disbelief cycling over his face. The moment his expression settled into repulsed acceptance, she released him.

His body sagged down. He caught himself and stalked over to stare down at the young ward on the floor. When he spoke, his voice was as hard as his face. "When?"

Free of Lena's hands, Marc shook his head. "I don't know. Soon. We were told final stages. Soon."

"Find Alex." Lena almost didn't recognize her own soft voice. It was flat. Defeat? No. It was her old standby, rage.

Jackson squatted beside Marc, ignoring the puddle of piss and the smell. His hand gathered a wad of the front of the ward's shirt, pulling up. "*How*?"

"*Get Alex. Now.*"

Jackson looked at her. Something in her face made him scramble up. "Don't kill him."

Lena flashed him a withering glare. "Alex's taking a report or prepping to leave. He's up on—"

"I know where he is."

"Then go. Make an excuse to get him here."

As soon as he'd gone, Lena rose. She stared down at Marc in his own excrement. His eyes tracked her. His chest rose and fell in little gasps.

"It should worry you, Marc," she told him softly, "that Jackson is so convinced I'm going to kill you. It should worry you a great deal."

She backed away from him until she reached the table. Perched on the edge, she kept her gaze locked on a spot above Marc's head.

A vision flashed into her head—a pale man with silvery blonde hair perched on the edge of her hospital bed, staring off into space as he waited. *I am nothing like Lucas.*

Lena twisted her wrists, almost feeling the bite of the restraints again. There was a difference between cruel sport and necessity.

She shook her head. It didn't matter. Lucas was dead. Alex had seen to that.

Footsteps in the hall outside brought her out of her reverie. She slid off the table to intercept anyone other than Jackson or Alex. When the door swung in, three familiar men entered instead of two.

Three familiar, angry men.

"What are you doing?" Thomas's pale blue gaze swept down to Marc on the floor and back to Lena's face in a mere second. Behind him, Alex closed the door behind Jackson and gestured for the younger man to stand behind Marc. Alex himself stood in the doorway, watching her, his face impassive.

"Rooting out the conspiracy you and Alex are so content to wait out—"

"This *again*?" He was furious. "All I hear about now is this threat. The threat, I'll remind you, that *you* didn't think was real enough to come share with us when you first learned of it—"

"That's bullshit," Alex spoke up, his voice flat. "Lena didn't know us well enough to trust us yet back then."

"Not even you?" Thomas's tone sank from fury to rebuke.

"Especially not me."

"Shut up and listen! It's not a few rogue guardians, Thomas." She flipped a quick look at Alex, but he didn't react to her words at all. He had his agent mask on. "It's guardians and agents and senior wards. It's not 'an infection,' like you said. It's a cancer. And it's spreading." She hated that her voice sounded so petulant, but dammit, she'd been through enough. She'd earned the right to be a full partner in the revolution, especially when it affected the safety of her girls. She'd trusted them. She'd given them what they needed. "They've moved it up. The attack on me. The girls. Moved it up to take advantage of Alex's absence." She tilted her head to look at Thomas. "It's not my imagination. And it's not *innocuous* talk."

Thomas's eyes narrowed. He crossed to Marc.

She tracked him, ignoring Alex, watching as Thomas stood over the ward. His toes were close enough to tap Marc's ear.

"Tell me." Thomas said only two words, but they seemed to chill the room by several degrees.

Marc made a small negative movement with his head. Though he'd conspired against the man, he was still intimidated enough by Thomas to try to opt for silence again.

Lena had the Dust give the student an internal reminder why he'd chosen to speak the first time.

When he was able, Marc swallowed. "Night attack," he gasped. "It's going to look like a night attack. By that Neo-barb's people. The woman? Rose. Get rid of her—" his gaze flashed to Lena "—then drag the rest away. They've got a place. Some of us—the juniors who've been training with them—were supposed to go, too. Make it look like they took boys and girls. We help. We go there. We get first choice. You hunt Neo-barbs."

There was a subtle aura of cold menace rolling off Alex now. She remembered it well. She liked it.

"Where?" he asked.

Marc shook his head. "I don't know." His gaze flicked up as Lena bore down with the Dust, pressure on his painful belly to remind him what she was capable of. "You can torture me all you want, but I don't know!"

Disgusted, Lena walked away, wrapping her arms around herself. When she looked back, Jackson stirred, though Thomas stood still and straight above the ward. Perhaps Jackson had realized that wishing wouldn't make the betrayal go away? It wouldn't lessen the danger to her girls.

"Is anyone on the Council involved in this plot?" Thomas asked.

"I don't know. I'm just a ward. They didn't tell us that."

"I want names," Alex gritted out now. "Tell me which guardians, which agents. Tell me which seniors."

Marc turned his head to stare up at the ceiling. "No."

"No?" Alex knelt now, placing himself in Marc's line of sight.

"Kill me if you want, but I'm done talking."

"Lena—" Jackson gestured her back so she could make the ward cooperate with Thomas and Alex.

She rolled her eyes. *Oh, now you're on board with torture and darkness?* "It doesn't matter, Jackson."

"It does matter, Lena! These are my friends. These are people I've spent my entire life with."

"It matters!" The echo of Jackson's angry sense of betrayal rang in Thomas's voice. "Don't be stupid. We need this information."

"Then you can figure it out how to get it on your own. I've heard all I need. I'm taking my girls and going." She walked back to them, waited until Alex rose to stare down at her. Was that agreement in his eyes? "Because no matter how many names he gives us, we'll never know if we have all of them. We'll never know how many others there are. It doesn't matter. We're done here."

Alex nodded.

"So now what? We kill him?" Jackson sounded almost eager.

"No, Jackson." She searched his face. "We don't kill him."

Thomas watched her, his gaze moving between her and Alex standing so close she could lean into him if she wanted.

Lena swept her attention over Marc and focused on the specific areas she'd caused the Dust to damage. Now it raced through, healing. "Get up. I've healed you enough for that."

Marc rolled over to crouch and stand. He wasn't terribly stable, and his hands were still clenched and pressed to his lower belly, but he could stand. He lifted his eyes to hers and they were sullen and afraid.

Marc focused on her, not Thomas. She flicked a quick look at the Councilor and saw he'd noticed, as well.

She leaned in, moving to stand very close to the ward so she could breathe her instructions up at him. "Stay in the infirmary. Speak to no one about this but the Councilor, if he should need any more information. If you try to tell, you'll feel pain that will put what you just went through to shame."

Marc stared at her. Hate pulsed from him. "Yeah? How will you do that? If I tell, you'll be *gone*."

Jackson moved beside her, hands coming up, but Thomas put his arm out to hold him back.

Alex turned to narrow his dark eyes at the defiant ward. "Stupid boy. The Dust will do it for her. Haven't you figured out yet that you all should have let her be?"

Lena laughed and tilted her head at Marc. "I won't have to do anything," she explained. "I've already done it, right now. The Dust inside of you will do exactly as I've told it, no matter what happens to me. It has its trigger. Even think of it in the company of the wrong men, and you *will* suffer. Speak of it, and you'll die terribly. Do you understand?" She waited until he gave her a sullen nod. "Good. Now come along, I need to leave you at the infirmary before anyone starts to wonder what's taking so long."

Lena waited for them by the door. After a moment, all four of the men followed her. Before she could lead the way, however, Thomas took hold of her arm at the crook of her elbow.

He held her back. When Alex opened his mouth and paused, Thomas shook his head. "Like it or not, I'm the Councilor, and I should have intervened weeks ago. The two of you can talk later." Thomas met Alex's gaze, his pale blue eyes steady on Alex's angry dark stare.

After a long moment, Alex turned to her. He seemed as if he'd like to say something, or perhaps do something. Was he going to reach out to her? Instead, he turned and left the room.

"It's hard to understand, Lena, but I've had reasons for everything this summer." Thomas's pale gaze, so hard for her to read, now held her own. It seemed important to him that she listen. “I hoped that you’d be patient until I could explain—”

“Silly me, believing everything you sold me about six hands holding everything together.” Lena tried to keep her voice low and even, but even she could hear the disappointment and hurt.

“You are a partner. Our focus right now is on ensuring your safety, and the best way—”

“Is what? To lock me up? Sorry. Been there, done that…my entire childhood.” She turned the hurt into angry bravado. “I won’t allow anyone to lock me away for my own good ever again. I won’t allow anyone to do it to my girls, either. But since you’re such a believer in the virtue of patience, you won’t mind waiting for me to let you in on *my* decisions, will you?”

So childish, Lena.

Maybe. But was she right?

“Lena—”

“It’s not about me anymore, and I won’t allow them to be hurt. Take your own advice. Don’t try to stop me, Thomas.”

Thomas went still before he nodded once and stepped away, releasing her arm. “I’ll send someone to clean up this mess. You can get him to the infirmary, yes?”

Lena dipped her head and swept away from Thomas. Alex was long gone, but Jackson and the ward waited for her in the hall. She led them to the infirmary.

Lena took a deep breath outside the cafeteria. Her gaze strafed over the men and boys gathered in the room. Their numbers overwhelmed her few girls and Rose. She needed to pretend she knew nothing; needed her calm to push back the rage beating in her temples so she could dissemble long enough to gather supplies and make plans to carry them to safety.

Jackson had left her outside the infirmary after she’d silenced Marc, at least in the short term, by instructing the Dust to keep his fever elevated and his stomach roiling. He was barely conscious by the time they’d delivered him. Jackson, so eager to kill the traitor back in the classroom, was less comfortable with the state she’d chosen for Marc.

He'd told her Alex had instructed him to go see what he could do about supplies. He had to calculate how long it would take to get them enough to make it away without drawing attention. They'd meet her back at their room after she'd finished her luncheon responsibilities. His voice had been rough with emotion. She hadn't even had a chance to answer him before he'd stalked away.

Now she slipped back into the cafeteria, head down. Once she settled herself into her chair, she took a breath and raised her gaze. She met seven pairs of questioning eyes, and one pair of knowing brown ones. She gave them a bright smile.

"Marc will be fine. I imagine he'll be himself again in a couple of days."

The boys nodded and went back to their meals, chattering among themselves. Marissa wasn't fooled. Lena winked at her. Marissa's little brows went up, and she smiled.

"Lunch's almost done," she reminded Lena in her little wise woman voice, "so you better hurry and finish if you want to eat."

Lena grinned back at her and nodded. She was right. Lena barely had time to finish half her cold meal. The bell rang out from the front. Though her stomach roiled with sudden nausea, she took a few last quick bites as a guardian rose from his seat and read out the day's announcements. When the second chime came, she handed off her plate to the boy who had pulled table duty and dismissed the rest of them.

Lena steered Marissa through the milling boys and men to Rose. Lena slipped the little girl's hand into Rose's and curled her friend's fingers around the smaller ones now safe in her palm. She leaned in and spoke directly into Rose's ear, keeping her voice low in spite of the boisterous voices filling the room around them.

"I have new information about our safety." Lena leaned back to be sure Rose could hear her. When Rose's startled expression smoothed into poker face, she leaned forward again and continued, "Make excuses, gather up the girls, and bring them to my room."

Rose pulled away to search Lena's face. Whatever she saw there, she nodded her head. "We'll be there as soon as I can grab them all."

Lena nodded and sent a last reassuring smile to Marissa. The little girl didn't buy it and neither did the solemn boy watching Lena from the other side of Rose. Lena's lips curved up. Marissa was too smart for her own good. And Leo…

Leo had decided almost as soon as he'd arrived that he didn't like Lena. That might be a problem once Alex left, but for now, she didn't have time to deal with it. She left them, hurrying back to her room.

Thomas was already keying the lock to her room. Jackson stood behind him. She didn't say anything as she approached and reached past him to open the door. By the time she had closed it and turned, Thomas sat in the seating area at the front of the room. Jackson stood with his back to her, shoulders stiff. His hands were clenched at his side.

Which betrayal bothered him more? That of his classmates and teachers in plotting against her and a group of innocent girls? Or hers—for having the audacity to push him away as she followed her own heart, however much he might hate where it led her?

She regretted being so hard on Jackson. She'd *known* Marc was guilty, and she'd been right. Lena ignored Thomas to approach Jackson. He didn't mean to be heavy-handed. He tried so hard to step out of Alex's shadow, and he did think that he had Lena's best interests at heart. He just didn't realize how insulting it was that he thought he knew better than she did. None of them did.

She reached out to place a gentle hand on his shoulder.

Jackson shrugged her hand off, dipping his shoulder to step away. She left him and turned back to find Thomas's keen, evaluating gaze on her.

She cleared her throat. "Alex is coming, isn't he?" She hated how tentative her voice sounded.

Thomas gave her a tired, humorless smile. "He is."

She waited. Instead of giving voice to her frustration, Lena tried a new tactic. She backed off. She stepped away to perch on the edge of one of the seats across from Thomas.

"Can you help with supplies?" Tentative again. Ugh! She wasn't wrong!

"Got it handled." Jackson's voice was still rough, angry. "We'll have a few weeks' worth when we're ready to go. Alex put a buzz in the Supply Master's ear that the Councilor wants the girls' abilities tested in the field, like the wards are tested each year. He's waiting for the formal approval from the Councilor's office—"

"He'll have it by tomorrow," Thomas promised.

"—but he's started putting together the provisions. By the time we're ready and have a plan in place, they'll be packed and ready to go with us, with no more questions than a testing exercise would ordinarily draw."

Her door opened, and Alex entered. He shrugged out of a huge rucksack and settled it on the floor. Alex ignored the men. He crossed the room to her and leaned down to wrap a long-fingered hand around the side of her head and tug it toward him. He didn't kiss her. He gently bumped foreheads with her before he plopped down beside her on the couch.

Warmth spread through her. She didn't know how he did it, but it had to be why they'd made it this long. It certainly wasn't due to her and her volatile temper.

"Our educational traditions provide you with cover. An excellent decision." Thomas gave Alex a nod. "Initial provisions aren't an issue, then. More will follow," Thomas continued, "brought to your location by a team we trust, who've been with us from the beginning. And Lena, I mean the beginning, when Alex and I were boys--our original crew of misfits. They're my personal eyes and ears, doing very different work than Alex."

"Your personal eyes and ears?" Lena almost didn't finish the scathing thought that had burst out of her mouth, but he wouldn't expect her to be circumspect, would he? The reminder of the work they were doing behind the scenes, work that she knew little about and had no input on, was like a bucket of cold water that drowned the warmth of moments before. There was no way to hide the quiet disdain in her voice, so she wouldn't bother trying. "You mean the eyes and ears that didn't know there was a conspiracy brewing under your nose? Or would the position of your nose be filled by someone else you grew up with, so that would be his job?" So much for that new tactic of backing off.

Alex sighed and shifted. A little more space grew between them.

Thomas didn't react, though, except to cock his head at her and allow the ghost of a smile to drift across his lips and then flee. "No, those who missed the conspiracy are now suspect themselves and will be kept busy elsewhere. The rest have been away, working on separate projects for us. You met three this morning. This'll be lighter duty than they're used to—following you out, helping to get you supplied and settled, then reporting back to me before escorting wards to your location to continue lessons. But their discretion is unquestionable."

"Escorting wards? After what you just saw? You've got to be kidding me."

"Young boys," Alex inserted, his voice smooth and easy. Charming. "The ones you've been lobbying all summer to replace the older boys with. Only those under the age of ten, handpicked by Thomas or me."

Lena turned to him. A long beat of silence passed as they stared each other. Lena shoved her hair back behind her ears. She could feel the imposed rules chafing already.

Alex's gaze followed the movement. He turned up one corner of his mouth in an attempt at a small smile. He must know she was upset. He knew how she felt about this. They'd been fighting over it all summer. Still, he obviously expected to charm her into cooperating.

"It's the cost of supplies, Lena." Thomas's voice was low and soothing. "The cost of building a new school. You don't trust the older boys? Fine, we'll send younger boys, but we will send boys. You promised to help us learn, too."

She didn't bother looking at Thomas. She kept her focus on Alex. "We all made promises we haven't kept."

Hurt flared behind his eyes. The little smile was gone.

She looked away. She had to.

Thomas sighed, then closed his mouth with a snap. A muscle

along his jaw tightened. “I’m sorry you feel that way. Nevertheless, this is one promise we insist you keep.”

“Then these will be the only qualifications you make. Otherwise, I take my girls and disappear. How many years did it take Alex to find me the first time?” She couldn't believe she'd said that.

Alex was still. He stared at the blank wall across from them, his face just as blank. Thomas pursed his lips, flicked a glance at Alex, then nodded.

She went on. “I expect supplies and assistance as needed in exchange for the access of two agents—the same two agents every time—and five boys in eight week rotations.”

“Five?” Even Jackson apparently thought five was unreasonable.

Thomas huffed a little laugh and shook his head. “At least fifteen to twenty. And the rotations should be much shorter, so we can expose more boys to what they need to be learning.”

“I will not have my girls outnumbered and deprived of attention and education they deserve. I will not accept more than five to ten, *period.* With shorter rotations you’ll expose more boys, yes, but at the cost of depth of understanding. There are only so many hours in each day. Do you want to substitute quantity for quality?”

“Eight weeks is a long time,” Thomas said. “Two months becomes a safety concern. We don’t want to lose any of you.”

Lena’s eyes narrowed. “I kept myself safe for ten years. I think I know the challenges and difficulties of life outside better than you.”

“Do you?” Another smile, this one seeming somewhere between knowing and sad, made a brief appearance. “That’s a discussion for another time, I think. In any case, it’s very different keeping safe a small, unknown person who didn’t make herself a target, and keeping twenty or more people safe, all of them already targets and hunted, many of them too young to help defend—”

“You’d be surprised what my girls can manage already.”

“Do you want them to have to?” Jackson's question was equal

measures indignant and incredulous.

"Yes." Even Lena was surprised by her passionate admission. "I want them to learn to defend themselves—we all know they're going to have to. I want them to learn they *can* protect themselves. They have the right to defend themselves using whatever they need to use. Because no matter how well we hide away right now, eventually someone will find us. I want to be damn sure when that day comes, the person who dares to come and try to hurt them will be the one bleeding on the ground."

She watched the men digest her words. Alex still stared at the wall, seemingly disengaged. When Thomas nodded, she couldn't help the relief that bloomed. She liked Thomas. She didn't want to be at cross-purposes, not now that she was about to have what she wanted. It was time for her to create her own system, and they'd have to deal with it..

"Okay, Lena. Ten boys," Thomas said. "Eight week rotations with our men traveling to and from to keep the wards safe. We provide supplies and help set you up. Do you object to Jackson accompanying you now?"

He'd conceded more than she'd expected. She opened her mouth to thank him, to reassure them all, but the lock of the door cycled. Rose held the door open for the small crowd of chattering girls and one small boy.

Rose shushed the excited girls and Leo, looking back and forth between Lena and the men. "What's going on? What's happened?"

"Alex!" Leo ran across the room, a grin splitting his face.

Alex tore his stare from the wall opposite himself and gave the small boy an answering smile. He leaned out with his arms open to welcome the boy. Alex held him close, even as he shushed him and explained in a whisper the adults were having a very important conversation.

"What's going on?" Rose repeated.

Lena glanced at Jackson. He hadn't said much, and his head was down, hiding his face.

She took a deep, focusing breath. "We're leaving. Very soon. As soon as we can make our final arrangements." Her gaze swept over the girls' now solemn faces. She managed a half smile to offer them some encouragement. She'd done what she had to in order to keep them safe. She'd keep doing it, without regret. Her half-smile grew. "I hope you ladies are ready to start our grand adventure. It's time for us to go find a space of our own."

She exchanged a long look with Rose. "Fort Nevada will have the supplies handled, at least enough for a few weeks. We have an arrangement for afterward. We'll be going in the next week or so."

"To your gas station in the desert?" Thomas asked her.

Lena shook her head. "No. Somewhere else. I'll show you on the map."

There was a slight movement beside her. When she glanced over, Alex frowned at her words.

Thomas nodded.

"Are we excited? Are we ready for clear skies and fresh air?" Lena asked the girls.

Their cheer was answer enough.

"And no more *guardians*." Marissa made every syllable an insult. Even the youngest was done with being controlled.

"No more guardians," Lena agreed with laugh. Jackson still hadn't said anything. She tilted her head to try to see his lowered face. "Are you ready, Jackson? You don't have any objections to going with us?"

Would Alex? He seemed not to care. He'd been involved in the plan.

Jackson lifted his head. "No objections."

"And soon, yes?"

He exchanged a look with Alex that she couldn't decipher. Then his gaze settled on Lena and stayed. His lips were still compressed, though not with anger anymore. She wasn't sure what the emotion haunting his eyes was. "Soon. Because the sooner we find our own place, the safer *everyone* will be."

"Am I going?" Leo's plaintive question was directed at Alex.

Alex grinned. "Of course you are."

"Are you?"

The smile faltered. "I hope so. Eventually." He ruffled Leo's dark hair. "For now, you and Marissa and the rest of our young friends have to have your quiet reading time. The big girls have to start getting their things ready. And we adults—we've got to hash some things out."

Leo wouldn't be distracted. "Why eventually? Why not with us?"

"Alex has to go on a trip for Thomas," Lena told the little boy. She understood the look in his eyes. She'd been feeling the same disappointment and dread.

Alex nodded. "I'm taking the train tomorrow early, so that I can get through my trip and come back. As soon as I do get back, you'd better believe I'll be on my way to go see you."

Alex rose to his feet, slinging Leo under his arm and bouncing him. "But now—I'm taking you for your reading lesson." Before he carried the laughing boy out the door, Alex turned to Lena and gave her a searching look. "And then I'm coming back to have a conversation with Lena about promises."

SIX

Alex

Thomas waited for him outside the classroom where he'd left Leo and the smaller girls.

Alex shook his head as he pulled the door closed behind him. "The rest of the night is for Lena and me. Without arguing." He kept his voice low. "No more meetings. No more strategy." He turned away to head down the hall to Lena's quarters.

"You *have* to intervene now. Things have changed."

"Nothing's changed." Alex kept going. "Except that Lena's right—no matter what we get out of that kid, you'll never know if it was all of it, most of it, or even enough."

"I can handle the ward. That's not the issue. The issue is you're leaving. She's leaving. She's taking our future with her. If anything happens to them…this isn't safe."

He stopped and turned to face Thomas. "Staying here isn't safe. She's not leaving. She's relocating. She's protecting *their* futures. She has every right to do it." Alex leaned in and jabbed his friend in the chest with a finger. "You told me to back off—that I was too close, and you could "handle" her better while I kept my focus on planning our next steps. You said you had it under control. You'd root out who it was she heard plotting to *kill her*. You'd find any conspirators. You'd end it. I trusted you to do that."

Thomas opened his mouth, but Alex wasn't finished.

"You didn't. You've completely lost her confidence." Alex paused to take a deep, calming breath. He expected Thomas to jump in, but his friend stared at him, stone-faced. "Now you're going to try to convince me to tell her to stay, because you can keep them safe while I'm away. But you won't be able to do that, either.

"Did you even bother to read the report Patrick and I handed you? There are parties in play now that we have no knowledge of—not what they want, not who they're working for, not what their goals are. For all we know they're wrapped up in the traitors here at the Fort. The only thing we do know is one of them delivered the file detailing Patrick's activities to Councilor Six while Patrick was standing right there, and Pat barely got out of the zone with his ass intact."

Alex rubbed his mouth in disgust. "Until we identify them, none of us are safe. Right now, there is one person with a target painted on her that everyone wants a shot at. Lena. I'm not any more willing to bet her life on someone else's eyes than she is."

"It won't just be me. Even before we heard from Patrick, I'd called back all of our original—"

"More secrets, Thom! I trusted you to be open with me, at least. Then I was surprised by Patrick because his cover was blown and he came in before you expected. Were you going to bother telling me you'd called them in? Or why?"

"You were leaving. It was irrelevant to your mission."

"Irrelevant to my—? You don't think it'd be good for me to know you're worried enough to pull everyone in? Fuck the mission. It mattered to my relationship!"

Thomas said nothing, but his eyes narrowed.

"It doesn't matter!" Alex swallowed and lowered his voice. "We've lost her trust this summer. That may be a challenge for what we're building, which I know is all you're concerned about, but it's bad for me, personally, Thom. It's bad." Alex looked off down the hall, where he knew she waited for yet another confrontation. "This is not what I want."

Thomas leaned away from him. His lips thinned. "If that's the way you feel, I'm surprised you're still leaving then. Why bother with a critical mission when you can take off with Lena and go play family?"

"Play family? Are you serious?"

"You're putting the needs of one small group—one small person—ahead of everything we've built. That's why we don't have families, Alex. We all agreed. Your priorities are questionable—"

"My priorities are exactly where they need to be. We made that agreement when we were kids, before we had any understanding of what it meant. If my priorities are any indicator, then we should all have one."

"We do. In each other." Thomas's face was so still that Alex, even after all these years, couldn't read the emotion behind it. He could see something simmering behind his friend's eyes. It was the same thing he'd glimpsed again and again as they'd argued this summer, but it was running hotter now.

Thomas was as close to losing it as Alex had ever seen him. *Because of Lena? Leo?* He broke eye contact and looked down, squeezing the bridge of his nose. He was done with this summer. He was done with turmoil and strife.

And jealousy. No. Thomas was above being that petty. When he heard a long slow breath easing from his friend as he, too, worked to calm himself, Alex looked back up, determined to make Thom see. "I'm leaving because there is nothing else I believe in like what we have spent all these years building. We built it together, but we've built it for them, Thom. For the boys and the girls like us. That includes those children. That includes Lena. We are all a kind of family." He shook his head and let Thomas have the truth. "And yeah, in a perfect world, I'd like to go with Lena. I'd rather be sure she's settled in somewhere safe and they're going to make it through the winter. But I trust you to help her. And I trust her to do it. You need to trust her, too."

"It's hard to trust someone that unstable." Thomas's voice was calm and flat.

"She's not unstable." Alex pursed his lips as he searched for the right replacement. "She's …volatile."

"It's the same thing." Thomas shook his head and held up his hand. "You made your point. She needs to do this her way. So long as it doesn't endanger the movement, we need to allow it.

But if her…volatility…proves dangerous, she needs to understand that I will protect us by protecting her, even from herself. So do you."

"I trust you. Just give her space." He flashed a grin. "She's going to surprise you."

"I don't like surprises, Alex. You didn't used to, either."

Alex laughed and twirled his fingers in a circular motion as he turned to continue down the hall. "We're all in a constant state of change. It's called evolution. It's what we're counting on, remember?"

Thomas didn't follow him. At the hall intersection, Alex glanced back as he continued through to Lena's door. Thomas still stood where he'd left him, staring down at the floor. He'd come around. He'd have to.

Things were changing. But change was what they were after, even if it was head-spinning at first. How could they expect the rest of the world to adapt to a new way of life if they weren't willing to do it themselves?

He opened the door and closed it behind him, then pressed his back against it for a moment as he watched her. *Change is good.* Lena was proof of it.

She leaned over a map spread across the small table. Jackson leaned in across from her, nodding as she pointed out geographic features. As soon as she'd finished, Jackson straightened. "The location works. It's a little high elevation, but if the canyon has a true micro-climate like you say—"

"It does."

Jackson nodded. Alex could tell from the set of his shoulders that he was still angry about what had happened that afternoon. Angry at her? Or at the situation in general? "It'll still be colder than here over the winter. I'll make sure to allow for that in requisitions." He glanced over at Alex. "I'll start my lists tonight." He left her behind then, crossing to the door.

Alex stepped out of his way.

"Safe travels," Jackson told him as he left.

"Likewise."

It looked like Thomas wasn't the only one resistant to

change. But it shouldn't be surprising. Alex's focus now, and for the rest of the night, wasn't any of them.

His focus was looking up at him, tapping the map. Her face was guarded. He locked the door behind Jackson and crossed to her. He crouched in front of her but didn't touch her. "Show me?"

Lena glanced at the map. She reached a finger out, sliding it across the northeastern stretches of Zone Three above Azcon. Alex looked around the map, noting locations he was familiar with—old Taos, the southern edge of Native Nations lands, and Eagle Nest Lake. When her finger stopped in the mountains, he used those other locations to triangulate and set their new home in his head.

"Jackson said there was a micro-climate?"

She nodded. "In the canyon, yes. It's a safe location. There are the shells of existing buildings, a bunker, a stream, an orchard. If we can get the supplies from Thomas, we could probably set up windmills on one of the ridges above for extra power. "

"If it's so great, why isn't anyone living there?"

"The Neo-barbs with claim to it moved east. They ceded rights to me."

"Rights?" Alex shook his head and chuckled. "That doesn't mean—"

"It's hidden. No one is there." She smiled, sure of herself. "And if there are people there, I'll handle it. It's what I do." She looked down at her lap then. She fiddled with the seam of her loose pants.

"You do, yes. Very well." He wanted nothing more than to reach out for her. But this had to be handled before he left, and his preferred way of handling things with her wouldn't cut it. He rose to back away from her and perched on the chair behind him.

She looked up. Her expression told him she was surprised. He waited for it to fade as she searched his face for the reason he'd parked himself across the room. When he was sure she was ready, he asked the question that had been eating at him. The answer to it held the key to all their arguments and frustrations over the past few months.

"What promises have I made and not kept, Lena?"

She stared at him, then closed her eyes. “Alex, I—“

“Lena. What promises?”

She sighed. “You don’t tell me everything.”

Of all the things he might have expected, that wasn’t one. He frowned. He was an agent. She knew that. If she expected him to tell her everything he knew, they’d be there a long time. “I never promised to tell you everything.”

There was a long pause as she looked down at her hands. She picked at one of her nails. After a moment, she made a sound somewhere between a laugh and a huff of frustration and shook her hands out. “You promised I’d be a partner. Both of you did. That didn’t happen.”

He nodded. He’d just expressed the same frustration to Thom. He opened his mouth to reassure her, but she wasn’t done. This time, she raised her gaze to his and stared him down.

“And you—you promised me us. I may be young, but withholding things, keeping secrets, that’s no way to build something real. If you want this…if you still want this…?”

He raised his brows. “I wouldn’t be here if I didn’t. But Lena, everyone has secrets. I’m an agent. If you sense I’m withholding something, it may have nothing to do with you.”

“But some do.”

Alex hesitated. “Yeah. Some do.” And some of them, things that seemed simple at the time, he dreaded telling her now that they’d made it through the summer. The truth about her brother’s position as the new Councilor Three ranked right up there.

“I need to know them. Because every time I let my guard down, every time I start to let myself just…be *here* with you…some secret you’ve kept pops up. It’s infuriating and destructive, and it hurts.”

He stared at her. She didn’t drop her gaze, but the fire he craved wasn’t there. Her voice, her face, her rounded shoulders, were those of a woman who was tired of this fight. Unease stirred within him. “You’re right.”

She blinked. “I am? I mean, I am.”

Alex laughed. “Yeah. You are. I’ll tell you the things I’ve been keeping from you. You deserve it, and they’re getting in the way of us. Just…not tonight."

Disappointment flared on her face. She shook her head in disgust and started to rise.

"Because tonight is for us." He held his hand out. "Tonight is the last night we'll be together for six months, and—"

"And I'm supposed to wait? Who knows when the next secret will pop, and you'll be off making more—"

"Okay." He eased forward on the seat. Not touching her was harder than he thought. "What do you need to know before I go? What can't wait?"

"I don't know, Alex. They're your secrets. What do I need to know?"

He bowed his head. "About the girls. And about my mission."

"I know about your mission."

He shook his head. "You don't know about the conflicts of information. You don't know our agents may be compromised in Zone Two. You don't know about the records Patrick found. He was embedded in Zone Six. A month ago, he discovered a records cache in Zone Six, going back decades. They record shipments of girls from at least around the time you were born. He thinks he got them all. We can't be sure, and Patrick's cover is blown. He can't go back."

"Is that why you're going to Zone Six on this trip?"

"In part."

"And Zone Two? You're going to discover what's happening with your men?"

He nodded.

"Both are dangerous."

Alex nodded again.

"Is that why you didn't tell me?"

"I didn't tell you because I was afraid you'd want to go yourself."

She pursed her lips, taking a moment to digest that. "I would have...before today. I have the right, Alex. When you get answers on this trip, if there are decisions, missions, that affect the girls and me, I have the right to know. I have the right to *go*. I've earned it."

He stared at her. His desire to keep her safe warred with what he knew she needed. Truth. Action. The ability to use what she could do to change things.

The same damn things you need, Reyes.

He nodded. "You have earned it. I'm sorry."

After a long exhale, she tilted her head and gave him a small smile. Relief bubbled inside. She'd known somehow his apology was real.

It didn't mean she was done. "And Zone One?" She prompted him. The steel was back in her voice. Had he really thought one "I'm sorry" would smooth things over?

"The stop in Zone One is meant to convince Councilor One to throw in his lot with us, whatever it takes. The strongest Sparks breed there—"

"Ha!" She smiled, and playfully narrowed her eyes at him.

The return of her feisty humor warmed him. He grinned at her. "Present company excluded. It would be a coup to get him to turn on the Council."

She nodded, taking a deep breath. Some of the tension eased out of her. She didn't want it all. She wanted to be included.

You're such an idiot, Reyes. He took a deep breath and dove in. He needed her to know his apology was genuine. He wanted her trust. "I am sorry. It's so easy for all of us to fall back on...*Lena's being headstrong again*...because you are. But you're not the root of the difficulty this summer. Our decisions—my decisions—are often made on the fly. Sometimes they're wrong. Usually, I'm the only one who has to deal with the repercussions. But there's a learning curve here. It's not just me anymore. We can make it through, though. Together."

She stared at him without blinking, blue-green eyes huge. He couldn't read her face. Unease crawled through him. What if she couldn't get over it? What if she didn't want to?

"Your family is there, right? In Zone One?"

He couldn't help the puzzled frown. He needed an answer. Not only was she not ready to give it to him, but she'd managed to surprise him.

Yes, it was his original zone, but that was so long ago… He could feel his brows draw in again. He shook his head. "They sent me away over forty years ago. I can't imagine those strangers have anything to offer me. No, Lena. My family is here."

And not everyone is happy about it. I'm not even sure you're happy about it. He pushed the thought away and held out his hand. He wasn't sure he'd given her enough to see her through the coming months, but he needed her touch before he went. He would share it all later. He needed her to take his hand now.

She lowered her eyes and chewed her lower lip. Her hand came up to slip her hair behind her ear. Instead of dropping her hand to her lap, though, she reached out. Her fingers twined in his. She watched their hands. The flare of Dust between them happened below the surface.

Was the sensation—the relief—as powerful for her as it was for him? It pulsed through him, easing, comforting. A sigh eased from him.

She lifted her face, and her tension was gone, too.

She feels it.

Even her voice was softer as she made her point. "Keeping me ignorant won't protect me."

"No, it won't. It will only break us. I want us, Lena. I won't do it again."

Her mouth fell open a moment before she laughed. Her head fell back, and her shoulders shook. Alex frowned. When she tipped forward again and saw his face through mirth-squinted eyes, she laughed harder, shaking her head.

Holding his hand, she hopped up, crossed the distance between them and plopped down on his lap. "Really? Never again, agent man?" She leaned in close, widening her eyes dramatically as she whispered, "Never, ever, ever?"

He snorted. "I'll try."

The skin around her eyes crinkled. "That's better."

He ran his hands down her back to circle her waist and tug her closer. "This is better." He leaned down, forcing himself to use the gentlest pressure to place his lips on hers. Sparks flared just before contact, popping into existence and then fading with the pressure of their kiss. No, it didn't fade. It became internal. The energy flowed, already a molten exchange of heat and Dust.

But it was more than that now. The feel of it had subtly changed over the summer, in spite of everything they'd been through. The contact flow brought more than energy. Emotion bubbled up with the Dust from deep within them both.

It eased something inside of him at the same time that it made him lift her shirt. He skimmed his fingers over her skin. The contact deepened the exchange. He flattened his hands on her skin and pulled her in closer to his chest. He craved this. He kept it buried. He hid it from everyone. But he needed her.

He loved her.

Tell her before you leave, Reyes.

Alex tried to pull back, to give voice to the words for what flamed between them, but her lips pursued his. He pulled his hand free from her skin, lifting a finger to get her attention.

She batted at it, shaking her head and laughing.

"Wait." He laughed breathlessly. "Just…give me…I need to—"

"I accept your apology, Reyes," she growled at him. "Now no more words." She slid her hands down between them and under his waistband to do something with her palm and the Dust and his skin that made his heart stutter.

She'd have to read his mind.

SEVEN

Lena

Lena woke to sensation—the slow, feather-light caress of a finger on her skin, dragging Dust along with it beneath the surface. The electric tickle stirred more than her mind to wakefulness.

Alex traced the freckles on her back. Belly-down on the bed, she faced away from him. She didn't open her eyes. She lay there, enjoying the feel of his touch like magic, and enjoying what that touch did to her inside.

She didn't want to move at all. If she moved, he'd stop. He'd get up, grab his pack, and head out to his next mission. She'd get up and plan her escape. They wouldn't see each other for months. She'd been dreading this morning, but nothing had prepared her for this feeling of loss. The night before had changed everything.

She'd expected a night like every other that summer. Even if they spent the day arguing, usually over something Thomas had done or not done, night would fall and somehow they always ended up wrapped up in each other, feeling right again. At night the fighting didn't matter. The world didn't matter.

But it wasn't like every other night. Alex wouldn't let it go this time. He wouldn't take the easy way of appeasing her with a touch. Or perhaps it was that he needed reassurance before leaving—reassurance that came from challenging her. It was the challenge that had gotten them where they were.

He couldn't keep things from her, even if he thought it was to protect her. She needed to be a partner. He'd promised her that. He hadn't seen what he'd been doing that long summer as outside of that promise. She had.

He'd finally shared some of it. She was under no illusions she knew everything, but she understood better. He'd been afraid that if she knew there were others, knew there were records of shipments of girls stretching back at least her lifetime, she'd go herself to Zone Four, where all of their people so far had disappeared or fallen off the grid.

She would have.

She couldn't now. She had to get her girls free of this danger, get them stable and secure and learning, and then she could think about what the next step would be. She would be directly involved, she'd promised Alex. If there were decisions to be made and missions to be achieved concerning girls, she wanted to be a part of them.

Just like that—after a few hours of honesty and fears and dread—the summer's frustrations were gone. She knew if she rolled over, they'd be a step closer to his leaving. There was no welcome in the thought for her. She didn't need the distance. She dreaded it.

His soft laugh told her somehow—a shift in her breathing, perhaps, or even the way the Dust changed their response once she was conscious—he knew she was awake.

She felt him shift in the bed and the warmth of his body pressed into hers as he leaned in and settled his lips on the back of her neck. "Wake up, Lena."

"No," she whispered. "I like it right here very much."

He leaned away. "Wake up."

"Don't stop."

"I have to leave soon."

Lena sighed and opened her eyes. There was no putting it off. She rolled over. As she'd expected, the moment their eyes met, she felt something settle into place inside. They simply fit.

Alex smiled down at her, eyes sleepy but content. He slid a hand up to begin tracing the freckles on her chest. "Are we still good this morning?" he asked, only half tongue-in-cheek.

She couldn't help the laugh that burbled up. "Or am I going to morph back into Dangerena, Magdalena's evil alter ego, under the light of the sun?"

He leaned in, laughing, and kissed her. The huff of his breath warmed her lips and cheeks before he pulled back again, still laughing. "It wasn't all you, remember? I'm one-half of the equation, so I get some of the blame." He raised his hand and spread his fingers apart a tiny space.

Lena reached up and spread his long fingers as far as they would go.

"Oh, I *see*." He arched his brows. "Well, I guess I'll try harder to make it up to you, then." He'd dropped his hand back down to trace with one finger again when he started speaking. Now he slid all five fingers across her skin in a feather-light caress that called the Dust to swirl around the points where they touched. "One of us should take the blame, right?"

"Why do you want me?" She stretched her arm up over her head, giving him better access to the sensitive skin beneath and to the side of her breast. "I'm completely insufferable."

He laughed softly, dipping his head to follow his fingertips with his lips. "I like insufferable."

"Liar. I'm serious. You deserve better." She brought her other hand up to trace across his shoulder and neck. "I'm moody and mean."

"Mmm. You forgot colossally stubborn and sometimes childish." He kissed her narrowed eyes, then continued dropping feather-light kisses down her face to her lips. "And funny...and smart...and strong...and beautiful."

"I am *not* beautiful."

"You are beautiful." He sealed her mouth with his, locking away any other protests, pulling power up through her body and into his through her lips and tongue. When he lifted his head, she knew her eyes were as glazed and energy-drunk as his were. "Would you like to know my favorite thing about you?"

She nodded.

His hand slid down her side. "My favorite thing about you, other than how insufferable you are," he chuckled and continued

following the curve of her body to her hip and then slid in, lifting himself to gain access, "is how very responsive you are." He pulled power through her, the Dust racing down now, coursing through her body to spiral out as his finger circled.

Lena's head tilted back. Her eyelids fluttered closed as her breath stuttered in her throat.

"No, please. Don't close your eyes. I need to watch your eyes. I've got to carry this with me. Let me watch you. Stay with me. I need this, Lena. I need you with me."

She stayed, eyes as open as her heart. She needed something to carry with her for the next few months, too.

It was colder down by the track tunnels, though no breeze flowed out from the dark. Lena had been cold since they'd rolled out of bed and dressed, sated and sleepy, and dreading good-bye. She scuffed her foot along the floor beside Alex as he opened the door and slung his pack inside.

At this hour, they were almost alone by the train. A few senior wards and agents—some of them Alex's men keeping an eye out for her—were on duty, but they were nowhere around.

"For the record, I absolutely could've handled the train to get you to your hike point and then get the train back here. Before all this...." She made a gesture meant to encompass the threats and her new plans to ready the girls to leave.

Alex laughed. He shook his head. "Even at good-bye, you have to have something to fight me on."

"No! That's not what I—" She groaned and grimaced. "I do, don't I?"

He nodded and leaned in to wrap his arms around her.

Lena glanced over her shoulder at the young men working in the train bay.

"I don't care who sees," Alex growled. "I don't care who knows. You're mine."

She blinked, then allowed a slow smile to curve her lips up. "Actually, I'm mine. I belong to me, but I choose to be with you. If you think about it, that's so much better than needing to be with you, like I can't handle my own—"

He laughed. "Even at good-bye."

She stopped and closed her eyes for a second. "But you like me insufferable and difficult and headstrong."

He kissed her, a feather light touch of lips and tongue on hers that turned her belly molten. "I wouldn't have it any other way. I'm grateful you choose me, Lena. I choose you, too."

She wrapped her arms around his neck and showed him that she didn't care who saw them, either. As she deepened the kiss and the Dust swirled between them, pouring into the connection, Alex stiffened. Lena pulled back, puzzled.

Alex looked down at a small hand tugging his shirt.

"Can we go now?" Leo yawned and gave Alex's shirt another tug. The little boy had sneaked down and waited for them. He wore a pack of his own and the field uniform the wards wore on exercises. It was small—even the youngest of the wards had to go. The uniform was still too big for Leo. Lena had no idea where he'd gotten either the uniform or the pack.

Alex huffed, and Lena knew humor and affection mixed with frustration in that sound. She'd heard it enough directed at herself. He squatted so he could look into Leo's wide eyes. "Leo. You can't come with me."

Leo set his jaw, and his bottom lip pouted. "I won't be any trouble. I can help you—"

"You can't. I'm going very far away, and I'll be traveling rough and hard for a large part of the trip. It would be dangerous for you. I need you to stay behind where you'll be safe. You'll be with children. And Leo—" Alex leaned in to look deep into the boy's eyes. "I expect you to listen to Lena and *be nice*. She has enough to worry about."

Lena snorted a laugh. So Alex knew the little boy didn't like her. She couldn't say she was all that surprised. Leo made no secret that he'd choose to spend his time in lessons with anyone other than Lena, and he regarded her as a rival for Alex's attention.

There was a genuine connection between the two of them. The little boy was unshakeable in his insistence that he belonged by the agent's side. Alex intimidated most people. The tall, dark agent had an air of menace, of danger, that even his smooth charming agent's persona couldn't erase. Leo being unfazed spoke to his strength of mind. Perhaps that was where Alex's abiding affection for the child came from?

Leo's chin trembled, but he sniffed his tears back.

Alex gave him a hug and promised to be back soon. He rose and gave Lena a half-smile. "I guess this is good-bye."

She nodded. "Come back safe."

"I plan to. I'll be home in six months-ish, wherever home happens to be. It'll be wherever you are." He leaned in to give her a last, more chaste, kiss good-bye.

"And me," a little voice piped up beside them.

EIGHT

Lena

It was far too late for Sam to be out, but he'd sent for Lena, demanding as only he could that she come visit him immediately. With her imminent absence from the Fort, she was inclined to give in to him. Besides, she enjoyed the old man and their visits.

The guard hurried over to unlock the door, apologizing for the delay. Once he pulled the door open for them, Lena turned Sam's chair around and backed through the opening. Sam's tremoring hand pointed the way to his favorite spot. They wound through the small park, empty at this hour. The night breeze was cool on her cheeks, and she let go of one handle to pull Sam's blanket up closer to his neck. He waved her off.

"I'm fine, Lena."

They reached his spot at the far end of the garden, away from the building. It seemed to jut out over empty air in an area where the cliff arrowed out at the top. Lena put the brake on the chair and sat on the ground beside Sam. The buffalo grass was tall and soft here. She ran her fingers through it and looked up. The stars poured across the night sky like a wash of wild water tumbling over unseen rocks. She needed this time with Sam, away from the worrying about supplies and safety and a winter away from civilization for girls who'd gotten used to living without deprivation.

Sam sighed beside her, a whisper of sound that flowed out and up to those stars. He crossed his gnarled hands over his belly and smiled. There was a sadness to his smile that alarmed her. He gestured up at the sky, a slow wave of his arm before bringing it back to his lap. “It is beautiful.”

She had to strain to hear him.

“Isn’t it? Like you, in more ways than you know.” He sighed, a world of weariness in the sound. “But I didn’t bring you out here to look at the stars.”

She waited.

“It’s time for you to know something. Only you. Do you understand?” He pulled his attention from the sky to look over at her. “They’re not ready for this yet, Lena.” Sadness weighted his voice. He turned back to the stars..

Lena waited, patient and at peace in his presence.

When he spoke again, he’d returned to the stars. He waved an arm again. “Do you know what a supernova is, Lena?”

“A supernova?” She wrinkled her brow and searched her memory. It was a kind of star? She hadn’t had much time to study the night sky. She’d always been hidden away. When she’d moved out to the desert and had the chance to appreciate the glory of the stars—well, there weren’t a whole lot of astronomy books at her disposal. She shook her head at Sam.

He nodded and cast his gaze back up. “A supernova is when a star explodes,” he explained. “To simplify it, the star builds so much energy that it bursts.” His hands made a small exploding motion.

It reminded her of the motion Alex had made months before when she had been so close to losing control. When she had built so much energy that she almost burst. Lena shivered.

“When it does,” Sam continued, “it outshines the whole galaxy. And then…” He swallowed. “It fades away. It happens when it is in its final stage of evolution, you see.” He held his shaking hands above his head, framing a star above him and then moving his hands apart. “The shockwave of its energy and radiation moves across the galaxy and causes new stars to form. The elements that formed the star are used again, in new ways. The light continues to shine.” He nodded his head as he lowered his arms. His gaze followed his hands back to his lap, and he studied them in silence.

Lena pulled her legs in to her chest and curled up, turning her head and resting her cheek against her knees as she watched him. She was cold inside. He hadn't brought her out here to talk about stars. He was talking about her.

Perhaps she was jumping to conclusions? She searched his face. Or perhaps his mind was slipping? He was more than two hundred years old, his life artificially extended by the Dust for its own reasons. Perhaps his mind had reached a critical level? Her skin prickled with fear. They couldn't lose Sam. He was Thomas's voice of reason. He was Alex's friend.

"Did you know that I was not originally a scientist, Lena?" When she didn't answer him, he turned to her, waiting for her response.

She smiled wanly. "I know, Sam. You were a soldier."

"I was a damn fine soldier. I believed in what we were doing, even if I didn't understand it. I understood that I was special, and being special would help me protect my family and friends." He drifted off again.

"You're still special, Sam." She smiled at him and reached out to touch the paper-thin skin of his arm with a feathery touch.

"Special." He infused the word with humor and laughed, a bark of sound across the empty park. Then he tilted his head back again to look again at the sky. "The science came later. Even when everything was falling apart, I knew the science would help me make sense of it all. That's why I saved John."

Lena watched, waiting, wondering who John was and how he was important enough to Sam to be saved. "John?"

"The man who caused all this." He turned to her, his eyes piercing. "What has Thomas told you about you, Lena? What has he told you about your role in all of his plans?"

Lena sat up. She shook her head. "My role? To teach. To show the students how to do things no one else can show them…he calls me the first. Says I'm Eve." She laughed self-consciously. "To be honest, it was more than a little creepy at first."

Sam regarded her, his eyes darker than the night. "You're not the first, Lena." His voice was final. It brooked no arguments. "You—and those girls like you—are the last." He kept his face turned to her, those eyes darker than the sky framed by his thin brows and pale skin. But his arm reached up and pointed to the sky. "Like one of those stars, flaring to brilliance before going supernova and going out forever."

He must have caught the consternation she knew was reflected in her face. "I don't think *you're* going out, Lena. It's the Dust that fuels you I'm talking about. All of these things that you can do, this brilliant light that glows from within you. You're a sign, a sign that the Dust has reached its final stage before evolution." He shook his head. "Thomas is wrong. You are not the first to be able to do these things, Lena. You are the last. And now that the flare has started, it is only a matter of time before all of it fades away."

"Fades away? Into what? If it's going to evolve, into what? Sam, I don't understand. How can a machine evolve?"

He kept his eyes up on the stars. "That I don't know. I can guess, based on formulas and programs that were used to make them. But so much has changed. I don't know. Maybe it's magic." His lips lifted enough that his eyes crinkled as he stared up at the light above.

"I used to think it was a kind of magic. But Erwin and the others convinced me I was wrong. Maybe. It's science. And machines don't evolve."

"Maybe science and magic are different words for the same thing. Maybe that's why they try so hard to understand what happened and why and where it's all going, but they can't quite get a grasp on it. They're thinking too literally. Too small." He grinned, his skin stretching across his face. "It would infuriate them to hear me say that."

Lena nodded with amused agreement then sobered. "You said I'm not going out, but…. Sam, at the big meeting a few months ago, I know they told you about it. I almost—well, we were afraid I was going to explode." She looked at him, but he kept his face turned up, away from her. "Sam, am I dangerous? Are my girls dangerous?"

"I don't know."

"Okay." Lena licked her lips. "Assuming we're not dangerous, how will everyone live? If we're the last who can do this? All the people in the cities, here, everywhere…they don't know how to live without us. How will they make it?"

Sam shrugged. "They won't, Lena. So many didn't, the last time."

"Are you sure about this?" Even as she asked, she knew that he was sure. He was their version of an oracle. He knew what there was still to know about the Dust. Still, she had to know what he knew, *how* he knew. "Where is this coming from?"

"Whispers. Voices from the past. I listened very well, Lena. To John. To Peller himself. He knew more than he ever let on—of course he did. And I was smart enough to listen, especially in those last years when he was so disappointed with what he'd created, but too proud to listen to us and dismantle it all. That was right before he disappeared."

"Disappeared?" Lena reached out and took Sam's hand again to anchor him to the here and now with her touch. "Sam, Peller *died*."

He turned to stare down at her. The bobbing started again in his arms and head. "He didn't die. And I'm not senile, so you can stop looking at me like that. My mind is as sharp as it ever was, just packed with memories. So much life. So many people and *plots*."

She knew a few things about plots herself, and she agreed with the disgust that infused his voice. He seemed sharp enough. He wasn't wan now. He was determined. He wanted her to have this information. He wanted her alone to know about the coming changes.

"Why did you tell me this? What am I supposed to do?"

"I don't know," he told her. He hunched in his chair, his back rounding. "My eyes only see in one direction now, and it isn't forward. What do you think you should do?"

She had no idea. She sat, even her fingers stilled in the soft grass, watching him, waiting for an answer. For more. He sat bowed over himself, looking like nothing so much as an ancient man, worn and tired. He avoided her eyes, looking out at the horizon. When he spoke, his voice was querulous. Cranky.

"All of this has already happened you know." He gestured out at the night. "All of this light happened in the past. It's already happened again and again. Loss. Transformation. Rebirth. We just couldn't see it." He took a rough breath. "I'm cold, Lena. Take me back to my room."

She had turned to stare out at the horizon. When she didn't respond immediately, he snapped, "I'm cold! I want to go back."

Lena rose to her feet, easing into the motion as if she herself had aged over the course of their conversation. She disengaged the brakes and turned his chair, wheeling him back toward the dark hulk of the building. She felt a thousand years old. Why had he told her this? What was she supposed to do?

Ahead of her, light flared as a man came through the glass doors. She squinted against the light and turned her head, trying in vain to see around it to the person who shone a hand torch in her eyes. Three shadows followed behind him.

"Lena?" His voice was crisp, but there was a sharp edge of relief beneath it.

"Thomas?"

He lowered the torch. She could see now that it was Patrick and two men she didn't know with Thomas. One of the strangers lit another torch and strafed it over the grounds.

"Ready to say goodnight, yes? On your way back in?" Thomas came and smiled down at Sam. "I'm afraid Lena must say her farewells here, Sam. I need her to come with me now." Thomas took Lena's arm above the elbow.

She looked down at his hand. His grip on her arm, though gentle, was firm.

She could feel her brows crease. His hand reflected a faint shimmer of aura. She looked up at him, and really looked this time. Yes, he had the Spark's latent aura. He'd used his Spark ability. Had he used it in the search for her?

Lena raised her gaze to his and saw something frantic and angry deep in the pale blue. His face, his surface, was calm. Beneath it? Something had happened. Fear pulsed within her. She glanced up at the other men. Patrick had changed from the joking, easy-going agent who'd been helping them plan their getaway. He and the other two men gave off an aura of grim efficiency very similar to that of Alex when he was in hostile agent mode and didn't give a damn who picked up on it.

"The girls?" she whispered her fear at Thomas.

He shook his head, a small movement. "Safe. But you need to come now. Say good night."

Sam's head bobbed, his hands tapping and retreating his agitation on the arms of his chair. "Good night? Or goodbye?"

Thomas didn't answer.

Lena stepped forward, letting go of the wheelchair and crossing in front of Sam. One of the agents with Thomas slipped into her place, his hands gripping the handles. Thomas came with her. The old man stared straight ahead, his lips compressed. His nostrils flared. He was upset—almost grieving. *What did Sam know that she didn't?*

Was it necessary to come out here and grab her? To upset Sam like this? She pulled loose from Thomas' grip.

Lena leaned in to place a kiss on Sam's cheek. "Goodnight, Sam."

When she leaned back to look into his eyes, there were tears gathered there.

"Goodnight, Lena." He lifted his brows, using this chin to point at the sky. "Remember."

"Of course," she reassured him. "I'll see you soon."

The agent pulled back on the chair. Lena straightened, frowning at him, but before she could say anything Thomas raised his hand to direct her back toward the doors behind them. "Please, Lena. We need to go."

She followed them out, throwing a look back over her shoulder as the agent steered Sam in the opposite direction to head back to his room. Thomas gestured her forward.

"What's going on?"

He shook his head. "Not here."

"Thomas—"

"*Not here.*" He stepped past her to lead the way. Patrick and the other agent with them closed in behind her. As usual, they took the entrance elevator down to the nondescript lower-level lobby, then walked through the halls to the main elevator bank.

No. Not walked, Lena corrected herself. They marched her through the halls. She stared at the back of Thomas's head. Thomas's agents closed in tighter around her. They approached a hall intersection, and Lena could hear a tumult of excited voices coming from ahead and to the left. Neither Thomas nor the men surrounding her slowed. Lena craned her head as they passed.

Guardians and students stood clustered, facing in, staring down at something. Voices were raised, speaking over one another, and several young men pointed in the opposite direction down the hall. In the beat from one second to another, one of the guardians standing at the fringe must have sensed their passage. The guardian turned his head. His hand fell on the shoulder of the man in front of him. Like a train passing through, a wave of silence and movement flashed through the group as heads turned and raised voices died to whispers.

Before she passed out of the intersection and out of sight, the men had parted enough to reveal a heap on the floor at their center.

Not a heap. A body, curled in on itself as if it had died in convulsions. His face was twisted, mouth gaping.

It was Marc.

Speak of this, even think of it in the company of the wrong men, and you will suffer. And then you'll die, terribly. She remembered her warning to the young man, and his sullen nod. She had warned him. But he'd still talked. To whom?

She had a millisecond to flash her gaze over the boys and men staring and whispering as she and the men with her hustled away. Was one of them a part of the plot against her?

Were all of them?

Then they were gone, and Lena stared back as if she could see through the wall. She tried to catch Patrick's eye, but he'd dropped back and kept watch behind them now. She turned her head to look at Thomas's set shoulders and tense, quick walk. *I'm in danger. So are the girls.*

Once they reached the main elevator bank, Lena and the men with her stood in silence. On the elevator, Thomas held a button on the console as they traveled. They passed the floor where her rooms were and continued to another level. Soon they exited, and the four of them hustled in silence down an empty, unfamiliar residence hall.

They turned a corner and traveled halfway down the hall before Thomas paused outside a door and pressed his hand to the plate, unlocking it.

Inside was a clean, sparsely furnished room like any other. It was empty. As soon as the door closed behind them, Thomas turned. Lena didn't give him a chance to speak.

"Where are my girls?" It was more demand than question, and she could hear the fear and fury vibrating in her own voice.

"You saw, then? Good. You'll take the risk seriously."

"Take the—? I'm the only one who's been taking the risk seriously!" Lena stepped up to Thomas, stopping inches away from him. "Don't play games with me, Thomas. I want my girls now."

"Step back." The agent she didn't know had closed in behind her. He grabbed her elbow to pull her back from his leader.

Lena was done being pushed around. She was done postponing what she wanted while the risks piled up around her and those she'd sworn to protect. "Don't touch me!"

She slapped at his hand where his fingers curled around her smaller arm. A visible flash of electricity, jagged and bright, flared from her fingertips. His hand flew back from her, jerking his body back with the force, wrenching his shoulder.

To his credit, he immediately turned back to face her again, though he curled his arm in to his belly, hand fisted in pain. His eyes were wide in shock.

Patrick raised his hands, palms out, though whether he intended to soothe or to try to grab, Lena didn't know.

"Stop." Thomas's voice was low with authority. He glared at all of them. "We don't have time for this." He focused his glower on Lena. "And that was completely unnecessary."

"Where are they?"

"In my room. Waiting to go." He jerked his head back to a closed door behind him. "Which you'll all do as soon as we talk."

Lena waited.

Thomas took a deep breath, calming himself. "Agent Lee is downstairs loading the train you'll take back to your home zone. There will be a wagon waiting for you. West scouted out to the location and back. He says it's secure enough, and abandoned, but barely habitable. You're sure about this location?"

Lena nodded, the motion curt. Of course he'd already sent someone ahead, in spite of her desire for secrecy. Perhaps someday they'd all stop questioning her judgment.

"The group of you will go ahead then. You'll have sufficient supplies to set up and carry you through the first few weeks. Patrick and Theo will follow in a week with supplies and to clear the route of anyone who thinks they're clever enough follow."

Lena raised her brows. "Do you think I'm incapable of doing that?" She kept her voice cool and glanced at the agent still nursing his hand.

Thomas's gaze darted to his agent, one of the original rebels who'd plotted with Thomas and Alex. His lip quirked up. "You are. Obviously. We'd rather you didn't have to." At the look on her face, he raised his hand. "I know. You can take care of yourself. Your goal is to teach the young women and girls in your care the same. You don't need to fight me, Lena. If I didn't think you were capable, I'd lock you all up somewhere safe until the threat had passed. Believe me, I considered it. You are capable. Your girls will be, too—and our select boys."

"If there's any chance of the rest of us learning that particular attack, I'd appreciate it." Patrick sounded so much like Alex with the soft, avaricious request for knowledge that Lena felt a pang. She missed the man, fiercely.

"Ask Alex. I taught him." She took a deep breath and pulled her focus back where she needed it. She returned her attention to Thomas. "Is there anything else?"

He shook his head. "Unless you're curious about suspects?"

Lena barked a laugh. "Curious? No. As far as I'm concerned they're all suspects. I'll let you deal with that, so long as you promise me one thing."

Thomas's pale gaze was wary.

"When you figure it out, kill them. Don't hang on to them. Don't try to root out more information. Just kill them. Okay?"

Lena turned away from him and went to the door to his room. When she opened it, she couldn't help the grin that split her face. Teenagers sprang away from the door. Rose didn't bother—she kept her position leaning against the jamb where she could've pressed her ear to the door to listen.

"Ready?" Lena hoped so. She wanted the school and all of the intrigues it held behind her for good.

Rose nodded. She dropped a hand to her side, and Leo poked his head around her hip. The little boy didn't seem happy. Of course, since Alex had gone, he hadn't been. It was as if he'd struggled to adapt without the one face he'd grown most accustomed to. It was why he clung to Rose. The blond Neo-Barb had a similar, fierce confidence, a no-bullshit, get it done attitude that both Leo and Lena were drawn to.

The boy had his own reasons, but for Lena there was a peculiar security that came from knowing the person by your side would do anything to keep you safe. And in a place that reeked of collusion and plots and ulterior motives, holding on to that confidence had been a hard thing.

Time for a change of scenery. It'll be good for you and me both, kid.

Lena was determined to carve a safe place for them all out of the desert. She'd done it once. Together, they'd do it again. And with their massed abilities, no one would be able to touch them.

NINE

Alex

"Damn, Agent. You look like shit."

Ace's honest assessment didn't make Alex feel any better. He paused in the entry of the train car to slick water off his rain-soaked hair. Cold water dribbled down the back of his neck as he shrugged out of his sodden coat. He handed it to the nondescript, middle-aged man waiting to take it. Man and coat disappeared into a closet.

Ace leaned against the wall at the back of the train car. He looked impeccable, as always, even the dark skin of his shaved head gleaming in the muted light. The clean lines and jewel tones of his clothes reminded Alex he was grubby and travel-worn. He'd spent an afternoon on the train, riding it as far as they'd managed to clear tracks, past Azcon and through the heart of the old country. The rest of the way to the rendezvous with Ace's Dragonfly House trade caravan had been on foot, and he'd been dogged by autumn downpours for the entire twenty-odd days.

"Leave your boots there," Ace told him as he eyed Alex's mud-coated feet, "and come on back. You look like you could use a chair and a hot drink."

Alex didn't have to be told twice. He toed off the boots and crossed the little hallway to enter the office behind Ace. Alex grabbed a blue and green glazed mug from the tray under the pot Ace gestured him toward and poured himself a cup of steaming, dark liquid. He wrapped his cold fingers around the mug.

He sipped. Tea. The best tea Alex had ever tasted, although

that wasn't saying much. "What is this?" He settled himself into a chair in front of the desk.

Ace grinned. "A personal gift from Herself. And I'm pretty sure it was a gift to her from the stash of her pirate-type contacts that sail across the wide ocean to ply the western coasts."

Ace referred to his boss—Kit Wallace, the granddaughter of the man who'd founded the first big trading house. Possibly the single most devious and intimidating trader alive, she'd promoted Ace to Zone Director over the objections of the other directors at Conclave. She'd made no secret, Ace had told Alex, of her reasoning. She was interested in Lena and her use of the Spark ability. So long as she hadn't decided yet whether she'd back the young Spark revolutionary who intrigued her or she'd throw the full force of her support behind the Council, she was hedging her bets.

Alex couldn't help but wonder if Ace took her at her word, or if he had the foresight to question everything he was told. If not, Alex felt certain Ace didn't have the devious mind he'd need to hold on to his position for long. Alex knew Kit Wallace wasn't all she seemed. He'd heard Councilor Three choke out her name as a conspirator while Lena punished the man for his crimes against her family. The devious old woman was playing both sides until there was a clear winner. It seemed Ace's position and good fortune were tied to Lena's actions, too.

Which meant he wouldn't be any happier with Alex than he himself was. He didn't know whether it was residual guilt from her pointed dig about broken promises that kept him up nights, or the dull ache he'd already identified as missing his little hellraiser. Either way, almost a month of poor sleep and crap weather had combined to create the perfect storm of irritability. It would make this first meeting interesting.

Alex took another long sip of tea.

"How's Leo?"

Ace's question made Alex wince in memory.

"Oh, damn. What happened to him?"

Alex shook his head. "Nothing. He's fine. Settling in. He just…didn't take a liking to Lena." His last view of them would have been comical if it didn't break his heart a little. He'd looked back through the window as the train pulled away and Lena had been looking down at Leo. She had her arm out, offering her hand to the little boy. Leo crossed his arms across his chest and peered up at her with suspicion, rejecting her overture—leaving her with tight lips and a raised brow. It was the same expression she'd worn when she'd first realized Leo had taken an instant dislike to her and she'd told Alex it was proof that she should never be a mother. He'd jokingly agreed neither of them was parent material.

Regret for what he'd meant to be a light moment burned through him. She'd taken it to heart after Leo's continued rejection. It was a problem. Alex fully intended the three of them to be a family once they'd changed the world and he could come home and just *be*.

"She's an acquired taste." Ace said.

His grin faded to suspicious narrowed eyes when Alex grunted his agreement. Ace had made it pretty clear that he hadn't been comfortable with the relationship back at the Conclave. Alex couldn't shake the feeling that Ace's subsequent cooperation—the cooperation that had helped them steal away the girls about to be shipped to a Zone Four prison—was based on the trust he'd gained through Lena.

If Lena trusted Alex enough to involve herself with him, then perhaps that was good enough for Ace? Alex tightened his fingers around the mug and settled it in his lap as Ace shot him a questioning look. "What?"

"Already issues?"

Alex smiled. "There're issues in every relationship, Ace. Do you think one between two people like Lena and me would be any different? Our issues were resolved before I left. We're fine."

Ace was silent. Alex had the distinct impression the younger man weighed his words for dishonesty. Alex hadn't lied. Things were fine. Yes, they'd fought. A lot. They'd also made up a lot. That went a long way, in his mind, to making the fireworks worth it. Lena was stuck with him. He might have to go away to achieve the goals that would make things easier, but as he'd told her beside the train, he had every intention of coming home again.

Home was wherever she was. Together, they could deal with anything.

We'll make it work. It's what we do.

With a focusing breath, Alex opened the compartment in his brain labeled "Lena" and put all of that away. He closed it with a promise to revisit the memories soon. He fully intended to return in five months with solutions to make her demands a reality. Thomas and Patrick would root out the betrayers within, and Alex would work from without to figure out how to keep her safe, productive, and happy. The road to getting there started with the woman he hoped to meet tomorrow.

"Do we have an appointment yet?" The question helped him focus on what he could work on at this point: the upcoming visit to two east coast zones as a representative of Daniel, the new Councilor Three. He had attached himself to an already planned Dragonfly House trade negotiation trip. He knew the implied connection and friendship between the newest Councilor and the most powerful trade house would grant him more access than he'd manage on his own. At the least, it would grant him more official access. Zone Two had one thing in common with Zone Four—the lack of trustworthy reports coming in from their agents.

In Zone Four, they no longer had agents reporting back. There'd been a series of disappearances, accidents, and reassignments, leaving the zone policed by older agents not a part of Alex and Thomas's network. Of course, after Lena's handiwork a few months ago, they now knew what they'd long suspected. Councilor Four was at the heart of the corruption and conspiracy against Sparks that infected the Council of Nine.

Zone Two was a different matter. Their reports had been coming in, but Alex suspected those reports were compiled from information their agents were being hand-fed. Alex intended to discover whether or not the agents were a part of the deception and how much Councilor Two knew about them.

Alex didn't like working at a disadvantage, especially not with an unknown operator. Councilor Two was very much an unknown. Oh, they knew the official line about Leng Sloan. She'd been Councilor here in Zone Two for more than thirty years.

When she'd inherited the title and the zone as a younger woman, she'd been handed a mess. Zone Two was historically second only to Zone One as the weakest of the zones. The east coast had been hit hard, and hit repeatedly, by disease in the years since the Great Disaster. Neither had ever really recovered.

Except Alex had had a long discussion with Ace when deciding which zones to target first. That discussion had made it clear to him how unreliable his reports had become. Sloan had been a busy woman, if Ace's reports of extensive infrastructure improvements to her zone were to be believed. Ace had informed him that Zone Two was careful—the surface of structures still gave the impression of want, and Sloan did not trade a greater quantity of goods than they'd traditionally had available. But the quality of life in the zone and variety of what they had on offer had been on a slow uptick in the last decade. What had changed? Nothing Leng Sloan had brought to the attention of the Council. Both the secrecy, and the new prosperity, made Zone Two the first stop on Alex's tour.

He hoped to make her an ally. It would make things so much easier if he didn't have to waste time planning another coup.

Ace made a face. "We have a standing appointment for the evening we arrive, although the bulk of negotiations will take place over the next few weeks. If you're asking if they know we're close, then yes. I sent word our arrival depended on the storms. I had to buy you time." Ace raised his brows.

Alex frowned in irritation. "Buy me time? I said I'd arrive today. I busted ass to make it true."

Ace smiled. "Never doubted you, but with this weather…."

Alex took another sip. "I thought we'd reached an understanding," he said flatly. "When you helped get those girls out. When you agreed to help us finish this as bloodlessly as possible, and do it without your boss's awareness."

Ace's smile faded. "Does it seem as if that is no longer the case? Am I not helping?"

Alex nodded. "Sure. But all this dancing around." Alex waved his hand.

"All this dancing around?" Ace laughed, the sound low and

mellow. "That's what men like you and me do, Agent Reyes. The game is on, and it's supposed to be the fun part. This is practice." The big man shook his head. "Don't tell me you're losing your edge?"

In the beat of silence as Alex stared at Ace, stunned by the question and wondering what had happened to himself, he heard something from below their feet—a quick, muted thump. He held up one finger for silence, gaze intent on Ace's startled face.

He rose, shifting his weight onto the edges of his feet to make the least amount of noise. Two steps toward the little hall the old train floor groaned beneath him. A long, barely audible rasp as something slid away beneath him answered the moan of the old flooring.

Alex flashed out the door and down the short hall to the car's entry. He slammed the door back on its track and leaped to the muddy ground outside, sliding in his socks in the muck. A moment later, he'd regained his equilibrium and crouched as he ran along the side of the train car, peering beneath it.

When he found what he was looking for, he stopped, turned, and stared at the dark tree line a few feet away. The trade caravan wasn't huge. For security, the cars circled up on the side of the old road, although the shape was more of a rough oval. The forest stood feet away, and the underbrush, the night, and the rain conspired to conceal tracks.

"Alex, what the Dust is going on?" Behind him, Ace held a coat over his head and shifted his feet in the mud.

Alex shook his head and swiped at his dripping hair and the water running down his face. "I heard something. Under the car. Under us." He turned back to point at a long, deep furrow in the mud. A body had slid out from beneath the car.

Ace stepped closer to look, then cast his gaze over the dark woods looming behind them. "An animal, maybe, seeking shelter?" He didn't sound like he really believed it was an animal.

Alex shook his head. "Animals don't leave footprints." He gestured at a deep indention where a foot had caught in a sucking patch of mud. The rain collected inside it, but hadn't beat down the sides yet.

Ace joined him in staring back at the woods. Alex cursed, but a one-sided smirk lifted his lips. He hadn't lost his edge. He'd heard the spy, even over the sound of the storm. He wasn't even pissed he hadn't managed to catch the culprit. He'd nail them eventually, and they'd tell him what he needed to know about who'd sent them and why. He'd discover whether it was one of the bastards in black that had stalked Patrick or one of Councilor Two's people. For now, it was enough to know Ace had been right about one thing. The game was on.

He glanced back at Ace and allowed the smirk to grow into a grin. It was about damn time.

TEN

Lena

Lena paused at the base of the juniper-covered hill. The walls of the narrow canyon that had almost stymied their wagon were behind them. Around this hill lay the craggy entrance of the valley opening. Tucked inside the valley, up a winding path forgotten by time and people, was the little rancho a friend had given Lena over five years before.

Lena scrubbed sweat from her brow and upper lip with a dusty arm and begged her stomach to stop roiling. She hadn't realized how nervous she was about bringing the girls to the rancho until her stomach started heaving a few hours before. The signs Jackson had pointed out indicating human travel through the area had added to the stress. Was the rancho occupied? Had unfriendly people—Neo-Barbs or even Scavs—moved into the area in the time between West's survey for Thomas and their arrival?

"You okay?"

Of course Jackson still hovered behind her. There had to be something to his native healing skill—if she was honest with herself, he'd already surpassed her skills at manipulating the Dust to diagnose and treat others. He was more in tune with the body, perhaps some empathetic skill. It was all that explained his ability to know that she wasn't sure if she was going to pass out or vomit.

"I'm fine." She plastered a smile over her face. "It's too hot for all this climbing." Had she just blamed the damn weather? Her? Desert hermit girl?

It *was* unseasonably warm. By this point in the fall, it should be cooling at this elevation. But that wasn't what had her stomach rebelling. She was afraid of their reaction to their new home.

She leaned to look past his broad shoulders at the young women and girls and little boy ranged across the scrubby grass behind Jackson. Rose drove the wagon. Leo perched on top of their supplies.

She raised her voice to call out, "We're almost there. I want to prepare you. It doesn't look like much at first glance." She managed a dry laugh. "It doesn't look like much at second or third glance, either. But there's an amazing surprise, so just…bear with me, okay?"

The chorus of assents ranged from enthusiastic to tired grumpiness. She didn't blame them. The hurried late-night train ride had been the first step of this journey. They'd had to offload the supplies in repeated trips between the underground train and the waiting wagon. It had taken more than a week of walking beside it the rest of the way. The children had spent the prior months becoming used to the easy schedule of regular meals, plenty of sleep, and classes that stimulated their minds more than their bodies. The sudden change was hard on them.

"All right then." She gave them all a jaunty nod. "Let's finish this so you can see your new home!"

The scenery leading into the rancho was beautiful. Inside the long, narrow valley, they entered a micro-climate. The temperature dropped by several degrees. Multi-colored deciduous trees packed in close with the usual upper-elevation pine, and above them on the ridge, silvery Aspen trees whispered in a breeze.

Behind her, Lena heard an indignant shriek, followed by laughter. She turned in time to see Jackson pluck another small yellow and red apple from a branch above his head and chuck it back at the girls. This time, his target caught it. Marin grinned at Jackson as she bit into it.

"Throw one to me! Throw one to me!" Marissa darted forward, waving her hands at Jackson.

He laughed and nodded at the much smaller girl, bending

forward so he could toss it to her underhanded.

She let it go past her with a scowl, and Leo hopped down to scamper after it with a crow.

"Not like that." Marisa glowered at Jackson. "A real throw. I can do what they can do!"

Lena nodded at Marissa as she stepped up beside Jackson. "Yes, you can, Marissa. Catch this one."

She took an apple from Jackson and threw it to the little girl. She didn't try to knock Marissa over, but she didn't baby it, either.

Marissa grunted as she took the force of it on her chest and curled her arms around it. The apple slipped through her elbows and rolled to the ground. In spite of this, she pounced on it with a grin of success and took her first bite as she rubbed her chest.

"Good one, 'Rissa!" Charity cheered for her small friend.

Her sister had reached above her to shake a low-hanging branch, raining the hard orbs down on the heads of the older girls with a laugh. The others cried out with laughter and playful shouts of pain as they bent to the ground, shoving apples into their shirts. They'd followed Phoebe's example and tucked their shirts tight into their belts, making a secure sack from their clothing.

Jackson laughed, and Lena heard him mumble the words "chips" and "block."

"You should know by now, little doesn't mean helpless. Neither does female." She raised her brows at him in challenge.

"You're absolutely right. I have no idea how I could have ever forgotten." He offered her an apple in apology.

Her stomach turned at the thought of putting anything into it. Lena swallowed and shook her head. "I'm good. Save it for later, will you?" She flashed him a queasy smile and turned to round up the girls. Their shirts were heavy with the apples, but there was a lightness on their sticky faces. It eased a weight inside Lena.

I was right. I was right to bring them.

Rose stretched up, her tall frame on the wagon allowing her to reach a branch well above her head. She plucked a golden apple and dropped it into her own shirt with a grin, allowing it to join the others rounding out the fabric. With her other hand, she lifted another to her lips and crunched out three large bites, finishing the apple.

"These are the best apples ever." Hania's voice was soft. "Do you know what they taste like? Freedom." She smiled self-consciously and dipped her head down as she finished her apple.

Lena met Rose's gaze over the girls' heads.

Beside her, Jackson chuckled. "Freedom tastes like apples, Hania?"

She lifted her head again and looked at him through her heavy, dark hair, and nodded. "It's better than anything else." She glanced at Lena, and a rare grin split her face. "Even maple syrup!"

Lena mock-gasped. "Bite your tongue, little girl! Nothing's better than maple syrup!"

They all laughed as they lined up to follow Lena again up the winding, narrow path. As she passed Jackson, he flashed her a wink and a small smile.

It was the first time in months he'd been able to relax in her presence. It was the first time she'd seen a genuine smile reach all the way to his eyes.

This will be good for all of us.

Lena felt nothing but relief when the path opened up before them. There were no signs of human passage up here. She lead them out into the broad, wide clearing. Behind her, the laughter and camaraderie died. Lena glanced back over her shoulder, mouth open to remind them to wait before passing judgment. She was stunned at the level of disappointment reflected back at her. Not a single pair of eyes behind her was still filled with hope. She turned around again to look at the rancho, to see it the way they must.

An old barn hunched in a ray of sunlight ahead of them, tucked in at the back of the valley. It had once been made of wood and adobe. Now its walls seemed all but melted, and the surviving beams were blackened from some long-ago fire. A trio of small out buildings grew out of the land in the middle range, none in particularly good condition. One was a frame with adobe walls so low Leo could step over them.

Closest to them on the right, half hidden behind an enormous rosemary bush, the remains of the main house slumped. Windows and doors long gone, slopes of sand, debris, and encroaching high desert flora were visible through the gaping wounds. Lena knew the damage was even more significant—the roof had almost completely collapsed over the rear of the building. What remained of the walls and floors were bleached by the sun and blackened by time and water in a diseased pattern of speckles and smears.

She took a deep breath and marched forward past the house, past the well, and into a wide, flat area in the back choked with wildflowers, low mesquite, and the tangled, twined vines of squash. A few feet past the well, she realized they had stopped. She walked alone. The girls were ranged out behind her, each of them having mutinied at a different point as they crossed the open space before the house. Rose had left the horses and wagon behind the house. They all wore the same unhappy expressions, a combination of disappointment, anger, and exhaustion. The condition of the rancho had burned through whatever joy the sweet apples had given.

Leo, walking along with his hand clasped to Rose's fingers, was closest to Lena. "I wanna go back," he said with a little-boy sniff that made him seem like a cranky old man. He lifted huge eyes to Rose.

She shook her head at him.

"We don't go back. We go forward." She lifted her face to Lena with one eye nearly closed as she stuck her tongue in her cheek. "Though it'd be nice to know how far forward we're expected to go."

Lena shook her head. She kept her feet moving, though she walked backward now. "It's not much further. Just right there, in fact." She gestured with her head over her shoulder to the middle of the open field.

Jackson spread his hands wide. "Lena. There's nothing there." His eyes, however, weren't exhausted. They were worried. He'd fallen back to walk with Phoebe and Marin, the two oldest girls. He left them behind now to hurry back to Lena's side. "There's nothing there," he repeated. He reached out as if to feel her forehead.

She ducked his hand and turned in place. Bile burned in her throat. The next several steps were torturous. She fought not to be sick. *Please, please, let them be happy here.*

She stopped in the middle of the field. Rising from the ground in front of her was a weathered, teetering cross. It was in bad shape, but better than it had been when she'd first arrived. She'd retied it with leather thongs, hammered it back into the ground as she left years before. Why they'd chosen to make it look like a grave she didn't know. It was a place of hope.

"We're not staying up here." She slid her foot across the top of the ground in front of the cross. It caught in some of the vines, but she managed to clear the top layers of earth. "We're staying down there."

Jackson squatted to pull the vines away, pulling several fat squash from it and rolling them toward Rose for keeping. Then he cleared the sand and soil away, revealing the steel door set down into the ground.

Lena knelt beside Jackson, settling her hand between the indented handle and the edge of the door. She reached out, feeling for the Dust in the lock.

Moments later, the lock mechanism ground into synch, each layer settling into the correct grooves. Lena pulled up, grunting with the weight of the door. As soon as she'd lifted it past the lip of the sealed edge, Jackson slipped his fingers in, taking the weight from her and pushing the door back. The staircase stretched down into the dark below them.

"Another hole in the ground?" Rose's complaint fell somewhere between good-natured and plaintive. She'd hated living below ground at Fort Nevada.

Lena couldn't help the laugh that burbled up. She wiped at her eyes. "Yeah. Another hole in the ground. But only until we get the rest of it fixed."

"Who's going to fix it?" Marin cast a disbelieving look around at the ruins around them.

"All of you are," Lena answered tartly. "You and the Dust. It'll make for wonderful lessons in both doing and believing."

Jackson laughed. The young people around them groaned. Lena exchanged a smile with Rose and then swung her legs around to climb down the stairs. They were steep and narrow in the darkness. The dirt that ground beneath her feet on the treads was what she'd tracked in herself years before. As far as she could tell, the bunker hadn't been used.

She pushed the thought from her mind as she paused in the first of the security foyers. It was a long, narrow tube-like structure with the base of the staircase at one end and another reinforced and locked door at the end. Metal benches lined one side. They were screwed into the metal floor, which was criss-crossed metal with another grate visible beneath it through the holes in the hatching. Lena had never figured out the purpose of the double-layered floor.

She waited until the rest of them crowded down behind her, filling the tube and lining the stairs. "Don't close the hatch, Jackson," she called out above their heads. "Give me a sec to get the lights up. The switch on this side is dead."

He called out his assent.

Lena reached out for the Dust in the metal of the door before her, caressing the lock plate for a second as she did, enjoying the answering swirl of Dust beneath her skin. The gears and levers within the door shifted and clicked, changing positions. When she sensed that they'd lined up, she spun the round handle several turns to the left, then pulled on it.

Air hissed out of the opening, stale and flat. She waited a moment, then slipped in and to the right to open a small panel on the wall and flip several switches. Lights went on around her, including out in the access tube.

"Come on, now." She backed up, making a follow gesture with her fingers at the girls so they'd cross the threshold into the wider space beyond.

Rose, in the middle of them, ducked down to cross through the hatch. Her gaze raked the cold metal walls and floor, a raised metal surface that clanged underfoot. Rose's lips turned up as she caught Lena's attention focused on her. "Homie, isn't it?"

Lena laughed. "This is another foyer. Wait."

Rose's glance took in the door across from her. "Another secured entrance?"

Lena nodded. "Four entrances, actually, if you include the back way out that dumps into the hills on the other end of the valley. Whoever built it really believed in security."

Rose looked around again with a new appreciation. Jackson joined her, his own glance measuring the space in one sweep. "Will you show me that exit later?"

"Of course." She looked around with a grin. "Are you guys ready to rest?"

Nervous laughter and nods supplied their answers.

She turned then and unlocked the final door. This one wasn't shaped like the two round hatches outside. It was a door—a thick, air-tight, metal door. When it was open, she reached again to the right and flipped open the panel that hid the controls. She rested her hand on the main plate, reaching for the Dust. With more systems here, getting it powered was a little more involved.

Last time she'd been here, she'd had to finagle the electrical systems. She'd built a large-scale capacitor and charged the Dust out of it—or rather, into it. Now she tested the available charge. Even with energy leakage, they'd have enough to get started tonight. With five firm shoves, she flipped the breakers and turned on the main systems. The lights came up, and ahead of her, deeper in the bunker, a fan pushed air through the vents. She straightened and crossed into the main living area—arms swinging as she turned back to appreciate the shock on their faces.

They entered a huge, circular room. One end of it was fitted with a quintet of comfortable surfaces, chairs and two couches that faced each other across a long, low table. The center was split with a door to either side, and the near space was filled with three rows of double-faced heavy cabinets. Drawers and latched doors lined their exteriors on both sides.

"Storage here." Lena pointed at the cabinets. "For non-perishables, mostly. The dangerous stuff—ammunition and like that—is in a locked door behind that room." She gestured to the door on the left. "It's kind of an office or a meeting room or something."

"A classroom?" Jackson offered with a small smile.

"It is now, yep. That door—" she pointed to the opposite side "—leads to a kitchen area. There's a utility closet and a machine room—where we'll have to take turns on the capacitor I built—and more storage for food. Though I had to clear out what was in there before. It was hundreds of years old. Still intact, down here, but not something I'd trust to eat."

Lena walked down the main room, sweeping her arm toward the door at the far end, beyond the sitting area. "Back there is a long hall with the back exit, more storage rooms—I haven't even explored them all—and a bathroom and sleeping quarters with bunks."

"Real beds?" Marin asked. She leaned into Phoebe happily.

Both girls laughed.

Lena understood. She'd be happy not to be sleeping on the rocky ground tonight, too. "Real beds. And enough for everyone, in two rooms."

Jackson blinked. His eyes shifted to the older girls. "I should set up somewhere else, so you all can have some privacy. A safe space away from the, uh, different energy." Jackson grinned at Leo. "What do you say, Leo? Should we drag some bunks into a space of our own?"

The little boy stared at him, then peered up at Rose.

She nodded at the boy.

Leo shrugged. "I guess. It'll be down here with them, though, right?"

"Yes," Jackson said gravely, "I think that would be best, too."

"So," Lena said, raising her brows at the crowd in front of her. "Are any of you interested in exploring?"

"You need to come sit down before you hurt yourself." Rose's voice echoed down the metal hallway from where she stood in the entry to the main room. Rose had handled finishing dinner clean-up in the kitchen.

Lena had had gotten their wards into bunks after she fled the smells of the kitchen. She wiped her wet, clammy hands down the front of her pants and swallowed. She'd been in the bathroom, unsure whether she dreaded being sick more than she hated the heaving of her stomach. She leaned against the wall, sweaty yet cold, until she decided she wasn't going to be sick, after all, and splashed icy cold water over her face again. She wasn't nervous anymore. Her stomach could stop rebelling now.

Power through it. She stepped out. "I'm fine," she lied, then flashed a smile. "I was already coming, anyway."

Rose nodded, but she didn't retreat back into the room. She watched as Lena walked to her down the hall. "You're not fine. You're sick."

Lena flapped her wrist in denial. "It's nothing. I've made myself finish forced marches with pneumonia before. This? I'll sleep it off tonight."

"Uh huh."

"Seriously—" She tried to laugh it off as she passed Rose and entered the quiet main room.

Jackson looked up from a pad he'd found in the office area. After settling the horses topside, he'd spent the last hours going through the supply cabinets in the main room making an inventory of what tools and supplies were useable versus what needed to be discarded.

"Seriously what?"

Before Lena could say anything, Rose answered for her. "She's not sick."

"Yeah, right." Jackson shook his head. He rolled his eyes, then frowned at Lena. "Who are you kidding? You need to be in your bunk."

"I want to make a plan for the next few weeks. We've got to have unified goals for rebuilding and for the school by the time Thomas's goons get here to inspect."

"Wait." Jackson popped up from his crouched position in front of a lower drawer. His frown deepened. "Thomas's *goons*? Get here to *inspect*? At what point did the Ward School become an adversary?"

Lena flopped down into a chair and settled her hands over her stomach. There was no way she could have this conversation standing up. She tilted her head back and closed her eyes. "When it became infested with people trying to kill me and those girls asleep back there. Have you not been paying attention?"

There was no answer. The silence stretched for too long. Lena cracked open an eye and peeked at them. Jackson and Rose exchanged an amused look. "*What* is that look?"

Rose shook her head. "Thomas's men are safe, aren't they?" She flicked a glance at Jackson, then back to Lena. "I mean, you agreed to them coming here. We trust Thomas. I'd trust Jackson with my life."

When had they become so close?

"I agreed to them coming because we'll need supplies in order to make this viable. I could do it on my own. So could both of you. But we have to support and keep the girls safe. I also agreed because I knew about the bunker." She lifted her head and pointed at Jackson. "Which they will not know about. By the time they get here, we need to at least be able to give the appearance of living up there. I'd rather we actually were. It'll be safer if no one from the school ever knows about the bunker."

Rose dropped her head, pursing her lips as she studied her feet. When she lifted her head it was to look over at Jackson with a small smile and raised brows. "Think the two of us can manage that?"

He laughed, a quick burst of sound and squatted to get back to work. "That's what we signed up for, isn't it?"

"Um. The two of you? There are three of us to manage and plan, and I— " She shot up and bolted for the waste receptacle in the kitchen. It was the closest thing at hand to empty her stomach into. Over the violent retching and heaving, she was aware of Rose moving in behind her, patting her back.

From the other room, Jackson snorted. "No," his voice came to them, "she's not sick. Not at all." He appeared in the doorway. "Do you need help boosting your recovery? Do you want me to check to see if you're…you know?"

Lena frantically shook her head and eased back onto her haunches. She wasn't ready to admit that she'd been trying to regulate her body all day and had only succeeded in feeling scattered and dizzy. She wiped at her mouth with the back of one shaking hand. "I can't be pregnant, if that's what you're worried about. I use the Dust to regulate that. I'll be fine by the morning. I have to be."

"You have to be? Why's that?" Rose had moved her hand to the top of Lena's head and smoothed the hair away from her forehead.

Lena gagged, half rose, then settled back again. "Because of all the work. Did you see it up there? And the capacitor down here will have to be charged in the morning, or we'll run out of power and air. I need to check to see what's left of the little dam I built to supplement with hydroelectric and check the wiring from there to here to see what's been dug up or chewed through—"

"You set up hydro?" Jackson's voice indicated he was both excited and impressed.

"Don't get too excited. Both the dam materials and the wiring were salvaged crap. It was more of an experiment to see if I *could* based on plans a guy traded me for some power work. The plans are in the office back there."

"We'll fix it." Clearly this was a project Jackson looked forward to tackling.

"Yeah, and Jackson and I are more than capable of starting without you." Rose gave Lena a pointed look.

"We can manage." Jackson rolled his eyes. "We've got skills, too. I'll be using mine right now to boost your immune system and knock you out. I want you sleeping this off."

Before Lena could open her mouth to protest, Rose added, "And quarantined. You don't want to infect your wards, do you?"

Damn. The woman knew exactly how to get Lena to cooperate. She wielded that guilt like a weapon. Lena shook her head. "I'll go."

Jackson pushed himself away from the door jamb and came to collect her. He leaned down to take both her hands in his and pull her to her feet.

She pressed her lips together against another wave of nausea and muttered, "But I won't like it."

ELEVEN

Alex

The pounding of the heavy downpour against the roof of the atrium hallway covered the clatter of their boots. With this many men, both their escort and the traders following Ace and Alex, it wasn't an insubstantial amount of noise to cover. So much for the easing of the rainfall the night before.

It wasn't the rain that had Alex simmering, though. For the first time since the rainfall had hounded him across the broad expanse of unsettled land, Alex was annoyed by something other than the weather. He'd known the information they were getting out of the zone was flawed. He hadn't known how badly, nor for how long Fort Nevada had been misinformed until this morning.

Ace told him about the building projects. He'd shared with Alex about the trade imbalances and Ace's own suspicions. It was one thing to receive a report, and another thing to witness it with your own eyes. The Zone Two Council Building had been refurbished to resemble an original governing building of the old country. The utilitarian cinderblock walls, low ceilings, and narrow corriders that were the hallmark of so many other zones had been replaced with tall ceilings, arched entries, and glass-walled hallways. It was nice to look at, sure. It'd be impossible to defend.

Zone Two had forgotten that need. This new prosperity, however deep it ran and from wherever it came, had made Councilor Two very sure of herself. Alex didn't enjoy the frisson of uncertainty that came with the knowledge. His men should have been updating him. Alex should have been out here himself…probably years ago.

What the Dust had *happened* to his men? *Why* didn't he already have this information?

As if he could feel Alex's thoughts, Ace turned to cast a look back at him. He grinned before turning away, confident. Clearly, Ace knew the way. Zone Two had been on his regular route before he'd been promoted. Of course, the last time he'd made this trip, he'd been just another bronze-pin trading rep.

They paused outside a wide set of double doors while one of their escorts slipped inside ahead of them. Alex fingered the bronze dragonfly pin Ace had given him the night before. It gave him trader's access. His agent's heart beat hard at the thought of using the privilege. But not today. Not for this meeting. He may be entering with the Zone Three Director of Dragonfly House, but he was officially operating as Daniel's representative this morning.

Daniel's and Lena's.

At the conclusion of the Meet that summer, when Ace had brought him the rumor of the powered girls being smuggled into then out of the Meet, Thomas had made a spur-of-the-moment decision to accelerate their plans. Alex and Ace had taken the girls to return to Fort Nevada and Lena's guidance. Alex had found the note Thomas had ascribed to Lena. In the questioning that followed, it was clear few Councilors believed Alex wasn't involved, though none made a direct accusation. He expected the suspicions to complicate this trip.

From inside the heavy double doors, a metal bell sounded once, deep and sonorous, warning those outside they were to be admitted and calling Alex back from his thoughts. The doors swung inward.

Alex focused on the dark floor as he entered to help his eyes adjust to the dimmer light within. When he raised his gaze, he took in the long room with no windows. It was empty but for a small, heavily carved, dark wooden desk behind a settee and a pair of low chairs. Between each chair and the chaise, candelabras resting upon small dark tables put out a dim, warm light. Four people waited like actors in a cozy scene from a play.

Two guards, one by the rear door behind the desk and another beside the desk itself, hulked over the smaller figures. Those figures worked at the desk without looking up—an unintimidating man with receding, silvered, tawny hair nodded as he took papers and quiet instructions from the seated woman.

A small woman with silver hair threaded with black held back in a knot at the base of her neck, Leng Sloan wasn't intimidating, either. Her cheeks and eyes spoke of her Asian heritage, while the small hook of her nose and prominent, sharp chin told of her father's genetic influence. She wore a loosely draped dun-colored tunic. An ornate golden collar curved snug against her neck and fanned out across the top of her bony chest.

As Alex came closer he noted the way her fingers came up to brush the edge of the metal torque as she raised her head to acknowledge their approach. The necklace was gold, he was sure, and meant to keep them guessing about the source of her prosperity.

Her gaze noted Ace's new Dragonfly pin. It moved past him to fall on Alex. The direct, unapologetic way she took his measure was almost discomfiting. Alex was willing to bet she knew a great deal more about why he was there than he and Thomas would be comfortable with.

When they reached the seating area of the room, the man who'd darted in ahead of them rejoined them, gesturing for them to halt while he made quiet introductions. "You remember Mr. Coffey, of Dragonfly House?"

Sloan nodded at Ace. "I do. Congratulations on your sudden and rapid ascension, Mr. Coffey. We are pleased that it is the representative who has been working so closely with us who took on the role of Director. I can only hope that our trade agreements rise in importance with you."

Ace leaned into a graceful bow. "Thank you, Councilor. It's been my pleasure to serve the needs of our zones. I share the hope that our agreements continue and prosper, as well." He turned his head in a slight twist to acknowledge Alex behind him. "Traveling with me is the personal representative of our newest Councilor, the Councilor of my own home zone. This is Agent Ale—"

"Yes," Sloan interrupted, "I am familiar with Agent Reyes's position with our new Councilor Three. And with his role in the…developments…at the Conclave several months ago."

Alex didn't respond to the provocation. He'd expected it. It was one of the primary reasons he hadn't worked to change his identity for this trip. He counted on them obsessing about Lena and the girls. They had no proof of his involvement. In an attempt to goad him into admitting to more, they might well give away details that would provide Alex with a kernel of new information to run with.

After a long moment of silence during which Sloan held his gaze, she continued, "It seems that controversy follows you wherever you go, Agent Reyes. I trust we won't have the same issues here in Zone Two?"

"I'm afraid I'm not sure what issues you worry I'll bring with me, Councilor. At Conclave I simply delivered a message."

"And how did you come to be in possession of that note, Agent Reyes?"

"I found it while investigating Zone Six's missing shipment of—" Alex paused. He managed to keep the sneer out of his voice when he continued, though it was close. "—trade goods."

"So you say." Her weighing regard didn't waver.

"I do. And with all respect, Councilor, considering that we now know those goods were not goods at all, but innocent young girls being traded like pawns in an obscene game, perhaps it isn't my word you should find suspect."

"An obscene game? The girls are sent from every zone, including my own, in accordance with law. I cannot control how other Councilor's handle the responsibility—" She pursed her lips in distaste, clearly knowing about the disappearances and faked deaths. "—but here it is no secret they must go away, just as the strongest boys do. Only their travel and destination—the *safe, humane* camps where they live apart for the well-being of all of our citizens—are kept secret to protect them, and all of us, from their instability. You maintain that acting in the best interests of the people is obscene? Am I also obscene?"

"I prefer to think—mistaken."

"Are you advocating for a change in law?"

"I'm advocating for an investigation."

"So we should give in to the demands of woman who is a thief—at best? At worst, she's a dangerous radical involved in the murder of a Councilor. Not the type of person to be believed, especially when she lacks the courtesy to simply petition the Council for an audience. If she was there and able to leave a note, then surely she could have done so. She either lacks conviction or honesty."

"I think that's unfair, Councilor. Perhaps she instead practices discretion. If what she says is true—"

"If, perhaps, you think... These are not the hallmarks of certainty the Council requires to act."

"No, ma'am. But I'm hoping they'll be enough to allow an investigation. I'm hoping they'll be enough to allow me free access to those who might best answer, and that they'll be enough to allow my results to be taken seriously, whatever they may find."

It was a bald statement of his goals and desires, and too close to his true mission. Alex could see that it was necessary, though. He couldn't help but wonder if she was the source of the mystery opposition Patrick had to flee in Zone Six. Wherever her information came from, it was solid. There could be no bald lies to this woman. It would be truths and half-truths cloaking one another, and perhaps he might not be ejected from the zone.

Leng Sloan leaned into the desk, reaching her arms across it to pull a slip of paper toward her and folding it over and over. A small smile hovered on her lips. "So, I'm to allow a senior security officer of another Councilor free run of my zone—no, not just another Councilor." She stopped and lifted her gaze back to Alex. "The senior security officer of a young Councilor related to the very woman who is suspect, a young Councilor raised to his position against all odds, and against all tradition."

Sparks were not meant to be Councilors. When the concern was raised at Daniel's confirmation, it was dismissed—there was no law in place to preclude Sparks, merely tradition. And while it might have been a shocking and distasteful development for some of the Councilors, Sloan herself had been a neutral voice amid passionate arguments on either side, and then had voted with the majority block to confirm Daniel. It was one of the reasons he and Thomas had chosen Zone Two as a starting point. There was a neutrality behind her eyes now, too. She wasn't raising the issue in protest, she was trying to rattle him. Or was she looking for a reason to confine him to quarters?

"Councilor Three has had no contact with his sister in years," Alex told her evenly, "and he is as eager to find her and find answers to the Council's questions as the rest of the Councilors. He has no idea where she is hiding. Before I left, he had already initiated a search of his own zone in order to locate her." It rang true because it was true. Daniel had no idea where Lena was, as Alex intended.

Sloan leaned back in her chair and regarded him with serious eyes. After a moment, she turned away to face the man waiting by her side. She spoke with him in an undertone.

While she was busy, Alex flicked a glance at Ace. The big man's shoulders were stiff. Was he concerned about the possible repercussions this borderline hostile conversation might have on his trade, and thus his standing in the Dragonfly House? Or was he worried about Lena?

Sloan turned back, and her movement reclaimed his attention. The man beside her moved to the bodyguard by the door. Before the larger man stepped outside, her assistant passed him a small, folded slip of paper. Alex swerved his gaze over Sloan's fingers, the fingers that had moments before been folding a slip of paper into a small square. They were empty. He returned his focus to her face, then, and saw that she'd seen his notice. She seemed almost pleased by it.

"You'll be happy to know that I've agreed to grant you your investigatory access to the facility where we hold our powerful young female Sparks before they're sent to the Council as required."

Alex felt his lips part in his surprise. He nodded, dipping his head in respect.

One side of her lips twitched up. “Thank you for gracing Zone Two with your trade,” Sloan nodded at Ace, “and your attention.” She turned an amused gaze back to Alex. “My assistant will contact you when an escort has been arranged to take you to the facility. I’ll look forward to continuing discussions with you both.”

She turned away, lifting a sheaf of papers from her desk and rising. She left by a secret door on the other side of the office that melded so seamlessly with the wall that Alex would be hard-pressed to find the edges of it again. Her assistant slipped in behind her, and the door closed without a sound.

The game was on. Not only was she playing, but she was so confident of her ability that she had shown a card or two to pique his interest.

Consider it piqued.

Alex followed Ace back out of the room. The same man who’d escorted them earlier led them deeper into the halls, to a long curving staircase that deposited them in an ornately carved lobby. The doors were wide, carved wooden panels. Installations of the same burnished carvings had been applied in a wide strip across each wall at waist height. Even the ceiling of the huge room was carved with the same figures.

As they passed through the long room, Alex tipped his head back. The stocky figures above them had wide faces and long noses. Their open, shouting mouths were filled with broad, sometimes sharpened, teeth. They raced, leaped, and twisted around snakes and leopards and an odd, feathered winged serpent. They reminded him of some of the carvings that could be seen on boulders in Zone Three, but were slightly different. Which bore the question: what were they doing here in Zone Two? How had Sloan come by them? Via trade? Or exploration?

Their guide turned and led them through a wide pair of doors to the side. A small landing opened in a semi-circle that lead to narrow stairs twisting down. The basement levels, formerly bunkers for the zone’s citizens, had been refitted as guest quarters. Ace assured him they were quite luxurious. The waste, and the risk, made Alex more than a little sick.

The Council had barely managed to pull its nine cities out of ruin. Those with intimate knowledge of the inner workings knew that at least seven of those zones were one hard winter, one long quarantine, or one disrupted trade season away from ruin. And yet Sloan felt confident enough to remove her citizens' last line of shelter in favor of luxurious quarters for traders. What was she thinking? And where did she get the assurance, or the audacity, to make such risky decisions?

The rooms themselves weren't far from the bottom of the stairs, though they'd gone down three levels to get to them. The room Alex walked into behind Ace gave no indication that it had ever been intended to be a bare-bones shelter. Layers of carpets in a riot of colors and textures softened their footsteps. Some were rough and appeared to be made of dyed grass. Others were fine woven cloth in bright jewel tones. Still others were heavy rugs with the same animals and squat humans weaved together in dark colors, like the carvings upstairs.

Ace stopped and turned to their guide with a wide smile. "Thank you," he told the man. "We appreciate the escort and the generous loan of such welcoming quarters."

Alex noted he kept his voice to the low, smooth, well-modulated tones he used when he was in trader-mode. He nodded in agreement and offered the guide a bland smile. "Indeed. Please convey our appreciation to the Councilor."

Their guide accepted the appreciation with no expression, simply crossing back to the door. "The Councilor has arranged for an afternoon tour of one of our production facilities. Someone will come for you in two hours. Until then, please refresh yourselves and rest easy knowing you are in the safest zone of all the Council." He left, closing the door behind himself.

Alex waited for the click of an exterior lock, but there was none. He turned back to Ace with a raised brow.

Ace's head tipped back as he rolled it on his shoulders and let out a gusty sigh. "Damn, but you like to make life interesting." The statement wasn't in an altogether happy tone.

Alex shook his head and shrugged, crossing the room to one of the coupled doors on the opposite wall. There was an identical pair to the left. He opened the door and leaned to take in a wide, soft-looking raised bed with ornate punched tin lamps dangling to each side.

"Bed here. Bath next door. Identical set up in the suite across the room," Ace told him from behind.

"They like pillows here," Alex noted. "And carvings." He raised his brows at Ace.

Ace answered slowly. "I told you about the changes in goods and infrastructure. She trades South. How far South, I don't know. I'm not privy to that information—not yet." He glanced away and then back at Alex with a one-shouldered shrug. "But there have been private shipments from Two for Kit Wallace. Whatever's going on here, she may have a hand in."

Alex digested the admission. According to the former Councilor Three's dying confession, Kit Wallace also had a hand in the Council's mistreatment of powered girls. Did this mean Councilor Two was involved in the prisons and experiments, as well? Or was their relationship one of convenience and trade alone? "But you don't know?"

Ace held his gaze. "I don't. Not yet."

"You might want to get on that, Director."

Ace rolled his eyes and turned away to stalk across the room. He dropped down onto the couch. "It might help if you didn't antagonize the Councilor before I got the chance."

"Antagonize her?" Alex barked a laugh and wandered back across the room, passing Ace to continue to the wide doors. "I'm pretty sure that woman likes to play as much as we do, and she's looking forward to the fun of the chase."

Ace leaned back, his brow furrowed. "Where are you going?"

"To check out the city. I need to be seen, make sure my people understand we'll be meeting up tomorrow. Time to find out why so much of this was such a damn surprise. They need to understand they *are* still my people."

"I'm pretty sure we were meant to remain here until they come for us."

"Yeah. I'm pretty sure we were, too. But they didn't lock the door. That might look bad." He grinned. "So let's see if I can create an obstacle course, shall we? She wants a chase. We'll give her one."

TWELVE

Lena

Jackson yanked at the roots of the last of the dried climbing vine that completely covered the one intact wall of the littlest of the side buildings. Lena gathered the brittle vines themselves closer to her body and pulled to clear his view.

He glanced over his shoulder at her, swiping the dripping sweat from his chin onto his shoulder as he did. “You can go check on the girls if you need to.”

The girls and Leo were cleaning out the lower levels of the main house while Rose worked on checking the upper levels for stability. Lena had left them perhaps twenty minutes earlier to come help Jackson.

She arched a brow at him. “Trying to get rid of me?”

“No. But I can handle this.”

He glanced up at her and saw what she’d seen in the mirror that morning—a pale face with dark circles under her eyes. She’d been pretending she was fine so they wouldn’t worry, but she couldn’t hide the exhaustion today. The responsibility for bringing them all out here, and the fear that she’d made a mistake, were taking their toll. Thomas’s men should have arrived that week with their extra supplies. They hadn’t. Jackson and Rose had been trying to supplement what they had by hunting.

A deer he’d shot had bolted. They’d followed the trail, but when they found the animal it had been butchered—a hack job, but the meat was gone. Two days later, a snare Rose had rigged for rabbits was destroyed. The footprint she found a mile up the valley told them it wasn't an animal. Someone was out there.

Lena's skin crawled every time she had to bring the children to the surface now. She didn't know if it was because they were actually being watched or simple paranoia.

The lack of sleep and the worry wasn't helping her recover from her brief illness.

Jackson tried again. "It's hot and miserable out here today. You should—"

"Do my fair share of the work." Lena finished for him. "I'm fine."

He sighed. "Okay." He turned his attention back to the deep roots and worked on them, rocking the root stem back and forth and then scrabbling to loosen the dirt with his fingers before rocking the stem again. He grunted. "This would be so much easier with the proper tools."

"Tools. Yeah." Lena tried to keep the amusement from her voice.

He let go and stood, narrowing his eyes. "Why is wishing for the proper tools funny?"

She cocked her head at him. After a moment, she chuckled. "You have all the tools you need, Jackson." She stepped closer and reached up to tap his sweaty brow. "Up here. You're as strong as I am. Use the Dust."

"As strong as you are? Oh, are we feeling generous today?"

She made a face and stuck her tongue out. "Okay. Nearly as strong. You should still be using the Dust as your go-to tool of choice."

He shook his head. "We've already established that we don't think like you do or access the Dust in the same way."

"So? You reach out differently. It shouldn't keep you from figuring out ways to use what you can already do in new ways. Think. What can you do?"

He wrinkled his brow. "What I can do?" He looked back at the stubborn root stem. "I can light a fire. But I'd rather not burn down the one good wall."

"So narrow your focus. Tell it what to do. How to do it. Dust, Jackson, you do it with human bodies. You can do this, too."

He squatted beside the hole he'd made and reached a hand in, feeling around the stem with his fingers. As he slid his fingers out of the hole, he lowered his head in concentration. Smoke rose from the hole, first a thin wisp and then a thicker stream that the wind picked up and carried away.

Lena coughed and stepped out of the way.

A few moments later, Jackson lifted his head. He reached out and grabbed the main stem of the plant and dragged it back. The root stem was gone. Bits of ash fluttered away from the blackened hole. He dragged the offending plant away and then returned to stand in front of her, hands on hips.

"See? That wasn't hard, was it?" She grinned up at him.

"I spent the morning clearing this entire building by hand, Lena. You could've come and told me that little trick earlier."

"I was hoping you'd realize it on your own," she answered tartly. "This is a school. We can all learn new things. And some of that should be by self-discovery. That's how I learned."

He shook his head at her and lifted his hands up to show her his scratched, bleeding skin. "All morning. By hand."

"Because you're trying to do things the way you were taught by the Ward School. It's a new world out here. It comes with a new way of thinking. Don't limit yourself."

He sighed and shook his head. "The girls are right. You're a mean teacher."

"*What*? I am not mean!"

"Tough," he amended. "And a little mean."

He reached down for the water and held it out to her. When she shook her head, he drank his fill and squinted at the remains of the building beside her. She could see him measuring it off with his eyes, calculating what he needed to do to make it weather-tight again. Was he also figuring out new ways to use the Dust to help himself? She hoped so.

When he spoke, though, it wasn't about the building. "Speaking of a new way of thinking…"

She raised her brows as he drifted off.

"Have you noticed the girls? How they—they always seem to be on the same page, even when they're given different tasks, in different parts of the valley? I know they're matched—"

"Whatever that means."

He looked at her and smiled. "I don't have one, so I couldn't tell you."

"I *do*, and I couldn't tell you." She shook her head. "It's…a connection. A closeness. I can't explain it."

"You know, at the Ward School, we're taught to carefully observe people—details, mannerisms—because almost everyone has a physical twin. Not really a twin, but someone who looks enough like them." He waved a hand dismissively. "The Ward School was all observational lessons, but it's helped a little. I wonder if we also have mental twins? If we have people who operate on the same wavelength for the Dust, or if being close to someone allows us to…? I don't know. Sync somehow."

She shrugged. "Rose and I were matched before we met. It's getting stronger, yes…"

"Right. But you don't anticipate what Rose is going to do. Where she's going to be. But sometimes when I'm working with the girls, one of them will get a faraway look and then—she looks like she's talking. Her face, I mean. Animated. Listening and responding. Like they're…"

"Talking to each other?"

Jackson nodded.

"I think they do," she said softly. "It's not such a stretch. I mean, we all talk to the Dust using our minds, right? And I think that's why Marissa has done so well. She still has the comfort of Jubilee. Have you ever watched her....?"

Jackson had raised his hands and cupped them behind his head. He nodded in agreement. "Have you ever done that? With Rose?"

"No, we haven't done it."

He opened his mouth to speak then paused, and it felt awkward. "Or Alex?"

Her gaze sharpened. "Alex?"

He sighed. "It's a connection, right? I'm just going off of what it felt like when we—it—the physical contact. I'm just saying. I have to imagine that more intimate contact, prolonged contact, like that, would mean—"

That they could somehow become matched? Talk to each other across the distance? She shook her head. Jackson stopped talking.

"I don't know what the match is. I know it gets stronger over time…or maybe with trust? The girls are so in tune—but it was like being in a crucible. They survived so much together. Rose and I are matched, yes, and I can feel it. A connection. It's getting stronger. But the physical connection with Alex feels different." A wave of longing passed over her. She missed him fiercely, and she wished more than anything that she had some magical way to reach out to him. She wanted his touch, yes, but she wanted his mind even more.

Even if she couldn't talk, to feel that wicked mind, to close her eyes and be near that presence—the essence of what was strong and unique and Alex. If it was possible, surely her need would have made the discovery before now? She blinked back the sudden flood of tears. She hated the way the stress and remnants of illness made her feel weak.

"It's just different, Jackson," she managed.

"I'm sorry."

She shrugged. "It's fine. I'll keep an eye on the girls. Experiment with Rose. It's something we should explore."

Lena woke uneasy, blinking her eyes to be certain they were open. Rose slept in the bunk above her, but Lena couldn't see the bottom of it. Here in the bunker, when they doused the lights, not a single glimmer of light eased the darkness. She held her breath and stared up in silence, waiting. Had their watching thief invaded? She thought she'd heard—

A low, moaning cry came again. Not a thief.

Lena kicked free of the blanket and slid from the bed. She left the room she shared with Rose, Phoebe and Marin, and Constance and Charity to the second bedroom. She moved through the pitch dark to the corner bunk and slipped her toes on the edge of the bottom bunk to boost herself up without stepping on Marissa, who was curled asleep on it. She reached between the bars of the top bunk and found a tightly curled and trembling back. Another shuddering moan of fear told her Hania was still deep in the grasp of nightmare. Lena flattened her hand across the girl's back.

Peace. Comfort. Warmth. Lena directed the Dust at the same time she murmured to Hania. "You're safe, Hani. You're safe. No one will hurt you here. You're safe."

She repeated the soft words over and over as the Dust worked to ease the terror and tension of the memories that wound tight around Hania in her sleep. Lena couldn't take the memories away…she couldn't change Hania's dreams or reality, but she could lower her heart rate, ease her breathing, relax her body, and hope that the girl's mind followed suit.

She kept her own rage and fear tucked down deep so the girl wouldn't pick up on them. Finally, Hania sighed and rolled onto her back. Lena slipped her hand free and reached up to stroke the girl's cheek in the dark. Her fingers caught in Hania's full, thick dark hair, and Lena slipped the strands back away from Hania's face. Lena waited, fingertips moving in small strokes over Hania's temple. The girl was calmed. She'd slipped free of the memories and into deeper, healing sleep.

Lena slid her arm back from between the bars and stepped down. She was silent in the dark room for a moment. None of the other girls needed her now. Most of these littlest girls had been rescued by Alex that summer. They might have been held for a time in their home zones, but they'd been spared the worst of the prison experiences. Lena felt a spurt of guilt that they couldn't be returned home to their families. It was quickly quashed. It wasn't possible. Not until the system had changed enough that there wasn't a risk that they'd be retaken. If that happened, Lena knew what waited for them.

Restraining collars. Experiments. Assaults.

Those memories sucked Hania down night after night. Those memories haunted the older girls. Heat—white-hot and merciless—flared in Lena's chest. The familiar burn was her own reminder of the promises she'd made to herself and these children.

Never again.

With the room quiet around her, Lena made her way back to the doorway and into the hall. Once she'd returned to her own bunk, she slipped down to perch on the edge. Her head hung down.

Across the room, Marin gave a hiccupping sob in her sleep. Lena could hear shifting and guessed Marin must have slipped down to crawl into bed with Phoebe again earlier in the night. She was likely in the throes of her second nightmare of the night—but this time, with Phoebe so close, Marin could curl into her and be calmed by their psychic bond.

Grief curled in Lena's stomach. It was fuel for the fire that burned above it. Lena smoothed her hair behind her ears and blinked away tears of her own. She was so tired. Now that she'd been up and moving, the ever-present stress churned her stomach to nausea.

Never again. Easy words to say, but how was she supposed to make sure they were true? She was one small person, and even her allies had been infiltrated by the enemy. The Ward School wasn't safe. She'd brought them all here, to the middle of nowhere, to keep them out of the grasp of the Council. But she had no illusions that the Council would give up and go away. The world was out there, waiting. The Council had men looking, watching for signs of them. They'd come. Perhaps they were already here—the source of her unease on the surface. Lena would burn the world outside this valley down before she allowed any of her wards to be hurt again.

A sudden flare of fear stabbed through Lena's head, freezing her. Above her, Rose made a soft choking noise. It became sobs that were almost lost to the thrashing that always accompanied Rose's nightmares. She fought them in her sleep. From her bruised and battered condition when she'd been rescued, Lena knew that she'd fought them in reality, too, in spite of the restraining collar. Lena stood now, in spite of the choking waves of gasping terror and pain that radiated from Rose.

Lena hugged herself. She couldn't climb into Rose's bunk to offer the woman the comfort of her presence. She couldn't even stand on the edge and reach in. Rose was bigger than Lena. Her strong, muscled limbs made her dangerous. Her trauma made it unsafe to wake her. Fists clenched under her arms, Lena closed her eyes. She'd tried this once before and failed. She'd fled from the memories locked within her friend.

Not this time.

The bright, anxious flares behind her eyelids coalesced into colors that ran together and became images. Images became real, pulling Lena in and folding themselves around her. The fragments jumped, each snatch of the nightmare vivid and real. The edge of a table or desk sharp against her lower back as she was forced down. A hand on her throat and the edge of the collar biting into her windpipe. The jar of connection as her fist made contact and then a man's angry grunt.

Laughter above and behind her.

"C'mon, man. You know she likes to fight. Neo-barbs like it rough."

Hands gripping her wrists while others pulled at her clothes. Air on her skin. Teeth sinking into her breast.

Lena's breath hiccupped out of her in panicked gasps in time to Rose's desperate, wheezed breathing.

Rose! The terrified mental cry made the images stutter. They swirled around her, parting briefly to reveal the real darkness of the room around her. The real room. Lena stood in it. No desk. No men. *Rose! I'm here. Can you hear me?*

Lena pushed through the vivid colors. Her hand made contact with the memory of flesh, solid and sweaty, before the feeling swirled away into nothing. *I'm here.*

Rose's breathing rasped in her ears. The sound was in her head, all around her, and above her in the bunk. She felt Rose's hands flailing. They reached for her both in the shared dream and in reality.

Here. Lena lunged forward, using the bunk to lift herself, reaching for Rose's hand. She couldn't see it in the dark. She could feel it.

Rose's fingers closed around her own. Lena felt a frisson of fear. Would Rose drag them both back down into the horror of memory? But the contact was all her friend needed to drag them both out. Lena could feel herself being sucked along as Rose clawed her way free of the terror.

She woke, with a long dry inhale like a drowning victim sucking a gulp of air after surfacing. Rose jackknifed up, sitting up and folding over herself. Lena's arm was wrenched against the bunk bars as Rose clung to her hand and pulled her in closer. She bore the pain.

Both of them were silent as their shared experience faded. Their breathing slowly returned to normal. Rose's death grip eased.

Lena knew she was back when Rose turned Lena's hand and pressed her lips into her friend's palm. "Thank you." The words were hoarse and low, raw. "I'm sorry."

Lena slid her hand up to Rose's forehead, easing sweat-damp hair back. She didn't know she was crying until she sniffed back the moisture. "I'm sorry. If I had come sooner. If I had made Thomas move faster…"

Rose shook her head. "What happened wasn't your fault. It was them. The guards. The Council—their laws and their damn sheep." Rose's voice twisted with disdain for those who chose to live in the cities, giving up freedom for supposed safety.

"I'm still sorry. You're not the only one suffering the nightmares… That's why I was awake."

Rose nodded in the dark. Lena couldn't see her. Somehow she simply knew. "Was it Hania again?"

"Yeah." Lena sighed. "I wish I could go back and change it for all of you."

"I wish we could go back so we could kill them all."

Lena moved her fingers from her friend's forehead to grip her hand, palm to palm. *We will*, she told herself silently.

"Promise?" Rose asked. Her voice was hoarse and plaintive.

It took them both a moment to realize that Rose had somehow heard Lena's thought.

"Did we just--?"

Rose cleared her throat. "Like the girls do," she confirmed. "That was…"

"Weird?"

"I was going to say, natural." Rose's voice was dry. It was a vast improvement over the lost tone she'd had after waking.

"Oh." Lena ducked her head, resting her forehead on the bar. "It was, wasn't it?"

"Yep. It was a little weird." Rose chuckled.

Lena joined her. "I guess we really are a match."

"Was there any doubt, after that time in the Ward School?"

Lena had over-extended herself and had built up a dangerous amount of feedback energy. She'd almost exploded. Instead, Rose had relied upon the supposed power bond between them and convinced Lena to dump some of the energy into Rose.

It had been a dangerous gamble. It had worked.

And now, somehow, they were psychically linked? Was it the full match manifesting itself? Or was it a matter of time and trust?

"No," Lena answered Rose. "I guess there wasn't."

Rose released Lena's hand and gave her shoulder a little nudge in the dark. "Go to sleep, friend. You're exhausted."

Lena nodded. She was exhausted. She was also overwhelmed. Jackson was right about Rose and her. He'd also suggested that perhaps Lena and Alex…

Lena forced herself to push the thought away. As if she wasn't already missing him enough, she had to pine for some secret ability to communicate across the miles? She silently wished Rose good night and ducked down to collapse onto her own bunk.

A moment later, she heard Rose's unvoiced response. *"Sleep well, Lena."*

A smile crept across Lena's face. She remembered the sensation she'd had on the train after rescuing the girls. There was a peace that came with no longer being alone in the world, with no longer being unique. The calm comfort that suffused her now was very like that feeling. It was like the last morning she and Alex had spent together.

With memories of that morning and Alex filling her mind, and still wrapped in the comfort of the connection with Rose, Lena slipped back into sleep.

THIRTEEN

Alex

Alex moved down the street, head up in spite of the fat raindrops that still spattered the flooded sidewalk. Ace could handle the negotiations without him that day. Alex had a different, specific goal for the day, so he'd slipped away after breakfast.

He was well aware of the two men following him. When he'd set out from the Council building, it had still been pouring rain and it wasn't hard to miss two men keeping pace with him on the mostly empty streets. At first he'd thought they were working together, tag-teaming him as he made progress away from the big building that loomed behind him like a glassy monument. Then he'd realized they were aware of each other, but they weren't pleased by the fact that there was another interested party stalking Alex. He assumed one of them was Leng Sloan's security.

Why did she not use the Council agents assigned to her as security? Alex wasn't certain who the other man was, but his demeanor was much more furtive and hostile. Perhaps he was a man from another internal security team here in the zone, one at cross-purposes with the other man following? Perhaps Zone Four had been investigating Sloan's new prosperity, as well?

If Brayer had discovered the changes within the zone, he couldn't be happy. Alex's tour of the production facilities here had been eye-opening. Sparks weren't merely the source of power here in Zone Two. They managed the power. Even in relatively liberal Zone Three, where Sparks could be sub-managers and senior aides, they were never solely responsible for any major operations that kept the people comfortable…and in line. Zone Two was different. It was as close as he'd ever seen to Alex and Thom's vision of a future. It would infuriate Brayer. The Councilor would absolutely send operatives.

Alex wouldn't put it past Brayer, and Ace had told him that the Councilor was thick with one of the Directors from Dragonfly House himself. Was that the root of the connection between Wallace and the Council's plotting?

That connection had been a detail Alex had been surprised to learn from Councilor Three as he questioned the man months before. Brayer was deeply involved with Dragonfly House—he had multiple connections and sources within the trade house, and he'd been instrumental in the House's successful acquisition of several of the large, favorable, multi-zone contracts they'd gained over the last two decades. Dragonfly House was the leading trade house on the continent. Kit Wallace could make for a dangerous adversary.

Alex had met the woman. He'd never underestimate the small, round redhead. In many ways, she reminded him of an older, wiser Lena—someone not to underestimate. Was it Brayer manipulating Dragonfly House to achieve his own ends, or was Wallace using Brayer's ambition to achieve her own domination? And if it was the second, could Ace be trusted?

That was the question Alex had been wrestling with since he left the Meet with the girls that Ace's cooperation had netted them.

He stopped on the corner of a now busy street. Earlier the torrential rain had slackened and then stopped for the first time in days, and people tired of being cooped up indoors over the previous days had poured out to hurry about their business. With the sun peeking through breaking clouds, the heavy traffic of pedestrians and bicycles moved in dedicated lanes beside horse-drawn wagons that splashed a fine spray of muck on all of them. There were no electric or steam vehicles here in the city center. Those were permitted only on perimeter roads in Zone Two.

At a brief break in the flow, Alex darted forward, moving across the crowd and then turning to merge with a larger group of tradesmen, inserting himself into their center. After a half-block, he slipped behind a wagon to move into a similar group of workers headed back in the opposite direction. From the middle of them, he looked ahead, marking both of his followers as they headed in opposite directions, one continuing up the street perpendicular to Alex, the other mixing in with a similar crowd, chasing Alex down the busy cross-street. Alex kept his head down as the man went past.

He was back to believing they were working together again. They'd each opted to follow a different possible track. Fortunately, neither was following Alex's actual path. He headed straight up the street, remaining burrowed into the center of the boisterous workmen. They carried him along to a loud, busy bar. When they went in, he continued ahead, slipping between people, watching his back for additional pursuit, and following the directions he had to the open-air market where traders and farmers gathered and the zone's citizens moved among them in crowds that offered protection from eyes and ears.

Every zone had one. Agents always kept a pair of eyes and ears ready there. They knew he was coming. Someone would be there. Someone would contact him, and then he'd have a chance to demand answers to questions he shouldn't have to ask. He'd find out why he didn't already *have* all of the information he needed to make this trip fully effective.

He moved with the people in the same natural ebb and flow between vendors. It didn't take long for one of his men to find Alex.

He glanced up from a display of bright woven scarves that were ethereally thin and dyed in colors that almost glowed. The young man at the display ahead of him paid for a small sticky bun. He took one bite, shook his head as if the taste didn't agree with him, and set it carefully atop a trash bin. As he did, his index finger pressed a tiny, hard case into the doughy center. He gave Alex a pleasant nod as he passed, and kept moving.

Alex paid for the scarf he liked and moved across behind the row of vendors, scooping up the roll as he walked through the people swirling around the bin. He split the roll with his thumb, removed the case, and threw the two halves of bread into the next bin as he traveled in the opposite direction from the young man. He paused behind a vendor's booth, glancing down at the furled paper after he unrolled it. It was a rough street map with darted arrows indicating the directions Alex should follow.

He shook out the scarf as if re-examining it had been the reason for his stop, then refolded it and tucked it into his pocket. Lena would love the bright colors, and the swirl of greens and blues would do amazing things for her eyes. He allowed himself a quick beat to remember the vivid dreams he'd been having. They played out as if they were part memory and part dream, except they felt *real*. An echo of her laughter and freckled skin made him swallow. Then he set his shoulders and refocused on the roads around the market square. He went straight ahead and then left, circling to a street one over, focused and looking forward to the answers that would help him keep her safe.

The moment he opened the door to the small building standing at the location marked on the quickly drawn map, noise roared around him. Men and women, young and old, rushed around the room, slips of paper clutched in their hands. They darted in to various bar-height tables set back from the main aisle, leaning in, shoving at each other to nod and wave paper and raise their voices above those closest to them to be heard.

Alex watched the mad swirl of activity for moment, noting the glint of bronze pins at collars and above breasts. He dipped his hand into his pocket, searching past the folds of scarf to draw out the Dragonfly pin he'd pocketed earlier. He clipped it to his own collar and drifted into the crowd. He allowed himself to be buffeted by the moving people, matching paces and listening to the bark and shout of the bottom rung of trade house operatives as they fought over goods and contracts.

Several glances grazed over his pin and did double takes. Their startled gazes made him wonder if he'd erred in affixing the pin to his shirt. He realized belatedly that there were no Dragonfly or Locust House pins in the lot. The two leading houses didn't send their traders down to fight over small contract businesses.

He was about to find a busy corner to hide in and

surreptitiously remove the pin again, when the young man from the park swung past and jerked his head in a nod. Alex slowly followed him in the direction of a narrow staircase on the back wall. The young man didn't climb up, though. He ducked into a small space behind the stairs and exited a barely noticeable door.

Alex turned twice to allow himself to be pulled back with the crowd so he could strafe his gaze over the crowd behind them. Alex wasn't sure he hadn't been followed. It was possible the men from earlier in the day had found him again. But he did know from those brief looks back that the young man himself had been followed. An intense gaze from across the room followed the young man as he exited out the back door. The watcher had then stalked to the front of the room and engaged in an animated close conversation with a second man.

While they were engaged, Alex exited through the door. His gut tightened as he stepped through and pulled the thin wood into place behind himself. It was an alley, and he was a few steps above street level, looking down aging metal steps and one intact railing to the street below. Only the center of the alley was uncovered by the wide rooflines here. A narrow strip of silvery water still ran off from the eaves of the buildings above. The noise of the water falling was amplified by the walls of the narrow street.

There were four men waiting in the alley behind the building. No, five—a fifth was moving down the alley to an area that narrowed before opening up again, a built-in choke point. Alex recognized the fifth man as one of his own, a young agent who'd graduated perhaps five years before. Rylie had come through very briefly to train with Alex before moving on to his permanent assignment. Alex felt some of his tension ease. This was the legitimate meeting he'd been looking for. They'd give him answers soon.

They'd better.

The others gestured Alex to follow. He shook his head and made a sign for silence and slid to the side of the door. He gestured for one of them to move to the mouth of the alley, twenty feet away, to keep watch. Several gazes flicked to the door in understanding, and then they scattered, one to the head of the alley and the others taking cover behind leaning piles of crates and garbage bins and waiting with Alex.

They didn't have to wait long.

Alex felt the scant vibration of the handle through his palm flattened on the door panel first and eased his weight back, pulling this hand with him, ready. The door opened into the building.

Alex waited, leaning back against the wall, hidden in plain sight. He waited a beat. Another.

The young watcher from inside eased his shoulder out first, his gaze strafing the far end of the alley where it connected with the street. He stiffened as he spotted the man at the entrance to the street. Alex watched as his lips tightened and he reached behind himself to his waistband. Alex couldn't hear the sound of the weapon being pulled free over the runoff falling in the alley beyond them, but saw the glint of the blade as the man lowered it to his side and hid it behind his thigh. He stepped through, his head finally turning.

It was a mistake that cost him everything.

Alex grabbed his wrist, slamming it against the rusting metal railing before them. The man's fingers loosened, but he retained the knife, so Alex slammed it down again. The knife clattered free. As Alex yanked the man forward by his arm, he wrapped the fingers of his left hand in the man's hair at the back of his head. Now Alex used momentum to smash the man's face down on the railing with a violent clang and crack.

The dazed man didn't resist as Alex dragged him down the steps and to the back of the alley. His broken nose bled down the front of his shirt, the bright stain spreading with help from the water beating down as Alex dragged him along. Alex could feel the man's muscles bunching as he regained some of his senses. But they were already in the protected space created by the narrowing of the alley. Alex pulled him to the side.

"Do any of you recognize him?" he asked through gritted teeth.

The men around him shook their heads.

Alex reached to grip the man's chin in his, intending to drag his face around so he could look into the man's eyes as he spoke. As soon as he'd lifted and started to turn the man's head, though, the man's gaze caught Alex's agent—the one he'd been following. He lunged, attempting to free himself from Alex's arms.

"Stop struggling." Alex ground the words out as he reeled him back, straining to hold the younger man. "Or I *will* kill you."

The man jerked his head away and let loose a distinctive three-note chuffing sound that rose to a howl that echoed off the sides of the building and down the narrow lane. He sucked in a breath to let loose the sound again. Alex smashed him on the back of the head to silence the warning.

The young man fell violently forward, his feet tangled with Alex's, and hit the wall a foot away from them. His shoulder connected with the wall and he collapsed to the ground in a heap.

Alex crossed to the unconscious man. Before he got there, he saw a flash of movement as a hand slipped down between the man and the wall, reaching for his ankle. Seconds later, his hand moved again, a blur of motion. Alex felt his muscles bunching. The faker would unwind from his supposed unconscious state and strike out at Alex with whatever weapon he'd removed from within his boot. But the man didn't leap up to fight a losing battle. Instead, a wide pool of red spread in the puddle the man was curled in, facing the wall. The red lightened as the water thinned it.

The young man had never intended for the weapon to be used against Alex.

Alex stepped forward and jerked the man back by the shoulder. His body fell back, his head flopping on his neck because of the gaping wound he'd slashed into his own throat. He fell onto his back, one hand clutching a knife with a curved edge.

Alex knelt, pressing his hand to the man's throat. He needed to question the fool. Avoiding an interrogation was a ridiculous reason to suicide. Alex closed his eyes, focusing and feeling for the Dust within the man. He felt the Dust, sluggish. Then he felt nothing. Alex opened his eyes and cursed. He rose, pulling away from the dead man and his own failure.

Blood still flowed from the man's nose and mouth into the water that ran on the dirty road. Alex stood over him, panting and furious. He squeezed his eyes shut and growled under his breath at the stupidity of the young man and the senseless loss of life before he turned to the sheeted fall of rain in the center of the alley. He rinsed the blood from his hands and then looked at each of the men around him.

He'd *needed* the answers the man could have provided, dammit. His appearance was far too similar to the description Patrick had provided of a young man dressed all in brown.

When he spoke his voice was quiet, so much so that he could see several of the men give each other uneasy looks as they moved closer to hear before he'd even finished his question. "What the Dust is happening in this zone?"

The men before him shifted feet and glanced at each other. They weren't comfortable with his furious question. He didn't care. He expected answers.

"What do you mean, sir?" one asked.

"What do I *mean*?" Alex felt his brows draw down even more. "I *mean* why were you—" He glowered at the young man who'd been his contact at the park. "—being followed by someone so hostile he'd rather die than be questioned? I *mean* why did I walk into a zone totally blind as to recent developments in its infrastructure, prosperity, and interested parties? I *mean* why have none of you been doing your damn jobs and getting us the information we need to be successful?"

"Wait. What do you mean you—"

As soon as the words were out of the dark-haired mustached man to his left, Alex's head whipped around at the start of the same question, and he growled low. Enough of playing the fools. He'd end them all if they'd turned on the movement. There was no way they didn't all know it.

But the mustached man had his hands up to hold off Alex's reaction. "Wait! I just—you should have been receiving our updates. We send them weekly, as required, without fail. We've been wondering why—" He looked over at two of the other more experienced agents. "We've been wondering why no one has taken any notice of the reports."

"Weekly?" At their vigorous nods, Alex barked, "Method of delivery?"

"Seamus."

Alex's eyes narrowed. "One man? The same man?"

Their reaction was enough. They'd been stupid. They'd also not followed protocol. No one was infallible, which was why no single person was ever meant to be solely responsible for any of the jobs they were expected to complete. No one except for Alex and Thomas, of course.

He studied them. Their reaction also told him that if there was a problem, it was likely limited to Seamus. It wouldn't help any of them keep their positions here; they'd all have to go back for re-training. But it would allow them to keep breathing. "Where's Seamus now?"

Heads turned to the mouth of the alley. The man closest to the natural chokepoint where the two buildings came together leaned out, his head parting the curtain of runoff rainwater that fell between the two buildings. His mouth opened as if he'd call out. Water ran down his cheeks and into the open space when he paused. His brows drew together in confusion, and then dipped further in anger.

Alex didn't wait for him to articulate why. He strode past the man, marching through the narrowing himself. Ahead of him, at the mouth of the alley. Seamus leaned belly-flat against the corner of the wall, head down, mouth moving. He'd positioned himself to see the street, yes. He was also speaking with someone out there with him.

Alex moved up behind him. He could feel rather than hear the others moving forward, too. At this point, he had to assume they weren't closing in on himself, but were following his lead on Seamus. If it was otherwise, he'd deal with them as they came.

Just before he reached Seamus, the young man must have sensed Alex's approach. He glanced over his shoulder, gaze focused on the rear of the alley where the chokepoint was—where Alex and the others were meant to be interrogating their suspect. Instead, his gaze caught on Alex's reaching hand.

Alex made sure he didn't have time to warn whomever was around the corner. He dropped his hand on the man's shoulder with an iron grip and tossed him to the men behind himself, rounding the corner at the same moment and reaching with his free hand.

The man there tried to scramble away. Alex's reaching fingers brushed the man's chest as he dodged back. The man stumbled as he spun. It was enough. Alex cleared the corner and reached with his right hand, grabbing the back of the man's shirt and yanking him back by the collar.

All of the fight went out of the man instantly. He didn't resist. He raised his hands up to either side of his head as Alex dragged him back into the alley.

Alex handed him off to one of the waiting agents and spared a moment to glance up and down the street outside. As before, it was busy with pedestrian traffic grateful for a reprieve from the rain. As clouds above moved back in, and rain began to patter down again, people hurried through the drenched street. Some lifted coats above their heads as they hunched against a new onslaught. Others lifted fabric umbrellas to ward against the water. If someone watched, Alex would be hard-pressed to tell who it was until he moved and had time to note a pattern of following.

Alex turned away in disgust. He stalked back down into the alley, feet splashing the growing puddles. Seamus was held between two of the agents. He wasn't struggling, but his head was down and his shoulders slumped. The watcher from the street—Alex had already identified him as one of the watchers who'd followed him that morning—was still, hands held up and behind his head to indicate he wasn't a threat. His dark eyes, stark against the paleness of his skin and his light reddish hair, were calm. "Where's the other man?"

"I could ask you the same thing," Alex answered.

He got a ghost of a smile in return.

Yeah. I can count. I know there was more than one of you this morning.

"Not the Zone Four creep. I meant the young man in brown

who followed you out into the alley. We have a stake in his interrogation."

"No stake. No interrogation. He's dead."

That got a reaction. "That was fast." There was a spark of anger in his eyes. He dropped his arms. "And stupid."

Alex shifted, sliding one leg back to present a smaller target and increase his directional options if he had to move.

The other man seemed uninterested in attacking. "Are you in the habit of killing men before you know their value? Are you so uninterested in what you might learn from a man like that?"

"I was very interested in learning his secrets. And he was very invested in keeping them. He slashed his own throat." Alex narrowed his eyes and turned his head slightly to address one of his own agents—assuming they were fully his own. "I assume by his disinterest in you and the lack of surprise that all of you are acquainted."

A man behind him coughed.

The voice that answered came from the side, from one of the two men holding Seamus. "Acquainted? No, sir. But he's native."

He was one of Sloan's homegrown security forces, then. And he wasn't interested in eyeballing the faces of Alex's men, which meant he already had them all identified. Alex shook his head. What a clusterfuck.

"I work for Councilor Two," the man confirmed, his voice almost lost to the sound of the rain. "She won't be happy about any of this. You need to return with me, Agent Reyes. We need to go back now."

Alex wiped rain from his eyes. Water flowed back in. Postponing the inevitable would be as pointless as trying to keep his face dry while standing under the onslaught of water.

He turned his head to glower at each of his agents, spending an extra minute staring down Seamus. Like a puppy caught chewing a boot, the young agent averted his eyes, darting quick gazes back to see if the most senior of the Ward School agents still stared at him in disgust.

Finally, Alex glared at the oldest of them. "We still need to meet. We have unfinished business. I expect this one—" Alex pointed at Seamus "—to be with you when you come. I suggest you don't let him out of your sight until then. If he goes missing between now and then, I'm holding you personally responsible."

The agent nodded, tightening his grip on Seamus. His glance flickered to the calm redhead standing beside Alex. "Should I pass word to you on a safe location?"

"They know who you are. They've been intercepting your messages. I don't think a safe location is possible at this point, do you?" Alex managed to keep the disgust out of his voice, but not the disappointment. "Just report to my quarters at the Council building."

"I'll leave word they're to be let through," the redhead said.

Alex wanted nothing more than to wipe the solicitous look from the man's face. "You do that. And be sure all of them get through, will you?"

Alex received a raised brow in response, the man's lips twitching.

Bastard thinks he's won. He doesn't know me. Alex played the Spark's game—the long game. And he was determined to win it, even if he didn't know what was at stake in this zone yet.

Alex tossed a last look back at the agents left in the alley as he followed Sloan's man back. To a man, they wore the bedraggled, angry looks of drowned rats. It wasn't how he expected to start his intelligence efforts in the area.

They took a more direct route back to the Council building. There was no more need for subterfuge at that point. Alex barely had time to start mulling over ways to recover the upper hand by the time they were walking through the halls again. He tried to shake the worst of the water from his arms, slicking it down his sleeves to his hands and then shaking the water away. He sure as Dust wasn't going to ruin the scarf he'd bought Lena at the market, tucked down deep in his pocket. He hoped it wasn't soaked.

They didn't return down the huge, impressive glass-roofed main hall. Instead, they traveled a smaller, darker hall. Alex reached out and trailed damp fingers along the dark-painted wall. Cinder block. They marched through the original building, then.

They were traveling to the heart of the Council building, where it had all started. Not just the zone—the Council. The zones had gotten their names from the old protection districts, Alex knew, not from the order of founding. Mark Peller had founded the Council of Nine here, in Zone Two. He'd been the one to build this building, and his government, on the backs of the Sparks that gave it all power.

His escort stopped outside a small, metal door. He turned to Alex with a grin. "Don't go anywhere."

Alex was tempted to attempt to make his way back through the warren of halls to spite the man, but he wouldn't give him the pleasure of bringing Alex back like a recalcitrant child. Instead, he waited, slicking his hair back from his face and getting angrier as the cold water slipped down his neck and dribbled along his spine.

The door opened. It wasn't the security agent who stood in its opening, however. It was Sloan. She stared at him, eyes cold and flat and lips so compressed they'd whitened at the edges. She held the door open, waiting for Alex to enter. When he did, she closed the door behind him with a brisk snap and then skirted him, walking to the center of the room. The security agent was no longer in the room. Sloan and Alex were alone but for one of her huge personal guards.

Sloan turned back, her arms swinging at her sides, hands clenched. "Was the death of the man following you necessary, Agent Reyes?"

He raised a brow. "He silenced himself after I knocked him around for either warning others or attempting to call in others. His death was his choice when he realized he was over-powered and about to be questioned."

"His choice?" Her voice was icy. "That choice cost me months of work to locate and be certain of the man and his employer. Now we'll have to ferret out the others and lose more time."

"It happens." He kept his face neutral, though he felt his pulse jump. She knew who was behind these men. Alex had decided in the alley that this man's clothing was too similar to the one who'd outed and chased Patrick across two zones to be coincidental. He would get that information from her, somehow.

"It does. But that loss of time has a very real price in C-notes and lives. I'd assumed you would understand this." She stepped closer, peering up at him. "He worked for an extremely hostile individual, Agent Reyes. I was able to feed him the information that I wanted him to have without any of them the wiser. Brute force isn't the only way to do things. You don't have to turn someone to use them, you just have to make them believe they are more competent than you are."

"Like you did with my men?"

She stepped back, turning her face to the side in a parody of coquettish movement. "Yes. But you did one thing better than I, Agent Reyes. You keep your soldiers ignorant of all but the terms of war. I have only the most basic information from them. I know you all believe you are fighting for the good of Sparks, but I don't know why you're moving now."

"Seems like a fair trade in ignorance, since all of the information I have appears to be wrong or manipulated."

"Tell me what you're really doing here, Agent Reyes."

Alex smiled, a smooth, practiced expression that meant nothing. "You first, Councilor Sloan."

The woman wore a cat-like expression that turned up the edges of her lips but failed to make any impression on the rest of her face. "You and I have more in common than you know. Perhaps in time you'll trust me."

"Perhaps in time we'll be in a position to trust each other." He shook his head. "Until then, I'm wet, I'm angry, and I'm tired of being manipulated. Unless you plan to torture me—?"

Sloan laughed, the first genuine sound she'd made since he walked into the room. "That's not my style, Agent."

"Then I'd appreciate being allowed to return to my rooms to dry off and lick my wounds, such as they are."

Her head tipped back with her laugh now. She flicked her fingers at him, indicating he could go, and turned away to cross the otherwise empty room.

Before Alex left, he let his gaze make another circuit of the empty room. What did Leng Sloan do down here? He shook his head. Nothing good, unless you were Leng Sloan. Whatever she was up to, it was clearly extremely profitable for her and her people.

He closed the door behind himself. The security redhead waited for him in the hall. He offered Alex a towel.

Alex took it. He ran it over his face, head, and shoulders as they made their way back up and then down again to his rooms.

Alex could have sworn on the way down they had taken a more direct route. The way back was more circuitous. He was being taken down different halls in an attempt to keep him guessing. Alex grimaced. It was an obvious tactic, but it didn't make it any less effective. He'd have a hell of a time reconstructing the routes and the building. Of course, that was the intention.

The redhead led him down the final, familiar, wood staircase with the elaborate carvings and left him in front of the door to his shared quarters with Ace. Alex didn't bother to bid the man farewell. He pushed the wet towel into the man's hands, opened the door, and then closed it again behind himself, not caring if the man waited to escort him inside.

He crossed the main room to his personal quarters, already stripping off his sodden shirt. He'd hoped Ace would be out, working deals or wining and dining those who made those deals possible, but he had no such luck.

"You look like a half-drowned street dog." Ace's face was amused. He must have caught something of Alex's simmering temper, because he barked a laugh. "I take it your meeting didn't go as planned?"

"No. It didn't go as planned, but it was informative." Alex threw his shirt across his sleeping quarters in frustration. It landed with a wet splat against the opposite wall. He took a deep breath and turned back around to Ace. "Leng Sloan has this place—not just this building, but this entire zone—locked down tight. She knew my men, she knew our meeting, she even knew that there was another interested party there. All of the misinformation, all of the issues I've had with understanding what's happening behind the scenes here…it's all at her hands. It's all deliberate."

Ace nodded. "I tried to tell you."

"She has eyes everywhere."

Ace made a gesture with his hands, spreading them apart to indicate agreement.

Alex growled deep in his throat and turned back to his room to go change out of the wet pants and boots.

"At least you got to use your pin. How'd that work out for you?"

Ace's question stopped Alex. He turned his head back, looking at Ace over his shoulder. "How did you know about that?"

Ace crossed his arms across his wide chest. He pointed into the room with his chin. "It's on your shirt. I notice house pins. It's my job."

Alex watched Ace in silence for a moment before he shrugged. "Didn't work as well as I'd hoped, as it turns out." He gave Ace a small smile and stepped into his personal room, closing the door behind himself. "Not at the trading house anyway," he said to himself.

Had Ace just given himself away?

There was no way he could have seen the pin on Alex's shirt, no matter how accustomed he was to looking for them, was there? Alex had been peeling his shirt off before he'd made it halfway across the room, and Ace hadn't come out of his room until Alex had almost made it to his quarters. Right?

Alex blew a gust of air out of his nose. Was Ace that good at picking out the glint of bronze on a shirt? Or had there been another set of eyes on Alex that afternoon? And if so, had those eyes reported only to Ace, or eventually to Kit Wallace herself?

Alex crossed to the middle of the room, removing his boots and pants as he thought. Layers upon layers, deeper and deeper, he stacked up the knowledge that he had with what he could extrapolate from recent events and snippets of conversation. Whatever the game was, it was bigger than he'd thought. He needed to know the stakes, and how they affected the plan for the Sparks. He needed to know it now.

FOURTEEN

Lena

Lena swiped at her hairline, dragging away the sweat that beaded there as she squinted against the sun at its zenith above her. It didn't matter how much she squinted, though. The ridgeline ahead wasn't changing, and neither was the oppressive heat, a last gasp before the cold of winter that the frosty mornings promised. The girls were hunkered down to rest for the afternoon in the valley behind her, taking cover in the patchy shade of a desert willow. They'd made excellent progress and had almost finished the interior of the big house, which was the only good news for the day. They were all tired, overheated, and itchy with dirt and sweat.

They were also in danger.

She could hear Rose's voice soothing someone below. Jackson approached up the side of the bluff she stood on, given away by the sliding rocks and loose sand dislodged with every step. Lena lifted her hands to her head, feeling the heat radiating off her hair.

"Please tell me again," she asked of him, "that coming out here was not the worst decision I've ever made." *You should have stayed. You could have helped Thomas drive out the traitors. You knew. They knew you knew. It was a matter of time. Now you've put everyone at risk again.*

There was no doubt they were being watched now. Whoever it was, they were good. Jackson and Rose together were better. They agreed that there were too many trace signs in the area around their valley. The fact that the watcher hung back without direct action against them was little comfort.

He let out a soft chuckle. “It’s not the worst decision you’ve ever made. They’re getting stronger.” There was that. “But we’re almost out of supplies.” He didn’t have to mention their concern about the unknown parties.

The resupply Thomas had promised, lead by Patrick, was long overdue. They’d been out here almost a month on their own, and they should have seen both supplies and agents at least ten days before. Had the agents been taken by the watchers? Or had Thomas reneged? Either way, they’d already started dipping into their reserves. Lena didn’t want to keep doing it. What if they had to make them stretch through the winter?

“And you’re still sick, which makes you doubt everything.”

Lena shrugged. It was true. Neither she nor Jackson had been able to get a handle on her illness. Jackson assumed it was related to stress and exhaustion. The Dust refused to cooperate, no matter how they asked or visualized the purging of the illness for her body. She’d feel better for a while, but then it would come back with a vengeance. It made her weak, unable to do her share of the physical labor of rebuilding. It made her angry.

As if Jackson could read the signs of her mood darkening at the mention of it, he moved back to the delayed resupply and the reason she climbed this bluff every day, twice a day, to look out from the top of the cliffs that protected their valley and across the view of the hilly high-desert country on the other side. “Still no sign of them?”

She shook her head and swallowed back her disappointment. “Not from anywhere that I can see. I’ve checked the southeast, Jackson, and the northwest. Why did I trust Thomas, trust in those supplies—”

“Because you can.”

“How? Nothing has happened the way he promised. Nothing.” She preferred to blame Thomas. The alternative—that the watchers were strong enough to take the agents—haunted her. She dropped her hands down and glanced back down the hill to the soft buzz of voices that carried to them. It wasn’t Thomas’s fault, though. It hadn't been his idea. "What was I thinking?"

"You were thinking you had to get them out to keep them safe." He kept his voice so even and neutral she couldn't tell if he meant the words. But he'd gotten them the supplies that were now running low. He'd come with them.

"Safe." The word tasted like ash in her mouth. "We're about to run out of food. Unknown people are watching us, and we don't know who or why. At this point, I can't even get them back to the Fort."

"We're not going back." The neutrality was gone.

She didn't really think going back was an option, either. How could they continue without food for the girls? Lena reached out to grip his lower arm, needing to be reassured. "They have to eat—"

"We'll find food, even if it's not the kind we've all become accustomed to. We'll find something." He raised his hands to his hips, pulling his arm from her grip, and turned his face away from her to scan the dry, rolling foothills that spread away before them.

Her hand dropped. She pulled her arms in to cross them over her chest, hunching her shoulders. "How can you be so sure?"

"Because I happen to know someone who did it before, when she was younger than some of those girls down there." He did turn back to her now, with a small smile.

"I only had to feed me, Jackson. And I had the Kewa next door to me to barter with. If I got hungry, I could trade on my ability. The Natives up here won't have anything to do with us." She'd tried to make contact. They kept slipping away. The only thing they knew was the Nations people weren't the watchers. She had no doubt they were keeping an eye on the valley from afar, but their territory ranged to the north, and they had no need to steal food.

"We'll find something."

"How can you be so sure?"

He cocked his head to the side. "Because between the three of us, we have all the skills we need."

When she started to shake her head and turn away in exasperation, Jackson took her arm and pulled her back. He didn't let go when he started talking again. "Lena. We have what we need. Rose was raised as a nomad. She has amazing survival and foraging skills, even if she's used to a different geography. She's already teaching the children. I have my training. You can do things no one else can manage. You said it to me once—you can make the Dust do almost anything you can think of, right?"

She stared at him. "I can't conjure food out of the air. What is it I'm supposed to be thinking of?"

"Well, right now, I'm hoping you can."

"I can?" She was wary. "And how is that?"

"Alex told me once that when he and Lucas went to pick you up, you had some kind of warning system? You knew there were agents coming somehow?"

Lena nodded. "The Dust showed me. It was…whispering at me." She laughed and shrugged at Jackson's expression. "It was."

"So…when it showed you…what did you see?"

Lena took a deep breath, thinking back. "Energy. Man-shaped energy moving across the desert."

"Man-shaped?" Jackson grinned at her. "Did you see anything else? I'm asking because I might have a solution to our food problem. Or you might. If you can sit and focus, ask the Dust to help you, I don't know, reach out and see? Maybe you can look for animal-shaped energy. Javelina. Or deer. Tell me where it is, I'll go hunt it without worrying about snares being broken or meat going missing. Bang. Food for all of us."

Lena blinked. Why hadn't she thought of that? She had seen everything. If it had heat or used energy, she'd seen its glow. She'd been focused on the men—and knowing the danger, so had the Dust. Could she ask it now to show her animals? Deer?

Could she ask it to show her the watchers?

Idiot. You should have thought of this yourself days ago!

Jackson tilted his head and raised his brows. "It's the best use of your talents and mine."

She nodded firmly. "Yes. Yes! When? Tonight."

Jackson laughed. "I was thinking now. Gives me the opportunity to take advantage of the mid-day heat." He gestured down the hill. "Animals resting from the sun in shade and shelter make it easier for me."

"Okay, then. Let's do it."

Jackson nodded back to the girls and the shade. "Let's do it down there, though. I'd like a minute or two to cool off before I head out."

Lena settled back against the homestead building, hands propped on her raised knees. The uneven curve of adobe bit into her lower back. It gave her something to focus on. As if she needed anything more to focus away with the ring of avid faces around her. Jackson rested against a rock off to her right—body relaxed, but his eyes sharp on her. Rose and the girls sat around her in a ring, quiet and watchful. Leo leaned into Rose.

Lena knew that each of them watched with more than just their eyes. They were almost as eager to see her try this new "trick" as she was to get started. At the thought, Lena's throat tightened and her breath hitched. That was Alex's pet term for the things she could do. He called them her tricks, and he'd been as eager to learn them all as the girls before her. She could see his face, lips twisted with frustration as he tried so hard to get the Dust to answer him. She remembered his reaction, too, after he'd accidentally knocked her on her ass—once he'd made sure she was okay, his amazed, proud laughter had filled the courtyard. Then he'd kissed her for the first time.

"Lena—are you okay?" Rose leaned in, brows furrowed.

Lena rubbed at her face with her palms. She hid her hiccupping breaths in laughter before she dropped her hands back to her knees. Damn, but she missed him.

"I'm fine, thanks. Just tired." Exhaustion made her fall victim to waves of emotion..

Jackson leaned in, too, his face worried. "We can wait—"

"No. I'm ready. I want to do this now. I'm ready to learn a new trick. How about the rest of you?"

Marissa's wide grin across from her was all the answer she needed, but if she'd had any doubts, Charity and Constance bounced with excitement. Even Hania, sitting cross-legged and leaning with her chin resting on her fist, was relaxed and intent.

Lena settled back against the heat of the building behind her and took a deep breath. She closed her eyes and breathed out again, pushing out with her mind, feeling for the Dust outside of her, around her, everywhere. At first there was nothing but the feel of the Dust, quiescent, waiting. As she probed and moved with her mind, she felt it waking, little flares like starlight in the dark of her mind. She reached further, probing out around her until it was as if her mind rested in a field of infinite stars. But these stars were waiting, listening. They were ready to help.

The moment the thought of what she wanted began to unspool in her mind, the blanket of lights on dark shifted, lightened, and then settled to a muted dusk over the desert. The starlight gleaming of the Dust was gone, replaced by darting flares of light against the darker background. Insects. Animals. The electric spark of life. Lena felt as if she were floating, lifting up to gaze down upon the undulating hills below. The bright noon light was gone, replaced by a darker haze against which the lights of the living glowed. Darting, fleeting lights were all around the brighter flare of human forms below—Lena herself, surrounded by Rose and Jackson and the girls. A smaller, dimmer light that must be the unpowered Leo curled beside Rose's bright form.

Lena watched them for several long moments, noting the differences in the light flaring from within them. They were all shimmering light, shifting and flexing like bright coals—Lena realized she saw more than their life force. Somehow, the gleam of the Spark was wound with and through the light of each life. One small form was brighter than the others, the shifting inside more brilliant. Her mind traced the small form's position and attitude and felt a spark of surprise. There was no surprise, but no pride either, as she noted her own bright form, her aura flaring into the air around her. But there was an odd, tiny kernel of light at her core, a brilliant fleck of blinding light shining whiter than the rest of Lena's glow.

Before she had time to do more than register the difference in the light within her own, something shifted in the corner of her mind's eye. It was as if the Dust had rippled, pulling her attention away from her body. Bright flares of life, larger than the insects and slower, moved through the hills to the right of Lena's own circle. She narrowed her focus and the Dust swept her in, flowing along the ground with it, following the eddies of air and rising heat from the ground.

Deer.

A small group moved in the shade of the same valley, but north of them, easing along the trickle of water. She turned to look further and saw a light glowing up through the darkness like a slender pillar, but so distant and so bright it speared into the sky. Though Lena's mind was far from her body now, she felt her face frown. The sensation wormed through her, jarring. What was the light ahead? Was it the watchers? Were they Sparks?

Lena tried to push her mind ahead, but something pushed her back. Lena tried again. She felt a stillness like the gathering of a storm, and then she was yanked back, her awareness rushing along the ground. Her consciousness sucked back to her body as if rejected by the very Dust around her. She gasped and her arms flailed up.

Voices.

Her name.

Lena coughed and shook her head, squeezing her eyes closed. The suddenness of sound crashing against her ears made her aware of the perfect silence of being she had experienced. Her own breath, catching in her throat, rasped, echoed. She opened her eyes.

"I'm fine." The words were soft, but they were enough to make the clamor stop.

Jackson and Rose both leaned over her. There was a ring of feminine faces behind them. Lena cleared her throat.

"I'm fine, really. That was…." She blinked up at them. "It was amazing."

"It worked?" Jackson was worried.

Lena laughed and looked at Jackson. "There's a small group of deer in this same valley, picking their way up the stream. They're north of us, hiding in the dark, cool part of the valley where the cliffs close in."

He grinned at her. “Of course it worked.”

She lifted her hands to her face, scrubbing at her skin to be certain it was real. The reconnection of mind and body was jarring. She was back. “It did work.” *And you, missy!* Lena’s gaze swerved to Hania, the brightest of them save for Lena, with pride. *You’ve been holding out on us.*

FIFTEEN

Jubilee

Jubilee crossed her eyes at Jacob's back as he stalked away to look out the window. He was annoyed at Lucas's refusal to give him the demonstration he demanded. Lucas caught her expression of defiance and his lips almost curled up into a smile.

Almost.

Then he must have remembered she was a filthy mongrel. That's what he called her, when he called her anything at all. Jubilee didn't know what a mongrel was, but she didn't think she wanted to be one.

She sighed and looked down at the table in front of her. She crossed her hands in front of her and crossed her ankles below the table. She was a good girl. The old man had rewarded her for being such a good girl—she was allowed to be a girl again, and not just a pet. She even had a little cot in her cage.

Now, if she was still and quiet, she got to sit up at the table with them instead of huddling beneath it. She flattened her palms on the *top* of the table with a happy hum before remembering herself. She laced her fingers back together to wait for the old man.

Neither of the old man's grandsons was good at being patient, though Lucas was better at pretending. He'd stare off into space and whisper to himself. Jacob, his big brother, didn't bother to pretend. Instead, he would snap his fingers and growl orders at people.

He did it now.

"You." He snapped his fingers at the assistant hovering in the doorway who'd just delivered the news that the old man was delayed in prayer at the chapel and would join them when he was cleansed. "I had a meeting scheduled with the special trade representative of Locust House. She's waiting in my office. Go and fetch her. If I have to wait, I'll conduct the business I must before we leave for the east in the morning."

Lucas blinked and glowered at his brother. "Isn't she going with you? Conduct your business in your caravan car."

"It involves her final preparations and my expectations for the trip. It has to be handled before we leave."

"Mmm. And the day before you leave is the best time to conduct such a meeting, of course. I can see why you're the apple of Grandfather's eye. Your efficiency makes you valuable, of course." Lucas had returned his gaze to the wall opposite him and spoke in a disinterested monotone.

Jubilee felt her stomach turn over. She hated when they fought. They always upset the old man.

Jacob crossed to the table and settled his hand between Lucas and Jubilee. He leaned in to put his face close to his brother's. "This from the creature whose only value to our cause makes him a monster. Careful, brother, or I'll have you put down like all the other Spark beasts who've outlived their usefulness."

A soft noise from the doorway claimed Jacob's attention. He straightened and smiled, showing his teeth.

Jubilee looked over. A tall woman stood in the doorway. She wore a dress in the same brilliant gold and brown and orange hues as the leaves on the trees outside. It made her yellow hair shine golden.

Jubilee thought she was the most beautiful lady she'd ever seen.

"Erika. Thank you for joining me here. I didn't want to keep you waiting on the day before we leave." Jacob's voice sounded funny—smooth and much deeper than usual.

Jubilee sneaked a glance at him and worried the skin over her fingers with her thumbs. Why did he sound nice? It was the people who tried to make you think they were nice who were always the scariest inside.

"Mr. Brayer—"

"Jacob." He smiled, his gaze moved down her before coming back up. "I've told you. Call me Jacob."

"Jacob." When the woman smiled she was even more beautiful. "I don't mind waiting."

"Absolutely not. I want to be sure we're on the same page as far as personal cargo provided by the House and what the manifest reflects. I don't want to have to make any more of these emergency trips to collect shipping records."

Erika dipped her head. "I understand, sir. I'm sorry it's necessary. My predecessor should have—"

"There's no need to apologize for someone else. Not to me." He gave her another smile.

Jubilee shivered.

A shadow fell in the hallway behind Erika, and fingers came around her shoulder. She flinched and spun, throwing up one arm to knock away the hand as she stepped back into the room. One of the Scary Boys stood in the doorway, watching the fast-moving woman warily.

The old man stepped around him, shooing him with a flick of a single finger and a baleful glare. He continued into the room, bypassing Erika without a glance and continuing to the table. He sat. After a silent moment, he raised his gaze to his oldest grandson.

"Why is there an uninvited guest in my conference room?"

Jacob met his grandfather's gaze without flinching. "She's not uninvited, sir. I invited her. She is the special representative I told you about. We had a meeting, and when you were detained, I moved it here to make efficient use of the time spent waiting."

The old man raised a hand for his grandson to stop speaking. He turned his sharp, pale gaze on the woman hovering near the doorway. "The representative from Locust House, hm?"

She held his gaze. "Yes, sir."

"And you've been here…four months?"

"Just under four months, sir. My transfer from our Zone Six office was a special request by the Director of Locust House here in Zone Four."

The old man nodded. "I am aware. I approved the request."

A flicker of confusion and maybe fear flashed across her face.

The old man's lips turned up, pleased. He looked like a cat. All he needed was the twitching tail of a mouse wiggling from the corner of his mouth.

Jubilee lowered her face to stare down at her hands. She had them clasped on the tabletop the way he liked.

"My grandson assures me you are as competent as you are beautiful. I hope that remains the case." The old man's voice sounded like a cat's pleased purr. "Since you are a *trusted* member of our household's business now, you should stay. Lucas is about to give a demonstration of what he's learned from his small instructor. He was tasked with learning to manipulate his Spark in new and aggressive ways. I think you'll find it enlightening."

Jubilee gulped. She knew Lucas's success or failure would reflect on her, in spite of his clear hatred and mistrust of her. They'd been forced to work together since he recovered from the second wound to his chest—the one she, and not the bear, had inflicted on him as punishment for his earlier failure. She healed him of his original wound. And then the old man had commanded her to tear his wounds open again.

So she had.

Now it would be Lucas's turn to show how he could use what she was able to teach him.

Lucas didn't look her way at all. He rose from his seat to stand shoulder-to-shoulder with his brother. At a nod from the old man, the Scary Boy in the doorway darted out and grabbed someone waiting outside.

When he returned, he dragged a shirtless young man behind him. Jubilee could tell from the glow around him that he was like Lucas and her—a hated Spark. The Scary Boy led him over to stand across the room.

Jubilee noticed that he'd been left to stand on the mottled sheet. It had been white, but was stained in various shades of brown and pink. It was the sheet Lucas always laid down on the floor when he practiced.

She took a tiny breath. She needed an extra sip of air to steady her. But she had to be sure the old man didn't know. She risked glancing at him, but his attention was claimed by the shivering young man in front of them.

Part of her wanted to slump down on the table at what came next. Another part, the part that liked that the Scary Boys avoided her now, the part that liked being a girl again instead of a pet, was pleased to sit up straight with her shoulders back.

Lucas was the one giving the demonstration, but *she* had done this. It was *her discovery.*

He stepped forward now. His head cocked as he moved closer. He stopped and glanced back to be sure his grandfather had a clear view. Reassured, he turned back.

There was no warning. There was no dramatic announcement, as she was sure Jacob would indulge in.

The young man's eyes widened and he clutched at his chest. He curled in on himself and a high keening filled the room. The sound choked away into wet gasps. A second later, he lifted his head. His mouth opened and closed, but no sounds came out. His first wounds were internal this time.

Blood ran down his chest, first in droplets as Lucas fought with the Dust. Jubilee could feel the Dust resisting Lucas. He redoubled his efforts. The blood became a steady stream as short, thin wounds like a cat's scratches widened. His chest looked mauled by dogs now.

It burst open. His skin separated in a fan of blood and peeling muscle that revealed the white of his ribs. The boy's eyes rolled back in his head and he collapsed. A bright new spatter pattern coated the sheet in a red that darkened with the flow.

Lucas turned around. His Spark's aura was bright and throbby—he wasn't anywhere near as strong as Jubilee. Doing this always took everything he had. Sweat beaded on his face and his hands hanging at his sides shook, but his face was filled with light. His eyes…

Jubilee shivered. His eyes looked like the old man's after

he'd finished his kneeling whispering chants.

Jacob cleared his throat in the silence. "That took a significant amount of effort from Lucas," he said. His normally hearty, decisive voice was almost tentative. "It won't do us much good as a weapon if he's only able to do it once."

Lucas narrowed his eyes. "I'll get better with practice. I'm already better."

The old man raised a hand and waved it to silence them. "I have a target in mind, Jacob. When I bring her to him, he'll only have to do it once. Until then, he can lead and teach my young men." He focused on Lucas. The old man's eyes were shining. "I knew your failure was an anomaly. I knew you could do this."

Lucas's answering smile was painful to look at. Jubilee turned her face away. The movement must have drawn the old man's attention to her. She felt a hand fall on her head and push her hair away from her forehead so he could see her face.

"You've done very well, Jubilee. I've prepared another reward for you in anticipation of this success. Would you like to see it?"

A reward? Jubilee looked up. There was kindness in his face now. He expected much from her, but he gave in return. She allowed her excitement to spill out in a smile.

"Yes," she breathed.

He nodded once and stood. When he turned, he started, as if he'd forgotten the woman still stood at the back of the room, watching. Of course, he hadn't forgotten. The old man missed nothing.

Her chest rose and fell in rapid gasps still. Her eyes were shocked. "They can do that? Your Sparks? I thought they just powered us, but *this...*"

They? Jubilee's brow wrinkled. Why was the woman separating herself from Lucas and Jubilee? She was a Spark, too. Didn't the others know? Jubilee could see the faintest of sheens on her skin. Yes, it was so faded and wan that she mustn't ever use her ability, but that didn't make her any less of a Spark. Not to the old man. Not to Jacob.

Not to Lucas, though he was a Spark himself. He should be

able to tell. Was he not strong enough to see the latent sheen that was there even though the woman must not ever use her Spark?

She looked at each of them in turn, tuning out the rest of the conversation as the old man gloated at his grandson's new ability to hurt and terrorize, and Jacob tried to soothe the woman's fears. They didn't know. Lucas couldn't see it. She looked again at the woman, focusing.

The woman was a Spark. A secret Spark?

Jubilee bit her lip. Should she tell?

Jacob had taken a few steps closer to the woman and raised his hand up. He smiled again. "We have full control over them. And this isn't something to be used haphazardly. As my grandfather said, we have a very specific thorn in our heel. We've been looking for creative ways to deal with the problem with the least amount of risk to innocent bystanders."

The old man's head bobbed in an eager nod. "A thorn, yes. And now we'll be able to yank it out." He turned to glance at Lucas and then focused on Jacob. "Perhaps Lucas should go with you on your journey?"

A look of distaste flitted across Jacob's face. "I'll bring the problem to you, Grandfather, so that you can experience the full pleasure of the moment." His smile widened. "Once I've retrieved our bait for you, let Lucas practice on him here, if you like. I want you to be able to enjoy this moment, too. We've worked so long and so hard for this."

The old man nodded, his eyes gone soft. "That would please me. Fine. Lucas stays home. Some of our special forces are already deployed. Be sure you meet with them." A moment later, he'd returned to himself and gave the woman, Erika, a quick smile. "So you see, this gift is reserved for our enemies. You are safe."

She swallowed and gave him a wobbly smile. "I had no idea—they were so dangerous."

"Why do you think we work so hard to keep them separate and contained here? It isn't because we're cruel. You cannot trust those who could kill you with a thought. Nurture them, yes. Control them, absolutely. But not trust." He stepped closer to her.

Jubilee could see a faint movement, like a quivering, that passed through the woman as she fought not to step away from him.

"I think," he said softly, "that you understand better why we do things the way we do here."

She nodded. Her eyes were filled with fear and a faint sheen of wetness.

He patted her hand. "Don't worry, dear. Soon every zone will be segregated like this. People will have safe zones. And Sparks will know their place. It's the only way to be sure of safety and comfort for our citizens."

He glanced back at Jacob. "Be sure you report before you leave in the morning. We have a few final items to discuss." He ignored Lucas for now.

Jubilee had no doubt that he would be rewarded, though. The old man always rewarded those who pleased him, even Sparks. That's what people like Erika didn't understand. She didn't have to be afraid to tell the old man she was a Spark. She wouldn't be allowed to keep doing her job, but they'd find her something else. And if she did a good job, they would be good to her.

The old man left the room without looking back, but Jubilee trotted after him. He'd said he had something prepared for her. This was her moment.

In her excitement, her mental shield slipped a little. Jubilee had figured out how to keep Marissa from seeing what kind of lessons Jubilee was learning and teaching. It wasn't that Jubilee was ashamed of what she did. It was just that she knew Marissa would be scared. She didn't want to scare her friend. Now she felt an immediate presence as Marissa's curiosity poked at her. She happily let her back in.

I earned a reward! I get a special present!

She could feel Marissa with her, watching. The tightness that was ever present in Jubilee's chest eased. She even skipped a little as she followed the old man down halls and upstairs to his private residence level.

The other people who worked here in the Council building lived outside. Jubilee knew that those who were high-ranked got to live in one of the inner rings surrounding the Council building. Everyone else lived outside, tucked safe within the walls of the city. Except the Sparks—they had their own little fortified village outside the walls with guards patrolling it to keep them safe.

The old man had moved from his outside residence to an upper level of the Council building. He led her there now. He stopped in front of a door and turned to her with a wide, kind smile.

Jubilee knew Marissa watched. She could feel the fear curl within her. Marissa was afraid of the old man. She soothed her friend.

The old man reached out and opened the door, pushing it back and nodding at her to go in.

Jubilee hesitantly entered. She glanced back over her shoulder as she crossed the threshold. The old man followed her in. His smile had become indulgent as he watched her.

Jubilee turned back. The room was small with a big, tall bed on one wall. It was soft, blankets and pillows in a range of pale, delicate colors piled upon it. Even the walls soothed, covered in pale green fabric. Across from the bed was a small chest with a stool before it and mirror hanging on the wall above it. Jubilee looked around, her eyes wide and unblinking. She crossed the room.

A window on the far wall looked down over a garden. There weren't bars on the window, only soft drapes of a darker green fabric hanging down from the ceiling far above her head.

But there was no surprise in the room. She'd looked for a box. There was nothing.

She turned back, folding her hands in front of her and waiting.

The old man's brows rose. "Well? What do you think, Jubilee? Do you like it?"

"It, sir?"

"Your reward." He spread his hands. "Your room."

She turned her gaze to look again at the bed, the walls, the window. She even looked down. Layers of carpets covered the floor. Everything about the room was soft. Everything in it was about comfort.

Her comfort?

She could feel a surge of admiration tinged with jealousy from Marissa. Marissa loved the people she lived with, but there was nothing there like this.

"It's mine?"

He nodded, his smile wide. She could see his happiness in his eyes. There was a gentleness there she hadn't seen before. He did want her to be happy, but he wanted her to earn it.

"I love it!"

The surge of joy was brief. Marissa withdrew from her mind. Her attention had been called away. The absence was always hard. In this moment of triumph, when she'd wanted her friend with her to experience it, too, those people called her away and left Jubilee alone again.

She could feel her face fall. Her chin puckered and she struggled to swallow back the sudden rush of tears that closed her throat.

"Child? What is it?" The old man's gaze strafed the room. "Does something displease you?"

"N-n-no, sir," she managed. "I love it."

"Well, then, what is it?" His tone was impatient now. This wasn't the reaction he'd wanted.

She shook her head, miserable and knowing she was ruining the moment. Would he take her beautiful room back?

"It's not that. I just—I miss Marissa."

"The other half of your matched pair."

She nodded. "I'm lonely. And I wish—together we could do so much for you. I wish I could share all of this with her."

His face gentled, but there was an anger beneath it. "I know. I wish it, too. If only they hadn't stolen her. If I could bring her to you, I would do it."

"You would?"

He nodded. His face was sad. "But they've hidden them away. They've taken them from one place and moved to another, and the man I sent to watch over Marissa can't reach her."

"But I know the way. Or most of it. I can see what she sees, sometimes." Jubilee felt a bright flare of hope in her chest. "If I can tell you how, can you send someone to get her?"

The old man stared at her. He was silent for a long moment. His chin came up, and his expression had shifted from shock to pleasure. She'd made him happy again.

Would Marissa be her reward this time? She was so lonely, and all the other girls had each other and Lena and Jackson. Jubilee had no one. All she wanted was to have Marissa back. They could share this beautiful room. Jubilee held her breath.

"Yes, Jubilee. If you can tell us the way, we'll go and get Marissa for you."

SIXTEEN

Lena

Lena woke slowly. She swam through a field of stars that flared to welcome her and then closed behind her again as she passed. Somehow she knew the stars were the Dust, moving against her and with her. She rose closer to the surface and looked back again to thank the Dust. Behind her, a light flared bright and bold, spearing through the dark. A ribbon of unease spooled out within her.

Who are you?

Lena opened her eyes, but the world outside her mind was no brighter than the dark she'd left behind. She blinked in confusion and reached up to wipe away grit. The smell of cooking meat was thick in her nose. Her stomach growled as she sat up.

"She's awake!" One of the twins called out from close by. Lena glanced over at the shadows of forms stretched out on the furniture.

Marissa and Hania were closest to her on the couch, but already asleep, tumbled together with Leo. Behind them, Charity and Constance grinned at her over the backs of the two smaller girls, their smiles gleaming in the dark. The rest of the smallest charges weren't in the room.

"Excellent news," came Rose's dry voice as she approached from the kitchen. "Now will you all go to sleep with the others?"

Lena turned to Rose, silhouetted against the light from the room behind her. Behind her, set up on one of the long metal counters to finish his work, Jackson worked a long knife across the remains of an animal.

"We have meat!" Charity whispered to Lena.

"It was so good!" Constance added.

Lena smiled as she tucked her hair behind her ears and rose to her feet. "Excellent news," she mimicked Rose's tone and words. "Now—"

"Go to sleep!" The girls chorused the words together and popped up from the couch to race each other down the dark hall.

Lena crossed to Rose. The other woman had returned to the kitchen to tend strips of meat from the oven. Jackson had another tray ready to go, and Rose slid it away from him and into the waiting heat.

"How long have I been out?"

Rose glanced at her. "All afternoon. We're a good three hours past dark now, so…."

"A whole day?" She punctuated the question with a long yawn.

"Well, whatever you want to call what you did today, I think it took a lot out of you." Rose turned the last of the strips to inspect the meat, then pulled the meat from a skewer and set it with the rest in a pile to the side. She wiped her hands down the front of her legs and then crossed her arms. "Do you think it's dangerous?"

Lena thought about the silence and the life lights moving beneath her as she floated above. "I don't think so." She remembered the sudden spear of light through the dark and the feeling of being pushed back before the Dust sucked her back into her body.

Lena turned her body to face southwest. She imagined the night sky outside. The details of her immediate surroundings here in the valley were lost to her, but she could visualize the bulk of the mountains that closed them in as a darkened hulk of earth blocking out the spinning patchwork of starlight.

"I don't think so," Lena repeated. "But something out there may be. I need to go back and look again."

"What? Lena—why?"

Lena shook her head. "I might have found our watcher." She

nodded ahead, out of the bunker. "It pushed me away."

"*What?*" Rose stared at her, then whirled. "Jackson!"

"Rose!" Lena rolled her eyes.

"What? He needs to know what's going on. This should be something we adults decide together. We're in this together, for them."

Lena glanced back over her shoulder at the living area. Two sets of eyes reflected the light from the kitchen back at her. Marin and Phoebe considered themselves too old to be sent to bed. Like the twins, they were awake, but they hadn't gone to their bunks. Instead, they sat together, keeping watch over the sleeping forms of Marissa, Hania, and Leo. They'd heard Rose's adamant declaration.

Jackson came across the kitchen, wiping his hands on the front of his pants. His arms were damp from being cleaned. Drying blood coated the front of his shirt and pants. "What's going on? What do we need to decide together?"

"I'm going back with the Dust to have another look."

Jackson grunted. His gaze flicked from Rose to Lena. "Why? You were passed out for more than six hours. We have meat. That was our goal. Why would you need to go back?"

"There's something out there. Someone."

"Someone? Could it be the team we're waiting on?" His brows rose. "What do you think—"

"It's not the team, but other than that…I don't know, Jackson." Lena tilted her head back in frustration. How could she explain the feeling? "It just—it was like there was something out there. When I tried to get close, it pushed me back. Or the Dust pulled me away."

"The Dust pulled you away?" Rose asked. "Like, saving you from something?"

Lena shook her head. "No," she replied softly, "I don't know how to describe it, but something was off."

"If something was off," Jackson began, shaking his head.

"Then you don't need to rush to see it again," Rose finished for him. "We don't need to rush into danger, any of us."

"That's my point," Lena said, her voice cool, "we don't need to rush into danger. But the thing—the feeling, the light—is headed toward us. I don't think it's that far away. Maybe a few days, at most. It's a good bet it'll be here soon, if it hasn't already been here. If we have to face it, whatever it is, I'd rather do that knowing what it is."

The others exchanged a look.

"You know I'm right. We need to know because if it is something dangerous, and we have to leave in a hurry to keep them safe—"

"You'd rather be able to go at first light than to have to wait again for you to sleep off another recovery period." Rose was becoming adept at finishing their thoughts for them.

Lena grinned at her. "It's almost like you're in my head."

"Now there's a terrifying thought," Rose teased her in a dry voice.

"You need to eat first," Jackson said. He nodded at the roasted meat piled on the counter, ready for storage. "And get some water in you."

Lena nodded. "It smells good. You did it!"

"We did it together." Jackson flashed a half-smile at her before returning to the carcass on the other side of the kitchen. Rose piled meat on a plate with a piece of rough bread and brought it to Lena while Lena rummaged for a cup and filled it with water.

It felt good to fill her stomach with substantial food. Lena considered the children asleep in the rectangle of light that speared across the dark room outside the kitchen. There was something out there. She'd be damned if she'd let it have them.

Rose and Jackson joined her. Jackson's clothing was sodden and his hands and arms were clean. While his clothes were stained, he'd done his best to rinse away the worst of the gore. Lena wiped the last of the grease from the meat from her lips and grinned broadly at Jackson. "It was really good."

He laughed, but shook his head as he raised an arm for her to precede him out of the kitchen. "Thank the cook. Rose knew how to roast and smoke, and she had the girls gather the wild onions, too."

Lena grinned at Rose. “I’m ready. We should head up. It might be easier outside.”

They followed her up and out of the bunker. She chose a comfortable spot in the grass nearby and sat, crossing her legs beneath her. Rose and Jackson, and Marin and Phoebe, too, settled in around her.

“We’ll keep an ear out for the little ones, but we want to be up here, too,” Phoebe told her quietly. From the look on her face, she half-expected to be told to go back into the bunker, but Lena nodded.

“I’ll be watching you,” Rose told Lena. “If you so much as gleam, I’m going to do whatever I have to so you come back.”

Lena took a breath to protest, but Jackson nodded his agreement.

“Whatever it takes.” His face was solemn. He wasn’t happy about her doing this, she knew, but he understood why she had to do it.

“I understand, but I’m going to try to look around, too, to see if I recognize the land from above. Maybe I can find Thom’s agents.” Lena’s goal was two-fold: figure out where the light was in relation to the rancho, and make sure there wasn’t any danger to them. “Give me time.”

Rose shrugged. “I’ll give you as much time as I can, Lena, until I think it’s a danger to you.”

Lena nodded. She trusted Rose—both to wait until she gauged there was truly a danger, and to bring her out if needed.

Lena gripped her own knees, fingers squeezing, focusing her energy on the sensation before closing her eyes and reaching out with her mind.

She’d been afraid the darkness of night would make the dusky view of the Dust-world even darker, and impossible to navigate. She was wrong—the Dust presented her with the same twilit dusk as it had during the brightness of day. Lena oriented herself in the flowing light of Dust. She noted the movement of life all around them, including the smaller forms of the four sleeping girls below ground.

Other than their small group, the only larger forms were

gathered well up the valley. The predators and scavengers were feasting on and fighting over the entrails and detritus of Jackson's first slaughter of the deer where it had fallen.

Oriented and content that there was no immediate danger to her group below, Lena looked up from the prowling movements of the large animals at the far end of the valley. She made a sweep of the immediate area, then widened her search. To the north, there were the dim life lights of the Nations settlements. The east was clear. She turned her attention to the southwest and the Neo-barb settlement at Old Taos. There were several brighter lights there—like Sparks, but somehow the light felt fragmented, scattered. Was this the signature of untrained Sparks among the Neo-barbs? She considered sweeping in for a closer look when a brighter light south of Old Taos caught her attention.

The slim column of light was gone, replaced by a diffuse glow that spread over the distant hills. Still bright, just quiescent.

Sleeping, Lena realized.

The column was a Spark. She'd hoped perhaps it was the land, an area of particular density of Dust. She turned now, to glance back at her friends.

Somehow, she'd moved farther from them than she'd realized. She hovered well above them. There was a bright, diffuse glow that eased through the valley like fog. The light crept up from the ground and out to cover the edges of their hollow like mist. It was very similar to the light she moved toward.

Another group of strong female Sparks? Perhaps another hidden Council prison? Lena's resolve hardened. She spun back and swam through the Dust. Unlike earlier in the day, when it had seemed to hold her back, the Dust now aided her. Lena flowed faster, moving like the wind that blew over the high desert. She strained her senses to see, to feel, ahead of herself.

Like the hollow far behind her where her companions waited, the light spread over the ground ahead, blurring out the details of the hills flattening into a high plain. It rose up into the dusky sky like a false sunrise. As she swept in, approaching the edges of that light, her eyes moved over the land, skirting the perimeter.

Lena reared back at the edge, stunned by recognition. She

turned to look to the north, to be sure. In the far distance, darkness plunged down into a gorge. There was the dark, cold, lifeless black span of an ancient bridge arcing out over the emptiness. She knew the bridge ended abruptly, a jagged, broken testimony to the ravages of time. Its fallen trusses were mangled, rusted lacework over the rubble of the former roadway that the river foamed around far below.

She looked back down. She'd been to this place, years before. It was the easiest crossing of the Rio Grande closest to the gorge. She'd used it herself on her first trip to the rancho after helping a young Neo-barb rescue his brother from the slaving Scavengers that had razed their village. The young man, Ghost, had sworn to avenge his family and recover his brother. He'd almost died to achieve it. He'd given Lena the rancho in thanks. Lena hadn't thought of Ghost in years, except for the sporadic wondering about the survival of the young man's new tribe.

She and Ghost had rescued the Scavengers' human cargo, including a young Scavenger woman and her daughter. He'd led them all away, forming a new family unit. Ghost had been determined to find some mythical safe zone deep in the charred ruins of Texas. She hoped he'd found them. She hoped they were all safe and well.

What had she herself found? Lena stared out at the light, close enough for her to reach out and touch if her body hadn't been left far behind her. She did know this place. Ghost had sent her to the rancho, and she'd warded it tight against intrusion. But she couldn't ward the path she'd taken. She couldn't ward the entire distance. They were on that path. And from the change in distance, they were making progress, moving toward the rancho.

Was the rancho their goal? Or would they keep moving past the narrow mouth of the valley? What was all this energy? Who was down there? How many were there to produce this much of a light signature?

Lena tentatively pressed forward with her mind, easing up against the edge of the misty light. She meant to explore the boundary of it—just a taste, to give her a sense of what hid below. She hadn't intended to wake it.

She felt the moment the mind—yes, the single, powerful, wild mind—behind the light woke. It jerked away from her touch. The light flowed back in toward the center. As it rolled back like a bright tide, it uncovered the details of the murky camp below. One mind provided the light, yes, but many people slept below, enough to be an entire tribe. There were the dark shapes of tents below. A few restless blobs of light padded around. Dogs? The larger lightforms of humans patrolled the edges of the little mobile camp, keeping larger animals close by.

Her vision tracked back with the receding light to one small tent near the center. The tall, slender column flared to the sky.

A restless fear animated the column. It twisted like an upside down dust devil, moving toward her, reaching.

It didn't mean to examine her. The energy sliced through her consciousness. It wasn't hot, but cold. The frigid impact sent her tumbling back, lost in the roiling air currents of Dust. Aching cold stunned her.

Lena imagined a bubble of heat and energy, a shield against the cold fear striking out. The Dust flowed around her, bright heat as an antidote to the frigid light of the wild Spark's powerful terror. The bubble deflected the next blow.

Lena tumbled back again, breathless and dizzy. She hadn't been struck, but the force had pushed her further away. Lena tried to catch the breath she somehow knew hiccupped from her lungs in panic and anger, but the disconnect between her far away body and her mind was too great. Dimly, as if a memory of sound, she heard alarmed voices calling out to her.

Her panicked attacker pulled back, regrouping. The light that had whirled away turned to strike again.

Please....

Lena's consciousness curled within her bubble. She shored it up now, drawing in more of the Dust surrounding her, using it to pour energy and heat into her shield. The voices called louder, a buzz that threatened to overcome the sibilance of the Dust at the back of her mind. She ignored them, bearing down with focus.

Whatever was behind the light was terrified. If she could reach it, reason with it....

PLEASE. Listen. It doesn't have to be like this.

The light coiled and struck.

Light and heat flared, crashing against each other. Lena flew back, twisting and rolling. Had she been whole, her body would have been broken. Instead, she was dazed. The explosion rolled over the camp and across the plain like angry thunder, an initial crash louder than any grounding or lightning Lena had ever heard. The after-boom went on and on, a low growling echo that chased Lena back as the Dust swept her away.

Her bubble had broken.

Pinpoints of light flowed into a smear as she rushed back. Some of it flowed into her, bolstering her mind. The Dust twined with her thoughts. She could also feel it back with the body it hurtled her toward, rising up from the ground to coat her, to swarm over her heart and lungs, to flow down to circle her hips like a wide belt, sinking in beneath her flesh, arrowing in to that bright pinpoint of light within her. The Dust was healing.

She had enough sense to feel a frisson of new panic.

The Dust filled her. Overwhelmed her. The power was rich, ozone-electric, and it was everywhere.

What would happen when she had to cram this power back down into her physical brain?

Seconds later, she found out. Pain exploded in her head and her chest. The last time she'd felt this near-to-bursting with energy had been after holding back all the combined energy of the men and boys of Fort Nevada. A vision popped into her panicked mind—Alex, explaining what had almost happened, his fingers flaring as he gestured to indicate her near explosion.

Lena jerked up, staggering to her feet and pulling from strong, restraining hands. She had to get away. She was a danger to all of them. She reeled away from a second pair of hands, alarmed shouts muted by the pounding in her head.

"Lena! Stop! This way. This way to Rose. Let her help."

"Please, Lena, remember. Remember how to share this."

Lena felt Rose's strong grip on her shoulders, stilling her.

Yes. This. I remember.

"Now. Rose. Now." The words were an animal whine, her

entire body taut with the effort to contain the energy. Her hands opened and closed, waiting for Rose's grasp. It was all she could manage.

Hands took hers. Their fingers entwined, but more than their fingers joined them. What they were—who they were—was entwined, too. Lena wasn't alone in her power, in her place in the world. Not anymore. There was Rose.

Lena let the energy go. She'd eased it into Rose last time, trying to bleed power off. Lena hadn't really believed they were equals, then.

Rose could handle it. Rose was her match. Lena had to trust that, or there was no way either of them could survive this.

The power surged from Lena to Rose, sizzling over and beneath their skin, dazzling bright, even with eyes squeezed shut. The light leaked through, the delicate veins of her lids silhouetted against it.

Then it was gone, replaced by a muted glow through her closed eyes. She opened them. Rose stood before her, hands still wound together with Lena's, body taut with the power she'd absorbed.

Lena now understood why everyone stared when she glowed.

Rose was lit from within, a glow that suffused her. The light was warm beneath her skin. It shone from her eyes, lighting up their pale blue. It was beautiful and unnerving.

Lena glanced down at their linked hands. She glowed, as well.

Rose pulled her hand free. She lifted it and rotated it in front of her own face, fascinated.

"Well. Look at me." Her glowing gaze moved from her hand to Lena's face.

"Yeah," Lena tried to smile around the nausea and the headache. "Welcome to the club."

Behind Rose, Lena could see Marin and Phoebe standing together. They watched Lena and Rose with a fascinated gaze.

"Oh, I so want to do that someday."

Marin nodded wordless agreement with Phoebe's pronouncement.

Were they craving the Dust-travel that Lena had accomplished for the second time, the glowing, or the depth of the sharing that she and Rose managed? Perhaps all of it.

She lifted her hands to her stomach, as if rubbing at it would rid her of the nausea growing stronger by the second. She remembered how debilitating it had been last time. Jackson's relieved worry was a palpable thing.

"Relax, Jackson," she whispered. "This has happened before, remember?"

"Yeah. I do."

She hadn't reassured him, but she wasn't feeling all that reassured herself. Her chin dropped to her chest, and she looked down her body.

Where the Dust burrowed in. Where the bright star of light hid. What had she done to herself? What had the Dust been so intent on healing? She needed to know if it was dangerous. Did it have to do with the supernova evolution danger Sam had warned her about?

"Am I supposed to feel like my head is going to explode at any minute?" Rose's voice was thinner than normal, more high-pitched, and tinged with a note of panic.

Jackson made a noise somewhere in the neighborhood of disbelief.

"Yeah." Lena took a deep breath, trying to calm both her head and her rebelling stomach. "That's how I was. And I think—I dumped more of it into you this time. Or the Dust did." She hadn't meant to give Rose this much. Had it been Lena? Or had it been the Dust again, protecting her?

"The Dust?"

"I don't know—I'm sorry. You should ground as soon you can handle it." Lena wasn't sure she could handle it. She wasn't sure she should.

"I think I need to ground now. This is—it's getting—*more*."

This was more. Much more. What had the Dust done? She fisted her hands over her stomach, unease growing with the sick feeling. "I can't," she blurted, giving in to the unease. "Not yet. But you go."

Jackson swore a steady stream. In a way, it reminded her of Alex.

"Get up over the top of the cliffside, now." When they didn't move fast enough toward the steep path, he barked, "Now—both of you! You need to be up and grounding *now*."

"I can't, Jackson." If she was a danger, she needed to know now. If the light inside could offer an explanation, Lena was going to have it. "I need—you have to check me over first."

That got his attention. "For what? What happened?"

"Are you okay?" Rose waited, unwilling to leave Lena to go ground no matter how much she needed it.

"Same as you," Lena grunted. She glanced over at Jackson flanked by Marin and Phoebe. "Rose, *go*."

Rose blinked, then turned to stagger up the hillside path. Lena knew she'd find the small, cleared area well away from the edge they'd all been using. It was close enough to be practical, but far enough not to pose a danger to the plants and animals—including the humans—that lived in the valley below.

Lena gestured with her head for Jackson to be ready to go up after her. "This is going to be a bad one for her."

Jackson waited for Lena to join Rose, face set.

Lena flashed the girls beside him a small smile. She turned and took a few steps before turning to sink down crosslegged beside the entrance to the bunker. A little light leaked up from the open hatch, although her skin outshone it. "When she's done, come check me," Lena told Jackson over her shoulder. "Then I'll rest and ground, too."

"Check you for *what,* Lena?" He demanded a second time.

She shook her head. "I'm not sure."

The thunder of Rose's grounding cracked into the sky and light licked up from the top of the cliff above them to the sky. The sound rolled back to them, covering the finish that all of them knew from personal experience was inevitable: the sound of her collapse to the ground afterward. Jackson postponed his questions to climb up the hillside to retrieve Rose. Marin went with him. Phoebe joined Lena by the hatch.

The young woman tentatively reached and took Lena's hand.

Phoebe's dark, doe eyes were focused on Lena's hand, and her shoulders curled in.

"It won't hurt you."

At Lena's words, Phoebe's looked up and their gazes met.

"I know," Pheobe said. A moment later she admitted, "It isn't the glow that makes me nervous." Phoebe was always direct, even when she had to push herself into whatever it was she had to say.

"I make you nervous?" Lena hadn't expected that.

"I think you make us all nervous—except Marissa and Marin."

"The youngest and the oldest of my own originals." Lena couldn't keep the disappointment from her voice. She'd never intended to be intimidating. She tried so hard to model for them what she'd never had…normal.

"Yeah, Marissa likes you a lot. I mean, we all like you. We just—we're afraid of not being as much as you are."

"As much what?"

"As much everything. Strong and brave and kind of scary. Tough." Phoebe shrugged. "Powerful."

Lena shifted her weight backward to pull her knees into her chest protectively. The pressure eased the nausea a little, but did nothing for the new anxiety blooming in her chest. She'd had no idea how they saw her.

"You're all just as much those things and more. I happen to know for a fact that at least one of you is more powerful than I am." She nodded at Phoebe's raised brows. "And that's only the Dust. You girls have been through things that I can't begin to…. You're all strong and brave and tough and scary, too. You shouldn't be scared of me. Be more like Marin."

Phoebe's eyes went wide for a moment and a bubble of laughter escaped her throat. She shook her head. "No, not Marin."

"Why not Marin?"

"Because she's—" Phoebe shook her head. "She's not in awe of you because…." The girl drifted off. It was almost as if she was afraid of sharing something.

Lena raised a brow. "Don't stop now, Phoebe."

"She's a little jealous." Pheobe was trying, in a late-teenaged way, to be circumspect for Lena. Or, Lena realized, trying to protect her friend's confidences. "She wants what you have."

"What I have?" Realization dawned. Was Marin jealous? "She wants Alex?"

"What?" The word was negative and highly amused. "Oh, ew. No. He might be kinda hot, but he's *old*."

"What?" It was Lena's turn to be indignant. "He is *not*." Okay, he was a little, from their perspective. "He's old*er*. That's not the same as old. And he feels young. No! I don't mean feels—I mean—he acts, he thinks—he looks—"

Phoebe laughed. "Oh, Dust, please…stop."

Lena ruefully joined her, settling her forehead on her knees. Their laughter dwindled away.

"I didn't mean him anyway," Phoebe offered. "I meant Jackson. Marin wants him to want her the way Alex wants you."

Lena kept her head down, but she shook her head. Her forehead rubbed against the rough fabric of her pants. "She doesn't need to be focused on that right now. None of you do. There's so much for you to learn and experience, and that's where your focus should be, not on…" Lena drifted off. She remembered herself at that age. She'd already been alone in the desert for a year when she was Marin and Phoebe's age. She'd already figured out that loneliness and sexuality were issues not to be ignored. She remembered the yearning that was an ache. She also remembered well that yearning for human contact and sexual experiences didn't preclude you from learning, or focusing, or building a life.

Becoming a woman doesn't make you a less capable human.

"Actually," she started again, voice soft and emphatic. She lifted her head to catch and hold Pheobe's gaze with her own. "Let me rephrase that. With everything you all have been through, I think it's a good thing to feel safe enough to think of others in that way." She glanced at Pheobe, whose wide eyes told her she was listening and wasn't sure what to think.

"Yes, we have a lot to do, and it's serious business, but I don't want any of you to feel bad for being attracted to someone else," Lena continued. "Thinking about sex, being interested in it, doesn't make you less—not less capable, not less serious, not less period. Not any more than not doing it would somehow make you more. We're all human, and all we can do is what's best for us without worrying about what anyone else is doing or thinking, so long as we're not hurting anyone else."

Lena stopped. Phoebe had averted her eyes, staring into the darkness.

Ah, Dust, I'm screwing this up. "I have no idea if any of that made sense. I'm sorry. I wish I could be wise. But I'm just…me."

Phoebe grinned. "That was pretty good. I wish Marin could have heard it."

Lena grimaced.

"It's okay. I'll tell her what you said." Phoebe's expression faded, to be replaced by a look that was almost haunted. "But—what if I'm not interested in that? After everything that happened, that's okay, too, right? I don't want to think about anyone touching me, not ever. Is that normal?"

Terror bubbled up inside Lena. Phoebe was the one of all the girls Lena would least have expected this from. She was the one filled with light and laughter.

Don't screw this up, Lena. Don't screw this up.

"I think that's okay, Phoebe. If you're moving forward, making new decisions and rebuilding every day, trying to feel your healing, then wherever you are is normal for you, for what you've been through. Maybe you won't ever want that. Maybe you will. Either way, so long as it's what *you* want, and not what *they've* done to you, then you're doing fine. But that's just what I think. What matters more is what you think." Lena held her breath, waiting.

Phoebe stared back into Lena's eyes. After a long moment, she nodded, a faint movement. Behind them, there was the sound of soft voices as Jackson and Marin guided Rose back down the hillside. They'd given her time to rest and dress before bringing her back.

Phoebe's eyes flashed. She leaned in toward Lena, her voice low but powerful. "Don't say anything!"

Lena wasn't certain whether Phoebe meant to silence Lena

about their discussions regarding Marin's affections, or about Phoebe's response over her own recovery. "I won't," she promised.

They waited for the others to join them, Lena's lips quirking up behind the shelter of her knees as she noticed for the first time how Marin responded to everything Jackson said, whether it warranted a response or not.

First love was a tough thing, especially unrequited love. Lena remembered the feeling well, and she still remembered the face of the young Kewa scout she'd pined for that first year on her own.

Jackson settled Rose beside the hatch on the other side and crouched beside Lena. "You said you wanted me to check you. For what?"

Lena didn't know how to express it. She stared back at him, then gave him a shrug. "When I go up with the Dust, it's like floating in a field of galaxies. And the Earth is dark beneath it. When I look down, I can see the energy of living things."

Jackson nodded, the movement quick and impatient. She'd already explained this part.

"So I looked down, and I could see how strong we all are. I could see us glowing, some brighter. And I could see a spark of something in me. Inside. Something different. Something very bright." Lena hesitated. That was the best way she could describe it.

Jackson frowned. "I'd expect that. You are different."

"No." Lena shook her head. "It wasn't the glow. And mine wasn't the brightest." Her lips curved up as she thought of the brilliant corona that was Hania. "This was—I don't know what it was. But it wasn't me." She glanced over at Rose. Her friend had fallen asleep.

Lena continued, her voice low. "I noticed it both times I went up. The first time, I went off and found the deer and then came back. The second time, I went toward where the pillar was. I scared it and it—" Lena stopped. Jackson wouldn't like this part. She took a deep breath, puffing her cheeks, then pushed it out. "It attacked."

"It attacked." His voice was flat.

Lena nodded. "I made a bubble to protect myself. The light mist formed back into a pillar. I looked down and saw a nomad camp—"

"A nomad camp? How many?" The questions were sharp.

"A lot. Enough to make a village."

He nodded. His lips were compressed.

"I had only a second to look down before it attacked. It lashed out, broke the bubble. Knocked me senseless for a second. The Dust pulled me away. Right before I popped back in, that's when I noticed it." She looked up and held his gaze. "The Dust was swarming me. It was healing. And it was focused on that bright spot inside me. There's something in me, Jackson, something the Dust wants to protect. Maybe it's what makes me glow. If it is, I want to be sure it isn't something that can infect the others. We already have Rose glowing now." Lena shook her head. "I don't know, but I want you to look. You're the best of us with healing."

It was the truth, and he acknowledged it now with a slow nod. He'd surpassed what Lena could teach him. Or perhaps her unorthodox training had spurred him to find new ways to handle the human body?

"Okay. But before I do—Lena, is there any danger to us here, other than the mouth of the valley? I can hide that. But do you think the pillar, the person behind it, could have tracked you back here?"

Lena frowned, thinking. She shook her head. "The attacks stopped as soon as I swept away. I don't think so, but to be safe, we should probably do what we can to hide the entrance up here, and then we should take cover in the bunker. We'll do this, and I'll rest for a bit and then ground. In the morning, we'll hide our presence. Whether anyone followed or not, I'll feel better if we're tucked in safe and sound below."

"Good idea. It makes a safe temporary solution, though it'll be clear someone has been here making repairs. We can't bring the horses down, and we can't stay down there indefinitely. If they find their way up here and decide to stay…" His gaze flicked over her. "We'll deal with that when the time comes. Are you ready now?" He lifted his hands.

"Yep." She glanced at the girls.

Phoebe and Marin both watched closely.

He settled his hands on her abdomen and back.

She cleared her throat and leaned back a little on one hand to stretch her body. "Just…try to figure out what it is and if it's dangerous. If the rest of you can catch it."

After one deep, cleansing breath, Jackson focused on his hands, on her skin and flesh cupped beneath them. When he went beneath the surface with the Dust, his eyes went soft and unfocused, the pale whiskey brown luminous in the firelight.

Lena could feel the Dust respond, a lazy swirling. The sensation was new, and it raised the hair on the back of her neck. It was as if she was somehow more in tune with the Dust now, more aware.

Jackson made a small noise in his throat. His hands pressed in, an almost painful pressure as they squeezed on either side of her. A moment later, the pressure eased. His hands slipped away from her, though his eyes remained trained downward.

Lena tilted her head to catch the edge of his gaze. "Jackson?"

What the Dust had he seen?

"It's not infectious." His voice was soft, but oddly flat. "And the only person it could be a danger to is you, especially with us living like this. It's not a knot of Dust or sickness. And I doubt it has anything to do with you or Rose glowing." He looked away into the dark of the night around them, still refusing to meet her eyes.

Dread curled inside her, working its way up to the center of her chest. What had he seen? Lena grabbed his arm and tugged on his sleeve to bring his attention back to her, though he refused to cooperate. "What did you see? What's the light?"

"It's a heartbeat, Lena."

Lena stared at him. "Huh?"

His face was serious. "The light is beating. It's a heartbeat."

Lena shook her head. "I don't understand. What—the Dust came alive?"

What is the Dust doing in there?

Jackson's mouth opened and his eyes closed. He shook his head. "And you made fun of me for being sheltered." He opened his eyes again. "It's not the Dust, Lena. It's a baby. Or it will be."

A baby...? Lena's thoughts stuttered to a halt.

She laughed, but the sound was too high-pitched to be amusement. "That's not possible."

"Um, you made it clear it's not my business, but I'm pretty sure it's abundantly possible." Lena watched his face move from strained to concern. "As sick as you've been, I'm surprised you didn't suspect. You do know where babies come—?"

"Oh, stop it. I didn't suspect because it's—I've never been around anyone pregnant before. I didn't—how would I know?" Lena levered herself up and to her feet, stalking away a few steps and then returning. "It's not possible. I was *careful*. I learned a long time ago what to tell the Dust to make sure that didn't happen, and I told it *every time*, Jackson. I told it." Her fingers tapped against her thigh as she thought back, tracking days and nights. "I told it," she whispered.

Lena stepped forward and plopped down in front of Jackson. "You're wrong. You'll just have to look again."

"I'm not wrong."

"Jackson, listen—"

"I'm not wrong." The words were barely audible over the background sounds of the night—the rushing and flow of the wind over the ridge, the songs of the insects active outside the reach of her glow. He looked up and met her gaze. "Congratulations."

It was Jackson's turn to push himself to his feet now as Lena gaped at him. "Get everyone below. I'm going to run a perimeter check, secure the valley, make sure we're all safe."

Lena was mute as he walked into the darkness, curving away from them and heading further down the valley. A wave of silence followed as the insects responded to his passage, only singing again once he'd gone.

"You heard him. He's right. We're going to have a long day of hard work tomorrow."

"Are you sure you should do that...now?" Phoebe asked,

voice tentative. Her gaze dropped down Lena's body before she brought it sharply back up again. They'd heard everything.

"Of course I will," Lena said. "This doesn't change anything."

This doesn't change anything. It can't.

There was no doubt in her mind that the Dust had done this. The men believed the Dust was simple machines. She'd always known better. The Dust had chosen this.

All that remained was for her to make her own choice. What would she do about it? And how would she explain whatever decision she made to Alex?

She didn't know. But she could feel herself teetering on the brink of no return. There was no going back—not to the way things were, not to the Fort. She had to build a safer world. And she had to do whatever it might take to make that happen.

SEVENTEEN

Alex

Alex turned his head and smiled at the woman who'd escorted him into the family visiting area. Internally, he seethed. Oh, sure, they were much more humane here in Zone Two. Everything gave the appearance of a school in the making—a boarding facility to train and prep the little girls who'd be sent to the Council, like those for the boys in the months before they were sent off. It gave the families time for the long, slow goodbye. It gave them the time they needed to accept their children were off to meet their destinies as the strongest of the Sparks, serving the Council and all of its citizens.

Except the destinies awaiting these girls was far different from that waiting for the boys in the facility up the road. There was no Ward School for them. There was a prison. There was torture and experimentation.

Did Leng Sloan expect him to be appeased by the set-up she'd created here?

A burst of laughter from the corner where a little girl wearing a royal blue uniform visited with her parents and a little brother turned Alex's head. The girl had a wide halo of pale brown curls against dark skin, a combination of her father's blond hair and her mother's dark skin and short curls. Her parents smiled at her, even as their hands were clutched together under the table.

They knew they were losing their daughter. Here in Zone Two, they'd been fed a line about it being an honor, instead of having her snatched away. They could put on a facade of being relaxed and happy and proud because they believed their little girl would go on to live a life of honor and authority, like the boys who grew into the Council's senior agents. What would they do if they knew their daughter would end up a traumatized shell of this laughing girl—at best?

"As you can see," his guide chirped with a limp flutter of her hand at the family in the corner, "our strong female Sparks are treated with the same respect and pride in their abilities as our strong young males. They are delivered in the best of health to the Council. It's important to us they be physically and mentally ready to embark on a lifelong journey of learning and service to us all."

Alex returned his focus to her. Was she serious? Even if she didn't know for sure what waited for these girls and their perfect health, she had to suspect.

Something in her expression, a faltering following a flash of fear across her face, told him that either his face or his eyes gave away his rage. He raised his brows, smoothing out the lines of his face. After three weeks of dancing around dealing with Sloan and her agents, the mysterious agents in brown who avoided his attempts to snag them, and his work to bring his own agents back into line, it wouldn't be wise to blow it all now, would it?

Yes, Leng Sloan had finally granted him escorted access to this facility. Was it because she wanted him to absolve her of blame if he was right and the Council was abusing them once they left her custody? Or did she have some other purpose in mind?

Either way, she'd put him here, even with her valid suspicions about his involvement in the loss of the shipment of girls from the Conclave. Would she expect him to be circumspect?

"What positions do the trained young women Zone Two receives back from the Council hold here in the zone?"

"I—I'm sorry?" Her smile didn't slip, but was that a hint of panic in her eyes?

"Well, you've said several times today that these strong girls are guaranteed the same experience as the boys. Those boys are sent to the Ward School for training and then are sent off to new zones to live and work. Each zone receives back fresh young blood according to how many they sent. Right?" He waited for her nod. "So, the young women who have come back to you to replace the girls you've sent…what positions do they hold? What is the Council training them to do?"

"Do?" She licked her lips. "I…don't know. I work here in the Developmental Facility. I don't have any knowledge of what happens to them after they leave."

"But you have received young women back?" He wasn't going to let this go.

She shook her head slightly. "I don't know their status. I'm sure we must. Perhaps someone in the Councilor's office could provide you that information?" She plastered the bright, fake smile across her face and lifted her arm to gesture him forward. "If you'll come this way, I'd like to show you our classrooms." Off she went.

Alex glanced back over his shoulder at the family in the corner. The little girl of about five had crawled onto her mother's lap to have her hair braided. Her father stroked her cheek.

Alex could dash over and warn them—tell them to take their daughter and flee. But where would they go? To another zone? To live in the wilderness, as Lena had done on her own? She'd still be found out. She'd be taken, one way or another.

He gritted his teeth. There was only one way. Alex had to convince the Councilors not directly involved with the prisons and experiments there was another way. Thomas had to be prepared to protect them. Lena had to be ready to teach them all.

First, Alex had to be sure which Councilors were approachable. He was treading close to outing his own treasonous activities now.

The door closed behind him. Ahead of them was a long open hallway with a sheltered play area on the left. Laughter and girlish shouts echoed across the opening to him.

He swallowed back his rage and bile, knowing what waited at the end of the caravan that would take them west at some point in the months to come.

Perhaps it was time to out themselves. Perhaps it was time to offer the world an alternative to the Council's way.

It was time for Alex to step out of the shadows. He was running short on time now. Their three weeks of trade meetings and negotiations were coming to an end. After the reception tonight, they'd begin packing and prepping for the trip north to Zone One. If he wanted to get through to Sloan, if he wanted to make a difference for these girls right now, he had to be ready to make a deal. The only problem was that even after three weeks, he had no idea what to offer Sloan to entice her to betray her position and the other Councilors.

What did a woman whose infrastructure and prosperity demonstrated that she wanted for nothing *need*?

After his tour of the Developmental Facility, Alex was in no mood for the reception, but he couldn't skip it. Any small conversation might lead to the clue he needed to coerce Sloan to cooperate.

Alex smiled and nodded at a lovely woman as she approached. He wasn't interested in anything she might be willing to offer except possible information. However, her gaze traveled up his body in a way that clearly brought her pleasure—until she reached the bronze pin he wore clipped to his collar. Her gaze swerved away at that point, as did the rest of her, off in search of higher-ranking prey.

He snorted and popped another canapé in his mouth. He'd never have thought to combine peaches and pork, but somehow the blend worked. He savored the morsel and the rejection. Wearing the bronze pin of Dragonfly House had been an interesting experience. With one glance, people knew he both worked for the most powerful trade house in Council territory and had minimal power of his own to bring to bear on their behalf. The only people who bothered with him were those who had even less power. It was a new and unique position to be in. It didn't allow him much opportunity to flex his muscles of any kind, but it did give him the ability to listen while being ignored.

What he was hearing was on par with the report he'd finally

received from his men—a real report with their true observations, not the packaged information Sloan had convinced one of their own to pass on. His gaze moved across the crowded room, noting, but not stopping, on those men moving through the gathered officials with practiced smiles.

At least they can handle this much of their training. It was a poor attempt at amusing himself, and it didn't work. A moment later, he gave his head a little shake. It wasn't a fair assessment, either. They had been handling things. They'd noted Sloan's movements. They'd noted people speaking languages none of them knew and trading in goods that didn't belong and shouldn't even exist anymore. They'd made note of whispers and rumors of Sloan's power and reach. They'd made one mistake. Out of convenience, they'd trusted a single man to carry coded reports back and forth to their drop point to be collected by a Fort Nevada courier on constant rotation.

Sloan had turned that young man to ensure no one outside of her zone and the traders with a vested interest in silence knew what she was building—or the magnitude of her potential empire. It was brilliant.

It was dangerous.

Alex still had no idea where she stood on Sparks. Other than a throwaway mention of his performance that summer at the Meet, Sloan had made nothing more of her suspicions of his greater involvement in the rest of his time here in Zone Two. She'd made certain he'd been unable to do more than confirm the suspicions of his men.

The "tour" of the Developmental Facility had been a farce. He'd seen the facilities. He'd seen the girls—from a distance. The only child he'd spoken to was an orphaned blind girl of about nine who was serving as a companion to the children he was actually interested in meeting. The adults he'd been allowed access to had been carefully vetted. The tour showed him what Sloan wanted him, and her own people, to believe—she was doing all she could to insure the comfort and well-being of the girls from her zone before they were shipped away to the Council.

Nothing he'd seen or heard had convinced him of her

sincerity. That worried him. He hadn't had the information he needed until he was here, trying to influence decisions. He was afraid it was too little, too late, even for him. Could he turn her?

A waiter offered another tray of canapés, but Alex turned away, shaking his head. As he turned, he caught sight of a young woman moving away from him across the crowd. The glimpse he had of freckled skin as she turned away combined with the halo of dark red hair was enough for him to move. He wove through the crowd, following.

After a moment, she turned again, smiling over her shoulder at someone she passed. She wasn't Lena. Of course she wasn't. The woman was too tall, and Lena couldn't be here.

He still had to swallow away the bitterness coating the back of his tongue. Was it the sight of those similar features that made him suddenly ache to see the real woman smiling at him, brow arched as she challenged him? Was it those vivid dreams?

Or was it that he was still worried they'd gone too far in handing the Council that taunting note attributed to her?

He took a steadying breath and glanced around the room again. There was nothing more to learn here tonight his agents couldn't handle. He doubted there'd be a scene or any random burst of information. It was all too controlled and orchestrated by Sloan.

If he had any hope of finding anything out before they left for the north in two days, he had to go find it himself. And he'd have to do it knowing it was what they expected of him.

He slipped from the room, well aware he'd be watched. He had a heartbeat to make his decision: try to fool them into thinking he was headed to his room and risk being backed into that basement, or take off in search of the utility hall and Sloan's secret room and let them give chase?

He grinned.

Like that's even a question.

He made his way confidently in the direction of the entrance they'd used when they came in that rainy afternoon. About halfway there, he recognized the intersection where they'd gone off from the usual public halls.

Alex darted down it, turning and then turning again from memory. Several turns and a few levels down, he allowed himself a half-congratulatory sniff. He was pretty sure he'd lost his pursuit.

Of course, he was pretty sure he'd gotten himself lost, too.

The dark-painted cinderblock walls were all the same. He'd felt confident until he entered an area where he traveled down two short ramps instead of steps. He didn't remember ramps.

Why are there ramps?

Voices ahead echoed down the hall from the intersection ahead—a deep voice soothing and a raised, querulous complaint. A soft, little girl voice answered the complaint. Alex darted into a nearby doorway, turning as if fumbling with a key to open the office. The voices grew louder as the three people crossed the intersection and moved straight through. Alex glanced over his shoulder.

Behind him, a young man dressed in a medic's uniform pushed a wheeled chair carrying a hunched, emaciated, ancient man. His shaking, gnarled hand pointed the way impatiently and wisps of white hair on his head fluttered as they passed. A little girl paced beside them, the fingers of one hand in constant, light contact with the arm of the bent, ancient man in the chair.

Wait. She was the little girl from the Developmental Facility, he was sure of it. What had her name been?

Corazon.

Yes. He'd made a note to remember because her name and coloring meant the orphan may well be from well south or west of the zone.

And the old man… Alex stared, rapt, as they continued on out of his line of sight.

Sam?

He stepped away from the doorway and moved to the end of the hall to lean around it.

The medic pushed the old man down another of the ramps, continued a short distance, then paused to open a door. The little girl stepped ahead of them, holding the door.

"We're back, Councilor," she soothed him. "Now you can

rest knowing your girls are safe, as I told you."

COUNCILOR??

The medic returned to his seated patient, spun the chair, and backed into the room. The door closed behind them.

Alex stared at it, incredulous. Obviously, it wasn't Sam here in the bowels of the Zone Two Council building any more than it had been Lena socializing upstairs.

But Alex would give up every joule of his Spark if that wasn't another of the original Sparks.

All of them had long since been accounted for. There were four survivors, including Sam at the Ward School—no, three. Ely Gracen had died the winter before, up in Zone Seven.

Except there was at least one more, and Corazon had called him Councilor. She'd also referred to the safety of his girls. Was he involved in the transfer of powerful girls, or was he showing paternalistic interest in little girls from the zone he'd no doubt lived in for hundreds of years?

Alex glanced around at the doors around him. Were these offices? Residences? Or medical treatment rooms?

Whatever they were, they weren't where he needed to be. Without the time to invest in this new puzzle, he'd have to put his men on it—carefully. He turned to retrace his steps back to the first ramp. Once there, he turned left instead of right and started again, moving lower down smaller staircases.

Just as he started to think this dark cinderblock was looking a little more familiar than the other dark cinderblock had, a throat cleared pointedly in the hall behind him.

Alex turned, a smile already pulling up the corners of his lips. The gig was up.

Sloan's redheaded security goon stood in the intersection behind him, hands on hips, lips set. He looked like he was trying to decide what to do with Alex.

"Oh, hey," Alex lifted his chin at the man in greeting, "How've you been?"

He didn't wait for an answer. He turned and continued the way he'd been traveling.

"Where do you think you're going?" The man now beside

him growled with displeasure.

Alex glanced over at him and smiled, nodding ahead of them down the hall. "To see your boss. It is this way, right?" He could read in the man's unhappy eyes that Alex was close to her secret office. "I mean, it's okay, you did a great job the other night when you brought me down here. All those twists and turns? You're good. Really. You are." Alex stopped and smiled before adding, "I'm just better."

The man's odd dark eyes went flat and emotionless.

"Did *you* need something?" Alex asked. "Or is our meeting down here a happy coincidence?"

"I was sent to collect you. Councilor Two would like to meet with you."

Alex nodded and grinned. "Excellent." He gestured ahead of him. "Shall I follow you, or would you rather follow me?"

Redhead didn't crack a smile. He stepped around Alex and walked with a stiff back to the end of the hall. He made two turns and then stopped halfway down a long hall. When he flashed Alex a hostile glance at the door, Alex made sure he had a delighted grin on his face.

The muscle in the man's jaw jumped as he pushed open the door. Alex followed him into the bare room from the week before. This time, Sloan wasn't waiting within. No one was.

Alex slowed, narrowing his eyes. It *was* the same room. It suddenly occurred to him why they might keep an empty, metal room. It made clean-up so much easier. Unfortunately for them, the metal of the room made resistance so much easier for Alex. He'd learned enough from Lena to be sure of that.

His musings were premature—though probably not wholly incorrect. The redhead didn't pause. He continued to the opposite wall and banged a quick, three-two-two note rhythm on the metal wall.

There was a faint sound of gears grinding and metal groaning against a track. A slit appeared in the wall ahead of him. It widened to a gap, then became a rectangle wide enough for them to pass through.

The room behind it was busy. Sloan stood halfway down a

wide, long table, staring down at a map. As the redhead ushered Alex in ahead of him, Sloan nodded to a man beside her, and he began rerolling the maps.

Alex worked his gaze along them as they slid into the roll. The maps weren't familiar…not even the shorelines. They weren't maps of Council lands. Where was Sloan headed, and what was she planning to do there?

The wall behind began to groan on the track again. A new whirring sound joined it. Alex glanced over his shoulder to see a pair of men twirling large handgears, working the mechanism of the hidden door. They weren't anywhere near the reclaimed technological level of Fort Nevada, yet they made do.

Alex looked around the large room with desks, the conference table, and plenty of people moving busily. They made do very well.

"Agent Reyes." Sloan watched him take it all in. "I thought it past time we put our cards on the table."

He nodded, sober. "Except allowing me in here is a little more than 'cards on the table,' isn't it, Councilor?" He had no illusions. This was a few steps beyond too much revelation. The only way he'd get out of this alive was to agree to whatever she was about to propose. Whatever he'd done to earn this *trust*, it came at a cost.

Alex had eyes on things only those employed by her got to see. He was willing to bet many people she worked with still hadn't seen this room and the possibilities it raised.

Sloan shrugged slightly. "Call me confident."

Alex exhaled and shook his head, darting another glance around the room. "What am I doing down here, Councilor?"

"We need to be able to talk, without reservations. Without half-truths. You needed to see what I bring to the table in order to make a proper decision." She swept her hand out and ushered him down the table to the end.

It was quieter at this end of the room. Alex took one of the two seats and tried to ignore the line of wooden crates set out nearby. They were out of place in the room. He had no doubt that whatever they held, they were for his benefit.

Sloan leaned in, capturing his attention and holding it. "I'm going to go first, as a show of trust." She waited for him to nod, then she returned it. "Based upon whispers I've heard myself—never mind what my people have discovered on their own and reported back—I feel confident in stating that there is a divide in the Council's agents. I believe that divide corresponds to the years during and after your attendance at the Ward School. But not only yours, am I right? There is a group of you. A cabal of powerful Sparks tired of dedicating your lives to the comfort of those incapable of the same special abilities. Why be a servant, when you have the strength to be a king?"

Alex held her gaze with his head tilted, but gave her nothing else. It was too specific to be mere conjecture, but she'd already admitted to him an inability to turn his young agents here in her zone. She was accurate, yes, but she still didn't have the full picture.

She smiled. It was a slow, confident spread revealing her teeth. "And, of course, kings require queens, am I right?"

She waited.

"I thought you said you were going first?" Alex prompted. "Because all I've heard is rumor and conjecture, but you've given me nothing."

She leaned back, laughing softly. "I've given you an opening. Take it, agent."

"An opening?" He spread his hands.

"Is she real?"

"Is who real?"

"The girl. Lena Gracey. The one to whom you gave the girls stolen from the Council at Conclave. Or is she a fabrication meant to claim everyone's attention while you move around the zones and gather up more girls, more support?"

"I didn't give anyone anything. I found a note. As to whether or not she's real—"

She leaned back in again, quick as a snake, and laid one finger on his wrist. "Don't lie." She tapped at his pulse point once. "Don't make that mistake, agent. You did not *find* that note. There is not a single Councilor who believes that, even if we don't have the proof. *Not one of us.* You were involved in the disappearance of those girls. You either wrote it for your own purposes or you are involved with this revolutionary.

"You are also more than an agent acting on behalf of our newest baby Councilor in Zone Three. You have access to and command over the young agents in my zone, and I'm going to assume others, as well, since they're not as aware as I am. You are known by reputation and name to agents everywhere, but recognized by few, most under a certain age. I am told that you have influence or control over Councilor Five. And now, of course, you have Three in your pocket. You also wear the bonze pin of Dragonfly House, so I assume you're embroiled somehow with Kit Wallace.

"You are either collaborating with revolutionaries. Or you are leading them. I think the missing link isn't the trade house. I think it's the girls. This isn't about power." She stopped and laughed. "Well, it is, isn't it? Simply a different sort than Kit Wallace is interested in. You're not embroiled with her. You're leading her on a wild chase." Sloan seemed delighted by the prospect. "This is about Sparks. It's about who holds the keys to the kingdom and who keeps it running. I don't even think you care who is in charge, so long as Sparks are free to live as they wish and not as the Council decrees."

"That's an interesting theory."

"You're dividing and conquering. And now…with this girl? You're instilling doubt, of our way of life, of everything we all believe, both the powered and unpowered."

Alex opened his mouth and started to shake his head, but she held her hand up to stop his denial.

"Oh, I know. We know where you've gone. We know to whom you've spoken. You've avoided interacting with everyday Sparks. But you don't have to. Rumors are flying through the Sparks—and the non-Sparks who resent them—like wildfire. The trade houses are tightlipped about what happened at Conclave, but not the everyday citizens. Not the independent traders and certainly not the Sparks there to work."

She cocked her head and drummed her fingers on the desk in

one slow fan of fingers. “They’ll rally to her, won’t they? All of the Sparks. We’ll be embroiled in a conflict that will destroy lives. It’ll happen as soon as enough citizens in the other zones realize the truth behind the Council and the girls. They’re not disappearing. They’re being shipped away like the boys.”

“*Not* like the boys. We’re given training. Rank. Power. They’re abused, tormented, killed.”

“You have proof of this?”

“I’ve seen it. The girls at the Conclave were not the first to be liberated.”

“But you can’t prove it.” She smiled. “She can. She will. Won’t she? The Sparks will rally, and the kingdom will fall.” She shook her head. “Except it isn’t really a kingdom at all. You know that, right?”

Sloan gestured over her shoulder at the familiar map on the wall, with each zone highlighted in blue and all of the open spaces between outlined in red. It made the land look like a patchwork quilt.

“The zones we use are remnants of a disaster relief plan for the United States of America. That country is dead. Soon, the Council will be, too.” She smiled at him to indicate that she was comfortable with the outcome. “Each zone is now its own country. People need to realize that and act accordingly. That’s what I’m doing. There’s a whole world out there, and we have no idea the condition of any of those places.”

She leaned back and gestured for a waiting man to move forward to the first of the boxes and crack open the wooden lid. “Well, *they* don’t have any idea what’s out there. I do.”

The man reached into the first box and lifted out a golden yellow mass that looked like thick fingers. At a gesture from her, he pulled one of the fingers off and brought it to her.

Alex watched as Sloan snapped the tip and peeled back the outside, revealing a creamy pale flesh inside. It was a fruit or a vegetable, he realized, though not one he was familiar with. She bent off the tip and popped it in her mouth, savoring the flavor. She held it out as she chewed.

Alex reached and bent off a piece. It was soft and gave under the pressure of his fingers. He smelled it first, trying to be subtle about his investigation before he put the piece in his mouth. The texture wasn't impressive, but the sweet flavor was.

"Bananas." Sloan told him. "From what was northern Brazil." She nodded as the man reached into the next box and lifted out a handful of dark, aromatic beans. They fell from his hand in a cascade that sounded like rain on a tin roof. As the man continued to show off the contents of the boxes, Sloan continued her description. "Coffee—north Africa. Sugar and rum—Carribean. Much of Europe is rubble, yes, but there's a whole world out there filled with resources. In the old days, America became powerful because of trade. It's key. Kit Wallace and the others are right about that, but their vision is small. They see only our little corner of the world.

"The truth is that the person who controls Sparks— whether through force or treaty—will control everything. It's the reality of the world we live in now. If you and your revolutionary are to be believed, Councilor Four and his cohorts have decided to consolidate their hold on power by eliminating the most powerful, the girls who offer the promise of a better life. I won't allow that. I don't have a humanitarian interest in the Spark population, but you catch more flies with honey than vinegar. If you can offer me loyalty and stability, then I can offer you freedom. Self-governing Sparks who answer to no one and treaty with me. Life, lived on your terms, in exchange for work. No more lives dedicated to one Councilor. No more sending children away from parents, never to return. They owe no one zone their fealty. No, not even me. Because I have faith in my ability to motivate them to stay with a better quality of life, with freedom, with respect for their efforts on our behalf. You've spent a week here. Are my people not happy?"

"They're the happiest of any zone I've seen." It was the easy answer. It was true.

"What is it you came here to discover? What is it that you hoped to win from me? Some concession, no doubt. Speak now, or lose the opportunity forever."

"Before I do, I need answers of my own." He waited for her

nod of acceptance. “Is that center I toured your own invention, or is it a new requirement from the Council? Is it merely an attempt by the Council to preempt Lena’s narrative should she decide to come forward?”

Sloan smiled. “That center is the only one of its kind in any zone, but it isn’t my invention. It was built before I came to my position by a predecessor who anticipated its need. I am not the first Councilor Two to want the best for these people.”

Alex digested her words. A predecessor who anticipated the arrival of highly powered girls?

And yet, she appeared to be telling the truth.

“Next question, then: who is the old man in the basement? And was his little Spark companion blinded deliberately to keep her dependent…and silent?”

“My,” she said very softly, “you have been a busy man.” She wasn’t pleased. Her fingers made another slow drumming fan on the table. “The old man is a relative, and none of your concern. The girl’s name is Corazon. She was found on the plains of Texas by a team of mine, already blind, lost, alone, and half-starved. They brought her home. Because she was a Spark, they brought her to me. Her care for my uncle offers her honor and security.”

Alex held her calm gaze. Except for the evasion about her “uncle,” he believed her. It was his turn. He had no doubt she intended to kill him if she didn’t like what she heard. She’d discover he was harder to kill than she thought, but he had a sense it wouldn’t come to that. Not any more.

“We are looking for allies. We’ve established a school for powered girls to help them reach their full potential. We’d like support for it—in the same vein as support for the Ward School flows from each zone.”

“Ah, yes. But that support comes at a price. Boys are sent to be trained, they are supported, and then an equal number of trained young men, new blood, are sent to each zone to be our Council’s police, spies. Enforcers. That is the system as it stands now. Am I to believe that you are not opposed to that system?”

“We’re not opposed to the training. There should be no severing of the child’s prior connections. There should be no forced recruitment. They should return home when they're ready."

"Where are they?"

Alex blinked. She'd digested his statements about the boys and returned to the girls.

"Safe."

"You think to win my support without telling me where they are?"

"I can tell you where they are not. They are not in Council prisons. They are not working in a forced camp with restraining collars around their necks. They are not buried in the ground, their talent and lives gone to waste and ruin because of the fear of old men."

Her lips turned up. "You cannot have my support without full knowledge. I want to know where these girls are, and how many there are, total. I want my people to inspect the school and to report back to me on what these most powerful Sparks have to offer us in exchange for our support. And I want to know my carefully and dearly procured goods are not being wasted on a project that does not serve my needs."

Alex raised his hands, already shaking his head. "I'm not returning there now. I have further stops—"

"Not now. But this year. We'll make arrangements at the Conclave. You bring girls; they'll tell their truth. Give us proof. We'll send representatives to inspect. I'll even lobby for full authorization with the other Councilors if I'm pleased. Be sure these girls—and what they can offer us—pleases me."

"You expect me to bring little girls back into danger? Bring them back to parade them in front of the men who were a danger to them in the first place?"

"If you can steal them, you can keep them safe."

"And what about the safety of the little girls in the facility I toured today?"

She shook her head. "They're not going anywhere. I will not ship them off to the Council until I've seen proof of your revolutionary's competence or that the girls previously sent are indeed captives and not students at a competing school."

"Competing sch—" Alex stared at her. "You don't know what you've sent your children to, do you? Even without ever seeing or hearing from these girls again? You just trusted…"

Her eyes narrowed to slits. "I trusted in that portion of the Council, yes. These girls haven't existed long enough to see a return on their training yet. And I did demand inspections of education sites—my people returned and reported the sites adequate, but not sufficient for long-term care and education."

"They were shown shells."

"I suspected as much, yes. That's why your activities this summer piqued my interest. If there is a better way—a *real* way—then I will support it. I will give my girls as well as my support to you and yours. But this time, I will be sure."

"What else do you expect from me—from all of us Sparks—in the future? For your help?"

"I expect?" She shrugged. "I hope to see you all opting to take advantage of the benefits of working here in Zone Two, for me. Expansion requires power."

"And power requires expansion."

"I'm too old a woman to expect to wield any obscene amount of power, Agent Reyes. I believe it's a matter of time before the Council implodes. You may think I'm operating in my own interests, but my primary concern is that my people not suffer when it happens." A shadow crossed her face. "I was…displeased…when the implications of the note and your actions this summer indicated the Council has been abusing my children and my trust."

She stopped speaking for a moment to swallow and glance away. Her nostrils flared with her upset. It seemed genuine and deeply felt.

She looked back up at him. "I believe you are motivated by the same desire to lead and protect your people. We don't have to be at cross purposes. We shouldn't be at cross purposes."

Alex leaned back, glancing over the crates again, taking in what they represented. The woman had reach. She'd traveled outside of the zone, sent people out to see what remained of the world and how it could benefit her people at a time when the rest of them were staring inward and merely trying to hold on to what they already had.

She had vision.

He wasn't sure if that vision included freedom for Sparks. It was true, expansion as she was describing took power. He'd seen it on his way in—the new dam being built using old plans and new methods, the windmills, the damn wall she was building around her territory. She knew the cost, and the issues with reliability, that came with non-Spark power.

She wanted Sparks, and she was ready to make an offer to get them as free agents instead of the enforced servitude that existed under the current system.

How far was she willing to go to have them? Did he dare risk Lena and the girls on a hunch?

He leaned forward again, turning back to face her. She waited, a gleam in her eyes.

"What's it to be, Agent Reyes?"

EIGHTEEN

Lena

Lena held herself still, head muzzy and filled with the anxiety of dreams of bright, pulsing lights filling her body as Dust swarmed through her, doing as it liked to her body, not listening to her desperate commands. She wanted to wake. She wanted to swim up and out of the darkness around her. Her heart swelled with panic.

Then she felt him. Alex's touch, there but not there, fluttered over her face. His fingers eased down her cheek, soothing. She leaned into it, heart still hammering. The Dust within her slowed, began to match the new rhythm of her heart. No, their hearts. She could feel his beating with hers as her heart slowed.

She opened her eyes. One hand lifted from the bed at her side, reaching for him. He was right there.

But he wasn't. Alex was far away, and it was nothing but a dream, filled with anxiety and longing. She told herself it was a relief to be awake. She rolled over to stare at the bland wall of the bunker beside her cot. This was reality.

Jackson had returned the night before. As soon as he'd reappeared out of the dark, he'd reassured the girls that all was safe and gave her a censuring look for not already having them in bed.

Why was he annoyed anyway? It was *her* body. She was the one who'd be dealing with this, who'd be deciding how to deal with it. She'd been the one sitting on the couch in shock, answering the questions the girls had worked up the courage to ask in monosyllables. How could she reassure them?

She couldn't reassure herself.

She heard stirring behind her, as if someone wanted to come over but instead hovered near by. She rolled over.

"How are you feeling?" Rose's fingers ran over a damp rag. She'd rested, and when she'd woken, clearly someone had told her the happy news. Had it been the girls? Or Jackson?

Lena made a small shrugging motion. "The same as yesterday, I guess. Except different." She shook her head and laughed. "Everything is different, and yet nothing has changed."

Rose didn't laugh. She stared at Lena, fingers moving across the rag, working it in a loop around and around. "I want to talk to you...when you're up to it."

Lena felt her smile fade. She sat up. "Okay." She indicated the end of the bed. "So come talk."

Rose glanced over her shoulder at the closed door, then came closer.

Okay. I guess we're really talking, then.

She hadn't expected it would be Rose with an issue. She'd expected it to be Jackson.

Her friend perched on the edge of the bed, fingers working faster than before.

"Rose."

She looked up.

"Stop." Lena looked down at Rose's hands. Those frantic fingers stilled. "Whatever it is, you can tell me. Matched, and all that."

Rose nodded, but Lena could see the strain on her face. "I don't want you to think less of me."

"Why would I?"

Rose shrugged. She looked down at her hands, still but gripping the rag so tight her knuckles were white. "I wanted to let you know you have options. *We* have options. Because we're Sparks. I, um—I discovered it. Well, Jackson discovered it."

"Discovered what?"

"The same way that we can heal, we can—we can change things."

Lena frowned. “I don’t understand. Change what things?”

Rose huffed a sigh and shook her head. She lifted her face to Lena with a small, pained smile. “You don’t have to be pregnant. Not if you don’t want to.”

Lena didn't understand. “I—what?”

“You don’t have to be. Not if you don’t want it. Jackson can help you.” Rose’s sickly smile fluttered. “The way he helped me.”

“He helped you?” Lena thought back. What? When?

Rose nodded. “I was going to leave. I meant to walk into the desert. I wasn't very clear on after that.” The laugh was as pained and brief as her smile. “He caught me. Made me tell him what was going on.”

“When was this?”

“Right after you two came back from the caravan attack on Councilor Three.”

“And you didn't want to talk to me....?”

Rose shook her head. “I couldn't. You had so much going on. The girls. I wasn't able to talk about it. I didn’t want it to be real. I never wanted children, ever. Not even when I was a girl. It wasn’t what I wanted for my life. And then…”

Lena waited when Rose drifted off and stared across the room. What could she have said anyway?

“I didn’t want it.” She delivered the statement in a brisk voice. “Didn’t want a child, period, but I certainly didn’t want a reminder of that time. Of the camp. The guards. Guards.” She laughed, but it was bitter and angry. “Rapists. I don’t even know which one—” She swallowed and shook her head. “Doesn't matter. Made my choice, and I'll live with it. I wanted you to know you have a choice. Jackson couldn’t do it. But he talked me through what he thought I should do, and it worked. I don’t regret it.”

Rose lifted her chin and turned to Lena, meeting her gaze with eyes filled with challenge. Whatever she saw in Lena's face—and Lena hoped it was the compassion and sympathy she felt and not a hint of the horror at what Rose must have gone through when she realized.... Whatever she saw, her face softened. She took a deep breath.

"Jackson won't do it, but he'll stay with you. He stayed with me. It meant a lot."

Lena nodded. She reached out and took Rose's hand, still mute. She had no idea what to say. She had to say something. Rose waited.

"Thank you," she managed. "For telling me. For trusting me and for—for putting yourself through the memory again to make sure I know about the option. I'm sorry I wasn't there before—"

Rose shook her head once, a sharp movement. "No. It was how I wanted. I wasn't alone."

It explained the closeness that had grown between them. It might explain Jackson's withdrawal the night before.

Either way, that was a shared experience between them, and it had nothing to do with Lena. She felt a brief surge of grief at the exclusion but angrily quashed it. That was the last thing they'd needed, or should have ever worried about.

Lena licked her lips. "Rose, will you—you wouldn't be upset, would you? If I didn't make the same choice?"

Rose searched her face. "You told me once you didn't think you wanted children, especially after Leo. I thought we had that in common. That's why I came to you. Are you sure?"

Lena laughed, and the sound was as hollow in her ears as her chest felt. "I'm not sure of anything. I need time to think. I need to consider the full range of options. I'm glad you told me. I am. Thank you. I'm not sure what I want to do yet. I haven't even had time to get used to the idea, or to think about what it all means."

"What it all means? It means if you do nothing, then in seven or eight months, you're going to be a mother. Do you want a baby and the responsibility for another life on top of everything else?"

Did she?

Rose leaned forward, continuing softly when Lena remained silent. "We haven't even made a home here yet. We're living underground."

At that, Lena scoffed. "We'll be above ground in another week. And the bunker isn't a liability in the decision. It's kept the girls safe. We've managed to keep everyone healthy. It's not like we—like I've—done a terrible job, even if Leo hates my guts. It's not like...."

Rose leaned back from her, brows raised.

Lena threw her hands in the air. "Why am I defending a decision I haven't even made yet?"

Rose leaned in and gave her friend a quick hug. She dropped a soft kiss on Lena's cheek and whispered, "Maybe you already have, you just haven't realized it yet."

NINETEEN

Alex

Alex perched in the vee between two branches high up on a mighty pine and stared down at the valley below. Miles behind him, the wall Sloan was building around her zone stretched off toward the horizon on either side. It seemed small from his vantage point, but when they'd passed under it the day before it had soared above them. He shimmied down to crouch at the base of the tree and jot notes on the rough map he'd sketched. He and Ace hadn't decided what approach to take yet, but they were in agreement on one thing: all was not as it seemed.

Once he'd finished a rough sketch, Alex turned and retraced his steps back to the caravan, hidden in a clearing ringed by a thick line of autumn trees and green pines. He scanned the camp for Ace and found him striding along the near wagon-line, listening to a man who was waving his arms.

Alex changed course to intercept them. When Ace saw him coming, he nodded, offered a few words to the other man, and then dismissed him.

"Trouble?" Alex asked.

Ace shrugged. "Personnel dispute. Nothing that can't be handled as long as it's nipped now. What did you find out?"

Alex shook his head. "We've been had. Or at least—that's what she intended."

"The Councilor?"

Alex shrugged, his gaze tracing the line of trees he'd come through. "She asked us to take this route instead of the usual trade road because she had issues with raiders north of the wall. She wanted me to look—"

"And didn't mind putting my caravan at risk."

"She compensated you. In advance." Alex smirked at Ace. "But my point is your people were right about the lack of signs of Scav activity in the area. And they're right that anyone with even an iota of experience would know it. There's no way that anyone could ever mistake the people I saw as anything other than a Neo-Barb village barely hanging on. No slave pens. No signs of typical Scav activity. There's no way they're making successful runs on trade caravans." He shook his head in disgust.

"So either someone has mistaken this group for another that's operating in the area—"

"With the network and training she has in place? And one that dodged her people, your people, and my eyes?" Alex snorted his disbelief.

"Or she deliberately primed us to take them out. Why?"

Alex chewed his lip. "I don't know. But I mean to find out." He flicked a measuring gaze at Ace. "Care to take a walk?"

"Take a—you're just going to walk in there? You're that sure they're Neo-barbs and not Scavs?"

Alex nodded. "You can bring a couple of your security with us if it'll make you feel better. They won't be needed." Alex stopped then held up a hand. "In fact, do bring them. They can carry a peace offering."

Ace's brows dipped into a scowl. "You're planning on giving away my goods? In case you hadn't noticed, Agent Reyes, this is a trade caravan. We are in the business of selling goods, not charity, and you are being hosted as a personal favor. You're not in charge and—"

Alex shook his head and waved Ace's growing anger away. "It was an idea. To save time. You can always send for supplies after you see their condition with your own eyes. C'mon. Let's go."

"Just like that?"

"Just like that." Alex held the younger man's angry stare. "They show all the signs of a dying village, Ace."

Ace's brows rose this time. "Disease?"

"I'm guessing starvation." He backed away, shrugged his shoulders. "I'm going in. I need answers, and as far as I can see, they're the only ones who can provide them."

Ace caught up not long after Alex left him at the caravan. Alex glanced over his shoulder as they climbed the rise. Four of Ace's security people were starting out behind them, a long crate held on the shoulder of each. He gave Ace an approving nod.

"You'd better be right." Censure filled Ace's voice.

When they reached the top of the rise, Alex paused to point out what he could without making Ace climb to the top of the trees above them. All but one of the trio of fields were overgrown and untended. The one was half planted with winter crops. There were no animals at all—no cows, no chickens, no goats. No dogs or feral cats roaming, either.

The village itself was quiet, even at midday. Three thin curls of smoke rose above chimneys and then thinned as they were blown toward the men watching from above. The smoke indicated the village hadn't been abandoned, but there was no bustle of pre-winter village life. There was no smell of anything cooking carried with the smoke on the wind.

Ace sighed, acknowledging the signs of distress. "It could still be a trap."

"Mm hm. It could be a very elaborate trap. Let's go see?"

It would be the only way for Ace to understand what Alex had seen from above. Alex had seen this before. Neo-barb communities, struggling on their own through drought or infestations of insects or a longer winter or summer than usual—there were so many things that could start the chain of events that lead to annihilation for those who lived on the sharp edge of survival. Once it started, it was hard to stop it.

Alex stepped away and continued down the steep side, angling across the hill so they came down closer to the village, but beyond the stand of trees and scrub that separated the mouth of the valley from the fields and the village beyond.

Just because the community here appeared to be dying was no reason to not be cautious. From what he'd seen, he didn't expect they'd be dangerous to six, healthy, Council-fed men, but it still paid to be careful.

When they'd descended, the field beside them was even more pathetic. The wilted tops spoke of crops that weren't tended often. Weeds grew in the path to the fields. Now they were left to weather the winter.

The houses could never have been described as luxurious. Made of hand-hewn logs and found materials, they were a mish-mash of faded colors and textures. Most of those here on the outskirts of the little settlement were abandoned.

As they approached the middle of the village, Alex called out. "Hello? Anyone about? We have trade goods."

Ace hissed beside him.

This would be the most dangerous point of this little operation. Starving people were dangerous, but hunger didn't always make them stupid. A few well-placed arrows, and these people could have all of their goods. Of course, firing a bow took strength and coordination. Alex was betting there wasn't anyone here with enough of either left to be a threat.

"Alex." Ace's voice was a low murmur. "We're being watched."

"I see them."

A few faces had appeared at windows as they approached.

Ahead of them, a tin door that had been banging in the cold wind suddenly stopped, as if held closed. Alex held up a hand, indicating that Ace and the other men behind them should stop. He waited, focused on the house ahead, trusting Ace's men to watch his and Ace's backs.

After several long moments, the door creaked open. An old man with loose, greasy hair appeared. His cheeks were reddened by weather or illness. He was bent, curled up on himself, as if he carried a heavy burden on his back.

His glance flicked to the men behind Alex and Ace, but he sighed and shook his head. "You can get gone from here. We got nothing to trade."

"You sure about that?"

Laughter wheezed into the space between them. "Look

around you."

"I have. I see a town awfully close to that big wall being built. I see people who sit pretty close to a crossroads where traders move and fortunes are built. If you have memories and mouths, you have what we're looking to trade in."

A hiss of noise came from behind the old man, and he tottered for a moment, tempted to turn around. Finally, he nodded agreement and made a beckoning motion. "Come closer, but not inside. You have food?" The old man's voice was hopeful. "Or medicine?"

Alex heard Ace's feet scrape in the dirt behind him as the man slowed.

"Ask them what illness. I can't take any plagues back to my people."

The old man raised his head. "Flu."

"Flu?" Alex could hear the skepticism in his voice. "Flu didn't cause this much neglect. Not that fast."

The old man nodded. "Flu's the most recent. Our water got diverted by that dam they built. When the wall went up, it blocked the game trail; scared off the game on this side. Our young men tried to go and reason with them. Got sent on to the Councilor in the city. It was a risk, but we needed our water. Only one of 'em came back, and he was sick. Said the councilor wanted one of our girls." The old man shook his head. "We don't trade off our young!" He spat in the dust.

Alex frowned. Was this why Sloan had sent them here chasing rumors? But why tell them it was Scavs? Why not just mention there was a Spark here? "She wanted one of your girls? Any girl or one specific one?"

The old man tilted his head to look up at Alex warily. "What difference does it make?"

"The Council is interested in a specific type of girl. Spark girls. You know what a Spark is?"

The man growled. "We don't have none of that here. Even if we did, the kids all got sick anyway after the second group of our men went off down the canyon to try to find a trade caravan—someone who could maybe carry word about what was happening here to another councilor. They say there's a big meet up where people can petition for help. None of them came back."

Alex understood the hopelessness that had them so listless. With the healthy young adults either sickened or gone for help and never returned, all that had been left here in this town were the old and the young—their past and their future. These elderly caretakers were now watching their future waste away. It was no wonder they didn't care.

The children were dying.

Alex eased up to the decrepit building and hovered in the doorway, casting his gaze around the room. He didn't see anything that might tell him what he needed to know. No tell-tale glow or glimmer of energy. "There may be a specific reason why you're being made to suffer. Are you sure you don't have a girl who has special things she can do?"

The old man glowered at him. He remained silent.

Alex tried again. "Sparks are stronger, and get stronger still as we get older. Do you have any children who aren't as sick...or who've been holding on longer?"

Nothing. The old man held his gaze but remained silent. Behind him two frail old women whispered together a moment. One of them leaned out then pulled back, as if she wanted to dart forward and talk to him but didn't dare.

Alex looked right at them. "C'mon. I'm here. I can help. Let me."

The old man looked back at the two women. Were they tasked with caring for the children? The taller of the women nodded at a corner.

"The healthiest is Paul, thought that ain't saying much. The one who's held on longest would be Bethany. That child won't let go."

Alex crossed to them, looking down at the children shivering on the cots. Judging by the faint dark fuzz on his upper lip and chin, Paul was almost a teenager, though he'd probably always be small. Alex noted that where he was frail now, he'd be wiry when healthy. Bethany was still very much a little girl. She might be nine under the matted reddish hair, flushed skin and thin cheeks.

She hadn't started out a small girl. But she was now.

Neither of them even glinted with a sign of energy.

"Did either of them show any sign of being a Spark? Before the illness?"

The elders exchanged looks.

"We don't hold with those powers here. Don't have nothing of the old world to charge anyhow."

Alex took a breath. "Okay. I understand. What I'm about to try is hard for me. It'll be easier if the child I try to help can help me back." He wanted to groan at the lack of comprehension on their faces.

"You're a Spark." The smaller of the old women, who might once have been plump and jolly, spoke from across the room, her voice sharp.

Alex nodded. "I'm going to try to use it to heal one of these children."

The old man had already taken a step back. He took another now. "I can't be involved in this," he whispered.

Alex wasn't sure if there was fear or regret tingeing the words.

"I am the spiritual center of this village, and I cannot be tarnished by this."

Alex stared after him as he left. The fear of Sparks in the Neo-Barb communities wasn't uncommon. Alex suspected Councilor Four used some perversion of religion to color his own zone's perception of the Sparks among them.

"Tarnished?" he echoed the old man's last word.

The women in the room lowered their gazes. One of them turned away from the children in the corner as if ashamed when Alex's gaze fell on her. "Both of these children are Sparks, aren't they? You keep them separate from the other children not because they're healthier, but because they're different?"

The taller of the women stepped forward and reached out. She hesitated, her hand extended. Then she dropped her arm without touching him. "Can you do it? Can you use the Spark to heal?" She didn't answer his question, but it was clear he had his answer anyway.

Alex shook his head and cursed under his breath.

"Can you?"

"It can be done. I'm not particularly good at it, but it can be done."

"You can teach one of them to do it?"

He nodded. "It's not a difficult concept. Just...different Sparks have different aptitudes. Mine's not healing."

"Heal Bethany." Her voice was firm. She gestured him toward the girl with an insistent swing of her chin. "She knows most about Sparking. She even grounded once."

Alex's brow furrowed.

"Her Momma was from the city. She had different ways. When Eugene found out—that was her man, the one she came to us for, and James's son—he sent her away, but made her leave the girl so she could be saved."

Made her leave the girl? Alex thought about Lena and about the likelihood of anyone separating her from any of the girls they'd saved together. Was Bethany's mother still alive? What kind of people was he was saving?

He glanced down at the girl and boy in front of him, struggling to survive. It didn't matter what kind of community they grew up in. Their destinies weren't sealed. People left. People changed.

"Save her," the old woman whispered. "Please."

He raised his gaze to her and saw the guilt there. She didn't want him to heal the girl just because she had the greatest chance of survival. She wanted him to do it because she had her own degree of guilt in the girl's life thus far.

He nodded curtly. "There's no guarantee I can do it. I'll try for her."

He moved closer, standing between the two children before kneeling beside the girl. Her eyes fluttered open. They were dull with pain, but aware.

"I'm going to try to make you better," he explained in a low voice, "and I'm going to use the Dust inside you to do it. Do you know about the Dust?"

Bethany glanced past him at the old women hovering,

watching. She gave him the barest nod.

"If you can, I'd like it if you can try to follow what I'm doing. I'm going to reach down, reach in, and try to talk to your Dust to see if I can tell it to make you better."

She nodded again, and her dull eyes sparked with interest. Now all he had to do was actually heal her.

Alex cleared his throat and shifted his weight forward to his knees. He raised his hands to show her, then settled them above her chest and belly, as near to the center of her as he could get.

He reached in, his mind reeling in past skin to the blood inside her and the Dust that rode it.

Please.

It was the barest thought intruding, but it told him that he was still cloaked in fear and that burning inadequacy. Lena's face flashed into his mind, coated with blood and dirt and bits of leaves in her terrible wounds. Her wide, pale eyes locked on him as she slid to the side, as he tried to heal her.... Alex flicked a glance to the girl's face.

No blood. Dark eyes. Yes, she matters, but she's not Lena. Focus.

He did. The Dust responded, sluggishly at first, and then it pulsed twice, in time with her heartbeat, and swirled. It flashed away, like a school of fish beneath the surface. But he hadn't told it what to do yet.

The little girl gasped in a breath almost like laughter.

Alex searched her face, seeing amazement, pride, and yes, fear. After a moment, she looked at him.

Her eyes weren't dim or haunted by pain anymore. The light only he could see shining from her was a bright halo. She was a strong little thing.

She'd healed herself. He'd shown her what he intended to do, but as soon as she'd understood, she'd done the heavy lifting herself.

Alex felt a smile lift his lips, and an answering grin spread across her face.

"You did it, clever girl."

She nodded. Her stare swerved around him again. Alex

turned himself this time. The two old ladies hovered there, holding each other. Twin looks of awe and horror mingled on their faces.

"The Spark isn't evil or a curse. It's a gift, given to those strong enough and stubborn enough to keep fighting for this world no matter what it does to them." He turned back to the little girl. "Remember that."

She nodded and sat up. Before he could even think about the boy, before he'd even had a chance to inspect her aura for signs of strain, Bethany turned to look at Paul. "Should I—"

Alex nodded. "If you feel up to it, yes. I'd like to know if you can manage others before I go." She slid off the bed and promptly fell into Alex's arms.

"Whoa. Take it easy, little sister." Alex couldn't help the laughter that colored his voice. "I know you're eager, but you haven't used your legs in how long?"

Bethany shook her head. She didn't know how long she'd been sick, and the two old ladies behind him murmuring about miracles weren't any help.

"Long enough," he told her. "You'll have to take it slow. Just you and Paul today. Then rest, food, recovery. Once you're strong enough, you'll need to ground, then you can try again with others. Do you understand?"

Bethany nodded. He lifted her onto the lap formed by the bend of his legs as he crouched and swung his body around so she could reach Paul.

Moments later, she was done. Paul sat up, blinking at them and rubbing his head as if he'd merely been sleeping hard and not sick for weeks.

Her aura still wasn't what Alex would term too bright. Bethany was one of the strong ones. She belonged with Lena. He told her so, trying to explain about a school for girls like her and a wonderful woman who was so strong she glowed like the sun. Before he could even finish, she looked over his shoulder at the other still bodies on the beds. He stopped talking after a moment and watched instead.

"Hey, kiddo," he told her after a minute, "do you mind

coming outside with me? We need to talk to your Grandpa James."

She frowned. "Mr. Carver?" She shook her head. "He doesn't let me call him Grandpa."

Alex nodded. "We'll add that to the list of things to talk about."

He rose with Bethany in his arms. Paul trailed along behind them, leaning on the wall. The two women followed. Alex squinted as they crossed from the darkened room and back into the pale sunshine outside.

"James?"

The old man turned. His eyes widened when he saw them. His head began shaking and his mouth opened.

Alex gritted his teeth. "Whatever you're going to say, don't. Close your mouth and listen."

Behind Carver, Ace turned from his men, his brows raised.

"These children are Sparks. They are not the incarnation of sin. They are not evil. They are not a curse. They're Sparks, and they're special." Alex waited, but Carver had shut his mouth tight and watched Alex warily. Alex nodded. "I didn't heal Bethany. I showed her what to do, and she healed herself. Then she healed Paul. Healing. Not harming. Not evil. She could heal all of those children in there, given enough time and recovery. She could save this village for you. Do you understand?"

"She could," James said, emphasizing the tenuousness of the verb. "There is an unsaid *but* after that could, if I'm not mistaken."

"*But* she has a rare power. A rare gift. She belongs with people who can teach her and not those who would revile her for existing."

"We won't revile her." The shorter of the two women stepped up, dragging the tall one with her. "Not anymore."

"You healed them so you could steal them?" James was suddenly indignant.

"I'm not stealing anyone. I'm letting you know that she belongs elsewhere. She's a treasure. I'll be sending my people back to check on her—regularly. Bethany made her choice. I've seen too many girls like Bethany who've had their choices, and their voices, silenced. I won't do it." He looked down at her.

Bethany stared wide-eyed at James. She brought her hand up to her mouth, as if to suck her thumb, but then seemed to realize and caught herself. She swept her hand back to push her hair behind her ear instead, in a motion that reminded Alex so much of his Lena that he thought his heart would stop. He swallowed and waited. He wouldn't have been able to speak then anyway.

"This is my home," the little girl said so softly that James had to lean forward to hear her. "These are my people. I belong here. To help. I know how to ground, if they'll let me use it. I know how to learn myself." She made a small shrug.

Alex wasn't surprised. James was. That was part of the problem.

Alex nodded. "Bethany, I'm going to honor your wishes, but I want you to know if you ever change your mind, or you feel unsafe, or something happens here, you get yourself down to a man named Gerald Parry in Zone Two. Not the Councilor. Gerald Parry. You use my name—Agent Alex Reyes—and you'll get help. They'll send word to me, okay? I'm going to send him up to check in on you, too, so you'll know him."

The little girl nodded. Alex handed her off to the taller, sturdier of the old ladies.

He smiled at the boy hanging back by the door. "They'll be checking on you, too, to be sure you get the training you need, as well." Alex turned back to James then and stalked down the three steps to the old man.

"You need to treat those children with honor. They'll be your salvation—in more ways than one—if you let them. So long as they're healthy and treated well, my man will ensure you have what you need, including water."

James swallowed. He tried to avoid Alex's eyes, but Alex was having none of it. He tilted his head to hold the old man's gaze.

"You *will* be the family that you and your son stole from that child. She's your granddaughter. Act like it. Or I'll come back myself. You don't want that."

James darted a look over his shoulder. He cleared his throat. "If all those children recover.... It's a long winter. I don't know how—"

"I said we'll help. We will. We'll leave some supplies now. And I'll send a note to my people in Zone Two. They'll help you."

Why hadn't Sloan done all of this? From what he knew of her, she wasn't a cruel woman. Her concern for her people was genuine. Alex wondered if he had the full story. Was that why he and Ace had been routed this way? Was that why she'd interfered?

But then why tell them the village was raiders? She couldn't have known how he'd react. What if he'd sent in a security team and wiped the village survivors out?

You're not the only one who can test the caliber of an ally.

He glanced over the old man's shoulder at Ace and saw the same slow realization dawning in the younger man's eyes.

They hadn't been played. They'd been tested. It remained to be seen if they'd passed or failed.

TWENTY

Lena

When Lena made her appearance at breakfast, the hum of conversation half-died. The littlest children—both the girls and Leo—were oblivious and kept up their conversations. But Phoebe and Marin stopped. So did Rose and Jackson. It had been happening every morning for the past week, since the night she'd gone up with the Dust. Little silences, sidelong glances, stepping in to take over heavy work from the repairs to the main house—it was all getting old.

Lena tried to ignore the silence and the looks, but halfway through the meal she'd had enough.

"Stop it." She made her voice as firm and stern as she could.

Everyone at the table froze.

Lena sighed. "Not everyone." She looked around. "You can keep talking. Just act normal, please."

"Normal?" Hania asked. She glanced around. "Um...us?"

Little girl laughter, smothered at first, and then growing, flowed down the table to her. Lena leaned down to cast a mock severe look at each of them in turn. Marissa sent her a shameless grin back. Leo shoved a piece of venison in his mouth and shrugged.

"Don't look at me," the little boy mumbled around the meat, "I'm the only normal one here."

The table erupted in laughter. Leo glanced around, startled, before grinning wide.

Lena laughed with them. She let the conversations flow

around her. This was what she wanted.

She glanced up, content, and caught Jackson and Rose exchanging a silent look of concern. They were still doing it. Lena shoved back from the table before anyone could notice and hurried into the kitchen with her plate.

Of course, all of them noticed. She could hear the questions and stood leaning against the counter, eyes closed.

"Are you okay?"

Lena leaned her head down for a moment and then nodded. "Yep. Go on back to your breakfast, Jackson. We have lots to get done today, assuming anyone thinks I'm fit to help."

"Okay." He drew out the word before he stepped closer. "Is it the sickness or are you—"

"I'm fine. If I can't handle the sickness, I'll go vomit. I'm fine." She didn't mean for her voice to sound so sharp, but they had to stop treating her like she was fragile. It didn't help with her decision.

"Listen, Lena, if you need it, I can help—"

"You can't help. I don't need your skill." She glanced pointedly out the door into the dining area.

"She told you." Jackson flushed and shook his head, lips tightening. "That's not what I meant. I'm not sure I could again, anyway, though I'm sure you could figure it out. I just meant, if you need it, you have whatever you need from me. My support. My friendship." He looked down.

Lena looked away, too. When she looked back, Jackson studied her.

"If you still want it?"

"Of course I do. It's not like I have so many of them that I can get rid of one. But if you'd rather go back, so you can be an agent—"

Jackson started shaking his head before she had even finished the thought. "No. That's done. I'm not meant to be an agent. I'm not sure what I am, but I'm not cut out for that."

"You're a friend, and a leader, and a wonderful teacher and guide for those children. Is that enough?"

"Enough?" He laughed. "I've been doing that for the last few weeks, and I've got to tell you, it's enough work for three lifetimes."

She nodded, giving him a half-smile. "If you'd let me do my share it wouldn't be as much of a burden."

Jackson sighed and leaned in, wrapping an arm around her shoulders in an awkward hug. She leaned into him. Even with the contact, her Dust didn't even stir. She wondered if Jackson noticed. She thought perhaps he had.

He gave her a small smile and tugged on a lock of her hair. "Congratulations," he said softly. "I didn't mean it before. But I do now."

Her Dust might not respond to him, but her heart could. It warmed now, filled with fondness and forgiveness.

"Are you guys going to come eat? Or are you going to stay in here and hug?" Leo stood in the doorway behind Jackson. He watched them both with mistrust.

"Lena didn't feel good, Leo." Jackson's answer was mild as he turned to the small boy and ushered him out.

"She never feels good. She doesn't get much done anymore, either."

"See? You guys have to stop. Even Leo sees it." Leo was partially right. She couldn't remember the last time she'd felt good. She'd been tired and run-down and nauseated for so long, she wasn't sure she could pinpoint a time when she hadn't been. Was this how she'd feel for the rest of the pregnancy? It didn't matter. There was too much to do. They'd had to give up a day on the house to build a gate at the entrance to the valley. They couldn't afford to lose more time. Winter was coming.

She followed them out and sat back down, nibbling at a piece of flatbread and some venison.

"Eat up, everyone," she said, well aware they were all watching her. "I plan for us to finish the main house this week."

There were groans all around. Jackson said something, but a deep buzz in her head blocked the sound of his words. She shook her head.

The Dust's electric alarms pulsed again in her head.

"Jackson!" She leaped to her feet. "Someone's coming—a lot

of someones. Up the track toward the canyon gate."

"I'm going. Stay down here. Keep the kids locked down."

"I'm coming, too!"

"No. You're staying here."

"I can help you. You'll need what I can do—"

"I need to know you're safe here, with the kids." He glanced down at her abdomen. "All of the kids, Lena."

Lena stared at him as he turned and took off down the hall. He didn't bother with the lights. He crossed through the living space and into the entry tube. Then he was gone.

Lena rounded on Rose. "That's exactly what I'm talking about! One of us going alone is stupid!"

"He's trying to protect you—"

"I'm not an invalid," Lena snapped. "We don't have the luxury to pretend I am. I belong out there."

Rose raised her hands. "I agree. But now's not the time to argue it." She looked over Lena's shoulder.

Lena turned. Marissa and Hania stared wide-eyed. Mae, the youngest of all of the girls, sniffled softly.

"You're shouting," Hania said in her soft voice. Her body almost hummed with anxiety, and her gaze flicked to the door Jackson had just run through. When she turned it back to them, she swallowed. "Did they come for us already? Do we have to go back now?"

Marissa's chin puckered, and she took a deep breath, trying to calm herself.

Lena's heart sank. "Oh, no. No, no, no." She hurried around to the girls, crouching in front of them and touching their faces with gentle fingers. "Those men will never take you from here. I will never let them take you again."

She pulled the three girls closer to her and took a deep breath. Leo probably wouldn't come to her—he preferred anyone to her—but she reached with her hand and gestured for him to come to her anyway.

He hesitated for a moment, and then like a shot, he was out of his seat and crowding close with the girls for comfort. Lena hugged them to her, her arms full of frightened children. After a moment, she stood.

"Come on. Rose is going to stay here with you. When you're done eating, I want you all to help clean up and then start working on your exercises, just like always. I'm going to help Jackson."

"I'm going because I belong up there," she told Rose.

Rose gave Lena a quick, tight nod. Lena left them. She climbed out of the bunker and crossed behind the bulk of the mostly repaired house. She'd expected Jackson to be just ahead of her, but he'd already disappeared into the long valley mouth leading down to the gate. She ran.

It was foolish to leave her behind. Jackson was a trained agent, yes, but his only weapon was his gun. She was the one who'd be able to use the Dust in more ways to help them than he could imagine. He had his gun. She had herself and her experience in the desert alone.

Jackson was just ahead now, moving through the orchard near the gate cautiously, gun in his hand. She could hear shouts from the other side of the gate. Were they responding to him?

"To where?" One shouted, his deep voice echoing through the valley. "We have nowhere left to go. We can't go back to Texas!" This last was said with vicious frustration and rage.

Back to Texas?

With a gasp of shock and fear, Lena realized who the interlopers were. She shouted her alarm. Jackson glanced over his shoulder and gestured her back with one arm. He raised the other and the gun.

She ran full out through the end of the canyon. She had to make it before Jackson attacked, or they did. She shouted as she tore through the orchard, screaming at the top of her ragged breath for Jackson to stop, for all of them to stop.

Lena was so intent on getting to them that she overshot where Jackson crouched and slammed into the reinforced wood beam and mesquite thorn gate he and Rose had built. It gave slightly, thorns piercing the skin of her side and forearms, before bowing back and throwing her to the ground. She lay there, gasping.

"Lena! Dust, Lena!" Jackson scrambled across to her.

"Lena? Lena!" A deep voice shouted from the other side of

the gate.

"Don't you move!" Jackson still pointed the gun at the men on the other side.

"Fuck that," the man shouted back. "We're coming in! I know Lena. I'm the one that sent her here!" In a lower voice, directed at the men with him, he said, "Take that damn gate out."

Jackson slid across the dirt and leaves to her side. She blinked up at him, still trying to retrieve her breath to tell him what was happening. So much for being a useful badass.

A cracking noise echoed over to them from the gate, and Jackson rose, spinning to aim at them.

"Jackson, no! I know them! I know them!"

"We know her!" The tall, lean man forced his way through, grimacing at the tear of the long, wicked thorns across his skin, but not stopping. He pulled through, yanking his rough, dun-colored shirt off a thorn as he came. When he saw Lena on the ground, he stared, then huffed a laugh. With a delighted grin that split his somehow familiar-unfamiliar sun-darkened and scarred face, he said, "Hola, Lena. I see you've fallen on your ass...again."

She eased up, pushing herself onto elbows and then palms and grimacing at him. "Ghost." She squinted at him, taking in his broad chest and shoulders, as well as the long black hair that partially obscured a face scarred by whatever he'd experienced since she last saw him six years before. "You grew up."

He laughed again. "And you didn't."

She mock-scowled, then noticed Jackson still had the weapon pointed at Ghost's chest.

"You can put that away, Jackson. You don't need it. This is Elias. He's called Ghost. We met six years ago."

"Just because you knew someone once, Lena—" Jackson was too nervous and angry to keep up.

Lena shook her head at him and pushed herself up to her feet. "I didn't know him once. I saved him." She smirked at the Neo-Barb in front of her. "Ghost owes me his life."

The Neo-Barb spread his arms wide, "Which I paid for with the directions to this amazing rancho."

"No, that was payment for helping you save your brother.

You still owe me for your life."

He tilted his head. "Lena. Really?"

She smiled.

Jackson made a huffing, frustrated noise.

"*En serio*," Ghost told him with a little frown, "put that thing away before you hurt someone." He looked back at Lena. "What's with the agent? You're not with the Council now are you?"

Lena laughed. "No. Very much not."

"Good," he said. He grimaced. "Good, because I've been looking for you. We need your help."

TWENTY-ONE

Lena

Lena couldn't help the trepidation she felt as Ghost led her down the track to his people. Jackson's simmering presence behind her didn't help. He wasn't happy about the turn of events. He didn't trust this newcomer, no matter how many times Lena had turned to give him an encouraging smile. She imagined he'd like it less when he realized, as she already had, that Ghost and his people were likely here to stay.

Whatever had happened in Texas, the fresh scar across his face and the somber relief at finding Lena told her it hadn't been good. Should she be worried at the six years of distance and life between them? Perhaps he wasn't the same Ghost? Perhaps he wasn't to be trusted?

No. What she'd told Jackson was true. She'd saved him and his brother. Neo-Barbs carried such things close to their hearts. Whatever else was true of Ghost, she could trust him.

"What happened in Texas, Ghost? Why are you all here?"

He didn't say anything for a moment. His head was bowed as he walked, but she could see him swallow. "Two different answers," he answered. "What happened in Texas... It started good. We made a home. A family. Allies." He barked a humorless laugh. "Enemies. It ended bad. Traders moved into the area from the east, pushing south. We—*I*—chose not to work with them." He swung his head around to look at Lena, glancing at Jackson first. "It was a poor choice, and unpopular. These new people…they were relentless. They took our crops first, then everything else. They turned us against each other. Divided us to make their attack easier. I lost my family."

Lena gasped. "Damar?"

Ghost frowned. "No. I still have my brother, of sorts." He gestured ahead of them, down the track. "I still have my larger family. They depend on me to make the right choices."

"It remains to be seen if you have." The soft words, delivered in an angry, insolent drawl, came from ahead of them. A young man of perhaps eighteen moved up the track toward them. He stopped now, his gaze moving over each of them. "'I still have my brother...*of sorts*.' Nice."

He looked like Ghost had at almost the same age, except Ghost's implacable rage had been directed at those who'd destroyed his family ten years before. Damar's ire, and the fire in his eyes, was obviously reserved for his brother.

"Damar." Lena spoke before Ghost could respond. "It's been so long. Look at you."

He stared at her for a moment, his hostility barely dimmed. Did he not remember that night?

"It's Lena." Ghost's voice was measured. "The girl who helped me come for you almost a decade ago?"

A flare of some emotion Lena couldn't name came and went on the young man's face. "The great hope. I owe you my life."

Lena shook her head. "Ghost paid that debt long ag—"

"My brother doesn't pay my debts." The heat in his eyes had died, and his voice had chilled.

"Was there a reason you came in search of me?" Ghost kept his voice even, though his shoulders had tensed.

Damar nodded once. "She wakes. It's working for less and less time." He turned his angry gaze back to Lena. "Now that we've found her, I hope she can help." With those cryptic words, he turned and went back the way he'd come.

Ghost's watched him go, face stony.

"What's wrong?" Jackson's voice had changed. There was still suspicion in it, but it was muted. "How do you expect Lena to help?"

Ghost looked back at Jackson. "I expect nothing. I hope." He shook his head. “We found a Spark. Rescued her, I think, but—” He shrugged. “You should come and see for yourselves.”

“Should see what?” Jackson moved closer. He gave Lena a look she understood—they were both thinking of the force that had attacked her.

“They broke her.” Ghost told them. His face was bleak.

“Who did?” Jackson asked.

Lena already knew. She remembered all too well what kind of people held young Sparks in the wilderness. She’d burned those that had taken Damar, but she hadn’t rid the world of all of them.

“Scavs,” she guessed.

Ghost nodded.

“Is she dangerous?” Jackson had reached out to put a light hand on Lena's arm in caution.

Ghost nodded again, the same weary head movement. “Sometimes. Often she is just a girl—sweet and confused. But then…it’s like she shares her body with another. That other is dangerous.”

“If Lena can't help her?”

Ghost took a deep breath. He firmed his jaw. “If we can’t help her, then we'll help the world. We'll put her down, just as we would a rabid animal. I'm hoping it doesn't come to that. There's been too much loss for my people. Too much division.”

He turned away and continued down the track.

Lena watched him, weighing her choices. Jackson moved closer. She didn’t want to meet his gaze, but she did.

“Before you say anything, just—you don't know what they do to Sparks out here. You don't know why her mind broke. I do. I've seen it. So has Ghost. That's why he came to find me. If he could save her, he would, no matter the cost. It's who he is.”

“It's cost him.”

Lena nodded. “Clearly.”

“It shouldn't cost you, too.”

“It's a risk I'm willing to take.”

“Still?” He challenged her, his eyes moving down pointedly.

“Still?” She laughed incredulously and leaned in to make her point. “Even more so. What if it's a girl? She'll be strong, Jackson, and dangerous, like all the rest of us. Should we give up on her, too? Perhaps we should turn ourselves in to the Council because they tell everyone we're all too much of a risk? You think?”

He leaned back. “That’s not what I meant.”

“I know you didn't. But others do. I won’t have it. Not while I can make a difference. Not if I can.”

“You're right.” He gestured for her to precede him down the track to where Ghost waited, looking back at them. “Just be careful.”

“I'm always careful.”

The snort that came from behind her back told her what Jackson thought of that. As she approached Ghost, she could see his lips were turned up, too.

Lena growled. “I haven't survived this long by being careless.”

“No,” Jackson retorted, “you've survived this long by being stronger than anything else out there.”

Lena thought about the pillar of light. It had rocked her spectral self with its attacks. He was right. A curl of fear mingled with the ever-present nausea in her belly.

She followed Ghost anyway. His people waited in a clearing to the side of the mountain track where the land spread in a gentle, even slope instead of an abrupt drop. Most of them took the opportunity of the stop to rest. Others moved about, checking on each other and their thin animals.

Lena recognized one of them. “Gabriela!”

“Lena?” She crossed to them, stepping around a child chasing a chicken.

Lena met her halfway. She had always assumed Ghost and Gabriela would find their way to a relationship. When he'd told her he'd lost his family, she'd been afraid he referred to Gabriela and her daughter, Corazon. Lena and Ghost had freed the two of them the same night they'd saved Ghost's brother. Gabriela had opted to throw her lot in with the young man who'd had enough courage and honor to pursue his lost family, no matter the costs.

After hugging Lena, Gabriela turned to Ghost. “You were

right. Thank you for this." She skimmed a look down Jackson, and her lips thinned when she took in his form and weapon.

Lena introduced them, and Gabriela nodded at him but clearly still reserved judgment.

"Where's Corazon?" Lena smiled, looking through the people moving around the open space for a blind little girl. How old would she be now? Eight? Nine? Lena felt a spear of hope. If they did stay, perhaps she could be a friend to Hania, who was the same age.

Silence answered her. Lena turned back and saw grief in Gabriela's eyes. An answering grief was written on Ghost's face.

He said he'd lost his family.

"Corazon was lost in Texas." Gabriela's face was strained, and she spoke the words through stiff lips.

"Gabriela, no." She breathed. "I'm so sorry."

Gabriela dipped her head, acknowledging Lena's words. A moment of silence passed between them before she lifted her head again to speak. The grief moved back to become a shadow behind her eyes. Lena had to imagine it was a darkness that never went away.

"Did Elias tell you about Karina? Can you help?" Gabriela asked the questions as if she was afraid of more disappointment.

Lena spread her hands. "I don't know if I can help, but I'm willing to try."

Gabriela nodded. "That's enough. She's like Corazon was. She's a Spark they made, but her group...they had her for a long time, Lena." Gabriela swallowed. "It doesn't matter to me what she did to them, or what she's capable of. If we can help her, we must."

Lena hugged Gabriela again. "We'll try. Take me to her."

Ghost pointed the way, but Gabriela took Lena's hand and led her.

Lena thought it was a tall tent at first. As they came closer, she realized it was a long, narrow wagon with a tarp of some kind stretched tight over a beam held above it by frames at either end. Several people were gathered around. Three people stood peering in at the end of it, speaking to someone inside, offering suggestions and making soothing noises. Several feet away, another small group of men watched, fear and anger on their faces. Damar was with them.

They each held a weapon—a club or an axe. They clutched things that could be used to damage a skull. They meant to stop a wild Spark. Their hostile gazes shifted between the wagon tent and the people who approached.

Lena met those gazes and held them, defiant.

"This is your help? This is what we came so far to find?" One of the men spat into the low, brown grass at his feet. His fingers flexed around the haft of a hatchet as he eyed Lena and turned his hostile face to Ghost.

"Go," Ghost murmured to her, nodding to the wagon.

"Are you sure? You may need someone at your back."

"I've got his back," Jackson said grimly, "and yours, too. See what you can do. But Lena—" Jackson took a breath and held her back for a second. "Be careful what you risk."

She nodded and stepped away. Gabriela led her to the wagon and lifted the end of the tarp that fluttered free. Lena ducked under after Gabriela. The sour odor of sweat fouled the air. She was struck by the feral appearance of the figure sitting up on a grass-stuffed mat. Even in the closed confines of the wagon, the slight figure was covered with a heavy woolen blanket. All Lena could see of her was filthy, matted hair that covered her face, and tiny, thin hands with broken nails clutching at the frayed edge of the blanket. A slight moaning came from her throat.

Karina shook her head over and over. Through the moaning, Lena heard snatches of words.

"*Dejame en paz…soy yo…por favor…quiero ser yo…*"

Gabriela moved to crouch beside the soiled mat. She murmured to the girl huddled on it, speaking soothingly. A woman beside her mixed powder in a pilon. While Lena watched, she poured off a measure of the substance into a small cup of liquid and used her finger to stir it in. She handed it to Gabriela.

"*Ayudame.*" Gabriela demanded assistance from a young man crouched on the other side of the raised mat.

He leaned in and placed a gentle hand under Karina's chin.

When Gabriela nodded at him, he lifted the young woman's face. Her eyes briefly met Lena's, but Karina was too deep within her own mind to note the strange face. Gabriela kept murmuring to her in Spanish, reassuring her and imploring her to drink. Karina opened her mouth.

They were dosing her with medicine to keep her calm. They were keeping themselves safe by rendering her helpless. Lena stole a glance at the young man's face. There was no revulsion. There was only fear. He was afraid of what would happen if Karina refused to drink, Lena realized. She wasn't fighting them. Her pleas for peace were somehow for herself.

Lena took a shaky step forward, uncertain if touching the girl would be the right thing to do. If she became more aware of Lena, would she attack? Would she turn on all of them?

Lena extended her shaking hand over Karina's bed until it hovered over a lump under the blanket that must be ankle and foot. She didn't touch the girl. She didn't reach out to her mind, either. She settled down into the Dust, first on her skin, and then in her flesh.

Show me. Show me, friends.

She let it carry her with it as it swirled through her body, lifeblood and life force that animated flesh and mind and energy. She made no demands. She simply observed, even when she felt a familiar presence recoiling from her. The force from the pillar was trying to hide. It was a mind that didn't belong. When Lena withdrew back into herself, she left a parting gift. She asked the Dust to lower the girl's heart rate, ease the breath quickening in panic at fear of losing herself to another mind.

Lena opened her eyes. Karina was calm, relaxed in the young man's arms as she sipped from the cup Gabriela offered. When she'd taken the last of the drug, he settled her back.

Karina raised her gaze to Lena and smiled. "*Que hiciste?*" She breathed the question as if afraid to disturb the spell.

Lena shook her head. "*No mucho. Ayude a relajarse.*" Lena glanced at Gabriela. "I had the Dust ease her fear." She didn't mention the presence that had her own heart hammering.

There were tears in Gabriela's eyes. "She's never been so

calm. Never." She stroked one thin arm.

Karina plucked at her blanket. "*Quiero banarme.*"

Gabriela turned to the woman behind her. "Quick. Get some warmed water and cloths. She wants a bath. We can make her comfortable. Quick, woman!"

The other woman scurried from the wagon.

Gabriela smiled at Lena. "Do you have any idea how long it will last?"

Lena shrugged. "How long does the medicine usually last?"

Gabriela's eyes darkened with emotion. "It doesn't ever work this well. Sometimes she'll still strike out at those close by. Little shocks. Pushes. Sometimes it's enough to sort of...make things go wrong outside in the camp. It's been hard."

"I'm sorry," Karina breathed in heavily accented English. The words ended on a sob.

"She's not always violent?"

Gabriela shook her head. "No. She has periods where she is Karina, just Karina. A lost, hurt, confused girl. But you can help her." Gabriela brightened. "Look at what you did for her with a touch."

Lena shook her head. "I—I don't know, Gabriela. I don't know how much I helped. I don't know how long it will last. I need to talk to Jackson." Lena shook her head, trying to find a way to explain that Gabriela could understand. "There's something else going on. Let me talk to Jackson."

Lena left the wagon, mind whirling. Outside, she blinked against the bright light. Several feet away, Ghost and Jackson faced down Damar. Ghost's brother turned his suspicious, skeptical gaze on Lena.

"Is all well now, Lena? Will she be okay?" Ghost flipped his hand dismissively at his brother with a growled warning.

Instead of answering, Lena asked, "What happened to the welcoming committee?"

Ghost grimaced. "I sent them off. Your friend here, with his Council weapon, convinced them today is not the day to challenge me."

"To challenge you?" She stared at him.

"Things have been difficult for us, Lena. Not everyone is happy with where I've led them, nor with how."

"But to challenge you?" Her stomach churned. That was serious. She hadn't seen Ghost in years, but she'd thought of him fondly and wondered how his little tribe had done in Texas. It had prospered. It had grown. But now, in difficult times.... "What will they do?"

"I imagine they will choose the strongest of them to formally challenge me. Either I will win, and he will leave and take his cronies with him, or he will win."

"If you need a place to go—"

His smile was grim, though his words were gentle. "I have no plans to surrender or flee. If I do not win, it'll be because I do not live."

"That isn't going to happen." Gabriela's strong voice came from behind them. She turned down her damp sleeves. Her cheeks were red with exertion and, Lena thought, anger. "Not ever."

Ghost chuckled. "I don't think so, either, but she did ask."

"Did you ask your friend about Karina?" Gabriela directed the question at Lena, though her gaze was on Jackson.

"No, not yet." She shook her head in apology. "Jackson, about Karina—"

"Not here." Ghost interrupted. "Come with us." He turned and led them away down the road. When he stopped, it was beside an area where the rough track passed beneath a tall cliff of stone. He leaned against the rock wall. Lena noted the way his gaze moved over the camp of his people behind her, marking individuals, before he gestured Gabriela to sit and crouched himself. The he spoke.

"I apologize, but anything to do with Karina is sensitive. I'll not give them more fuel for their madness if the news is bad." His face was bleak. "Is it?"

Lena took a breath.

Before she could speak, Gabriela did, her words running over themselves in her excitement. "It can't be bad. Karina is calmed. She's calmed and responding to the medicine in a way that she hasn't since we started using it!" Gabriela looked at Lena and

Jackson. “We've been afraid to increase her dose much more. The valeriana and pasiflora barely work now, but she is at a dose that is becoming dangerous for her. It will be toxic soon, and then...then those bastards get what they want anyway, and they don’t have to find the courage to lift a finger.” She stopped to take a deep breath. “Whatever you did—you calmed her. She is sweet Karina again.”

Lena held up one hand in warning. She didn’t want to give the woman bad news. She also couldn’t give her false hope. “Calmed her, yes, because that’s a physical thing that I can tell the Dust. But with what the Dust showed me—I don’t know if we can help her more. I don’t know if we can heal her.”

Gabriela and Ghost both sagged. They believed what they must have been telling their people—if they found Lena, she could fix Karina.

Unfortunately, there were some things Lena didn't fully understand.

A memory of Marissa skipping away on a break and talking happily to herself filled Lena’s mind. They’d figured out she wasn’t talking to herself. She was communicating with her match, Jubilee, lost so very far away.

“Lena!”

Jackson's sharp voice brought her out of her reverie.

“I'm sorry. What were you saying?”

“I asked what the Dust had shown you. What's wrong with her? Did she—is she the one that attacked you?”

“Attacked you?”

“How could she? No!”

Lena made a calming motion with her hands. “It wasn't a physical attack. I think she—or rather, someone else—felt threatened by my presence. I was with the Dust, and I was drawn by her energy. It's hard to explain.” She laughed ruefully at their twin expressions of confusion. “But no, Jackson, I don’t think it was Karina. Her mind is broken, and she didn’t recognize my energy. But someone else did…”

She took a breath and focused on Jackson, knowing the others wouldn’t understand. “I think it was her match. Karina’s injury isn't physical, it's a psychic wound. I don't know if her match is also broken or just violent, or if she steps in to protect Karina. I—"

Lena looked up at Gabriela now, an apology in her eyes. "I'm not sure that anything at all can be done, and even if Jackson can manage something—I don't know how successful it will be."

Jackson wore a thoughtful expression. "I'm not comfortable with you trying anything else right now, anyway. Of course I'll try."

"Why would he attempt it and not you?"

She shook her head and smiled, and knew the expression was tinged with pride. "Jackson is ten times the healer I will ever be. He surpassed his teacher months ago."

Ghost seemed newly impressed, and he offered his hand to Jackson for the first time, clasping the hand and wrist of the young agent who extended his hand. "You use your gift for more than that weapon, then? For more than the Council expects?" He gave Jackson's hand a firm shake. "You're welcome by my fire anytime, Agent."

Jackson held himself very still, then dipped his head. It seemed he understood the honor, though he'd only ever encountered one other tribe of Neo-Barbs that Lena knew of, and that had been fleeting. And not altogether positive, though they'd gained Rose and they'd become friends.

"Thank you. You are welcome by ours."

Lena gave Jackson a small smile. He'd said exactly the right thing.

"Should we go back now?" he asked. "So I can examine Karina? That's what you intended, yes?"

Lena nodded.

They rose. Lena stepped out to lead the way back, but Gabriela held her back. Ghost gestured for Jackson to follow him, and the two men continued to the wagon.

Lena raised her brows at Gabriela's serious expression. "There's something else wrong?"

"I don't know, yet." Gabriela answered. "I'm trying to figure that out." She started walking back, but slower than the men ahead of them. Her head was down. “You and your people—you hold the valley and the rancho Ghost intended to make our home?”

“We do.” Lena kept her response muted. She was afraid she knew where Gabriela was going, and she wasn’t sure what answer to give the woman.

A smile fluttered over Gabriela's face. “You could defend it against us taking it, that I know.” At the startled noise Lena made, she turned her head. “Ghost wouldn’t do such a thing. He wouldn’t take what he's given a friend, but if he tells them this—if he tells them we must keep going through the winter, they will challenge him.” She fell silent.

It was Lena's turn to hold Gabriela back. “He seems confident he can best the strongest of them.”

“Can he best him? Perhaps. But it would break him. Damar is the strongest of the men against him.”

Lena stared at her. Could Ghost beat his brother in a physical match? Ghost had grown from a wiry young man into a tall, lean, powerfully built man. If she didn’t know him, she would be wary of the corded muscles and frightening countenance of the Neo-Barb with his long dark hair and the scar that crossed his brow to the bridge of his nose.

She did know him. She knew what he had gone through for his brother, knew he’d almost paid the ultimate price to reclaim his brother from the slavers who killed the rest of their childhood tribe. She'd seen the Scavenger leader sink a piece of metal rebar through his knee to torture him for the audacity and ferocity of the attack on their camp. Without Lena's help, he would have died of infection before he ever caught up to them. With her help, the zone had one less Scavenger slaver group to worry about, and Ghost got Damar back.

He'd saved Gabriela and her daughter from their lives as slaves, as well as those in the slave pens. They'd all stayed with the brave young man who had the tenacity and loyalty to succeed where their families and villages had not.

Lena didn’t know where the rest of the people now in Ghost's tribe had come from—presumably found along the way—but she had no doubt every one of them knew him for his best qualities. They'd been drawn to his group because of it. Were they all so quick to forget?

Was Damar so eager to destroy the man who'd risked everything to save him from a life of slavery and torment?

What had happened in Texas?

She opened her mouth to ask Gabriela but realized what had happened to this tribe in the past didn't matter. She had to worry about what they meant to the people she'd sworn to protect—the girls waiting at the rancho.

You can't be impetuous now, Lena. Too much is riding on you. Too many lives are at stake.

When she did speak, she went slow and careful. "I know what you are saying—you need the offer of winter shelter, at least, to keep the tribe stable. I want to be able to make that offer. I would have before, without a second thought. But I have my own responsibilities to those who rely upon me now. I cannot bring potential violence and upheaval into our safe zone. I need the tribe stable before I can make such an offer."

Gabriela's lips twisted. "We're caught then, aren't we?"

"I'm sorry. I wish I had a better answer. I'll do what I can to help you."

Gabriela exhaled and nodded. "And Jackson will do what he can now for Karina. It's all I can ask and more than I expected when I woke this morning." She offered Lena a genuine smile, though sadness lurked behind her eyes.

"Gabriela—will Jackson be safe here now?"

She looked at the wagon, and then back again, "Of course. Why?"

"I left suddenly. The rest of us will be waiting for an update." Rose must be furious with worry.

"Of course. Go back. I can get someone to take you—"

Lena laughed. "I don't need help."

Gabriela's gaze, which had moments before been scanning for an escort, now sharpened. "Where did they go?"

"Who? Your rabble-rousers?"

Gabriela nodded.

Lena looked around. She didn’t see them, either, and she hadn’t since Ghost had scattered them.

“They wouldn’t go up the road to the rancho, would they?”

Gabriela looked at her. “Ghost has forbidden it.”

“They're on the verge of challenging Ghost, yes?”

Moments before, her concern had been appeasing Rose and prepping the girls to meet outsiders. She'd thought of bringing them all above ground, so the access to the bunker was restricted. Anxiety clawed at her now, and it had a very different flavor. Those men had clubs. They knew Sparks used their minds to control the Dust, and they knew to disable quickly.

If they went to the rancho, if Rose and the girls came above ground to look for Jackson and her...

She turned and started back up the track that wound past the entrance to her valley. Behind her, Gabriela called for Ghost.

Lena didn’t stop, and she didn’t wait. She managed a quick trot until she was past the bulk of Ghost's camp. When she reached the narrowed cliffs, she ran.

TWENTY-TWO

Alex

Ace curled over his desk in the ornate little office at the back of the caravan car, scribbling notes. Alex leaned against the door and waited. He'd finished another early-morning circuit of the caravan while everyone slept. He'd noticed the candlelight flickering in Ace's tiny office window.

Ace flicked him a glance and finished what he was writing, then leaned back and stretched. "What's up?"

Alex shook his head. "Nothing in particular."

Ace leaned forward again, focused on Alex. "Any more tracks or signs of the men in brown?"

Ace's security men had caught glimpses of young men dressed in mottled brown through the trees—the same kind of mottled brown uniform Patrick had described. The travel on this section of the route was rough. Roads hadn't survived well, and the terrain was rocky, hilly, and dangerous. Both zones one and two shared responsibility for maintaining the roads. Closer in to the zones, they each did well. As the caravan traveled further into the no man's zone between them, the vegetation creeping across the roads grew thicker, and the pebbled pavement was spread less evenly across the old highways.

By the time Ace's men moved into the trees to investigate, the mysterious figures always disappeared.

Alex knew Ace was frustrated. It was clear someone had them under surveillance. They were heading into the halfway point of the journey. If there was going to be an attack, it would be best to have it happen when they were weeks away from both zones and any possible help. The tension had Ace on edge.

Alex shook his head again. "No men in brown. No tracks."

"Maybe they were Sloan's men, sent to make sure we cleared her territory?"

"Maybe." Alex shrugged, feigning indifference. They weren't Sloan's men, unless she'd sent them to Zone Six that summer to wreak havoc on their plans there. One of them had destroyed Patrick's cover and dogged his trail home. "If not, I'll catch one of them eventually."

"They don't seem sloppy."

"Everyone gets sloppy."

"Yeah? Even you? Is that what that was back in the village?"

Alex frowned and sighed. He left the doorway and crossed in front of Ace's desk to drop down into one of the chairs. "You want to talk about this?"

The muscles in Ace's jaw jumped. He looked down at his hands and steepled them. "We shouldn't have left her."

The thought of the girl left behind in that dying village haunted him. Yes, they'd left the boy, too. Yes, those kids had each other. The boy was a mid-range—worthy of training, sure, but not in any particular danger if he was discovered. If anyone outside that village discovered *her*, there was a good chance they'd take her. She was worth a great deal to the Council. She was a Lena.

That was why Alex left her, though everything in him told him to take her with them and bring her back to Lena for training. Clearly Ace thought Alex had made a mistake, because he hadn't stopped questioning the decision since they'd left the kids and the village behind almost a week before.

"That was her home. She wanted to stay."

"She needed to get the Dust out of there. She needed to be protected."

"She wasn't in any immediate danger, Ace."

Ace raised his gaze then, and it simmered. "How do you classify immediate danger? That girl was in as much danger as Lena was when she was—"

"She's not a zone girl. She's not being hunted. We have no evidence anyone even knows about her. If they did, with the weakened state of the village, she'd have been removed a long time ago." Alex held up a finger to make his final point. "Since we're on the subject of the village, she *is* strong enough to heal the others. There was no justification for forcing her out of her home against her wishes. That behavior is precisely what I'm fighting so hard. I won't be a party to it."

"She was a *child*."

"She was old enough to make her own decision. She had a reason. She'd thought it through. I respected that."

Ace rubbed his eyes. "Children aren't old enough to know what's best for themselves, Alex. They have to be told. They have to be taught."

"What do you know about it? It's not like you have a kid."

"I have nieces and nephews." Ace tilted his head in a *beat that* motion.

"I have Leo."

Ace snorted. "Thank you for making my point for me. You can't just do what a child wants because he says he wants it. You have to consider his best interests."

"It's a rough world. The Ward School is a helluva better place for him than an Azcon orphanage. He ran away from that place three times. You think he should've been forced to stay? Live in misery?"

"It happens. Like you said, it's a rough world."

"It shouldn't. Not if someone is willing and able to change that. Children aren't meant to be orphans."

"Not all adults are meant to be parents." Something in the sudden tension tightening Alex's shoulders must have caught Ace's attention. "Wait—you want him? You want kids?"

"Do you?"

Ace frowned, but melancholy replaced the frustration in his eyes. "I do, actually," he answered. "But it's not likely to happen spontaneously for me, is it?"

Alex shrugged his shoulders to relieve the tightness across the back of his neck. "Leo's a distraction Thomas would rather I didn't have," he admitted. "Bringing more on the scene would cause…difficulties. We're not meant to *have* children. Agents, I mean. We're meant to father them, but not to raise them. They're a liability. A weak spot that could be used to gain access to Council secrets."

"Maybe that's for the best."

Obviously, Ace didn't think much of Alex's potential skills as a father. Hadn't Alex said much the same to Lena? It had been a joke, playing off her pretend despair when Leo rejected her overtures of friendship. He'd agreed with a laugh that neither of them was parent material. A quicksilver flash of hurt had flared in her eyes before she'd turned away. When he'd pulled her back to apologize, it was gone. He'd almost managed to convince himself it hadn't been there.

Except he knew it had.

He shook his head now, chewing on the inside of his lip in irritation at the memory. "It doesn't matter," he told Ace, his voice a little rough, "Lena has that locked down. *She* doesn't want children, and I respect that decision."

Ace nodded his agreement with that assessment and bent down to pull the file folder with the daily security log to note Alex's observations.

Alex looked down at his hands clasped in his lap. It was for the best, wasn't it? Relationships in general made an agent weak. He'd learned that early. He'd taught the message himself to younger agents. Dust, he'd rid himself of the complication of Erika because he believed it was best for what he was working so hard to achieve. Why was he questioning it now?

If a relationship made you weak, the parent child connection could prove devastating. It wasn't something he needed. It was just as well that Lena was so adamant that she wasn't interested in that particular complication herself. It was her body. It would have to be her decision.

If there was one thing Lena had taught him, it was that she craved autonomy more than anything else. Alex worked at giving it to her. He hoped Thomas was smart enough to give it to her on other decisions that mattered to her in Alex's absence. Alex winced now, remembering how often and how loudly he'd had to run interference before Thomas did something Alex knew would set her off. He shook his head. She thought the summer they'd had had been tumultuous? If only she knew.

He wasn't sure if it was the challenge of Lena's strength and headstrong intelligence that set Thomas on edge, if it was that no one else had ever bothered to question Thomas, or if it was, as Thomas referred to it, "the distraction of the dalliance."

Dalliance? Thomas had no idea of the strength of what was between Alex and Lena. Or of how ultimately distracting she was.

Isn't that the fucking point, Reyes?

Perhaps that's why he'd caved when Thomas had told him it was time for him to head east. He'd been right. It was time, and there were too many little issues that called for Alex's attention. So many little issues pointed to the possibility of a larger, unseen issue looming in the dark where they couldn't make it out yet. Alex left to shine a light on them and figure out the larger picture. He knew he'd discovered a part of that picture with Leng Sloan. The fact that he was almost certain it was just a part of the picture frustrated him no end.

So why was it the girls—not merely Lena, but all of them—claimed Alex's attention more and more?

Because of how they survived and thrived despite what had been done to them. Because of what would continue to be done to them if no one put a stop to it. Because of what otherwise good men were willing to do to claim that strength and with it, the future.

Otherwise good men? Alex snarled at himself internally. *Good men would never even consider doing what's been done.* Dust, Alex would never consider himself a good man, by any stretch of the imagination—he worked for good, yes, but he wasn't good himself—and the thought of participating in any of the programs to take the strongest of the girl Sparks made him sick. Prisons? Breeding programs? No. Call it what it was—sanctioned torture and rape.

That was a part of the larger picture, too. He had to bring it into focus.

Because he'd be damned if he'd allow the threat to continue to exist, nebulous and constant and hungry for the woman he loved. The revolution he and Thomas had built was for all Sparks. Destroying this element of the Council's activities was intensely personal. It was for Lena. Alex would destroy it, or he'd die trying.

TWENTY-THREE

Lena

Lena heard the Neo-barbs who dared to invade her home before she saw them. Low male voices laughed as they stomped through the main house of the rancho. She held back for a moment, well aware these men were Ghost's responsibility and that he couldn't be far behind her.

As soon as she'd broken free of the valley entrance and rounded the path up from the orchard she'd seen that Rose had kept the children below ground and closed the door to the bunker.

Lena hung back, trying to decide whether to wait for support from Jackson and Ghost or whether to force these men out of her future home alone. She watched the house from her position crouched behind the trembling branches of a juniper.

Should I wait?

Her hand slid in from where it rested on her thigh and hovered for a moment over her belly before sweeping up to push her hair back behind her ears.

I should wait.

Laughter echoed back to her from the open door. Jackson had made and hung it just two days before. They'd kicked it in. A thumping echoed out to her, followed by the rending, crashing sound of breaking wood.

The shelves Rose built!

Lena sprang up and pelted for the door. She slid to a stop outside it and peered in around the edge of the frame. If they'd smashed Rose's shelves, they were in the storage area off the kitchen. She slipped inside, heart pounding, and tried to remember how many of the disaffected young men had been gathered together outside that wagon. Had it been four? More? She tried to count as she made her steady, silent way to the back of the house. Damar, and at least one more to either side of him. There had been another behind them. She was sure of four. Had there been more?

"You said there'd be food. Where is it? I'm hungry."

"There is food." She recognized Damar's voice from the conversation on the track down to Ghost's people. "If they live up here, there's food. We just have to find it."

"Look around you! No one lives here. I don't know what she's trying to pull, but this place is empty."

"They live here." Damar's voice was angry and resolute. The scuffing steps from inside, as if someone paced to and fro, stopped. "They just don't live up here. They're in the bunker."

He knew. She'd be damned if she'd let him anywhere near that bunker. Lena stepped forward, into the open frame of the kitchen's entrance. One sweeping glance around the kitchen and she slid to the right, keeping her back against the wall and the exit of the room beside her. Damar stood in the middle of the kitchen, and the three others were ranged out behind him, the four angry men between her and the back door exit from the house.

"You think you're clever, coming up here, forcing your brother's hand?"

Damar hadn't taken his stare from her since she'd stepped forward. His gaze was steady and cold. It reminded her of a mountain lion she'd encountered once, many years before.

"I don't care what my brother thinks. I'm not afraid him."

Lena smiled. "He's not the one you should be afraid of. This is my house. This is my land, given to me as payment for saving you. You should go. Now."

"I never asked for your help. I never made that arrangement—"

"No, but he did. Should I have let him die? Should I have let the Scavs rape the boy you were and sell you to the highest bidder, so they could do the same? You'd rather a lifetime of torture and pain than show a little bit of gratitude?"

"A little bit of grat—" He laughed, swinging his gaze around to the angry young men lining up behind him. Their stares were hard on her and much more familiar than she would tolerate for much longer. Damar swung back around to face her. "You have no idea what he expects of me."

"I have an idea. Not to be stupid. Not to be a thief, too, I imagine. Very unreasonable."

He turned up one side of his mouth in an ugly smile. "I'm not the stupid one. And like you said, he's not the one who should be feared. By you." He took a slow step forward.

"Attacking me would be a very bad decision."

"Only if they found out."

"They?" Lena laughed. "Do you have so little memory of that night you think *they* are the ones you need to be afraid of?"

Damar shook his head. He took another slow step forward. One more, and he'd be close enough to reach out. One lunge now and he might have her.

If she wasn't herself.

Lena was tired of the game. "If you want to be stupid, fine. Don't condemn your three friends with you."

Now Damar's smile grew from a one-sided slash to a grin of delight. "Three friends? Oh, did you think there were only the four of us in here?"

Lena's heart thumped and she did what she should have as soon as she entered. She reached out to the Dust to see how many were in the house.

The heat signatures made no sense. The Dust's impressions were jumbled—too much movement and heat for her to sort. More bodies than should have been there. There was nothing for it, she'd have to attack first. She'd explain to Ghost later and—

Damar's glance flicked minutely to her left.

She turned her head, already reaching out. She caught the shadow of the club descending. *I'm too late.* She gave the command anyway.

The club didn't come at her in a controlled arc. It had been dropped as he started his downswing. He was frozen, panic and pain in his eyes. She jumped back, and the club thunked on the floor. It bounced twice before rolling away.

Rose stepped out from behind him.

Lena snapped her attention back to the enraged men in the room. *Muscles only!*

Damar froze, fingertips brushing her throat. Rage pulsed in his gaze, now locked on her.

She leaned away from him, stepping to the side again. "Where did you come from?" The question was for Rose as she checked to be sure the three other young men were also held firm by the Dust.

"Where do you think?" Rose's voice was equal parts annoyed and amused.

"But how did you know—"

Rose stepped past the Neo-Barb, her gaze following Lena as she checked the men. "You called me." Her voice was even. "Clear as day."

Lena stopped and stared at her. " I—what? I didn't."

"You did." Rose raised her hand and tapped her forehead.

Lena stared at her. *Call her? I didn't—* But she had thought about her, hadn't she? As they smashed the shelves Rose built? She'd been so angry.

"We'll—talk about that later."

Rose nodded. "Okay." She glanced over her shoulder. "You can come in now."

Phoebe slipped past her into the room. Her shoulders were tense, her jawline clenched. The girl who'd spent too many nights filled with terror wove through the frozen men now, head down, making herself as small as possible so that she wouldn't brush against any of them. Lena's heart broke a little more for the girl who'd been through too much in her seventeen years.

When she reached Lena, she let her breath out in a long, relieved sigh. "We came to help you. Marin stayed with the kids. She didn't want to, but there wasn't time to argue, and I was by the door already." Phoebe's huge dark eyes shone. She was as proud as she was fearful.

"I'm glad you were ready to go, to come and help."

Phoebe gave her a smile, though it was wobbly. "I was so scared. But I came. I came right up."

Lena cupped the taller young woman's cheek with her hand. "You did good, Phoebe."

Lena turned back to Damar. She ran her hands through her hair, exhausted and angry and sick at heart that the little boy Ghost had been willing to give everything for had somehow become this bitter, angry young man.

"Do you think Jackson and Ghost will get here soon?"

"Yeah," Lena answered. "I'm surprised they're not already. Jackson must have been in the middle of helping Karina." She felt a curl of unease. Had something happened with the Spark's dangerous match?

Jackson shouted from the front of the building. An answering brief scuff came from outside the back door. Lena spun.

There hadn't been five of them. There had been six.

A young man stood framed in the back exit. His eyes were more than a little wild as his stare darted from one to another of his frozen friends. His chest heaved. His gaze tracked back to the one familiar face he could blame. His stare caught on Lena. His slitted eyes and tight coiling posture made Lena's stomach tense.

He has nothing to lose.

"Don't be stupid."

Phoebe stood between them. Lena grabbed the girl's shoulder to shove her behind, but Phoebe turned to look. The young woman's eyes widened in a spurt of terror. She was taller than Lena, and stockier with soft curves covering hard muscle, but the man in the doorway was bigger still.

"Get away!" Phoebe's shout was instinct.

His snarled negative response was, too.

Behind him, Lena could see Ghost closing. He'd been stalking closer, scanning the far tree line as he circled the ranch house. His head turned to them, and Ghost ran.

"He promised us we could do what we want!" The furious shout was directed in equal parts at Lena and Damar. His lips curled, and he leaned forward, ready to come for them.

Lena reached for the Dust. She felt an odd pull as Rose did

the same.

It didn't matter. In the span of two breaths between turning and his shout, Phoebe screamed wordless rage at him. The pain and strength of years of survival filled her raw voice. She stepped in, raising her arm to strike his face.

Lena's reach for the Dust stuttered as her concentration broke.

Phoebe's hand was encased in white, sparking energy.

The man instinctively caught her hand to push it away. His eyes widened, and his mouth opened in a shriek of shock. He curled down, eyes trained on his hand wrapped around hers, both now glowing white.

As he twisted lower, Phoebe slammed her other fist down over his ear.

He collapsed to the floor, but couldn't roll away. She still had hold of his hand.

Ghost filled the entrance. Barely winded, he went still as he stared at Phoebe. She lifted her head. Perceiving a new threat, she twisted her hand free of the other Neo-Barb and raised it again.

"Phoebe, no!" Jackson's voice came from behind. He simultaneously spoke the same words as Lena.

"He's a friend, Phoebe." Lena slid closer and moved around to where Phoebe could see her.

Lena stepped over the moaning man on the floor as he cradled his forearm. Spittle and tears rained on the floor around what used to be his hand. She ignored him. There was only one danger in the room now, and she'd never forgive herself if she didn't keep Phoebe from doing something she couldn't recover from.

Phoebe's eyes were wild and darker than normal, filled with moisture and memories. Her face was empty. Lena stepped closer, moving into Phoebe's line of sight. The girl looked at her, eyes moving away from emptiness to awareness, and then to vicious joy. A moment later, she recognized Lena. The joy faded to be replaced with despair.

"It's okay, Phoebe."

Phoebe turned her horrified face down to the moaning man at her feet and then back up again. Her focus darted between Lena and Ghost behind her.

Lena hoped with everything she had Ghost's face held no judgment. Phoebe was all too aware of what she'd done. She didn't need censure. In fact—

Lena flicked a hard gaze at Jackson. He stared down at the man on the floor, face disgusted.

"Jackson, please run the perimeter and make sure there are no more surprises, and then go check on the children."

He raised his gaze, and it burned into her. "Don't you think I should tend to the wounded man at your feet?" he asked.

"I think you should follow orders."

Orders?! She swallowed, then raised her chin. "I can handle what everyone in this room needs."

She pulled her gaze from his and focused on Rose. "Do you have them?" she asked her friend, referring to the three Neo-Barbs still frozen in the kitchen.

Rose nodded. "They're not going anywhere."

Jackson turned on his heel and left.

Reassured, Lena focused again on Phoebe. She reached out to take one of the young woman's trembling hands, then led her from the kitchen. Ghost stepped back to allow them out.

Had she been afraid he'd judge Phoebe for what she'd done? All she saw in his gaze was respectful appreciation for her ability and censure when his gaze fell on his tribesman. When Phoebe stepped into the sunlight, and he caught the despair on her face, dismay flashed across his own.

"No—please." Ghost lowered his head to be sure he had the tall young woman's attention. "Don't blame yourself for what his choices forced you to do. Don't blame yourself."

"He's right," Lena told her.

Phoebe shook her head. "It wasn't—It wasn't his choices I was reacting to. I was—I went back, and I— Oh, Lena, did you see what I did? I hurt him, and it wasn't his—"

"You removed a threat. He was determined to hurt us all. He wanted what we have." She moved in close to look up into Phoebe's face. "And that was his choice. You protected us." She smiled. She understood the anguish and the internal conflict, but

Phoebe hadn't been wrong. Unfiltered, but not wrong. "Look at me. Say it."

Phoebe looked at Lena. Her gaze darted back to the man behind them.

"I won't heal him until I'm sure you're okay first. Look at me."

Phoebe focused again on Lena and took a long, shaky breath. "I should do it. I should heal him. I damaged him. And you—you're almost glowing again anyway."

Phoebe was right. Lena hadn't grounded since the night she'd gone up with the Dust. She needed to discharge the excess energy. Anxiety bubbled up. Pregnant Sparks were given lighter duty so they had to ground less often. Lena didn't have that luxury. What would the energy she drew through her, built up, and then discharged do to her unborn child? She'd have to take that into account if she decided…

Later. Not now.

She shook her head. "You don't have to—"

"I do." Phoebe's voice was firm. "I do. I hurt him. It was his choice to be here, and I was protecting us, but I hurt him. That was my choice. It's my responsibility."

Lena smiled as Phoebe took another deep breath. The young woman's eyes cleared. She was still hurting, Lena had no doubt, but she'd dealt with the immediate horror. She'd made herself cope for the moment. It was all Lena could ask for.

Phoebe leaned down and startled Lena with a quick hug. Then she stepped past Lena and back into the kitchen. Lena watched as she crouched beside the now shivering man and whispered to him. Her face was grim as he whimpered and tried to pull away, but her grip on his arm was implacable. She'd done this. She was determined to undo it, as much as she could.

"Immobilize him first." Lena advised her. "So he can't strike out at you as soon as he's no longer insensible from pain."

Phoebe nodded and frowned as she focused. Lena could feel the Dust inside the man responding to her commands. Satisfied, she turned back to Ghost.

There was no censure in his expression—not for Phoebe. He

was focused, yes, but with appreciation, even admiration.

"I thought you were unique," he said now. "Even after we found Karina. She was strong like you, but it could well have been her power that drove her mad. But now—" He shook his head in an expression of amazement.

"It wasn't power that made Karina weak enough to control." Lena's low voice was filled with loathing for the evil that drove the Council to put a bounty out for women and girls like her, and for the evil of the men willing to do anything to earn it. "It was the same thing that made Phoebe react like that the first time she faced a dangerous man now that she knows how to fight back. And no, I'm not unique."

She looked around her at the meadow now brown with autumn, the buildings they were still repairing, and the mountains that enclosed it all. "The rancho will be—*is* a school for girls like me. It's a haven. I won't compromise their safety. Not for anyone."

"You said children to Jackson. There are more?"

"Hidden, yes. All of them freed from men who thought they could take what they wanted."

His jaw tightened, and he nodded, his head turning to glance over his shoulder at the entrance to the bunker. He knew where it was. He was the one who'd told her about it and about how none of his people had ever been able to get it open. "That's even more reason for us to stay. We can help you protect them, build a community for them."

Lena huffed a small sound of amused scorn and flipped a hand at the kitchen and the men in it.

Ghost's face hardened. "They are no longer a concern. They've sealed their fates. They'll be shunned tonight."

Her heart skipped a beat. His face was twisted with both anger and grief. He was going to shun Damar, too?

"Ghost…"

"It was a long time coming." His voice was rough. He looked at the ground, allowing his thick hair to fall over his face and shield his eyes and the pain and moisture gathering in them. When he looked up again, he was in control. The pain had been tucked beneath the anger. “More than one of my people think it should have been done in Texas. It’s been a long time, and a lot of pain, coming. We saved him Lena, but we can’t live his life for him. We can’t make him see the value of community, of living and working and believing in the sanctity of lives lived for and with each other. We can’t allow him to spoil those things, either.”

“I’m sorry, Ghost.”

“As am I.”

A choked sob of frustration and the sound of Rose’s murmured reassurances drew his attention back to the kitchen behind Lena.

She turned to see Phoebe kneeling on the floor, the man’s now shortened arm laid across her knees. She curled around it in her focus. Frustration and despair came off her in waves. Lena crossed to her and knelt beside her. She glanced up and got a reassuring nod from Rose.

She placed one gentle hand on Phoebe’s shoulder and reached with her other to take his arm from Phoebe. The young woman resisted briefly then let Lena take it.

Phoebe lifted her face to Lena. Tears tracked through the dust on her dark cheeks. “Look what I did to him. How will he live on his own?” She’d heard Ghost’s plans.

“He will live marked on the outside for the kind of man he is on the inside.” Ghost’s voice was implacable. “All of them will be marked for their choice tonight. Not a moment of that, or what comes after for them, is your fault.”

Phoebe raised her face to Ghost. She held his gaze, needing to believe him. Whatever truth she found there, Lena hoped it would help her. She knew the need to believe, and how important it had been to find that reassurance and acceptance of what she’d done and why.

Lena inspected the end of the man’s arm. His thumb and first two fingers were gone. Pink new flesh covered what would have been blackened, red wounds. He would have to cope with the loss of his hand, but he wouldn’t have to worry about infection or death. It wasn’t insurmountable. Difficult, yes, and no doubt traumatic…but he was alive. It remained to be seen what he did with that gift.

When she looked up to assure Phoebe that she'd done a good job for the man, Phoebe was still staring up at Ghost. Lena turned her head.

The movement pulled his attention to Lena. He flicked a glance back at Phoebe and gave her a small, sympathetic smile, then turned his attention back to Lena. "Do you have rope that I can borrow to bind them?"

"We have rope, but not that we can cut. Our supplies are limited," she told him apologetically. "Our resupply is delayed." She shook her head. That was a concern for another day. "I can limit their ability to do anything other than walk, then come down tonight and release them when you're ready to be…done."

"We both will come." Rose added.

Ghost took full notice of the other woman at the back of the room. His gaze swept over her tall, muscular frame and golden hair. Was it something in her manner that caused him to smile in recognition, even as she arched a brow and gave him a look that was emphatic in its lack of encouragement.

"You're one of us," Ghost said with delight.

Rose shook her head. Without even pausing for thought, she said, "Not anymore. I was one of the People, but I'm one of them now." She indicated Lena and Phoebe with a nod. "Now and forever."

Lena grinned at her.

Phoebe looked up and gave them both wobbly smiles. "Now and forever."

"So you can take your boys," Rose told Ghost. "They can walk, and that's about it. We'll see you tonight. Midnight?"

He nodded.

"At midnight, then. We've got clean-up of our own, now. And decisions, too."

Ghost nodded respectfully. "I hope we'll be part of the discussion. We need a home. You and your children need a family."

"We have a family." Phoebe's voice was strong again. In fact, it was little tart.

"He meant a community," Lena soothed. "A larger community," she added for Rose's benefit, when the other woman opened her mouth to say, Lena was sure, much the same thing Phoebe had voiced.

Lena turned to Ghost. "We'll discuss it, I'm sure. I'm making no promises."

"I don't need promises. I trust your judgment."

Rose snorted.

Lena wondered whom that snort had been directed at, the speaker, or the one whose judgment he was trusting.

TWENTY-FOUR

Lena

"Where did you find him, and how do you know him?" Rose's pointed question was filled with layers of disdain that Lena wasn't sure what to do with.

She stood there, looking at her friend with pieces of the shattered shelving in each hand. As soon as Ghost had left with his prisoners shuffling beside him, Lena had turned to the shelves Rose had built to see if they were reparable. She lifted the pieces in her hands as if they were a peace offering.

"Forget the shelves. I'll make more. How do you know him? Are you seriously considering allowing a village of People to settle here with us?"

Lena exchanged a look with Phoebe. The young woman had gotten to her feet and was attempting to use dirt and the toe of one boot to scrub blood and bits of charred flesh from the floor. Phoebe flicked a look over at Rose and then shook her head, returning her attention to the floor. Lena was on her own.

"I wasn't aware that was such an issue…?"

Rose closed her eyes. "It's not. It could be. My people were different. They didn't follow the more traditional view of tribal structure."

"I thought all Neo-Barb communities were similar? You knew what he meant by shunning, and you guessed when it would be done. So…not so different?"

Rose sighed. "There can be similarities. Probably more between those of us in the west than between my people and, say, a group from out east. When he used that term, I guessed. I don't know him. You do. How?"

"Six years ago—no, almost seven now—I saved his life. Scavs had attacked his tribe. They killed everyone except Ghost and his brother Damar—the kid who attacked me. They took Damar."

"They had an order for a boy from a rich Zoner." Rose's voice was flat and filled with disgust for those in the Council zones who provided the business that fueled Scavengers.

"Ghost was wounded. It would have been mortal wound. He found me. I healed him. We both went after his brother and saved him and several others from the Scavs."

"You killed them?"

At Lena's nod, satisfaction spread across Rose's face.

"Ghost rewarded me with this rancho—it had been one of his people's stops on their route north and south each year."

"They're nomads?"

"They were. The survivors wanted to stay with him, so he took them and his brother to Texas. Built up his own People. From what he told me, it sounds like they'd found a good place to settle, but something happened. They left. On their way back to familiar territory, they found a girl like us, but…broken. I think her match is using her weakness to control her somehow. Ghost made the decision to keep her alive and try to come find me to see if I could help her. From what I gather, it wasn't a popular decision. It's cost him, especially with some of the younger men."

"Who rallied around his brother." Rose sighed. She didn't seem surprised. Was it a common Neo-barb dynamic? "This girl—she's the one who attacked you when you were up—?" Rose pointed up at the sky, indicating when Lena was traveling with the Dust.

Lena nodded. "Her match."

"And now she's…?"

Lena shook her head. "I don't know. I was coming back to check in with you when I realized the, um, disaffected youth from Ghost's tribe had beat me here. Jackson was working with her. I'm hoping he was able to help her. I don't know. She's—

damaged."

"Damaged? Where did your friend find her?" The question came fast and sharp. Lena knew it was the memories that woke Rose in a cold sweat lurking under the words.

Lena shook her head. She either didn't remember what they'd told her or hadn't been told. So much had happened in the last few hours, her head was spinning. "Scavs?" she guessed.

Phoebe got to her feet. "Do you think Jackson was able to help her?" Her voice was soft and filled again with the weight of all that she and the other girls from the prison camp had been subjected to.

"I don't know. I hope so."

"Let's go ask him." Rose brushed her hands against her thighs and looked around at the wrecked kitchen they'd worked so hard to get ready to be used full time. "This'll keep. And for Dust's sake, Lena, leave the shelves."

Rose led the way back to the bunker. They descended to find the children lined up at the table eating lunch. From the sounds coming from the kitchen, Jackson was cleaning up.

Marin sat up straight as soon as they appeared and her gaze locked onto Phoebe. "Are you okay?"

Phoebe gave Marin that wobbly smile.

Marin knew something had happened above ground. Did she know what? And how? Lena turned to exchange a look with Rose. Rose shrugged and tapped her forehead the way she had when she'd told Lena how she'd known to come help.

I called her. Lena shivered, remembering her conversation with Jackson and the morning she'd woken Rose from her nightmare. How was that even possible? The men of the Ward School had made it clear what the Dust was and where it came from—their ability to interface with billions of tiny robots. Even Sam's implication to her a few weeks before that the machines were evolving didn't explain this.

Was it their inherited ability to talk to the Dust that allowed them to interface with each other? Or was it the machines in their heads? And what did it mean to be each other's matches, anyway? How was Karina's match using her to reach through, to strike out through her? And how was it that when Lena had gone up with the Dust she got the distinct feeling it was hiding things from her?

Lena sighed and tucked her hair behind her ears. She didn't have any of the answers. All she could see right now were two young women who had a supernatural connection that brought them comfort and gave them a safety net.

"Go on," she told Phoebe, who leaned toward Marin in her need for her match. "Why don't the two of you take your lunches to the back and eat in your room so you can talk."

Marin flipped Lena a startled look, then nodded and rose. Phoebe flashed her a grateful smile. The smile faded as she stepped forward and her gaze caught across the room.

Jackson had come out from the kitchen to lean against the jamb of the doorway. His arms were crossed, and his face was set and unhappy. The heavy weight of his gaze and its censure fell directly on Phoebe.

Lena felt a flash of anger. She marched toward Jackson, pushing past him to enter the kitchen as she hissed, "Step back. And stop staring at her like that."

"Excuse me?" He turned to follow her. If his face was anything to judge by, he was a thundercloud of emotion waiting to burst free.

That was fine. She was ready to have this out.

"I won't have you look at her the way you looked at me for months." She kept her voice low so it wouldn't be overheard, but her hurt and fury, long held in check, throbbed below the whispered words. "She defended us, but your self-righteous morality sees nothing wrong with guilting a survivor of things you can't imagine because you don't like the way she did it."

"Self-righteous morality? She burned a man's hand into a blackened stump. Don't you think a little guilt is in order?" His voice was low, too, but almost as venomous.

"Would it have been more acceptable if it were one of the boys from the Ward School? If he'd put a bullet in that man's hand, instead?"

"What are you talking about?"

"Would it have been more acceptable to you if one of the

wards had done as he was trained and shot that man's hand, instead? It's a simple question, Jackson. Yes or no."

"I don't know." He raised his hands up in confusion, then let them fall. "All right. Yes. It would have. It would be less—"

"Instinctual?"

"Violent. Inhumane."

"Bullshit. The end result would be the same. He'd still lose the use of the hand and probably a few fingers. He'd still be incapacitated for life. You don't have a problem with what happened. You have a problem with the way we do things, with the way *our power* affects things. You have a problem with the fact that it's *us* doing things."

"That's incorrect."

"Is it? You're a trained killer, Jackson Lee. Just because you've chosen to heal, doesn't change what they made you, like all the rest of those boys. But because what you do is cold and controlled, is codified into law, is delivered secondhand through a gun, because what you do isn't based in feelings and emotions, somehow that makes you better than us?"

"That doesn't make me better than you. I pay a price in conscience for everything—"

"Oh! You're mad because we don't feel guilty enough for what we do to the people determined to hurt or control us?"

"I'm not angry because of what you do or how you feel. I'm angry that you revel in it, that you—"

"We have a right to defend ourselves. And to be proud of it."

"Proud of descending into darkness? Of being more and more twisted by—"

"Why do you *care* if I'm dark or twisted?"

"Because I care about you—all of you."

"Then let us be." It was time to be as clear as possible. If he left, then so be it. "This is who we are. It's what we do."

"It doesn't have to be this way. You don't have to revel in darkness. It makes you—"

"Happy. I am what I am. I came out here to be free and to give the girls the same gift. I'm not going to change or hide or lie to your face about what lives inside of me so you can feel better about the world."

She held up her hand when he opened his mouth to protest. "I know you love these girls, the same as me. I'm telling you now if you really love them, then you will allow them to be angry, to be hurt, to strike out at those who hurt them. If the way they do it disturbs you, you will show them another way to heal by what you do, not by telling them they are bad. You give them balance and light by being light, Jackson, not by forcing it on them."

He stared at her. She had no idea if she was getting through.

"That's what you will do for those girls, or you can get out now and go back to the Ward School. We've had this discussion before, and you keep telling me you want to stay. Fine. But this is the last time. I mean it. If I ever see you looking at them the way you just looked at Phoebe, judging them for what they are because of what good, moral, controlling men like you gave bad men permission to do to them, I will send you away forever."

Jackson still stared at her. He leaned back against the counter behind him and crossed his arms. He said nothing.

"Everything I've said went completely over your head, didn't it?"

"No." He said the word quietly. He shook his head for emphasis. "I get it. Your way is the only way. Right? Your girls. Your school. Your darkness. Your way. Am I wrong?"

She sighed. "If that's how you choose to look at it. You can't wrap us in ropes and chains and tell us that because they're made of goodness and light that you haven't bound us."

"I'm not trying—"

"No, you're not *trying*. It isn't what you intend, but it's how it ends up. I don't need to be controlled. I don't need to be held back. I *do* need your light. We all need it. As an example. In the form of advice. So long as you can understand I won't always choose to follow it. Sometimes the dark path is the way. Those are our decisions. You can't make them for us. You can't erase that part of us. Not if you really love us."

Rose's quiet voice startled them both. "We don't need a keeper, Jackson."

She'd entered behind Lena and they'd been so engrossed in

their argument that Lena had no idea how long she'd been there.

"We need a friend and a partner and someone who understands that though we may *hear* what you're saying, we won't always choose to *listen.* That doesn't make us bad. It makes us human. It makes us independent. And yes, it is *her* school, because she's the only one who's ever had the courage to stand up and say, 'Enough!' She's the only one who can teach us to just be what we are. She's the only one who's ever been a strong female Spark in tune with the Dust and herself. Can you teach the girls how to do that?"

He stared at Rose. The heat faded from his face, and it wasn't defensiveness that replaced it. It was thoughtfulness. He was trying. "No. I can't. I have no idea what that feels like." He switched his gaze back to Lena. His shoulders tightened, but he took a deep breath. "I guess I owe you an apology."

Did she dare trust that it was real this time? They all needed what he had to offer.

She shrugged and gave him half a smile. "I like the fight. I don't like being made to feel like I'm *less than* because we're different."

He took another deep breath. "So fighting is good. Just be respectful. And back off when the decision is made, even if I think it sucks."

"And love those girls no matter what. They're doing the best they can to deal with stuff no one should have to."

He swallowed and nodded. "That I can do." He pushed off from the counter. "I need to start by apologizing to Phoebe."

"Wait!" Rose said. "We've got stuff to discuss—the Neo-Barb girl, and whether or not we want them to live here, too."

Jackson shook his head as he crossed the room. At the door he stopped and looked back. "Karina is her name, and I have no idea how to heal a brain. The emotional damage? The control by someone outside? I don't know what to do for that."

Lena nodded understanding. She'd been stunned by the realization—and she'd had no idea what to do, either.

"I can keep her calm, probably enough so she can keep control herself, she can be up and out and less drugged. But I can't fix her. And as for whether or not they should stay…assuming the problem of the gentlemen upstairs has been resolved?"

They both nodded.

"Then I think I'll let this be one of the first decisions you make, and I deal with. I don't know the man well enough to offer any input either way. I'd be throwing in my bias."

Lena let her mouth fall open in joking amazement. "Are you admitting to bias when judging another man?"

He snorted. "Ha! I'm admitting to possible bias when I don't know a man. I know Alex. I know he's a jackass."

"Alex is a jackass," she admitted. She widened her eyes in an exaggeration of breathless excitement. "That's what makes him so perfect for me."

Rose grinned and ducked her head to hide it from Jackson.

Jackson stared at Lena for a moment. "I'm going to leave that alone right now."

"Good choice."

"Yes, it is. You see? I'm trying."

"I do see." She leaned out to call after him, "Thank you, Jackson."

"Have fun making a decision that will affect the safety, health, and future for all of us!" He called back.

Lena leaned back against the counter. "Wow. That was a little hostile. He's kind of a jackass, too."

"We all are, Lena. That's why we fit so perfectly."

Lena held up her finger and pointed at her friend to indicate she had a point.

Rose laughed then sobered. "Well done, Lena. I was a little afraid you'd push him too far. But—it all needed to be said."

Lena ducked her head. "Yeah, well. I don't want him to go away, but I don't want him to make them miserable, either. No one could live up to Jackson's expectations."

Rose clapped her hands, putting an end to the rough conversation. "Ready to fight with me now?"

Lena covered her face and groaned. Rose simply laughed.

Lena stood back, close to Rose for both warmth and emotional support. They hovered at the edge of the firelight, witnessing from a distance. It was cold back here near the edge of late-autumn night, enough that Lena shivered under her layered clothes and the blanket Rose had tucked around her.

It was nothing compared to the cold that rolled off Ghost closer to the firelight. It was a cold that had nothing to do with the season or the time of night, and everything to do with deep disappointment. He used that frigid demeanor to insulate himself against the pain he must cause—to the young men and their families, including himself.

The small tribe of perhaps fifty gathered around a bonfire. The crackling of the flames was the only sound. Lined up in a double row, three deep, the young men were bound and made to kneel beside the fire. Lena was glad their backs were to her. She didn't want to see their faces. It was difficult enough to see Ghost's.

He approached the first of them, a long, curved knife in the hand that hung at his side. His words were carried to them in snatches by the wind.

"...made your choices...live in violation of...send you now to the wild." Ghost leaned down to the first of the young men and grabbed him by the hair on the right side. He brought up the knife and sawed down between the hand that held out the hair and the skull of the kneeling man.

Lena gasped, wondering for moment if he took his ear. But when he raised his hand, it was only a full hank of long, tangled hair in his hand. Now he shouted, lifting his face to the sky lit by stars above. The words flowed like white heat as his breath puffed into the cold mountain air and the wind whipped both breath and words away across the mountain. He threw the hair into the fire. It rose on a current of wind and heat before shriveling into ash.

Ghost continued quickly to the man beside the first. Two older men moved in, lifting those who'd been banished to their feet and cutting their bindings. A skin of water and a pack was thrust into their hands. They threw one angry, shamed, defiant look round at the ring of faces staring at them and bolted into the dark, back down the mountain. They didn't wait for the others. They ran.

Ghost repeated the brief ceremony for the next pair of traitors. One of them was the now-disfigured man that Phoebe had burned in defense of Lena. When Ghost was done, and the hair from the right side of their heads was shorn, the same two men moved in to equip them with whatever the village saw fit to give them. They ran into the night, as well.

Ghost stood now before Damar and a younger man. The younger man sobbed, his face down. Lena could hear answering sobs coming from somewhere in the crowd as a mother or girlfriend—perhaps wife?—also wept. When Ghost stepped forward, the young man raised his face. He shook his head and spoke low words, rapidly.

Ghost hesitated.

The young man leaned forward, his shoulders straining as he tried to make himself heard, believed.

Ghost spun in a slow circle, taking in the murmuring of his people, assessing their mood, until he faced the fire again. He lifted his hands to it. The fingers of one hand splayed, clear against the light of the flames. The silhouette of the knife was a dark shadow in the other.

Lena looked at Rose.

"The boy asked for forgiveness." Rose's face was impassive. "And now your friend must weigh that request, and whatever is in his own heart, with the needs of the whole." Rose turned in the dark and her pale eyes shone down at Lena. "He has to try to figure out if you'll deny the lot of them if he forgives one of the men who attacked us."

Lena swallowed. Would she? Her gaze moved to the rigid back and shoulders of Damar beside him. There was no shaking of his body as from tears. There was no softness or weakness to him. If Ghost forgave the younger man, would Damar ask for forgiveness, as well? And if Ghost granted it to him, would Lena turn them away?

She would. She'd have to. She'd seen the hatred in Damar's

eyes for Ghost. If he remained, there would be no peace for any of them.

Ghost turned back. “You disobeyed me. You attacked an ally. You endangered the future of the people. I will not offer you absolution.”

The young man’s shoulders sagged.

“I will offer you a choice. You demanded freedom at the side of the men you conspired with. You may have that now—as a marked man for the length of time it takes for your hair to regrow, and as a free man thereafter, forbidden to return to us. Or… You may remain among us. For the span of one year, you will be the least among us. You will do whatever we require. You will not speak, you will not conspire, you will not act of your own will except what we demand of you. You will be as a dog among us, for the span of one year.”

Silence fell. There was only the fire and wind.

“At the end of that year, your name will be restored, as will the rights and privileges of one of the People, debt paid. What do you choose?”

The young man spoke, his head nodding.

Ghost regarded him, eyes unblinking, face somber. “I hope you understand, Timbor, those will be the last words you speak for a year.”

Timbor’s head moved up and down again, a jerky motion.

Ghost nodded. “Then go and sit at the feet of your master.” Ghost pointed at a man at the edge of his people. He didn’t watch as the young man struggled to his feet and his bindings were cut by a man who stepped forward to help him. Ghost turned his face toward the fire again.

Lena thought he might have missed the moment when Damar reared back and then forward, spitting on Timbor’s back as the man walked away from him. Then he turned his head back to his younger brother, bound before him on the ground. The distant, cold air around him flared to enraged heat. He must be using his grief over what he was about to do to fan the flames. This was no neutral leader meting out punishment he didn’t care for in order to preserve order.

This was a betrayed brother who had once given everything he had to save the man before him. Lena shivered. She remembered Ghost's desperation. His determination had kept him going even as infection raged through him. It kept him conscious and looking for a way out even as the Scavenger leader who'd taken his brother shoved an iron spike through his knee as punishment for the damage Ghost did to his camp and his men. Damar had been forced to watch.

What had happened between then and now to lead these two to this point?

The shadows and light from the fire played over Ghost's face as he stared down at Damar. "Have you anything to say?"

"I demand satisfaction. I demand the right to take these people from you by show of strength."

"You've lost that right forever. You are selfish and stupid, and I was a fool for forgiving you once because I love you. This…" Ghost stopped, swallowing. "This is a lesser crime, and yet I will not forgive it. I will not fight you. You have not once in your life earned the honor."

"Coward!" Damar tried to surge to his feet, but they'd tied him at the ankles, too. The two men who'd been assisting came over and used hands and knees to press him to the ground as he writhed and spit.

Ghost himself pressed his brother's face to the earth with one hand. He twisted his brother's long hair around his fingers while he intoned the ritual words.

"I return this man to you, sky and wind and earth. I send him to the wild. He is not now, nor ever again, of our people!" Ghost flipped the knife in his hand so that the curved blade rested along his wrist and curved out. With a long, slow slash, he ran it along the base of the twisted hair next to Damar's scalp.

Damar's keening shriek of rage and shame rose gooseflesh on Lena's skin.

Ghost stepped back. The anger was gone. There was nothing in its place. Ghost seemed remote, like nothing could touch him. He took another step back and then tossed the hair into the fire. He watched it burn to nothing.

The men cut Damar's bonds. He lunged for his brother, but they caught him again and carried him over to the edge of the village to press a waterskin and a pack into his arms.

"Go," one of them shouted at him, "and don't come back. You know what will happen if you do."

Lena looked at Rose again. "What will happen?"

Rose shrugged. "It depends on their customs. Some ignore them, treat them as a ghost in their midst and refuse to acknowledge them until they drift away again. Some shame them. Some stone them. Some hunt them."

"So…nothing good."

"Nothing good," Rose agreed. "Which is what they've earned. This is a shunning, yes, but they have a chance at a life. They can shave their heads, wait for the hair to grow back in wild again in a few years. Then no one in any other group would ever know about their unfortunate past. Life is hard, out here where we People live. So many things could happen to someone's people and lead one to go in search of another family. They could start again, somewhere else. Spend those years alone learning from this mistake." She shrugged. "It's a chance."

"But not one they take?"

Rose shook her head. "Not usually, no."

Damar started down the track away from his former people. He kept turning back, walking backward, watching them. As Lena and Rose spoke, some movement must have given away their position. Damar stopped. All Lena saw of him was a vague outline in the dark, and his eyes reflecting the fire light in a glow. That glow focused on them now.

He said nothing. He did nothing. After a moment, he turned and ran down the track, as if he had not a care in the world and was eager to be away.

What are the chances that's the last we see of him?

Slim to none.

She sighed. This was none of her doing, but it would all come back to her new home. She looked back at the people, moving in to close in on Ghost now, to touch and offer reassurances or condolences. One woman offered thanks for her son.

What kind of damage did making that kind of decision do to a man?

Could she have made the same decision? She tried to think of her brother, her betrayer. Alex had tried to bring him up over the summer. She'd refused to hear of him. Even now, she pushed away the mental image of him. Instead, an image of her sister Teresa's face, spitting with anger and twisted with a jealousy Lena could never have done anything to alleviate other than cease to be, rose in her mind's eye.

Yes. She could make Ghost's choice.

She was so caught up in her own thoughts she didn't notice Ghost making his way to them. Rose touched her elbow and brought her back to herself as he approached.

"I'm sorry," Lena said softly to him.

He nodded in acknowledgment.

"I'm proud," Rose told him. The words, and the finality of her tone, took Lena by surprise. "It took courage and dedication to the rest of your family to do what you did. I'm proud to know you."

He nodded again, and looked down for a moment, as if to collect his thoughts. When he looked up, his face was clear. "Did you make a decision?"

And just like that, he's moved on. What happened, Ghost? What happened in Texas?

Rose looked at Lena.

"We did. You and your people are welcome to share our rancho." She glanced at Rose, calling up the formal words Rose had shared. "We offer our home, in exchange for your blood."

A smile crinkled his eyes, though his lips remained still. He darted a glance at Rose, knowing, no doubt, that she was the one who knew how to bind him and his people. He took the tip of that curved knife and dug it into the soft flesh at the base of his thumb. Blood ran free as he pulled it out, and he tilted his hand so the blood ran across his palm.

Rose reached down and lifted Lena's hand.

Ghost slid the tip of the blade across the same spot on her palm. It was a much smaller cut, but he and Rose both seemed satisfied.

It's a good thing Jackson didn't come. And Alex? What would he think?

Ghost took her hand in his, clasping it palm to palm as he said the words that joined their two worlds.

"One blood. One home. One family."

He turned back and raised their clasped hands up for the crowd peering into the dark at them. A soft cheer and clapping rose up, spiraling into the night.

When Ghost turned back, Lena flipped his hand around and bent over it, intent on healing the deeper wound. He tugged it away.

"This wound I'll keep. This is a good pain, to keep the other at bay this first night. Heal it tomorrow, Lena. Heal it tomorrow."

He gave her a lopsided smile that had both contentment for his people and the deal he'd struck and shades of the deep personal pain he carried now. He nodded at the crowd around the bonfire behind him.

"Come. The celebration will be muted because of what came before, but we can all use a little fiesta tonight before the hard work of building a new family tomorrow."

TWENTY-FIVE

Alex

Alex stretched both arms above his head, barely conscious. His eyes remained closed, and he drowsed, drifting halfway between sleep and awareness.

He slid one of his arms back down to drag the blanket across his chest. Before he could hike it up and roll over, he felt the soft, familiar caress of small fingers chasing along the edge of the blanket. His breath hitched in his throat.

Dream again. The thought was muzzy and half-formed.

He ran his fingers along the blanket's edge. There was no hand there. But he knew her touch. He could smell her—maple syrup sweet and southwestern spice. This was more than memory. It was a dream, perhaps, but it felt real. He sank into it easily…gratefully.

She rose above him again, straddling him at the waist. He slid his hands over her belly, enjoying a new softness there he didn't question. It was a part of the dream, a reflection of difficult discussions and secret longings. Above, her breasts had the same new fullness in his palms. He used his thumbs to trace a circular path to her darkened, peaked nipples. She shivered in response, and he couldn't wait to taste her anymore. He ran his hands up her to her face, cupped her cheeks, and his fingers tangled in her hair as he pulled her down to him.

She stared into his eyes, the haunting blue green of hers inches away. Before she could press her lips to his, he left a string of wet kisses across her nose and cheeks, adoring her freckles.

Her breath as she laughed whispered against his cheeks. It was real. This was real.

She was real.

Lena.

She claimed his lips, and he hungrily responded as sparks flared. Dust surged, flowing between them. He pulled her down, naked chest to naked chest, the energy swirling and pulsing. The contact, the sensation, was more than skin deep. Their connection flowed, renewing their bond.

It was electric, erotic heat slicking over his nerves at the surface, below the surface, deep inside. It was pure Lena. His need for her touch, for this renewal, was an ache that throbbed in his head and chest and dick.

He wasn't the only one feeling it. "I need you inside me." Her words were a husky, hungry gasp against his lips. "I need you deep." She slid to the side, freeing him of her legs, and pulled his arm so he'd roll to his side, facing her.

"Deep, Alex. Now." Urgency made her even more demanding.

It's the dream. Never enough time.

She pulled him up and raised her hips. She wanted him behind her. Alex gripped her hips and pulled her toward him.

"No." Her voice had become throaty. "Be still now. Let me. Let me."

She eased herself back onto him, painfully slow. It was exquisite. It was torture. His head fell back and his eyelids fluttered.

"I love you so much." His truth was a whisper from his soul to a dream. It made him shudder.

Her soft laugh was his answer. "I know."

Three hard raps on the door of his private room on the caravan car crashed through the room, discordant and final.

No!

Alex was still, only the sound of his own labored breath in his ears. Lena said nothing. He couldn't even hear her breath. He opened his eyes. Lena was gone.

The unwelcome knocks came again. The door opened.

"You're not up yet?" Ace peered around the door's edge. And blinked.

Alex was naked and alone, fully aroused, kneeling upright in the bed. His thighs trembled with the effort to keep himself still for her and his hands… His hands gripped air.

Fuck me.

"Hmm. I guess…you are up." Ace shook his head, his lips twitching with amusement.

Alex stared at him. Ace stared back, brows raised and laughter in his questioning eyes. Alex reached up to scrub his face and hair in frustration before he launched himself forward. He fell face down onto the pillow. Pain shot through him, and he flipped onto his back, grabbing for the blanket and pulling it up to his waist.

"Ungh!" The inarticulate cry was filled with longing and frustration. And it wasn't muted by the pillow.

"Sorry for the interruption." Ace tried for contrite, but his voice was still filled with that damned amusement. "We're ready to break camp. Thought you might want to do your spy thing. I was surprised you were still, uh, sleeping. In bed. Whatever."

Alex growled at the ceiling. Would the man not leave already?

"I'll be with you shortly." His response was an angry rasp.

"Yeah." Ace finally pulled back behind the door. Before he closed it, he added, "Take your time, man."

Alex blew out a long stream of air, trying in vain to call his Lena back to him as real as she had been moments before they were interrupted.

It never worked. It didn't this time, either. The feel of her, the smell of her, was gone. He was awake and alone again.

He reached down. It might not be as magical, but memory would suffice. He wasn't leaving without some relief. It wasn't like it would take all that long in the state he was in, anyway. Ace could damn well wait.

"That was fast." A large mug dwarfed by the larger dark hand holding it was settled in front of him. Alex raised his gaze to Ace's amused face.

"Really?" Alex heard the irritation in his answering question. "Are you going to bust my—?"

Ace laughed and dropped down beside him. "Nope. I understand. Life on the road. It's hard, man." He winced and snorted a quick laugh. "I didn't mean—"

"Uh huh." Alex lifted the mug to sip from it. Tea. He grimaced. "Dust, the only thing this has going for it is that it's hot. What happened to the coffee Sloan gifted us?"

"You drank it."

"All of it?" At Ace's bland smile, Alex grimaced again. "Not much of a gift."

Ace barked a laugh. "It was enough of a gift that I started to wonder what you'd done for the woman." His eyes narrowed playfully. "Got a better idea now…"

Alex shook his head, rolling his eyes.

"You've been on edge and guzzling that stuff non-stop." Ace was silent for a beat. "Seriously, what's going on?"

Alex closed his eyes and sighed. "Nothing… Missing home."

"Agents get homesick?"

Alex's lips curled grimly. "Not usually."

"It's that girl from the mountains." Ace held Alex's stare without blinking. "She reminded you of Lena. It's your subconscious telling you we should've intervened."

Alex gritted his teeth. He did not need this. "We've been through this. She's safe enough where she is in the middle of nowhere. It's not like a zone girl where she'd be discovered on the grounding platforms or through school."

"She's a child. She needed to be protected."

Alex sent Ace a cold look. "Like Lena's dad protected her?"

Ace looked at the wall across from them.

"Mm hmm." Alex took a gulp of the hot liquid, risking scalding his mouth. He settled the mug back on the table and pushed it away from himself. "We've been through this." He stood. "I'm going to make my circuit, and then we can head out. We'll make Macopany in what, two days?"

They'd entered Zone One's territory days before. Now they were closing in on the capital relo-city that housed most of its citizens.

Ace nodded. "Rain stopped chasing us north. If the roads stay dry, we'll make better time now."

"That's a good thing with temps dropping."

"For damn sure. I have no desire to get caught in Macopany by snow. And we definitely need to get you back to Lena."

Alex shook his head in answer to the gibe. He had a dim memory of the kind of snow Ace referred to. It had been bitterly cold the winter before he'd been given to the Council. The drifts had been almost as tall as his father.

But there'd been sledding. An echo of laughter only he could hear chased him out the door. It was the sound of a man and a woman cheering him on, and the sound of his own little-boy delight.

Alex shrugged his heavy coat up closer around his neck, as if the cold air made him shiver. It wasn't. It was the past, creeping closer with every mile he traveled toward Macopany. He'd been having dreams about them, almost as vivid as his Lena dreams.

His parents' voices were always muddied in the dreams. Their faces were always turned away from him. He danced around, trying to see them. It was important that he see their faces. When he woke, it was to frustration and grief. He knew why his dream self kept trying.

He'd long since forgotten what they looked like.

He hadn't thought it bothered him much. They were just people. They'd had him in their lives for a brief period of time, and then faded out of it. He was forty-nine years old. What weight could those first five years hold? His subconscious told him otherwise, and it was getting louder the closer he came to the place of his birth.

He hiked away from the main trailer and down the line. At the tail, he turned off and moved into the tree line, gaze scanning.

He told himself they were just dreams. They were no more real than the fevered dreams he had of Lena. Of course, those elicited an entirely different response. He grinned, and hopped across a wide muddy pit via a large, well-positioned rock.

He glanced down to be sure of the foothold right before his foot came down on the faint brown outline of a footprint already there.

Alex tapped the rock instead of bringing his full weight down and twisted his body so he came down to the side, splashing down in the mud. Ignoring the muck, he bent to examine the footprint, running his finger over the outline of it where his own boot hadn't contaminated it.

The mud was fresh. The sun, now peeking over the horizon, hadn't had a chance to dry it yet. And the print itself had been missed in the dark of pre-dawn, when whoever had left it had been skirting the caravan. He stepped free of the mud and made a slow circuit of the area, being careful to inspect every bit of it before he put his own muddy feet in an area. It took twenty or so minutes of moving in an ever-widening arc, but he found what he was looking for.

A bent stick.

A little further up, the low-hanging branch of an evergreen shrub was crushed.

He followed the little tells, backtracking when needed, then moving forward again, away from the caravan. A little more than a quarter mile out, he found the cold camp. No fire pit. Just an indented, beaten down area beneath a long, bare branch that had been bent low by a tarp and still hadn't fully recoiled.

He resumed the search. If they'd made camp here, and that mud was fresh, then they'd camped, checked the caravan, then withdrawn again to a distance safe enough to follow. This was no random camp of another weary traveler. The subtlety of the signs left behind agreed. Whoever was out here had been trained to be out here. He was on the trail of the mysterious brown-clothed young men.

Alex broke through a mass of vine-covered shrubs and stepped onto a long open area. The ground here was raised in odd humps and dips and covered in the brilliant colors of fall foliage dumped atop wilting vines. He stepped out, lifting his foot to step up onto one of the humps. His foot slid in the rotting vegetation along a harder surface beneath.

Alex reached beneath a knotted brown vine to the surface and scraped aside the thick growth. Dull, mud-coated metal hid beneath it. He raised his head to look up again at the odd humps and the long open space in the trees. It had been a road, once upon a time, packed with cars. Both the road and the cars were abandoned in the years after the cataclysm, forgotten like countess other back roads and the people who'd tried to escape on them. How many skeletons were buried under the rocks and soil of the surrounding countryside as people fled from the road on foot?

A slithering, scraping sound had Alex's attention snapping ahead of him. It was followed by a hollow, metallic ping. Someone had slipped. He crept along, moving carefully through the thick growth on the sides of the road. His gaze raked across the undulating vegetation. Someone else was here, hiding.

About fifteen feet up, he hopped onto the rear of a low car and then onto its roof for a better view. The moment he did, the man hiding between two cars another thirty feet away leapt up and sprang across the road, using the rear and front end of two cars to propel him across. He disappeared into the forest on the other side.

Alex was right behind him. They both dodged through the undergrowth, crashing through thick fallen leaves and dried vines. The man ahead of Alex was small and quick, but Alex was a born runner. Long and lean with legs that ate up the ground in front of him, he had both the reach of his limbs and endurance in his favor. As soon as the rabbit he chased started to tire, Alex would have him. It seemed the rabbit knew it, too. He glanced back and blanched at the closeness of Alex's features.

Someone's sending kids out to play at spy. The rabbit wasn't just small. He was young.

He ducked under a low branch now. His feet slid in the detritus of the forest floor. He changed directions.

A moment later, Alex was under the branch, too. He saw the little rabbit's goal—the road had curved and was ahead again. Rabbit seemed to think he'd be able to outrun Alex on the weirdly undulating surface. He was wrong. Alex changed course, too. He followed, but planned to come out at a slight angle ahead.

When he broke through the tree line, the kid was gone. Alex slid to a stop. His breathing echoed in his ears. He looked up and down. To all appearances, the road was empty. But back along the curve, a flock of birds whirled up into the sky and then curved back, spreading low and retaking positions in the trees alongside a large, long vehicle.

Alex smiled. Scared from their hiding places, the birds returned to a position as close as they dared. Alex jogged along the tree line where the ground was less treacherous. He approached the big vehicle, noting the paint long faded to a haze of what might be yellow with darker smears along the side. It had been ditched, or crashed, to the side of the other vehicles. It still teetered at a slight angle, held up by branches grown through the long-broken glass of the windows.

A faint aroma of musk and waste reached Alex. He frowned, considering whether or not his rabbit would have been foolish enough to seek shelter in an animal's den. Had the kid noticed the signs?

Alex crouched before he reached the bus. He tilted his head and ran his gaze along the bottom of the bus. Smart rabbit.

Smartish, anyway.

A portion of the dried foliage had been crushed as he slid underneath from the opposite side. He hadn't gone into the animal's lair. But trying to hide from Alex beneath the bus—beneath the den itself—was only marginally smarter. He'd have been better off if he'd kept running.

He was certain it was a bear's den. Days were still warm enough that the occupant was probably out foraging. Still, when he called out to the kid, he kept this voice low.

"Here's how this is going to go down, kid. I'm going to go back to the big tree over there and climb it to keep a watch over you. One of two things is going to happen today. Either the bear that lives here is going to come back from looking for things to fatten himself for the winter, smell you invading his home turf, and drag your sorry ass out for me. If there's anything left after he's had his way with you, I'm going to check it out and get some information. Or you're going to try to wait me out. My friends from the caravan will come looking for me, and I'll have them bring me something nice and warm to wait you out. When the temps drop tonight, you're going to become hypothermic. You'll crawl out, and I'll drag you away and have my way with you—informationally speaking, that is. It's me or the bear, kid. If you come out now, the odds of you surviving today are much better."

It was bullshit, of course. Even this long after the Cataclysm, the only bears with any real presence in this area of the country were black bears, and they weren't generally aggressive. They weren't aggressive enough that Alex could rely on one dragging his rabbit from its hole. But Alex was betting on someone the kid's age not knowing that. He was a city kid and not Neo-Barb stock. A Neo-Barb never would have risked sliding in under that vehicle. But then, a Neo-Barb wouldn't have slipped up with the footprint back at the rock, either.

Alex waited for a moment, then rose and walked away back to the tree. Before he even got there, though, he could hear the rustling behind him. The kid wormed his way out. Alex expected him to bolt. He didn't. He didn't head over to join Alex, either. He sat there, his back tight against the bottom of the bus. His eyes were closed. His lips moved silently. His hands were fisted at his sides.

What the Dust did the kid expect to happen now? Alex squinted at him. He glanced around, wondering if there were others out there the kid awaited.

He froze. He'd been right about the bear coming back. It had paused on the other side of the road. Its head swung back and forth. Its sensitive nose flared, taking in their scents.

It might be true that most black bears weren't aggressive. But it was a bad idea to crowd one anyway. Invading its home turf and then hanging out there? A really bad idea.

Shit.

"Kid. The bear came home." Alex kept his voice as low and non-threatening as he could. He eased his feet back, one at a time, backing away. If they could move diagonally, they had a chance of escape without the bear deciding they were a threat.

The kid's eyes popped open. He raised himself up to peer over the front of the vehicle. Once he'd seen the bear, he turned back to Alex.

Alex flipped his fingers at the kid, telling him to come over. "Slowly. To me."

The kid glanced around, his gaze moving up to the treetops of the area around them. When he looked back at Alex, he swallowed and nodded.

Alex waited while he eased over. Once the kid had made it over, Alex took another step back and to the side. "Follow my lead. We'll talk when we make it out. Got it?"

The kid shifted his weight to follow Alex to the side. His head lifted back in the start of a nod. Then it disappeared in a warm red mist that spattered across Alex and everything around him. The crack of the shot fired echoed from the treetops.

Alex dropped. The bear darted back, smelled the blood, and charged. Alex scrambled up then. Up or down, he was in mortal danger. He pulled his own gun out and raised his arms, squaring his shoulders as the bear made it across the road and gathered itself for the final leap. Alex fired a moment behind whoever had shot the kid. He saw both bullets impact. A third one, from the same angle high in the woods, took the bear down. It dropped and slid through the blood and leaves, its momentum carrying it almost to Alex.

Alex waited. There was nothing. If they were going to take another shot, now would be the time. Keeping his gun up and ready, he stepped around the bear. The kid had looked up at the treetops, the same angle from which the shot had come. Alex scanned the tops now, but the mix of evergreens and bare deciduous trees showed him nothing. Alex stepped back and knelt beside the kid.

He made a quick one-handed search. Of course, there was nothing he could use to identify him. He had looked like he was around twenty years old, give or take a few. Too young to end up with his life's blood pouring out his neck onto the forest floor.

Alex focused on the image of the kid after he'd slid out, as he leaned against the metal hulk. He'd been waiting for something to happen. He'd known he'd failed and had expected to die. They hadn't been aiming for Alex and missed. They'd killed the kid to keep him from talking. They'd killed the bear to keep Alex alive.

Who were they? The gunshot told him at least some of them were Sparks. What did they want? Alex stood up and made a last check, looking for birds, waving treetops, anything. But the forest and the mountains beyond it were silent now. It kept its secrets.

Alex looked back down at the body of the young man who'd been tracking him. Now he'd keep his secrets, too.

"What a waste." Alex turned and headed back. His skin crawled as he did. They were out there, they were Sparks, and they were highly trained. But by whom? And what role did they play in the grand picture he was piecing together? He didn't have the answer.

The day was seriously pissing him off.

TWENTY-SIX

Lena

She tugged the blanket higher to cover her shoulders and curled onto her side. It was still grey outside, the twilight time when dawn was starting to be seen outside their little valley but would take a little longer to get to them. She'd been dozing off and on. She'd slip into sleep, and then some new concern would pop into her mind, and she'd wake to worry at it like a stone.

Building a new village—and blending the family units into one—was easier than she'd anticipated. They'd finished the repairs to the big rancho house already, and it was the center of their blended village and the school. She, Rose, and Jackson stayed with the children in the house full time. Within a week of finishing it, the smaller out buildings had been repaired and re-purposed and several other buildings were in various stages of being built.

However, their long-overdue first Fort Nevada supplies had not arrived. Lena anticipated that despite the silence of the last ten days, they had not heard the last from Damar. And she worried over making sure the shelters going up were adequate to keep her larger, new family warm through the winter. Because even though the little valley made its own micro-climate, winter was coming.

With the weather turning soon, she'd thought to contact the Native Nations people a few days to the north by horseback. Surely she could trade her services as a Spark for some wool, perhaps even some blankets? The tribe refused to deal with outsiders. They'd had their fill of broken promises and violence at the hands of the Neo-barbs that held old Taos to the southwest near the Rio Grande Gorge and their Scavenger allies.

Lena had never heard of a Neo-Barb tribe doing business with Scavengers. Were the Scavs their unseen watchers, those she knew were there but hadn't been able to find, even with the Dust? Had she brought the girls into an area where there was a risk of attack and they'd be, at best, returned to the Council?

She flipped onto her back and breathed deep to try to calm her pounding heart. Perhaps Thomas and Alex had been right? Perhaps the danger she knew, and could guard against, was better than the danger she didn't.

The thought of Alex caused her chest to constrict with a physical pain. She missed bouncing ideas off of him. She missed butting heads with him. She missed his mind that never stopped working and that complemented hers so well. She missed his touch.

She wanted another dream visit with him. She'd never been a vivid dreamer, but the series of dreams she'd been having were beyond vivid. They were real.

She could feel his skin, the spark of current moving between them, his shiver as she touched him and demanded he touch her. She could smell his unique fine tequila and sex scent.

Lena swallowed. The one yesterday morning had been the most real yet. She could taste him. She'd needed him inside her so badly—missed the feel of him and the Dust working together to drive her wild—that she'd taken charge.

When she'd looked over her shoulder to watch the play of pleasure and emotion rippling over his face while she'd slid onto him with delicious, langorous slowness, he was gone. One moment she'd run her gaze down the long line of him, admiring the way his torso flexed as he controlled himself, the way their bodies fit, and the sound of his choked, "I love you so much."

The next she was awake in her bed, on all fours, gasping with need. His sudden absence crashed over her. Her need for him was a hot ache.

With a mumbled curse, she sat up and flung the blanket off. The chill in the air woke her more. There was no point in staying in bed now. Once she reached the I-miss-Alex portion of each morning's misery, there'd be no more sleep for her anyway. She'd either end up with her hand between her legs, trying not to wake the rest of the house, or with her face in the pillow wet with frustrated tears she'd have died before she let anyone else see. It was best to get up and get on with it.

She left her room, rubbing her arms, and stopped to listen to the silence of the pre-dawn morning. Lena tilted her head in the direction of Rose's small room and waited for any sound of distress. She turned to face the two doors across the hall to the rooms that held the bunks of the girls. There was no sobbing, no cries in the dark, no whispers of reassurance from one to another. Her relieved breath hissed out between her teeth.

She stepped lightly on the stairs and went to the fireplaces in the common area and the kitchen to pile on more wood and re-Spark the glowing embers. At least she could get the area warm for the girls before they came down for breakfast.

Lena crossed her arms against the chill in the air and urged the Dust to increase the temperature of the fire. It burned higher and hotter. She leaned down to pull out the wide, flat pan they'd brought up from the bunker. Perhaps she'd start breakfast before Gabriela and the women and men who alternated helping with breakfast came into the kitchen and filled it with bustle and voices. It seemed they'd all had a good night's sleep. Well-rested children meant hungry children. Hungry children, she'd discovered, were loud and demanding.

The front door slammed open, and running feet crossed the entry and headed up the stairs. Lena frowned and left the kitchen for the entry, ready to head up to see who'd galloped up the stairs.

"Lena?" It was Ghost's low voice.

A gasp of frustration sounded from upstairs and then rapid footsteps moved down the hall to Jackson's room. Ghost didn't bother to knock. The door opened. An alarmed voice and a sleepy voice conferred in low mutters.

A moment later, Jackson was in the hall upstairs. "What do you mean she's not in her bed?"

"I checked and she—"

"She's down here." Lena called up.

The two men appeared at the top of the stairs.

"And if you could please *not* wake everyone early, I'd appreciate it." She gestured them down.

Ghost was already halfway to her. "We have a problem." His face was grim. "One of the watch woke me. Your delayed supplies are coming up the track. They'll be in the valley soon—men with a wagon and a small group of boys?"

Jackson grunted his assent.

Lena nodded. "Why is that a problem?"

"*Cuantos*? How many men were you expecting?"

"Two." Jackson answered for her. "With ten boys. And that's all they needed, believe me. Did something happen to them along the way?"

"Something must have," Ghost answered, heading out the door.

Lena shoved her feet into her boots crumpled in the large pile by the front door and joined him and Jackson. She shook her head to clear it of the Dust's trilling alert, now going off in her head. "What do you mean?"

"Your two men and handful of boys—not ten—are being escorted by People that we don't know. Damar is with them."

Lena hurried to match Ghost's long stride. A young man waited for them in the pre-dawn dark. Beside him, still a shape in the darkness but for her voice giving low orders to three people who melted away to wake others, Gabriela turned to them. Her face was dark and closed, and her hand was on a young woman's shoulder.

"Lena, is it all right if I send Patsy to wake Rose and the others? If Damar is returning, it is with very bad intent." She gave a look simmering with frustration to Ghost. Had she wanted Ghost to kill his brother? "You'll put your children below ground in the bunker?"

Lena nodded. "Get all of the children down there. There are still supplies below they can eat."

Gabriela flashed her a grateful half-smile and nodded. She whispered an order to the young woman before giving her a soft push toward the rancho house. Gabriela nodded at the rest of them.

"I've got to gather our own little ones. There aren't many of them—"

"Get all of them below. And then—" Lena glanced between Gabriela and Ghost. She had no idea what their standard plan was in the event of attack. She knew only that while Ghost was very much the leader of their group, Gabriela had as much power and voice as he did. "Can you help Rose with them?"

Gabriela shook her head. "My place is up here. But I will send two of our young men and women down."

Ghost didn't wait. He turned and loped toward the opening to the long narrow route down via the orchard. Lena and Jackson followed. Lena didn't look back, but she had no doubt that as they wakened, Ghost's men and women were joining them, as well. Everyone had a role.

Before they reached the mouth of the narrowest portion of the valley, Lena could see several of Ghost's men and women hunker down, setting themselves defensively.

She grabbed Ghost's arm when the Dust alerted her again. "They've entered the valley below."

Ghost cursed. "They come too fast. Damar will have told them how to enter and about our defenses."

"Will he have told them about Lena and the girls?"

Ghost turned to give Jackson a long look over his shoulder. He opened his mouth to answer, then shook his head. "I don't know. I don't want to assume—"

"I do. And I assume so." Lena interrupted. "He blames me. Of course he told them. That's why they've come."

"We don't know that. They could have just found the re-supply. He may be here to barter for position or to demand a chance to fight for the People again. It may not be a full tribe he's found, but another group of Lone rejects. We can't assume anything."

They arrived at the mouth of the path. The sunlight penetrated the valley finally. Below her, she could see them coming. There were no more than a handful of them surrounding the wagon. Six boys rode atop a mound of supplies.

What happened to the rest of the boys? Four were missing. Lena shifted her gaze to the two agents sitting in the open wagon. Patrick drove and Theo stared sullenly ahead. They were both haggard from lack of sleep and, unless she missed her guess, mistreatment. Both men were collared. Where did Neo-barbs get Spark restraint collars?

The Scavs.

Theo dropped his hand between his legs and flashed his fingers. Five. Three. Three. Lena flicked a glance at the men surrounding them, walking up beside the wagon. There were five of them, including Damar. Were there two more groups of three men somewhere above or behind them? Lena turned to Jackson. He looked up, already tracking along the cliffs above.

"We have people up there," Ghost breathed to them. He'd seen it, too. "If there are others above, they'll be dealt with."

"But won't Damar know you'd have stationed people up there to watch?"

Ghost shrugged at her, a slight movement. "It won't matter. My people are still angry."

The horses pulling the wagon didn't fight when Patrick slowed them on a shouted order from a man on the left.

"It begins." Ghost waited for Lena to join him. They walked together, Jackson a step behind. Ghost's people closed the gap, sealing the valley behind them.

"You're late," Lena said to Patrick as he and the Neo-barb to his left approached. She ignored the other man. "What took so long? And who are your guests?"

The Neo-Barb snorted.

Patrick waited a moment, as if making certain he was permitted to explain. The Neo-Barb waved his hand, indicating the agent should get on with it.

"We were delayed out of Azcon. Shortly after crossing the Rio Grande below the gorge, our attention occupied by something behind us…" His story trailed off and the disgust in his voice was clear.

Lena turned her gaze on the Neo-Barb. “Are you in the habit of ambushing and stealing from travelers?”

“We’re in the habit of surviving.”

Lena knew from the man’s hardening face her disgust was mirrored in her expression. Before she could speak again, Ghost broke in.

“What do you want?”

The Neo-Barb smiled. “A man who comes right to the point. I like that. Maybe you should do it more often, instead of allowing your women to waste my time.”

Lena bit the inside of her cheek to keep from snapping back at the man.

“We didn’t ambush them. We had the right to know why armed men were in our territory. Imagine our surprise when we found enough supplies to feed an entire village. A new village.” His stare strafed up the valley behind her, lingering on the entrance blocked by bodies. “One that exists without our knowledge or permission.”

“You have my former brother with you.” Ghost didn’t bother looking at Damar. His voice was even and steady, as were his eyes. “He’d have told you this valley and the rancho in it belonged to my people. It has for generations.”

“You were nomads. You gave up the claim.”

“We ceded it to another. Now we all use it, as is our right.”

“It’s our right to make sure these lands stay safe. We don’t want Council men and their whelps parading around. Someone could get hurt.”

The Neo-Barb smiled when he said the words. Instead of looking at Patrick, he leered at Jackson, who refused to rise to the bait.

Lena had been surreptitiously examining the collar on Patrick. It was exactly like the ones she’d removed from the girls, like the one that had been snapped on her own neck briefly. Council made. Council supplied?

“You’re here now, as are the supplies and the boys…but not all of them. Why?”

The Neo-Barb shrugged and smiled, spreading his hands wide in a gesture of magnanimous innocence. “When the boys explained what the men would not—they’re establishing a branch of the Ward School right here in our mountains—well, I knew I couldn’t stand in the way of that progress without attracting the Council’s attention.” He shrugged, and his gaze fell on Lena again, piercing and evaluating. “But when we made our way north, escorting these fine men and boys to their destination, we met your brother.” The Neo-Barb paused, his face filled with put-on wonder and shock and betrayal. “He explained to us what kind of school was really operating up here and, well, with the alerts and messages sent out by the Council, the real Council, mind you, not whoever you all are, I realized the true situation. And how well it could serve both of us.”

Of course the Council is sending out alerts. That threat hasn’t lessened because you’ve been focused on the Ward School traitors.

“And how is that?” Jackson finally spoke, his voice skeptical.

“Well, you all want to run an illegal school to train girl Sparks to be spies and what-not like they do the boys over at Ward School. And we want to live a little more comfortable and with a little less worry about where our meals are coming from.” The man smiled again, but there was no warmth or friendliness in the expression. “We’re not inhuman. We know winter is coming and you’re counting on these supplies, but you moved into our territory without our permission. We’re stronger than a ragtag group of Neo-Barbs and a handful of little boys and girls. Prior claim on the land. Prior claim on the supplies. We claim half as tribute. We kept some of your boys to keep you honest.”

Ghost opened his mouth to protest, but Lena was done with playing cooperative little woman. “You collared these men because…?”

He smiled, showing his yellowed teeth. “Because you might need an example of what’ll happen if you don’t accept our terms.”

“We don’t. We’ll be coming for the supplies and the boys.”

The Neo-Barb’s gaze flicked between Lena and Ghost, as if trying to figure out who she was and why she was being permitted to intervene. He was annoyed, but a wide, condescending smile spread across his face.

"Well, then, how do you expect to keep us from rounding up all of you and putting collars on the Sparks? How are you gonna pay us?" He lowered his stare down her body.

She met his leer with a smirk of her own. "With your lives."

Beside her, Jackson sighed. From the corner of her eye, Ghost's head turned toward her. His face wasn't happy. How had they expected this to go?

But in front of her, Patrick's eyes glinted. He'd had one taste of her abilities. After his time with the Neo-Barbs, he was obviously ready to see more. She was glad someone agreed with her methods.

"Our lives?" The Neo-Barb sputtered with laughter.

"Yes." Lena stepped forward as she spoke, and casually reached up to Patrick's neck. She slid her fingers beneath the metal and the Dust separated it. "We'll allow you to leave with them. We'll allow you time to go back, gather *our* goods and boys, and give you enough independence that we won't require payment from you…contingent on your cooperation, of course."

Patrick pulled the collar from his neck. Lena took it and asked the Dust to compress it down. When she tossed it to the Neo-barb, it was a misshapen, dull ball that bounced off his chest and fell heavily in the dirt between them.

He stopped laughing. He also stopped flicking glances at the men. All of his attention was focused on Lena. He paled, then flushed almost purple. "How about this—" He snarled the words, but he backed away from her. "How about I let my Scavenger friends know there is a whole mess of powered girls with a heavy bounty on their heads hiding up here? I can feed my people for a long time with what they pay. You want to make this hard? Fine. We'll make it hard."

He turned back to his people with a shrill whistle.

"Don't forget," Lena called out to him. "We expect the other half of our goods and the boys. You harm any of them and you'll answer for it. Why don't you ask Damar's fingerless friend what that'll feel like? *We* don't tolerate dishonor."

She watched his shoulders jerk and tighten in response. *Good.* Patrick's gaze was speculative as he examined Lena and her calm. Jackson hissed his displeasure, and Ghost rounded on her, eyes ablaze.

"You have no idea what you've done."

"I know exactly what I'm doing."

Ghost breathed hard. His hands fisted at his sides. "My people do not need to relive Texas."

She opened her mouth to respond with equal heat, but she closed it again. She had no idea what happened in Texas, but it was clear that it had been terrible—and Ghost was still dealing with the repercussions of it in the loss of his brother. Perhaps that had even re-opened the psychic wound.

"Ghost." She said his name softly, intending to soothe.

He shook his head. He wouldn't be appeased.

"Listen. Let me explain. There's no need for our children to go hungry—"

"They wouldn't go hungry," Jackson interrupted. "We're capable of supplementing with hunting and foraging. We've done well so far. We've managed. The last thing we need is a fight."

"You'd let these asses get away with this? What's coming will hardly be classified as a fight—"

"What's coming—" It was Ghost's turn to interrupt. It was getting old. "—will be a rout. Scavengers plus a whole, healthy group of People, supplemented by five of my own warriors who know our weaknesses. Against what? Some girls and my people, tired and—"

"Those girls are more than capable of defending all of us. Maybe if you'd shut up and listen, you'd realize why I did what I did." She swept her gaze over all of them, including Patrick, who was still giving her that evaluating stare. He wore a small smile now.

Lena turned to look back down the valley. The outsiders were still walking out, though they'd turned to watch over their shoulders as the men had exploded. Lena shook her head in disgust. Jackson and Ghost better not have undone what she'd achieved.

"We'll finish this discussion back at the rancho, in privacy." She gave them withering looks. "And this time, you'll listen to me with the same degree of respect you'd give one of you if you had my abilities. No more interrupting!"

She stalked over to the wagon, gesturing Theo down with an imperious wave. She removed his collar and crumpled it into a metal ball that she tossed beside the other one as she marched back up the path. As she passed the men, she added for Patrick, "Please bring the boys up so we can get them settled. I'll want to hear what happened in detail from you and Theo."

He nodded, the one among them who'd kept his temper.

Lena marched herself back up to the rancho, fuming. She couldn't believe the men had been so prepared to cave to the demands of the interlopers—they'd kidnapped wards, for Dust's sake! She didn't care if they were boys or girls, no one would mistreat children while she drew breath to stop it. And she was damned certain that no one would be mistreating Spark children.

When she reached the wide, flat meadow that spread out away from the narrow path, she ran into Gabriela, who'd been heading down.

The woman's eyes widened. "Already? Or did they send you back? Is there fighting?"

"Send me back?" Lena stopped and regarded the woman with a tilted head. "What is it about me that makes people forget what I am capable of?"

Gabriela stared at her. Before she answered, her gaze flickered over Lena's shoulder. No doubt she saw the men and the wagon approaching now.

Lena didn't wait for an answer. She didn't trust herself to not show her disgust with them all. Instead, she looked at the men who'd opened up to allow her through. "Pick several men and send them after those Neo-Barbs. Make sure they leave and keep an eye out for two more groups of three to rejoin them at some point. Figure out where they've come from so we can watch for more of them."

The men nodded. One of them turned to the others to give quiet orders.

At least they listened to her.

Once at the rancho, she dragged a new wooden stool over to the fire so she could warm back up, then perched on it to focus. Letting her breath out in a long, slow exhale, she reached out to search for the feel of the Dust in Rose. She wasn't quite sure what she was doing, but she narrowed her thoughts to Rose.

"Come on up. It's safe."

Lena felt a surge of startled emotion that washed into amusement. She got the dim sense of a response…*"On our way"*…and then lost the tenuous connection.

She blinked and sagged down. Her heart thumped in her chest.

Rose was right. It had worked. Could it work with Alex?

Before she could put it to the test, the men scuffed their way into the rancho. They came in silence and took up places around the room. Ghost took the other half of the pair of stools, sitting over by the opposite wall. Jackson leaned up against the wall by the wide entrance to the room off the main hall. Patrick entered, followed by Theo and six tired, haggard boys.

Lena stood and offered the boys a smile. "Would you rather have breakfast first, or a bed and then breakfast?"

The boys were dazed and cast looks at each other and then her.

"Beds, I think," Theo offered. "They've had to keep awake all night balanced on that wagon because those bastards were determined to make it here at dawn. They had minimal time to rest from a day of hard travel before we packed up again and moved on last night."

Lena nodded agreement, though she felt her lips tighten at the news. "Up the stairs to the left. There are three larger rooms with what bunks we managed. The room with five sets is for the boys. They're clean and ready to go. The facilities are outside, though, if any of you need them." She pointed in the direction they'd need to turn to find the outhouses.

Several boys nodded.

"The rest of you go on up. I'll take you guys out," Theo said.

"I'll take them up," Patrick offered. He nodded at Lena. "I'll be back down to give my report."

"Thank you." She waited for the room to clear again. Soon, it was Jackson and Ghost in the room with her. The former stared at the floor. The latter kept his stare on the flames in the fireplace beside her.

Lena rolled her eyes. She waited for Patrick to return before saying anything, content to allow the silence, and the anticipation, to grow.

A few moments later, Patrick returned. He eased into the room, his gaze making a circuit of them.

"I take it I didn't miss anything?"

Lena shook her head, amused. "Is everyone ready?"

Three gazes of varying degrees of defensiveness met her own.

"So," she began, "all of you thought that I unnecessarily antagonized him and put everyone in danger. Jackson thinks we can make do without the supplies, and Ghost is unwilling to subject his people to risk of more violence. Is that about it?" She waited for their slow nods. "Patrick, did you have anything to add to that?"

He shook his head and shrugged. "I could give a damn about the supplies, though I understand you all need them. But I *am* getting those boys back alive."

"How did they take you all in the first place?" Jackson asked. He shot Lena a look. "Assuming I'm allowed to ask a question?"

"There's a difference between asking a question and talking over someone," she told him tartly. "Patrick?"

He glanced at Jackson, acknowledging that it was his question but returning his focus to Lena.

"We were delayed out of Azcon, like I said. We were being followed. We took time to go south, trying to lose them. Neither of us ever got a chance to see who, or even how many there were, but they were agents. They were using the same methods and techniques. We thought we'd lost them, turned north, then figured out they were still with us. We decided to ambush them. We'd gotten the wagon and the boys tucked away in an arroyo beneath an overhang of mesquite. We were heading back to our choke point, where whoever it was would have to come through, when we heard the commotion behind us. The Neo-Barbs took the boys. When we got back—there were almost twenty of them to our two. No firearms, but armed to the teeth, and they had the boys. There was no choice but to surrender and wait for an opportunity."

"But it never came. They had collars." It wasn't a question, and Lena made sure her words were voiced in a neutral tone. Was that why she'd seen such odd energy when she'd examined Taos through the Dust sight? The collars disrupted the Dust in a Spark to the point that they were harder to see?

He nodded. "We fought the minute they pulled them out, but at that point… They separated us and broke the boys into groups. We expected what came next—the questions, the beatings. We had no way to know what was happening with the boys. By the time they piled us up back on the wagon and we realized one of the boys had broken, they'd separated out the oldest."

He paused, remembering.

"Do you have any idea why they'd keep those boys? Are you certain they're still alive?" Ghost's voice was sympathetic but implacable.

Of course he'd want to be sure there were boys to go back for.

Patrick nodded. "They were alive when we left. I saw them. They kept our firearms. I assume they kept the oldest boys because they've started weapons training. There was a Spark there, not a Neo-Barb, and he was strong enough to have been an agent at one point. I think he's a Scav."

Jackson gasped and recoiled in shock. Neither Ghost nor Lena reacted. Neither was surprised. They'd already encountered such a possibility, together, six years before.

"They don't want the boys to control us, they want them for their own purposes." Lena was certain of that.

"We have to get them back."

Jackson's soft comment drew a snort of scorn from Patrick. "As if that was ever in doubt."

"It wasn't." Lena assured him.

"You still didn't have to antagonize them into attacking us

here. You didn't have to push him into drawing in Scavengers. We'll be fighting two enemies instead of one." Ghost wasn't ready to let go of his indignation.

"The Scavs were already involved. I knew it the moment he mentioned the girls, and Sparks, and the Council. He had too much information—more than Damar could have given him." She held Ghost's angry stare. "There was a reason I antagonized him. I pushed him deliberately, Ghost. They had men in reserve. There's no reason he couldn't have attacked. Except for fear. He wants the sure thing—like the opportunity to control a situation because he controls innocents. Like the opportunity to send in others to do his dirty work."

Patrick nodded in agreement. "And that last taunt you threw at his back—you called him a coward. He didn't come back. He didn't respond."

"Because he already planned to have his revenge," Jackson sighed. "He knew he didn't have to do anything today."

"The Scavs are coming. That was never in doubt. His plan was to return these boys and half the supplies to throw us off, then send in the Scavs to clean it all up. Dust, the half they brought back may be payment for them when they come. But we'll be ready. We control the fight here with weapons they can't even imagine."

"They'll be anticipating our defense." Ghost was thinking out loud now, working through it all. "Damar will tell them our methods. We'll change them up."

"The real action will be going on at a level they can't see. The Dust will be acting in our favor." She smiled grimly. "So we need to go over everything your brother might tell them to expect."

Ghost nodded. A slow light grew in his eyes. "You'll need a defensive contingent around you to keep you safe from stray bullets."

Lena laughed, but winced in memory of their shared battle against Scavs almost a decade before. Yeah. Being shot wasn't fun. It added the possibility of things going awry. "Keep them off Rose and me, and it'll be fine."

"Rose and you?" A sharp voice came from the hall. Rose and Phoebe came around the corner. "What about me?" Phoebe demanded. "I can fight."

Behind her, Marin hovered, eyes wide. "Who are we fighting?" She sought out Jackson, face pale. Her voice was high and thin. "Did they find us?"

Hania peeked around the corner. Lena could only see half of her face and one eye, both nearly hidden by the fall of thick black hair.

Lena closed her eyes. When she opened them again, she shook her head at Rose.

"You said come up," the other woman answered. "You didn't say alone."

Lena strafed a glance over the faces of frightened girls. "They haven't found us. The boys from the Ward School have arrived. Someone decided to hurt *them*, and now it's our turn to be protectors." It wasn't a lie. She met Phoebe's eyes and the darkness in them was more than brown iris and wide pupil. "But this fight is for the adults."

"Why?" Phoebe's posture was part of her demand. She wanted answers. She wanted to participate. "I'm seventeen—practically an adult. I can do it. I won't lose control. I want to be a warrior."

"Marin," Rose murmured, "could you and Phoebe please take the girls and Leo out to ask what you can do to help the People outside?"

"That's an excellent idea." Ghost's rumble was calmer now. "I'll join you and check with Gabriela to see what reports have come in from our people watching above."

"No!" Phoebe brushed off Rose's request and stepped into the room. "I've heard you fighting with Jackson because you want to teach us to fight. You want us to be able to fight. So why not now?"

Lena exchanged an uncomfortable look with Jackson. He raised his brows at her.

Why not now? Why was she so uncomfortable with the idea? She'd fought and fought for this. She wanted them to learn to fight. Phoebe had the aptitude.

"I'm not saying we're not." She made her voice hard. "I'm saying the adults have to figure things out, and once we've done that, we'll have a discussion about what your role will be. You want to prove you're ready to fight? Do as you're told. Warriors follow orders."

Phoebe searched Lena's face for signs of a lie before dropping her gaze and nodding.

"Come on, Phoeb." Marin tugged at her friend's hand.

Phoebe stepped back and away, and the two older girls led the smaller children away.

Lena let out the pent up breath. "Why can nothing be easy?" she asked no one.

Patrick laughed. "Because then people like us would lose our minds." He grinned. "And I've spent all of two days total in your presence, and I can tell you, you losing it would be a very bad thing for the rest of us."

Ghost dipped his head, but she could see a slow smile spreading across his face.

"Okay," she said dryly. "Laugh. See if I care."

At that, they did. Even Jackson's grim face lightened.

"I do need to check on reports from above," Ghost told her.

Lena nodded. "And Patrick needs rest." She gave him an apologetic grimace. "Though it'll have to be brief. They won't be back today, but our preparation needs to begin yesterday."

"I'm used to operating on power naps. I'll update Theo, then we'll join you all—?"

"For lunch," Lena decided.

Patrick gave her a jaunty salute, and he and Ghost left the room. Jackson didn't budge from his position over on the far wall. Rose crossed the room to join Lena in front of the fire.

"I take it all went well?" Her voice was light and joking.

Lena groaned.

"You wanted a school away from everyone. And that means away from help." Jackson's gibe was soft, but it was still a gibe.

"I thought that's what you were doing here? So help."

"Being the voice of reason is helping. We already had this

discussion, remember?"

She looked away, shaking her head. Rose saved her from having to respond by leaning into Lena and nudging her.

"You need to catch me up."

Lena leaned back into her friend, accepting the support, and explained what had happened below. She tried to frame the indignation of Jackson and Ghost in neutral terms. When she was done, Rose had a thoughtful look on her face.

Lena scrubbed at her own with her hands and groaned, "What am I going to do about Phoebe?"

Rose grinned. "You're going to train her, crazy woman. Just like you—like *we*—planned before we even came out here."

Lena lowered her hands and stared at Rose. "I know. But what will it do to her?"

"Does it matter?" Jackson asked.

She looked at him. "Of course it matters. You've *seen* why it matters." She paused, collecting her thoughts. When she continued, she spoke slowly, feeling her way through expressing what had changed for her. "I am what I am. That doesn't mean she should be the same. I want her to have the freedom to be what she wants, but I guess I'm afraid of her choice." Lena leaned away from Rose's support, bowing forward with her back rounded. "I'm afraid for her. I keep seeing her face after she responded to a threat without thinking."

"You don't have the right to agonize over this." Jackson waited until she looked up at him, shocked that he was the one advising her to forget the horror, before he continued. "I've spent a lot of time thinking. You were right to tell me I had no business trying to change who you are. You need to take your own advice." He sighed. "I've focused on training Phoebe over the last week. I thought—maybe if I could help her learn to heal better… Except that's not where her aptitude lies. She's not a healer. Marin is. Hania is. Marissa is, too. Phoebe is a fighter. If you refuse to train her, you'll be doing to her what I tried to do to you. We all know how that turned out." His lips quirked up slightly, as if he was trying to find amusement.

Rose nodded so hard her shoulders rocked. "I agree."

Lena took a breath. “Yeah, but....” She lifted her head again, but this time she focused her gaze on Rose. She’d need her friend’s honest reaction to deal with this concern. “We all know how deep and dark I can be, and I don’t have half the pain Phoebe has to avenge. What if I train her, and I make it okay for her to dip into that well, and she doesn’t come back up?”

Rose’s eyes were the dark, deep blue of a lake reflecting a sky about to rain—nearly black with pain. “Then she doesn’t come back,” she whispered. “But that’s her path to take.”

Lena shook her head. “I can’t do that to her. It’s one thing for me. But not knowing where she’ll land?” She looked toward Jackson for help.

His brows were high, but he gave them nothing else.

“Oh—now the voice of reason is silent?” Lena’s tart words made them all smile, but the basic dilemma was still there.

“It’s not always about revenge, Lena.” Rose took her hand. “You obsess about what happened to us, because that’s who you are. But it’s not always about *them* or what they did to us. Sometimes it’s just about us. It’s what *she* needs. Training her native talents doesn’t mean she’s going to go out in the world to hunt them all down and lose her way. Think about it. Why are we here?”

“We’re carving out a safe space so the girls can be what they need to be.” She stopped. After a moment, she swallowed. “And then protecting it and them.”

Rose smiled. “Well, there you have it. Will you deny one of them the chance to be what she needs to be, just because she’s suited to do the same?”

Lena shook her head. “I can’t.”

“Exactly,” Jackson said. He crossed his arms over his chest and shook his head, eyes widening in mock-amazement. “And look at you now. Listening to reason. Proof that anything is possible.”

TWENTY-SEVEN

Jubilee

Jubilee sent her thoughts deep into the old man's chest. She focused there, refusing to acknowledge any discomfort. This work took everything she had. She wouldn't mess it up. She wanted Marissa here with her.

The old man had promised to make it happen.

So Jubilee held her small hands to his chest. She leaned into the hard wooden arm of his fancy chair. She pushed closer, ignoring the discomfort. This time he would feel a difference. This time the healing would be obvious, and he wouldn't be able to question it.

She could see his blood, tinged with Dust, pumping sluggishly through his damaged heart. Jubilee had been working every day to correct the diseases that afflicted him. His skin was no longer yellowed. His joints were no longer inflamed. His stomach no longer bled.

Today, she would fix his heart.

He wanted to be young again. He wanted to surprise his grandson when he returned from traveling. The old man planned to keep his hold on this zone for a while longer. Jubilee helped him with that.

He was so happy with her. He told her that his men were working on bringing her Marissa. Jubilee pushed the bubble of excitement away. She focused on the pumping thing in front of her. She'd discovered she didn't have to know how something worked to fix it. The Dust knew. She had to ask it. She had to focus it.

She could see it happening—parts of his heart that were shrunken and weak filled back in. Another area that was thick and swollen slowly shrank. His heart became more symmetrical again. It beat stronger, without skipping or racing. The blood pumped rich and full of air and Dust through his body.

She knew the moment he felt the difference. He inhaled. A moment later, he took a long, deeper breath, and when it came out of him, it was a laugh, deep and filled with joy.

Jubilee opened her eyes and stepped away. He liked a respectful distance to be kept. He didn't like to be touched, but he bore it for the healing. The old man looked better. His lips were no longer tinged bluish purple.

To her shock, he reached out and grabbed her by the wrist and pulled her in to him. He wrapped his arms around her, still laughing. Jubilee held herself stiff, not sure what she was supposed to do or feel now. He was happy. But was she meant to heal more? She felt his hand, still spotted, but no longer swollen or gnarled, patting her head. Jubilee swallowed. Just as she was about to relax into his hold, he slid his arms to her shoulders and set her back from him.

But he didn't release her.

"Child. Has your life been so difficult that you don't recognize affection?"

She blinked at him, afraid to pull her gaze away. How was she supposed to answer? She didn't want to make him angry. She wanted to answer, to have words to keep him happy, but it felt like her mouth was sealed shut.

His hand slid around to cup her cheek. "Well, no more. You are a treasure, young lady." He wagged his finger in her face. "And I won't have anyone telling me otherwise. You're like Lucas."

What? *Lucas?* She didn't want to be like his younger grandson. He hated her. He hated himself, too.

The old man leaned in, as if sharing a secret, "We use the holy tools sent us, even if we don't understand why they've been chosen. It isn't our place to question it. You are a precious tool,

Jubilee. Thanks to you and your teaching, Lucas will soon be leading my new army. You're meant for great things, too."

She was saved from having to answer by a quick knock at the door to the old man's office. He pulled his shirt closed and buttoned it, then nodded at her to retreat to her stool in the private alcove off his office. Jubilee scurried back to it, and the old man told whoever was at the door to enter. Jubilee risked peeking around the corner. One of his assistants came in, fear and anger on his face, and quickly closed the door behind himself.

Before the assistant could get out a single word, the door opened again. It bumped into his back. The door was pulled back again and then flung open, slamming into the assistant and sending him stumbling.

"Sir," he managed, "you have a—"

"Visitor." The old woman marched serenely past both a small, dark-haired woman holding the door open for her and the assistant. She flicked a glance over the assistant. "You may go."

This old woman had short silvery hair and green eyes. She was round and seemed merry, but there was something about her that had Jubilee's body easing back away from the corner she hid behind. She didn't want to be near the woman, but she was afraid to stop looking at her.

The old man seemed more amused than angry. He flicked his fingers at his assistant, and the young man scurried out. The young woman at the door closed it behind him and took up a position to the side of it. Her gaze swept the room. It caught on Jubilee.

A second later, she stepped forward and bent to whisper in her mistress's ear. The old woman tilted her head in the direction of the little hidden alcove.

"Thank you for coming." The old man seemed more amused by the discovery than upset. He was in a very good mood. "Would you care for tea?" At her nod and raised brow, he raised his voice. "Jubilee. Come here, child."

The old woman still hadn't said anything.

Jubilee crept from the alcove and came to stand by the old man, face down as he preferred.

"Heat the water for our tea, Jubilee. You know how I like it."

Jubilee nodded and walked over to a side board. There was a pot of water there, and several small tea cups. She focused on the water and brought it to the perfect temperature. If she made it too hot, he made her stand with her hand in the pot until it cooled and then start again. It hurt, but she could heal it once she was alone again, so he didn't worry about the damage to her skin. It was a lesson, he told her, in paying attention to the small details that mattered.

Jubilee lifted the tray and balanced it so she could cross to the desk. She poured them each a cup of hot water, and they selected their tea from small tins in a row. She scooped out the leaves and placed them in the muslin bag, then dropped it into their water. When she was done, she returned the tray to the sideboard and stood waiting.

The old man felt the side of his cup with a finger. "Perfect," he told her, beaming. "You may return to your place."

Jubilee scooted back to her alcove. She plopped down on her stool, her heart pounding in her ears. Her skin felt crawly after being watched by the old woman. She wouldn't peek again. She didn't want to see the woman. She'd be happiest not to have to go back in there until after the old man's visitor had gone.

"I'm shocked," the woman said now. "I can't believe you of all people have one here, in your private office."

Jubilee could hear the smile in her voice. She just didn't believe the smile. She hoped the old man didn't believe it, either.

"You'd be surprised what I can tolerate in the name of righteousness. Besides, Jubilee is special. She is chosen. I'm molding her into my perfect companion."

"Well," the old woman laughed, "I suppose each to his own."

"Indeed. You have your Ang Li. I have my Jubilee."

"I hardly think that child is as perfect as Ang. The comparison is—"

"Accurate." The old man laughed at her now. "But I didn't ask you to come here to discuss our companions."

"I hope not. It was more than a simple detour. You know that I winter in Zone Three. And it is *quite* the place to be right now."

"Mmm." The old man made a noncommittal noise. "What information do you have about young soldiers? Sparks. Trained as well as Council agents, but not agents."

"Young agents/not agents? Dressed in unattractive mottled brown? Able to use the Spark as a weapon? And when discovered—very rarely—they either suicide or are killed? Terrible waste of training and resources, even if they are Sparks." She made a tsking noise. "Why on earth would you train them like that?"

"So information about them is leaking out finally. My people did a magnificent job keeping them well-hidden until it was time to use them, even from your Ang's eyes." He chuckled. "I keep my people well-motivated."

Jubilee shivered. The old man's motivational techniques could be hard. It was for his workers' own good—the zone ran so much more efficiently when all of them were working at their peak performance, after all. That's what the old man said.

But those techniques were still brutal. And they weren't always applied to the worker. He had used Jubilee's skills a time or two on family members of those requiring motivation. The old man used whatever technique would be most effective with each individual who was beholden to him.

The old man had paused, waiting for the woman to volunteer information. When none was forthcoming, he asked, "Do you know who these young soldiers are? Where I got them?"

A long, loud slurp was his first answer. A moment later, the old woman answered, her voice a little irritated. "No. But I can guess. Don't toy with me."

There was a long silence that stretched between them. Jubilee had no idea what it meant, but her heart pounded in her ears. It was a physical relief when they spoke again.

"Do you see now? That you're not the only one capable of keeping secrets?" There was an amused tension in the old man's voice.

What secret had the woman been keeping from the old man? It couldn't be serious, or she would be dead.

There was a rustle and the sound of a teacup being placed on a saucer. "Regardless of their secret breeding, you've stepped up the program very recently. My roving spies tell Ang you are moving beyond devoted young men and technology from the east and into…newer skills."

"We are."

"You've made a breakthrough with your other program, then? The powers the girls are capable of?"

The old man made a noise somewhere between a hiss and a scoffing huff. "In a manner of speaking. I found a new ally for us. We'll be able to work around the obstacles of training soon."

"A new ally?" Her voice was sharp.

"Of course. I'm always looking ahead. A new piece in our little game came to me himself at the Conclave. A major piece, from the Ward School."

She laughed now. It was a tinkling sound. It made Jubilee shiver again.

"How major? Is the war over before it began then? Perhaps we should all go home." Her voice was mocking.

She didn't believe him?

"Major." The old man gloated now. "We are recruiting at the Ward School now. Of course, he thinks he's in control, and I'm letting him. He believes he's playing with us—but he isn't even playing the right game. He's so easily manipulated by the promise of what he most wants that he cannot see beyond it. Having him under my control changes everything."

"And makes it more enjoyable."

"It does, yes." His chair creaked as the old man leaned back. "Tell me about Zone Three now. Everything is in place?"

"Of course." Now she sounded cross. "If I wasn't invested in our dual achievement, I wouldn't be here in the cold and wet instead of enjoying the relative warmth of a more southern zone. My employee understands better now the role he is to play. He doesn't like it. But he understands that I require it."

"Good. I was most displeased when he helped those girls slip away. The others are well hidden?"

Always back to the girls. Jubilee risked peeking around the corner. The old woman leaned forward to pick up her cup again.

She sat back and nodded. Her nail tapped against the fragile cup. "I'm not sure about this next move. If we are going to the effort to infiltrate—"

"I want to draw them out. I want them at the Conclave, where everyone can see for themselves the monstrosity that science created. This isn't a battle for territory and trade, Kit. It's a war over hearts and minds. You can have Zone Two and her trade networks. I want the people. And they must come to us willingly. They *will* come to us."

"Yes, but to go and take one? If you have that kind of access, why not bring back all of them?"

Take one? Marissa! Jubilee felt a spurt of excitement. He'd promised her, and now it was happening.

The old man gave the woman a sharp look. "I've told you why. Since the Conclave, too many have heard about these girls, too many have heard the Spark rumors about changes and easy lives. Too many doubt us. I want there to be no question. Those creatures are violent, feral, and prone to madness when they're left uncontrolled. The people need to see that. And soon, they will."

"How so?"

"I've arranged for their young leader to be presented with choices that will draw her out. No matter which way she goes, someone will need her. And no matter what road she chooses, I have no doubt that she'll provide a spectacular demonstration for the public on why these mad young girls should be controlled."

"And your new ally? Has he signed on for this?" Her voice was skeptical.

The old man laughed in a way that made Jubilee shiver. "He just has to sign the order. He doesn't need to know where it will lead. I'm ready for this to begin." His voice was a soft rasp. "It's time to draw the circle of revolutionaries into my grasp, starting with their leader."

"This is a dangerous game you're playing. And the potential for disaster—"

"Is worth risking." The old man laughed. "When my new player makes his move, it will change the entire board. The play has already started. Their infallible network…isn't. They have no idea what's coming. We'll have them."

"Good. There's too much at stake to loosen our grip now."

"It's all coming together." His voice was soothing. "All the pieces are moving into their assigned places."

The old woman laughed and it was an oddly young, trilling sound. "I love a long game."

Jubilee shuddered. The woman's laugh, her voice, her *joy* was dangerous. It was poison, Jubilee was sure.

She shoved her fingers in her ears. She didn't want to hear any more. She didn't want to know.

TWENTY-EIGHT

Ace

Ace tucked the sheaf of newly stamped shipping papers into his leather folio and grinned down at it. "Finally," he murmured loud enough for Alex to hear, humor tingeing the words, "having a gigantic pain in the ass agent along for a ride begins to pay off."

When he raised his amused gaze, Alex arched a brow at him. "Did you forget the gifts and extra cargo you took on in Gartenn due to my close, personal relationship with Sloan?"

"You drank up one of the most valuable of those gifts already," Ace reminded him. "And I'm pretty sure when the cost of *donated* supplies is offset, the rest of the cargo's value will be accounted for, as well."

Alex snorted. "You got more face time with Sloan than even a Plat trader could ever have expected. Can't put a price on that kind of exposure."

"Mm. And only half of that time was spent making promises to calm her because she was livid at some stunt you pulled. I'm surprised you made it out alive."

On some levels, Alex agreed. He grinned sardonically anyway. "Sloan loves me."

Ace laughed and clapped him on the shoulder as he turned back to his caravan master. "Sure she does. We all do."

Alex threw his arms wide and feigned hurt feelings. "Why do you have to be like that? I'm a loveable guy."

Ace shook his head and glanced back over his shoulder, amusement glinting in his eyes. "Whatever you've got to tell yourself to get through the day, Agent Reyes."

The two men walked back to their caravan so it could pull through the gates and into the warehousing area hugging the eastern wall of the Zone One relo-city compound. Macopany was the least impressive of all of the cities Alex had seen. The buildings were small and dingy, the stonework and bricks covered in smoky grime. The streets were narrow, and the people hunched against the cold that was already bitter and howled along those streets as if making promises to the people about the harsh winter coming for them. It even smelled like wet ashes.

It was just as he remembered, and yet…it wasn't. Everything was off, smaller and greyer, as if his perspective and his memories swam.

He turned back to the young gate supervisory agent who'd hurried from his office the moment he'd recognized Alex striding along with Ace. The local security forces and trade consortium were responsible for manning the gates and conducting inspections, which was generally a long, tedious experience. But local security answered to and was overseen by Council agents assigned to the zone. The agent who held the position here was young. He'd graduated perhaps five years before? It was convenient, because it meant that the agent was one of theirs. He'd made sure the process for the caravan was quick and painless. But it also spoke volumes about the desperate situation here.

That lined up with the information Alex had coming in about the zone. It had always been one of the hardest hit by disease. Influenza had decimated the population twice in the years since the Cataclysm, and anything else that got a foothold raced through the people. Five and a half years before, another severe strain of flu hit hard. It hadn't been as bad as in years past, but it had been bad enough that Council had imposed a zone quarantine. Those that hadn't succumbed to illness had been forced to survive winter with severe rationing.

Alex stared out at the streets, tracing the shapes of buildings and following after the people bustling around the busy entry to the city. He looked for anything familiar. Finally, he shook his head and turned back to rejoin Ace and get the caravan underway to the warehouses.

As he strode back along the line, his attention caught on a shout out to the retreating supervisory agent returning to his office.

"Zone Six delegates arriving…"

Alex glanced around. A trio of men approached from the other direction, heading for the gate offices. One of them was a zone inspector. He was questioning the late arrival of the caravan, as they'd been expected the month before.

"It was an unavoidable delay," a travel-worn caravan master answered in a loud, hoarse voice clearly used to shouting orders to his caravan workers. "We were waiting on the arrival of a special representative from Councilor Four, sent to inspect and take possession of special documents here in Zone One."

The smaller, sharp-faced man with him shushed him. He glanced around, checking individuals within earshot.

Alex swept his gaze away but continued to watch from the corner of his eye. The small man stopped walking when he caught sight of Alex moving along the side of the caravan. He cocked his head and narrowed his eye, then took a step as if to pursue.

Alex didn't look back and continued walking, swinging his arms as if he hadn't a care in the world. When he reached the end of the train car, he swerved to move between the cars, stepping over the train coupling and moving on.

He didn't know if the little man had recognized him. Alex remembered him well, though. He was the Zone Six trader he and Ace had stolen the smuggled girls from at the end of the Conclave. He was the trader involved in the disappearances that were being engineered, Alex was sure, by Councilor Four. How convenient that he he'd been delayed by a special rep of the Councilor.

Four had sent a representative to take possession of special papers, had he? Was this in response to Alex's trip to each of the eastern zones? Or was it out of an abundance of caution after one of their deliveries had been interrupted? They'd never been able to prove Alex was involved, even though Sloan made it clear that many suspected his involvement after he'd delivered the note he'd said Lena had left during the subsequent investigation. Perhaps this was an attempt to gather evidence?

Either way, Alex had a new secondary mission: figure out what the documents were and find a way to intercept them. He was willing to bet every C-Note he had that those documents were records of shipments made. He could only hope they made reference to destinations.

A slow grin spread across his face. He'd have them. By the time the annual Meet rolled back around, he'd have the proof he needed to start dismantling the Council.

Ace leaned in close to him in the back of the courtesy vehicle sent by Councilor One. "We're getting close to the Council building. They have adequate guest lodging in a separate building nearby."

Alex nodded, though he kept his gaze on the city rolling by outside. He'd already known they were getting close—a memory? Something in the buildings to remind him? He wasn't sure what it was until they passed a wide square where people gathered. There were a few make-do stalls for trade. It was mostly homemade goods on barter in those stalls, he remembered. He'd once been one of the urchins running free between the stalls and in and out of the tired people. The adults were hunched against the cold and against the chill of life. The children were still free, even if they were thin.

Alex tracked along the square. His gaze caught on a door—faded lavender. It had once been vibrant purple. A younger Alex had passed it every day on his way to the park. He'd go in the evenings to wait for his father to come walking home from his shift at the power plant. Alex crossed in front of the door every day on the way to wait at the park and then back home again, his hand in his father's larger palm as he skipped and ran beside his tall father.

The driver was talking now, attempting to point something out to them. Ace made noncommittal noises in response. Alex ignored them both, leaning closer to the window and craning his neck to look back as they passed the square and turned right, away from it.

It was still there, just beyond the lavender door. A little bar with a cut-work golden goose for the sign. And beyond it…

A small, narrow side street, little more than an alley, led away from the square and the main road that went around it. Three blocks down that alley, Alex and his father would have gone inside his mother's bakery, climbed the steps at the back past the kitchen with its warm ovens, and up to their little apartment where she'd wait.

She'd be making dinner, yes. But she'd also be waiting to give his father hell. There was always something, some sharp question and waving arms. His father would walk into the kitchen and wrap his arms around her, pulling her close and dancing around the kitchen with her.

He'd liked her fire.

"Alex. Are you okay?"

He turned his head back, staring at Ace. After a moment, he cleared his throat and shrugged. "I'm good. Thought I saw something I recognized for a moment."

"You recognized? Zone One is your home zone?"

Alex nodded.

The driver glanced back at him through the rear-view mirror. "Oh, yeah? Most agents don't get to come home. Welcome back, sir."

Alex gave him a thin smile. "Thanks."

Ace watched him with serious eyes. "Is this a problem?"

Alex shook his head.

"Does it have the potential to be one?"

Alex laughed softly. "No, Ace. Our stop here will be quick and uncomplicated. In, out, and heading home via Zone Six before the first snow falls." Alex glanced away from Ace's concern, focusing his attention on the worn people outside the window.

They passed a single girl standing on the corner. She looked to be no more than six years old. She was crying. As they passed, a young woman with dark, mussed hair hurried up to her and took her hand, pulling her close to her side in comfort as they turned away.

That's why you're here, Alex. Those girls are the key to freedom for all Sparks. Remember that.

In, out, and back home—with the proof that would change everything. He nodded his head, eyes no longer seeing anything out the window. That was the plan.

TWENTY-NINE

Lena

Lena curled tight around herself, buried under blankets. She'd woken some time ago and had been desperately trying to go back to sleep. It wasn't that she was tired or felt the need for more sleep. In fact, her body demanded she get out of bed and relieve her bladder.

Lena wasn't ready to give up yet. She craved those twilight dreams of Alex she had when she was waking or falling asleep. She knew she was ready to start her day—there was so damn much to do to get ready for their fight against the Scavengers. She just didn't *want* to start it without him.

Which was a ridiculous thing to want, considering he was hundreds of miles away. It wasn't like the dreams were real.

Except she had the increasing sense they were real.

If only she could somehow force them to happen when she was awake. If only she could reach out to him like she did to Rose now.

Well…why couldn't she?

She had to believe the Dust was somehow linking the two of them while they both slept. The Dust wanted to help, didn't it? She'd known that forever. If she believed it, then why couldn't she at least try to reach him consciously?

Lena rolled over onto her back and took a breath, then another, steadying herself. She forced herself to relax, let her eyes drift closed, and reached. It wasn't like traveling with the Dust. If she went that far, she was afraid she'd lose the anchor of her body and be lost to the Dust forever.

Instead, she tried to do what she did when communicating with Rose over a distance. She thought of Alex—thought of the things that made Alex uniquely *him*—and focused on his smell, the way he cocked his head at her, the crinkle of his eyes, the timbre of his voice. She focused on his mind, the poet who masked his pain with dark amusement. And she reached for him.

Alex. Where are you? Can you hear me? Can you feel me?

Lena pushed herself out further. There. Just there.

She had a vague sense of him and reached out. The nebulous sense became suddenly concrete—not his mind, but his smell. She saw a flash of skin—his arm flung above his head as he opened his eyes, staring up, puzzled.

Then he was gone.

She lifted her hands as if to waft the smell toward herself, to cling to that one real thing for a moment longer, but it was already gone. If it existed at all, it was in her nose alone, not in the air around her. Lena rolled her eyes at herself and sat up, swinging her legs over the edge of the bed. There was no use pretending. It was in her memory. There was no mystical connection. She was a lonely, pregnant woman missing her man, like centuries of women before her. She had too damn much to do to lie in bed and make wishes—they had plans to make and boys to rescue.

Besides, she and Alex had agreed to this. They *both* had agreed. Alex needed to be out in the world, working the angles that would make the world a better place. And she needed to be here, protecting these girls and teaching them to protect themselves in the comfort and safety of anonymity.

Lena stood and moved across the room, dressing swiftly in her layers of clothes against the late fall blustery morning. She slipped downstairs before any of the children woke and tugged on her boots at the door.

Once she was outside, she didn't have to creep for silence. She strode across the grey valley, enjoying the hint of dawn rising. To her left, south of the outhouses tucked into a stand of trees, the Neo-Barb village woke. She could hear the echo of voices in the clear mountain air and smelled wood smoke.

Once she'd relieved herself, she wandered more slowly back to the big house. She turned to watch the village. The dull *thunk* of an axe in wood called her attention to a figure bent over beside the wood stand. A young woman struggled to pull a heavy axe from the wide, flat trunk used to chop wood.

Lena squinted. It wasn't any young woman. "Karina." Lena called out to her and shook her head as she crossed to the wood stand. Why on earth was the girl up alone, chopping wood? "What are you doing?"

Karina looked at Lena over her shoulder, irritated. "Being useful," she gasped out. She reached down to grip the top and bottom of the blade to tug it out of the wood.

"Don't!"

Karina's fingers slid along the sharp metal. Blood immediately spurted.

"Ah, Dust! Give them to me." Lena reached for the girl's hands.

Karina stepped back, jerking her hands away. Blood ran down her wrists. "I can do it," she said. She leaned in close to growl low in Lena's face. "I can do it myself. See?" She thrust out her hands. Lena stared into Karina's hostile eyes for a moment, startled. She dropped her gaze to the girls' fingers as her skin knitted back together.

No. It flowed together, blurring, looking almost silvery and liquid.

Lena blinked. She stared down, but Karina's fingers were merely fingers—dirty, thin, but whole. There was nothing liquid there. There wasn't even blood.

"Told you. I can do things, too." Karina curled her fingers to her palms. She gave Lena a small, defiant, secretive smile before she turned away and ran back to the village to dart into one of the homes.

Lena took two steps to follow her when movement to the left caught her eye. Gabriela exited her tiny adobe house with a roof made of skin stretched tight over a round wooden frame. The Neo-Barb woman stretched and yawned. She spotted Lena and waved.

Lena waved back.

Gabriela glanced around, taking note of the empty village. She ducked her head for a moment, then looked back up, holding out a hand to tell Lena to wait. She slipped back into her home. Lena turned to look after Karina again, but a moment later, Gabriela ducked out of her home, clutching something small in her hand as she strode to Lena.

Lena walked over to intercept her, curious.

"Morning, Gab." Lena hesitated, wanting to ask about Karina.

Gabriela smiled her greeting, but she glanced away and down again, as if embarrassed. If something was bothering Gabriela, perhaps Lena should wait to talk over what she'd seen with Jackson and Rose. She didn't need to upset her unnecessarily. Perhaps Jackson had seen something similar before? And as for the attitude…everyone had a bad day. Clearly they needed to give Karina more to do, to make her feel like part of the community.

Lena smiled. "What is it?"

Gabriela laughed softly at herself. "I found a basket hidden within a basket yesterday. From our journey here."

She meant from their hurried abandonment of their life and village in Texas.

"It held some stones and wire that I used to make jewelry for trade. I wanted to see if I still remembered how—and I made a piece. I don't think about what I'm making when I start. It takes shape and just becomes. It's meant for you, I think."

Gabriela dropped a small soft skin bag into Lena's hand. The stone within was heavy, and the weight of it was firm in her palm. It fit. She pulled open the mouth of the bag and dropped the stone into her hand.

It was a speckled blue green, pale with deeper tones, like the shades found in her eyes, and crisscrossed by silver wire that wrapped around the edges. She laughed.

"The color is perfect. My eyes, right?"

Gabriela tilted her head and shook it. "Yes…but no. That's the back. Turn it over."

Lena flipped it.

Her breath caught.

On the front, the stone wasn't crisscrossed by wire. The silver branched across the stone in sharp angles from the top center, where a curved bail was meant to hold a leather thong so it could be worn around the neck.

It was lightning.

It was a Spark's pendant.

"It's lovely," she breathed. "It's perfect."

Gabriela beamed. "I'm glad you like it. It's good to see you smile. You've seemed so…"

Lena raised her brow, her smile fading.

"And there you go again." Gabriela gestured at Lena's face. "Angry. Sad."

"Um…confused?"

"Why confused? It was a gift, meant to make you happy. You gave Corazon and I the gift of freedom years ago." Gabriela rarely spoke of her daughter, so when she did, Lena paid attention. "I thought of you often as we built a life and a community in Texas. I never expected to have the chance to repay you." Gabriela looked down.

Lena swallowed and glanced away. "You don't owe me anything—"

"I owe you more than I could ever give. If you could have seen Corazon there, you'd understand. She was happy and free. Just a girl. She had six years of being a happy girl."

Gabriela's words were uncomfortably close to Lena's mother's frequent lament that Lena had never had a chance to be normal.

What was normal, anyway? Lena was herself. Her life had unfolded and brought her here. She regretted none of it. It was the one thing she wished she'd had a chance to make her mother understand. If only she could see Lena now.

Her mother had always wished Lena at least had a circle of women to depend upon. She was afraid Ace would outgrow their childhood bond. Lena had never been comfortable around girls because of her sister's contempt, not that she'd had many opportunities in her life. Now there was Rose and Gabriela. Soon there would be a daughter, or so Jackson told her. Her mother might finally have been happy with Lena's choices.

Lena still felt like an awkward child, not sure what to say. She didn't say anything. She tucked her hair behind her ears.

She could build a school out of ruins and dreams. She could hunt vengeance for her family. She could seduce an agent who was arguably the sexiest man ever created. But she couldn't figure out how to talk to a friend who'd given her a simple gift.

Perhaps she didn't have to say a thing. Lena looked down at her scuffing feet. Or she would have, if she'd been able to see them. The soft swell of her belly was suddenly big enough that she couldn't see her small feet peeking out beneath anymore. Lena laughed in disbelief.

She glanced up, mortified. "I'm not laughing at your memories," she blurted. "I—I noticed that I can't see my toes anymore. I popped overnight. This is real."

A slow smile spread over Gabriela's face. "She's real, yes." She stepped away from Lena, pointing to the pendant in Lena's hand with her chin. "Perhaps someday you'll give her that to wear."

The Neo-Barb woman turned and strode back to the village she and Ghost had built for their People, leaving Lena behind.

Lena turned and made her slow way back to the house. She had to get breakfast started. She had to prepare herself for the lessons of the day. But first she had to find a bit of thong for her new necklace.

None of it took her long. The smell of breakfast woke the girls, and soon, Lena was surrounded by voices and bodies and the warmth of the stove. As she leaned over the table to pull a plate toward herself, Charity shrieked with laughter at something her sister said.

Something of the sound must have rolled through her belly, because it turned over in response. Lena straightened. She looked down.

The little life inside her swished again and then settled, still.

Lena swallowed. There was a life inside her. She had chosen it, if only by default. She'd never discussed it with Alex. She hadn't thought about what he'd be like—what either of them would be like as parents. She'd never consciously *decided.* Panic stirred in her chest.

Lena slid her hair behind her ears and closed her eyes. In the midst of voices and laughter, she reached out for her calm and found it in a memory of lying on top of Alex in the back of a small electric vehicle.

They'd made the first of their promises that night.

They may not have a mystical connection, but they would have time together again, brief, precious interludes that belonged to them. Until then, she'd do the work she'd promised to both of them. She could focus on work when the enormity of her decision-not decision weighed on her. She tapped her small belly and then reached up to grab at the pendant hanging between her breasts.

"Be still. Or something. Let me focus. Okay?"

She nodded to herself.

It'll be okay.

She looked up, and her gaze caught on Rose's solemn face. She didn't smile, but Lena felt her presence wash over her mind, though Rose stood in the kitchen door.

"It will be okay." Rose repeated her own thought from moments before, but it was somehow soothing and much more real.

"Thank you." She mouthed the words across the room

Rose laughed. The woman tapped her head. *"Okay, then. Thank you. Better?"*

"Better."

THIRTY

Alex

Alex gritted his teeth and glanced around the reception again. They'd been told Councilor One would greet all traders new to the zone together, as equals, at the monthly reception. All personal audience appointments would be set this evening, via lottery, for the following three days. He wouldn't play favorites, nor bump up any appointments, not even for the newest Platinum director of Dragonfly House.

It was bullshit. The Zone Six trader was nowhere to be seen. Everyone was prompt to this reception, Ace assured him, because Councilor One offered a limited number of appointments. It was a carrot to induce attendance and to be sure traders hustled to arrive in time for the reception. If you didn't get your name in the pool before the maximum allowable appointments were reached, you were out of luck. You could conduct your business—buying and selling with existing customers—within the zone. But you couldn't try to induce new rates, or new cargo, or any changes to existing agreements with the zone itself.

The sour man from the gate was an experienced trader. If he wasn't here, it was because he was already dealing with the councilor.

Alex excused himself from the small group Ace was entertaining with a travel anecdote and deposited his drink—an oversweet pale wine from Zone Seven—on a side table. He moved through the crowd, giving small, practiced smiles to anyone who tried to catch his eye as his gaze slid away. He gave the appearance to each of them of a man who'd seen someone he knew across the room.

He'd reached one of three side doors up the long side of the room and had his hand on the handle when three booming knocks sounded through the room from the closed front entry at the far end. Alex turned with the rest of the crowd. The door swung open, and One's aide entered, announcing his imminent arrival.

Alex had seen plenty of Councilors making dramatic entries. Instead, he watched the crowd, noting who strained to see because they were new, who kept whispered conversations going because they were not, and who watched the door with disdain. As he marked the last man as someone worthy of conversation, the side door one up from Alex opened, and three people slipped through it.

First came a man, blond and pale with high cheeks and thin lips. A woman, similarly tall and blond, slid into the room and sidled up next to him. Her back was to Alex. The Zone Six trader took a position on the other side of the tall blond man. When he turned his head to speak to the man, Alex could see the satisfied smile he couldn't quite hide.

Alex slipped his hand off the handle of the door, and he stepped away, back into the crowd. He ducked his head and said a word or two to an older woman standing at the edge of the room, using her escort's tall, wide body as a shield.

The Zone Six trader glanced over the blonde's shoulder, frowning. He looked around. The woman with him said something to him, and he shook his head, waving his hand at her as if to tell her not to worry. He turned away to focus on the Councilor, who finally made his entrance at the front of the room.

The woman watched the trader over the shoulders of the blonde between them, then she turned to look around, trying to find what had caught his attention.

Alex froze. A moment later, he forced himself to turn his face away casually and glance back out across the room. Her familiar features, a memory until the second before, were all he saw.

When he turned back, Erika had returned her attention to the front of the room.

Alex eased a breath out. He'd sent her to Zone Eight, about as far from Three as he could think to ship her, years before. Now she was here, accompanied by a trader from Zone Six, and unless he missed his mark, the special representative from Councilor Four.

What was her mission? Why didn't he know about it?

Alex made his way back to Ace. He wove in and out of the people listening to the Councilor's welcome speech, cutting across the room diagonally.

"You need a refill?" Alex nodded at Ace's half-empty glass and then at the bar. It was noisier over by the bar area.

Ace lifted his glass and finished its contents. "As a matter of fact, I do." He nodded and smiled at those around them and followed Alex to the bar.

"Making good contacts?"

Ace eyed him. "That's what I do."

Alex grinned at the taller, darker man and turned to glance back at the trio along the wall. Erika was gone, but the men were still there, pretending to listen to the Councilor. "Do you see the blond man with the Zone Six trader?"

Ace glanced over then focused again on Alex. He nodded as he raised his finger for the barman's attention.

"Do you know who he is?"

Ace leaned in to order another round of drinks. When he leaned back, he shook his head slightly. "Nope. Should I?"

"Maybe you should make your way over and introduce yourself to the two of them. Do you remember the trader's name?"

"That one? Hende. Locust House." Ace made a small expression of distaste at the unofficial name of the Blacketer Trade Group. Locust House was a younger trade house. They had a hungry reputation of sweeping in and destroying the contracts of other houses. "He's the one—?"

Alex nodded. "The very same. But I'm the only suspect in that debacle, so you're free to do your thing."

Ace reached out and took their drinks, handing one off to Alex. "So maybe I'll go introduce myself to the competition."

"That would be a very bad idea." Erika slid between them and raised her glass to show the bartender the red liquid in it before she finished it and set the glass on the bar top. She leaned in, stretched her shoulders. "Wait for me to report in, please. I'd rather you didn't undo all my work by sending in a Dragonfly and turning Jacob's head. I've worked hard to cultivate the relationship between them."

She accepted her new, full glass from the bartender with a smile and turned. She stepped forward to leave and bumped into Alex. "Excuse me," she murmured with a demure smile for any onlookers as she stepped away.

No one noticed the hand that trailed across his lower abdomen before she went.

Except Ace. He watched her go and then cocked a brow at Alex.

"Don't ask," Alex growled low as he moved away and into the crowd.

"Not a chance." Ace responded from behind him.

THIRTY-ONE

Lena

Lena didn't look up from her fingers working the needles and yarn that had been delivered with half of their supplies three weeks before. She waited for the patter of small pebbles cascading down the hillside in front of them to stop. Then said, "Again."

Pheobe groaned. She sweated with effort in the cold morning air.

"I'll go again," Charity offered quickly.

"You will not." Lena eyed Charity's knitting and nodded the girl back down to the cold rocks she, Marin, Constance, Hania, and Lena were perched upon a safe distance away. "You'll focus on your stitches, especially since you just dropped half that row."

It was true. When the girl had half-risen, too-loose stitches had slipped from the working needle.

Charity gasped in dismay and groaned. "My fingers aren't meant to do this. And my butt is frozen."

"Practice makes perfect, Charity. Knitting is like working with the Dust. And just as useful."

"Is not."

"What good is defending yourself if you freeze to death because your toes get frostbitten and you can't walk home? Toes matter. Socks matter. Keep knitting." Lena looked up at Phoebe, who had paused to collect herself and listen to the debate. "And you—again." She nodded at the hillside, where a large boulder embedded halfway up the path was fractured and blackened.

"Are you sure I'm not glowing? I feel like I should be

glowing already."

Lena snorted and didn't look up from her hands. "You're not glowing."

"One of these days, I'll glow like you do."

"Not if you keep taking breaks. Again. And then once more after that to make up for all this wasted time."

"Ugh!"

"Exactly!" Marin agreed.

The thing about teenagers, Lena had discovered in the last few weeks of working exclusively with them, was that they liked to have the last word, even if it was a grunt of disgust. She shook her head and smiled, waiting for the crack of sound as Phoebe used the Dust to form a channel of visible lightning to strike out at the rock above.

When it came, it rolled across the valley below them, as it had all morning long as she'd worked with the five girls. Lena cast a quick glance over that valley. The animals still moved restlessly, but the people below didn't even pause at the sound. They'd become used to it.

There were two gathered groups of students below—all the youngsters Lena herself wasn't teaching. Half of the boys and girls encircled Rose as she taught them defensive measures. The other half gathered around Jackson as he worked with them on healing techniques. Lena had decreed that only the oldest of the girls would be taught offensive techniques. She refused to teach any of the boys anything but defensive and healing work.

Patrick had warned her before he'd left, borrowing one of Ghost's horses and promising to return with it in a few weeks. Thomas had made his deal with her understanding that the boys would be taught everything the girls were being taught. Lena had argued she was doing that—she was teaching them the same thing as the girls in their age category. Until they knew who was operating at the Ward School, she wasn't comfortable sending back future weapons to be used against their teachers and peers.

So long as they got back the missing boys so she could teach them, what difference did it make? All the young Sparks were receiving lessons in techniques they had never had before.

Movement caught her eye.

Karina wandered on the periphery of Jackson's group. She liked to watch the lessons. Perhaps that was how she'd learned to heal, albeit in an odd way? Lena reminded herself again to speak to Jackson about the blurring of Karina's healing. She'd been so busy…

She looked back at the girls partially responsible for her hectic life. Phoebe's strike was loud and powerful, and the fractures had spread. Lena stood, setting her knitting to the side.

"Excellent. Now do it again, right now!"

Phoebe gave her a startled look.

"Now, Phoebe! You missed."

The girl's brow furrowed as she looked back up the hillside, still raining pebbles.

"You missed, and he's coming for you. There's a little boy who's counting on you! Strike again, right now!"

Phoebe gulped at the make-believe scenario that was all-too-possible. She growled and focused, sending out her command, reaching—

Energy buzzed and the rock above them shattered with a roaring crack. Pieces of it shot away into the trees and brush, landing short of the women below.

No one said anything for several long moments after the pebbles and dust settled.

"You exploded him." Hania sounded very pleased with the idea.

Phoebe let out a long, satisfied breath.

Lena glanced at Marin, Charity, and Constance. They were appropriately unsure of how to react. But Phoebe and Hania…between the two of them, there was way too much satisfaction.

"That was very thorough, Phoebe. Of course, if it had been a man, it wouldn't have been flying pebbles you'd have been dodging. That's important to remember. Right?"

Phoebe turned enormous doe eyes on her. Lena recognized what she saw in them. There were so many memories for Phoebe.

"Why don't you come on over and we'll go over what we

learned today?"

Constance groaned, and Charity giggled, looking at her sister. Their moment of uncertainty gone, the healthy sense of mischief had returned.

"I've learned that rocks are cold in the winter." Charity's murmur made Marin huff with a suppressed chuckle of her own.

"It's not winter yet," Lena reminded them. "It'll get colder."

Hania's face stilled. She turned to look out over the little valley, her head cocked. Lena knew she was listening to the low hum they could all hear if they focused.

They'd all helped Lena create the invisible net that ran beneath their entire valley. It was a warning system, defensive web, and their first line of attack. Lena had planned it and drawn on each of them to help, even Patrick before he'd gone. She maintained it herself, and the energy it required meant she was grounding daily now. She had no idea if that was dangerous for the baby. Every time she begged Jackson to check for her, he said everything seemed fine. She hoped that the smaller daily discharges were safer than if she waited and released a huge burst of energy. She had no way of knowing. There was no one to ask.

Rose had tried to share the burden, but Lena had no idea how to share it once it was built. Not without taking it all apart again. That was the problem with doing something new. The hum meant none of the Sparks could forget the lesson.

It was also a constant reminder of the attack they still awaited.

Hania turned back to Lena. "Will they still come if it gets much colder? Ghost said it should snow soon. Won't that keep them away?"

Lena settled back onto her rock, patting the space beside her for Phoebe. The girl joined them, and Lena pulled her knitting back onto her lap.

"We don't know," she told them the truth in a quiet, calm voice. "If they're familiar with the area, they may be waiting for snow, thinking that it will make us—new to the area—less able to respond."

"They'll think that if we're trapped here by the weather that it'll make getting us easier, even if they have to face the snow themselves." Charity was all business now.

"It's possible."

"It's possible they're waiting until Spring, letting us sit and wonder and worry." Phoebe's voice was filled with disgust.

Lena nodded.

Hania frowned. Her gaze flicked up and then down again. "But we won't let the bad men keep the boys all winter, will we?"

Had she been listening to the adults hashing through these very issues in the evenings when Ghost and Gabriela came up to the house for strategy sessions? Lena cocked her head at the girl and saw the guilt on her face.

She had. That was the problem with the quiet girl. She had become used to moving and waiting in silence. Apparently she wasn't averse to using that ability to sneak around.

"Hania." The censure in Lena's voice was enough to make Hania flinch.

Lena was surprised when the girl raised her face and said more than a little defensively, "We have a right to know, too. We'll be fighting. We're the ones they want."

Lena sighed. "We won't be leaving the boys there all winter, no. We're waiting for Patrick to return from the Ward School. It's dangerous to split up and leave the bulk of you here unprotected. It's possible they're waiting for *that*, too. So Patrick is bringing some agents back with him." It was a concession Lena wasn't happy with, no matter how many times Patrick reassured her that the men he returned with would be those personally vetted by both him and Thomas.

"Is he coming soon? What if it snows before they get here?"

Lena nodded at Phoebe. "He should be here any day. They can travel quicker on horseback than with a big wagon."

And hopefully they'll be aware of anyone following. Lena couldn't shake the fear that the Council already knew where she and her girls were living. There was the watcher who'd somehow slipped away. She shifted her shoulders and let the hum flow over her. The net would protect them from anyone who came. It had to.

The sense of its energy flared now, as if recognizing her

concern and offering comfort.

"Okay, if there aren't any more questions about the boys and our plans, let's go over the lesson. Phoebe's…exuberance…at the end should give us all something to think about. What do you think it'd be like to have that happen to a man? To know that you did that?"

The girls avoided her eyes as they thought.

"What was it like for you?" Hania asked her.

Lena frowned. "Excuse me?"

"The day you came for us. There was a man on the cliff. The one who—" Hania stopped for a moment, overcome at the thought of Lydie, her lost match. The man on the cliff had shot Lydie and killed her.

Lena knew what Hania meant. She'd done much the same that she was teaching the girls to do now. She hadn't used focused energy to form a bolt of lightning. She'd used energy itself—a shockwave of rage. She'd torn the man to pieces with it.

"It was…" Lena looked at them. These girls had been through too much. She wouldn't add to it with lies. "It was satisfying. I was glad. I was so *angry*. But…" She held their gazes in turn, making sure they understood. She held Phoebe's the longest. Phoebe ached to do the same. "But I have dreams about it. About him, sometimes."

"I have dreams about Lydie." Hania's voice was flat. "Every night. I don't care about him. I hope it hurt. I hope he felt himself break into every little piece. I hope it wasn't fast." Her voice was thick.

Lena reached for her hand. Hania let her take it, but the girl had raised her gaze to meet Phoebe's. Phoebe nodded her head, a slight movement, but it held a world of meaning.

What am I doing? How can I teach them without helping them forget first?

"Look!" Constance pointed out across the valley below them.

At the distant narrow mouth to the path through the orchard and down to the mountain track leading away from their sheltered valley, men on foot led horses. Lena picked out Ghost making his way to them.

The flare of energy hadn't been the net comforting her. It had been the net recognizing the energy of one who'd helped create it. Patrick had returned, and he'd brought the agents he'd promised.

Why did the thought make her even more anxious?

"And with that bit of distraction, I think the lesson for today is over. Grab your wool and needles, and let's head back down."

The girls squealed and jumped up, shaking the feeling back into chilled legs and rear ends. They preceded her down the path, congratulating Phoebe on her big boom.

"Hania and Phoebe," Lena called out, "We'll finish this conversation later. It's important."

The girls glanced back at her then looked at each other and turned away, whispering together. Marin trailed them, keeping her own watchful, uncertain gaze on her Match.

She was pleased with the timely interruption. It allowed her to move her own frozen bottom and hips. And empty her bladder. She wiggled, rubbing her free hand on the soft, small swell of belly that had made a sudden appearance a few weeks before. She splayed her fingers over her abdomen, measuring the distance between them. She was getting visibly bigger. No wonder she needed an outhouse. The new growth and the cold meant she felt a constant urge to pee. It was damned inconvenient.

The path twisted round and deposited them halfway down the length of the meadow. They were closer to the big rancho house than they'd seemed from up high.

She trekked across the meadow, trying to decide between greeting the Ward School visitors first or heading straight for the outhouses. She squinted ahead. Patrick hadn't just brought agents back with him.

He'd brought Thomas.

She couldn't help the little leap of hope. She scanned the valley, searching.

Alex wasn't with them. The disappointment was a weight on her chest that threatened to set off the nausea that had left her a week or two before. She gulped, forcing back both sickness and threatening tears.

Stop it. Of course he wasn't with them. Alex would be gone for at least five months, but realistically it would be six or more, depending on weather and events. It had been just over four.

The men stood in a rough circle, Ghost and Patrick towering over the others. In their midst was the shorter, wiry figure of Thomas. Even from a distance, his energy was palpable. He was asking something, his hands gesturing toward the end of the valley where she and the girls had been perched halfway up the cliff side moments before.

The girls bobbed across the meadow all together. Jackson turned and smiled at the little warrior class, then nodded for Thomas as he caught sight of her smaller form behind them. Lena lifted her hand in a small wave. Thomas's lips quirked up, and he shook his head in a small movement, as if in wonder at all they'd managed. Or disapproval.

Lena laughed at herself. What difference did it make? She tucked her heavy sweater closer around her and into the belt holding it closed. At least the cold weather served one purpose. It allowed her to wear heavy enough clothes to camouflage that small baby swell. She wasn't certain she wanted to share that information with Thomas.

He smiled at her as she stopped in front of them. "Hello, Lena. Mountain living seems to agree with you as much as the girls."

"Free living, Thomas." She gave him a cheeky grin. "What are you doing here? Not that we're not happy to see you, but it's a long way for you to come."

"Some of my wards are missing."

Lena took a deep breath. "They are. But not for much longer. We'll be going for them now." She swallowed and tilted her head. "I hope you haven't come to take that privilege from us?"

Thomas shook his head. "Let's talk about this inside."

"Thomas. This is something *we* need to handle."

He nodded. "I know that, which is why I didn't bring all the men I wanted. Let's talk inside."

She still hovered there, watching him.

Just ask...

"How's Alex? Have you heard…?"

"Messages home indicate all is well. The mission's on track."

Of course that was Thomas's sole focus.

As if he knew her thoughts, his brows dipped down—a flash of emotion that was quickly gone. He gave her a smile. "I'm tired and cold and hungry. The horses are loaded down with extra supplies. I'd appreciate it if we could talk over a meal."

Jackson gave her an encouraging smile.

"I'm sure we can put something together," she told them. "I'm hungry, too, now that you mention it."

Jackson raised a brow at her. She knew it wasn't because she was already hungry again. He'd gotten used to that. She had a feeling he was wondering if she'd mention her condition.

She eyed Thomas. He'd dubbed her the Spark's Eve when they first met. As creepy as that was, she wasn't ready for him to know about the baby yet.

"I'll meet you all at the house. I'll join you as soon as I get the girls settled in another activity." And pee. The girls were gathering by Rose, and Rose was near the facilities.

She shook her head at Jackson as they crossed paths so he could lead the men to the main house. He gave her a barely perceptible nod. She didn't know if he was indicating he understood or that he agreed with her decision not to say anything. Either way, she felt a little better.

She felt much better by the time she rejoined them. She crossed to the wide, long table that had been fitted together over the last weeks and perched on a stool. Once she was seated, she loosened her belt and shrugged out of the sweater, allowing it to pool in her lap.

Thomas, Patrick and Jackson had helped themselves to what they could find in the kitchen. All of the men were eating, lined up across one side of the table. Of the other men, Lena only knew Theo and West, the agent she'd met months before in Thomas's office.

Jackson fiddled with the edge of a plate that held their staple diet—dried venison, flat bread, dried apple slices. He picked up a piece of meat and popped it into his mouth. With a mischievous grin, he slid the plate in front of her.

Lena didn't eat right away, though she was hungry. "So…Alex is well?" At Thomas's nod, she continued on. "I don't suppose there are any messages? For me?"

Thomas's gaze flicked up and then back down to the food in front of him. He shook his head before returning his gaze to her. "No. Not yet. But you will be happy to know that our investigation at the Fort is bearing fruit. We're rooting them out. It'll be safe soon—"

"It doesn't matter. This is our place now."

His face stilled. He glanced down the table to West, then looked down again at his plate. He didn't look back up.

After a long moment of awkward silence, Lena decided she might as well eat. She layered a thin slice of venison around the apple and ate it, leaving the flat bread. Before she could swallow, the door opened again, and a blast of colder air circulated the room. Ghost and Gabriela entered.

Ghost's little shadow, Leo, was right behind him. Leo had attached himself to Ghost almost as readily as he had to Alex. He hadn't been happy when Lena had sat down the children to discuss her pregnancy with them. He hadn't been happy at all when he'd realized what it meant, and who the new baby's father was. Just as they'd reached a point of trust, where the boy was no longer treating her as an enemy, it had all fallen apart. It didn't matter that she'd tried to tell him that it wouldn't matter to Alex. She'd tried to make him see that this child and Leo were not in competition. Leo was having none of it.

He'd found a new father-figure. And like Alex, Ghost was content to have the little boy follow him around and teach him what he thought the child needed to know.

Gabriela absently settled the child between her and Ghost and looked around the room. Her brow furrowed. "Where's Rose? Shouldn't she be a part of any discussions?"

Lena nodded, but her mouth was still full.

"She will be," Jackson reassured Gabriela. "I'm going to relieve her in a few minutes. We'll keep each other abreast of any decisions."

Gabriela nodded, appeased, and turned to look at the men,

offering Ghost a glance. He ran his gaze over the new men at the table. Thomas did much the same to the two Neo-Barbs, his pale eyes moving back and forth between them.

Lena swallowed. "Thomas, this is an old friend, Elias, known as Ghost. He is the Father of these people. And this is Gabriela. She is their Mother." Lena used the formal designations that gave their ritual and political roles within their tribe. "We are blood sworn. They share both the valley with us and the responsibility for the physical safety of the people within it. Ghost, Gabriela, this is Thomas, who is Councilor Five, the head of the Council's Ward School, and leader of a movement to free us—the Sparks—from Council control."

She internally winced, waiting. Bringing the girls to the wilderness to grow up among Neo-barbs hadn't been part of the deal. Revealing his true identity to these people would be an issue for the secretive man.

However, Thomas didn't spare her a glance. He dipped his head deeply, offering them respect. "I'm honored to meet you. I'm pleased that Lena and the children found such a fine people to watch over them. I'm pleased that you found each other."

It had the sound of a formal greeting. Ghost and Gabriela exchanged an amused glance.

"Thank you. We found each other and this family that we guide, though we did not *find* each other," Ghost corrected. He and Gabriela were equally quick to correct those who assumed they were a couple.

"Why don't we all eat?" Gabriela suggested. "I'm sure you could do with finishing your meal. And Lena may be hungry, as well."

Leo sighed dramatically from between Ghost and Gabriela. "Lena's always hungry now. It's that *baby.*"

Every eye swiveled to the little boy.

"Leo!"

Thomas turned his head, almost in slow-motion, to stare at her. "I thought you looked different," he said softly. His glance flickered down to her breasts, almost as full as her belly hidden below the sweater and the edge of the table. "But apparently it's not mountain living that agrees with you. Keeping secrets?"

Lena nudged at a slice of apple before looking up. "Not a secret, no. Just…not your business."

His face flushed.

"Or anyone else's," she added.

Thomas settled his hands on the table, palms down, and leaned in. Lena noted from the corner of her eye how Ghost tensed.

Thomas, as he spoke, focused all of his attention on her. "It is the business of everyone at this table."

"No. Like everything else to do with me and my girls, it isn't everyone's business." She managed to keep her voice even and steady. She mentally congratulated herself.

Thomas ruined it. "This child belongs to all of us, it is—"

She laughed incredulously. "This child belongs to me. My body. My baby."

"I'm saying…" Thomas made a calm-down motion with one hand that pissed her off even more. "This is an important development for our movement. It changes everything."

"It does not. This has nothing to do with you or the movement."

"Lena, you must come back." It wasn't a request. There was a dangerous glint in Thomas's eyes and an edge to his voice.

"I will do no such thing."

"Don't make me order—"

She laughed again, still shocked, and growing angrier. She noted that she wasn't the only one. Ghost and Gabriela weren't happy with the new man and his declarations. Lena couldn't see Jackson's face. His chin was tucked and he stared down at the table. *Say something.*

Jackson might be still too cowed by his upbringing and training to speak up, but Lena had no such issues. "You have no power to order anything here. We are not subjects of the Council or the Ward School."

"You are dependent on our goods."

"No, they're not." Ghost spoke up, his voice a controlled but very angry rumble. "They survived well enough when your goods didn't arrive. They welcomed all of us and gave us support until we were able to hunt and forage after building homes. She's been working on a plan to secure trade that will make our lives even more comfortable. She doesn't need your goods in order to lead. She doesn't need you. You need her."

Thomas's jaw pulsed as he ground his teeth. He turned to glower at Patrick. "Did you know about this?"

Patrick held up his hands, absolving himself of any involvement.

Thomas turned to Jackson accusingly. "You should have sent word."

"About which? The baby, the ability to fend for herself, or the plans for trade?" Jackson's quick response had been directed at the table. He had been studying the table while the argument raged around him. Now he raised his gaze to Thomas. "And why?" He shook his head. "She's right. This isn't a development, it's a child. Her child."

Thomas's eyes narrowed. "Have your loyalties changed, Agent?"

Jackson swallowed. His lips thinned. "Yes."

Lena's heart thumped in her chest and then soared. He'd made his decision. He'd chosen them.

Thomas sat back, a thunderstruck look on his face. His angry stare bored into Jackson and then moved back and forth between Jackson and Lena. It even turned to Ghost at one point, considering. Leaving the issue of Jackson's loyalty, he returned his desperate grab for her baby.

"But not only *her* child. Right?" He looked down the table at Lena. "Unless the father is sitting at this table—and based on your physical development, he is not—then it isn't entirely your decision to make." He nodded his head briskly, a final movement like an exclamation point. "We'll see what Alex has to say about his child being raised in filth, deprivation, and constant danger—"

Lena stood up, knocking the stool back. The sweater slid down her legs to the floor. Her hands were shaking. She had so many words she wanted fling at Thomas right now, but they stuck in her throat, mixed with bile and betrayal, and caught together.

"That's enough," Gabriela said. She rose, too, reaching out a hand to tangle her fingers with Lena's in solidarity and comfort. "You came to get your boys back, not to steal an unborn child." She lifted her chin. "We don't need you for the first, and I would strongly advise against the second."

Ghost shook his head. "First you offer us respect, and then you insult our lives as 'filth and deprivation'?" He rose, too, preparing to leave the table in disgust.

Once the Neo-barb left, he wouldn't be back, and the visitors would no longer be welcome to move freely in the valley. At the moment, that wasn't a problem for Lena. She was ready for Thomas and his men to get the Dust out, too.

Before he could leave, Patrick extended a hand asking him to wait. The agent looked down the table at his leader. "*Thomas*." Censure and disbelief at what he'd witnessed filled his voice as if the agent couldn't believe his leader had lost control.

Lena could. Alex had mentioned his friend's obsession. She'd experienced it, too, but never like this.

Thomas didn't look at his agent. He lowered his head and she saw his eyelids flutter down as he closed them. He raised his head again and met Lena's gaze. His expression was filled with regret. "I'm sorry." He turned to look at Gabriela and Ghost. "I apologize. I lost myself. I mean no disrespect."

"That is what you offered, however. You have no idea how we live or what we've built." The Neo-barb wasn't ready to let it go.

"I do. I was raised among People. They saved me after a Scavenger attack killed my family. Raised me as one of them, until Scavengers again took a family from me. I do know. And I know better. I am sorry." He shook his head at his own stupidity. "This is a high-emotion issue, but you're right." He darted a glance down the table at Lena. "It isn't one for me to decide."

Somehow his words didn't reassure her much. The look he gave her when he said them seemed to offer a promise to her of more difficulty, and with someone whose opinion would matter, when Alex returned. The knot of nausea and anxiety coiled in her belly again.

What will *Alex think?*

"If we could all sit down," Patrick said. He spread his hands. "Lena's pregnancy is her concern, not ours." As soon as he saw Thomas open his mouth to speak, Patrick raised his voice and spoke over his leader. "You wanted to see how the students here were doing. You've done that. They're learning and prospering. Our focus right now should be the wards who've been denied the opportunity to do both. We need to get them back. That's what we came for."

Thomas nodded. Ghost took a breath and looked at her.

They were all looking at her.

"Please, Ghost. Gabriela." She squeezed her friend's hand and then released it to gesture at the table.

The big Neo-barb flashed another look around the table, ending by spearing Thomas with a disgruntled stare. He resettled Lena's seat, pulled his stool out, and took a seat. Gabriela joined him.

"Has the plan changed at all from when we put the net in place?" Patrick glanced at Thomas as if to remind him of an earlier report.

West. seated down the table, was clearly not in the loop. "Net?" he asked.

Lena played with the next venison-wrapped apple she wished she could be eating. "I used the energy of the Sparks here in the valley to create a defensive net of energy beneath the surface of the earth. I've told the Dust what to look for—Scavengers and Neo-Barbs that aren't native to our valley. When they come, I'll know. And when we're ready—" she gave him a thin smile "—I'll use it to tell the Dust to find hostile forces and reject their life forces. Violently."

She allowed him to use his imagination as to what that might entail. Based on his throat movement as he swallowed and paled, she thought he had the right idea.

"You've progressed in your own abilities, too," Thomas noted.

She glanced at him. "I have, though the net is based on something I'd already done for myself and by myself when I was on my own in the desert."

"So are we supposed to wait here until Scavengers decide to attack?" another of the agents asked. "Because we need to get those boys and get back to the Ward School before snow—"

Thomas flicked him a look of disgust.

"Traps you here in our filth and deprivation for a winter?" Ghost rumbled.

Now Thomas sighed. At least he didn't try to deny his own words, Lena noted. He was willing to take it on the chin when he'd earned it.

And he had.

Before the conversation could spiral back into another argument, she spoke up. "That's no longer a concern. You're here now, the sky doesn't look like snow regardless of the cold, and we'll be able to make a decision based on…reconnaissance…by tonight."

Jackson nodded. He assured the men, "Depending on what intel we get, we'll either be prepping for an incoming attack by the Scavs or we'll be free to make our own move to get the wards back."

Ghost offered his portion of the plan now, though whether it was because he wanted to be helpful or wanted to deliver the bad news himself, Lena didn't know. "If the Scavs are not close and we're free to go, half of you will remain behind here to protect the non-warriors, and half will come with us to assist."

"Half?" West spoke his indignation before Thomas could even respond.

His leader flicked him a look of annoyance, and the agent subsided.

"Half?" Thomas asked. "We're far more equipped to get in and handle a delicate operation."

"It's not going to be a delicate operation, Thom." Lena responded. "We aim to make an impression. It's going to be direct and brutal. They'll hand over the boys or we'll take them. Ghost and his warriors will help us use the environment to keep us hidden, which in spite of all of your training is a talent very particular to Neo-barbs. The girls and I will get us in through their defensive wall." She nodded at Patrick and Theo, noting their contribution via descriptions of what they'd seen of the Neo-barb holding at Taos. "And then we'll use all of the talents very particular to us to make our points about cooperation and neighborliness."

Thomas ran his finger in small circles on the surface of the wood table. He leaned back and stared up at the ceiling, thinking. Lena was familiar with this now. She took the opportunity to shove the bit of meat and apple into her mouth and crunched down.

Thomas's pale gaze turned to her. "So who's bringing us intel, and when will we have it?"

Lena shifted the apple in her mouth to speak around it. "I am. And I'll get started as soon as I've had a chance to finish eating."

THIRTY-TWO

Alex

Alex flipped the now damp towel over the top of the shower rail and left the bathroom, padding into his room. He'd dress, grab something to eat, and be on his way. Ace would already be gone from the room up the hall. They'd outlined their plan of attack the night before. Their trade appointment was set for the afternoon. The morning was dedicated to gathering information.

Ace had his duties as a Director—and he'd promised to keep an ear out for anything coming out of Locust House. Alex planned a different method of gathering information. He meant to stalk the warehouse and caravan cars belonging to the Locust House trader. And he hoped for a contact from Erika. Sooner would be better than later. He hated going into an op blind.

He should have known she'd have anticipated that. He paused in the doorway, then shook his head as he continued across the room to his bags.

She was on the bed, propped up against the wall, long legs crossed at the ankle. She was wearing some high-necked, long dress in a material that technically covered her but left little to the imagination as it draped over her long, lush curves. She was still a beautiful woman.

But not his woman. Not anymore.

"I guess it would be too much for me to hope for you to respect my privacy?" Alex pulled on his pants and fastened them before glancing over at her.

She watched him shamelessly. "It's nothing I haven't seen

before."

He grabbed his undershirt and pulled it on, covering his skin. The irritation and the need to cover himself was new. A woman, even a strange woman, appearing in his room would not have been cause for prudery before. He would have taken advantage of the situation. Things had changed more than he'd thought. "It's nothing you have a right to see now."

Erika laughed. "So I guess it's a good thing that I resisted the temptation to join you in the shower?"

"It would have gotten you thrown on your elegant ass."

The laugh quieted into a satisfied purr. "Ohhh, you still think my ass is elegant, do you?"

Alex turned away from her, shrugging into his black button-down shirt and giving each button his attention. "Report, Erika. Then return to duty."

"When did you lose your sense of fun?"

"Report." He gave his voice an extra edge of steel.

"Fine." She sat up and swung her legs over the bed. Her voice became brisk. "You knew I was placed as a non-Spark trader with Locust House in Zone Eight? Thomas arranged for my transfer to Zone Six two years ago, when the alliance between Six and Four became more obvious."

Alex nodded. It made sense.

"I worked my way up, gained confidences, gained a pin of my own. Six months ago another transfer came through, but this one was initiated through Locust House. They needed me in Zone Four. They had a special project. A sensitive trade agreement, requiring a delicate touch, and in order to be given the assignment, the rep they chose had to be approved by Four. I sent a message to Thomas, and off I went."

"This trip a part of your approval process?"

"I believe it's a sign that I've made it through the process, though nothing official has been said. I've been assigned to Jacob Brayer as his personal trade liaison."

"Four's oldest grandson?"

Lucas's brother.

"And his protege. If this trip goes off as planned, I will

have—well, if not the keys to the kingdom, then access to them."

Alex turned and gave her the first real smile since he'd seen her the night before. "Excellent."

"It is excellent. And then you showed up…right on time."

"On time?"

She nodded. "They kept referring to 'a thorn in their heel' and made references to finally yanking it here. They have something planned. Jacob is anticipating doing something that will garner him a great deal of favor. The moment I saw you I realized to whom they were referring."

"I'm the thorn?" He smirked.

"Aren't you always?" She rolled her eyes. "Of course you are. Were you delayed on your trip here?"

He frowned at her. Sloan's request they take a different route. The side trip to the town. And then they'd been delayed all along it. Sloan's hand in it all? Was she involved?

He grunted and nodded. "So what's the trap?"

She shook her head. "I don't know yet. But—" She stopped, huffing out a breath and biting her lip.

"But?"

"But it might have to do with the documents we're here to take possession of—shipping manifests. Records of personal cargo shipments belonging to Councilor Four from this zone through Six and onto Four."

Alex could feel his eyes light up. "I knew it. Proof."

She made a small noise of confirmation. "That reaction is exactly what they're expecting."

"It's a helluva bait."

"It is bait. You know that?"

He nodded. "The key will be to get it without springing the trap. That's where you come in. You need to find out everything you can about this package—where it is, how it's hidden, when they're taking possession of it."

"Without compromising the position I've worked so hard to achieve, right?" Her eyes narrowed.

"That goes without saying. In fact, I expect you to do whatever's necessary to consolidate your hold on both your position and Jacob Brayer."

"Whatever's necessary? Is that code for fucking him?"

Alex shrugged. "Assuming you aren't already. You were never particularly squeamish when it came to getting the job done. Has that changed?"

She stared at him, her posture rigid and her eyes icy. "I despise him."

"We all do things in the name of duty that we find distasteful."

"Distasteful?" She laughed. "Do you have any clue—?" She stood. "If this is punishment for me not caring enough for you—"

"Do you understand that every agent that we have sent to Zone Four has either disappeared or gone native? You got in. Brayer doesn't even know you're a Spark. They won't suspect you. We'd be fools not to use this advantage."

"It's a funny thing. When you sent me away, I was excited." She looked back at him. "I didn't care that you were ending things. New adventures awaited. I never cared for you like you cared for me." She shrugged. "It's why I didn't see the point of sending me off at first...until I realized how strong your feelings were. You were living even more of a lie than either of us knew, weren't you?"

Alex looked away with a heavy sigh. "Can we please not do this? All of that is completely irrelevant. It has nothing to do with this situation or with my request that you apply pressure by—."

"Nothing? You're pimping me out for the cause, Alex. Please don't tell me that has nothing to do with your feelings for me—."

"I have no feelings for you. Not anymore. And if Jacob was Four's granddaughter and you were a male agent, I'd be making the exact same request. It's not personal. It's practical."

"Oh, please. A man like you? You may fool everyone else with the tough guy act, but I know the real you, poet." She sauntered over and reached out to grab his hands and slide them down her sides to her hips. Her body was as long and lush and rounded as it had been when they'd been together years before. "I remember what you like. No more pretense. No more wasting time." She grinned at him.

He pulled his hands away and stepped back. “You’re a beautiful woman, Erika. But that’s not going to happen.”

“Don’t you want to make up for lost time?”

He shook his head. “There’s nothing to make up for. No time lost. That decision was made.”

She laughed. “Bullshit, Alex Reyes. I know you.”

“Why does it matter? You didn’t care for me, right? Not like that? No more than a stepping stone?”

“Right.” She swept a narrow-eyed, evaluating gaze over his features. “It doesn’t matter. I figured it was a workaround—make you realize what you’ve missed, and you wouldn’t force me to do this.”

“I’m not forcing you to do anything. You signed up for it. A hand in the re-shaping of the world, remember? This is your job. If you can’t handle it, then fine, don’t. We'll figure out some other way to get that access to Brayer. Someone will be willing to do whatever it takes.”

She stared at him. Alex couldn’t figure out what was going on in her head. She'd always been the one person who could hide things from him. He'd thought back in the day it was charming. It was a game. Now he needed to know where she stood. He wanted answers. He wanted that bait, so he could be done. He was tired, but he needed more than mere rest.

He needed his home. His one home.

“You're right,” she finally said. She nodded. “It is my job. I'll get the information no one else can get. I'll do the impossible because that’s what I do.”

“Excellent.” He echoed the earlier praise he’d given her. “I don’t want anything to compromise your position. Don’t attempt contact again until you have the information I need. And be careful.”

“Yes, sir,” she said softly. She turned away and headed for the door. When she reached it, she made sure the hallway was clear before slipping out. She didn’t look back.

Alex shifted in his chair at the long conference table. The hard wooden seat was too short for his frame and it bit into the backs of his thighs, numbing his legs. Was it deliberate?

He glanced over at the Councilor at the head of the table a few seats away. Councilor One's hang-dog eyes watered as he waited for Ace to finish thanking him for the favorable terms to which they'd agreed. His shoulders slumped in a habitual terrible posture. Everything about the man reflected the feeling of defeat that permeated his zone. Was he the source, or merely a mirror of centuries of disease, death, and Council neglect?

All Alex knew was that he was looking at a living argument for why existing within the status quo was so unacceptable. The Sparks of each zone were complacent because they felt safe in the false value granted by the Council. The minute they joined the cause in any great numbers, the crack-down would be swift and brutal and designed to reduce all of them to *this*. It was what Alex and Thomas were working so hard to avoid.

It was almost impossible to rally those with broken spirits.

How could Alex achieve it now, with this man? What subterfuge or threat of force could he bring to bear on this man that hadn't already been applied to him and his people?

Nothing.

All Alex had left was the one thing none of them had been given a taste of in a very long time: respect. No, not the trappings of respect the man earned as a Councilor while being worked over by Councilors, traders, agents like himself. One had the opposite problem of the emperor in the old story. He had the clothing. He lacked the power it was meant to clothe.

Both problems were rooted in the same cause. No one had ever given the man the truth. Giving it to him now would go beyond calculated risk to foolhardy. But the potential payoff—to cut off Four from a rich source of the one thing generations of death in the general population had managed to achieve, consistently strong Sparks? That was huge.

Alex blinked himself free of his reverie and realized the object of his thoughts was staring back at him with those moist grey eyes. Alex flicked a look around the table and realized that Ace and the other Zone Three traders from various houses ranging up and down the table were all staring at him.

Shit.

"I apologize, Councilor. I was lost in memories for a moment."

The Councilor roused himself enough to raise a brow.

"I don't know if you are aware, sir, but this is my home zone. You are, to me, the first Councilor in more ways than one."

Councilor One blinked. Alex didn't know if the semblance of surprise was because he hadn't known or he hadn't expected Alex to admit it. "I did not," he said, voice soft. "Isn't it forbidden for an agent to return to his home zone?"

"To live, yes. But this is a brief visit, in pursuit of benefits to all of us. I'm not staying."

The Councilor didn't take the bait and ask about the benefits. His was silent for a long moment and then asked, "Have you been to see your family? Or do you not remember where you lived as such a small child?" He gestured to a man standing in the corner behind him. "I'm sure I could have my people look into—"

"No, sir." Alex cleared his throat. "That's a very generous offer, but unnecessary. I decided before I arrived that such a visit would be…unproductive. After all these years, and the history of the zone…" He stared into the man's eyes, knowing the Councilor would not miss his reference to the disease and deprivation his people suffered. "I can't be certain my family is even still living. I'd rather not rouse again any loss long since tucked away."

Alex was startled by the quick flare of pain and compassion in the man's eyes. Was this a Councilor who genuinely cared for his people?

"I understand," the man told him. "That constant potential for loss is a heavy pall on those of us who live here."

Alex nodded respectfully, watching the play of emotions across the man's face as he shifted in his seat. He was either the best of all of them, or he might be that most rare of things: a good man. When Alex spoke again, he infused his voice with respect. This time, it was genuine.

"That's why I've come to you now, sir." He glanced down at his hands and then carefully searched the faces of the other men ranging down the table. “But…what I have to say is a personal message of hope from Councilor Three. If your Zone Three trade negotiations are complete, perhaps we could speak in private?”

There were pinched brows and murmurs from around the table, but Alex turned back to the only man who mattered. The Councilor stared at him. Alex forced himself to breathe in and out, steady and even, even as his heart hammered in his chest. It had been so long since he’d dealt in the truth the anxiety of the decision was almost cramping his stomach.

The Councilor nodded. “Gentlemen, I’m sure you’ll understand that messages of hope and prosperity are hard to come by here. If you’ll withdraw to the anteroom, my aide will escort you to a reception, where I will join you shortly.”

Alex didn’t look at any of them as they rose. He focused on the table in front of him as they rose and filed from the room, still muttering. When Ace took his feet to join them, Alex glanced up at the man.

Their gazes contacted for less than an instant, but he relaxed. Alex had cast himself as apart and deliberately excluded Ace from this conversation. It gave Ace the opportunity to vent about his “uninvited guest” and curry sympathy from the others. It gave him an opening. Ace was on top of his game. Alex was confident Ace would use it.

Once the door clicked shut behind the aide, and it was only Alex, the Councilor, and the Councilor’s personal Spark security guard hovering in the background, the Councilor smiled.

“So what are these glad tidings our newest young Councilor has sent? And will I be pleased or sorry after I hear them?”

Alex took a breath. “Both, I think. I hope you’ll consider what I have to tell you. It’s about the girls and the future of both Sparks and those who rely upon them for survival.”

The Councilor frowned. “The girls?” He cocked his head at Alex. “Girls like the ones stolen from the Conclave this summer? You *were* involved.”

“You know about them, of course, and that it wasn’t ‘delicate personal cargo’ that went missing?”

“We all know about them. The girls are a danger—”

Alex held the man's gaze. He leaned forward. "Only to the machinations of a certain faction within the Council, the same group that convinced all of you that it was necessary to ship them away in secret to Zone Four. Sometimes new eyes can find truths long hidden. Councilor Three has discovered what happens to them. Have you ever wondered about their fate? Have you ever asked yourself what becomes of these smallest citizens of yours?"

THIRTY-THREE

Alex

"No." There was a hardness to One's voice, a steel that hadn't been there before.

"Sir, wait, please. I saw your reaction when I told you the truth. You can act now to protect your citizens—"

"That's what I'm doing, Agent Reyes. I have a duty to all of my citizens. *All of them*. You're asking me to put an entire population at risk for the sake of a few based on mere supposition and rumor."

"It's neither supposition nor rumor. I've seen one of the camps."

"Where are they, then? Can you show me?"

Alex gritted his teeth. "He's moved it."

"So, again, you ask me to risk everything with no proof at all. I will not."

"There is proof."

"Where?"

"I believe some of it is here now. The records the Zone Four representative—"

One reared back and gusted an exasperated sigh. "Are no more than cargo manifests for private shipments of goods—"

"Of girls."

"The fact that girls are shipped to Zone Four is not news to me."

"But where they end up, I believe, would very much be."

One lowered his face and rubbed his watery eyes. "There is a madness that infects them. They are a danger," he began.

"*No.*" Alex shook his head and slapped the table for emphasis. "*That* I can prove is bullshit."

The Councilor raised his head. "How?"

It was a chance.

"One of them escaped notice. She was raised free."

"The radical that attacked and killed a Councilor?" One huffed a laugh. He clearly couldn't believe that Alex would point to someone who was a criminal and everything Councilor Four had warned the rest of them against.

Alex swallowed. He was inching out onto a precipice. "I've met her. She's not mad. She's not dangerous, except to men who would imprison and torture those like her. She wants to be free to raise them herself, to teach them—"

"You've met her?" One was aghast.

"She's building a school. Is that the act of a dangerous madwoman?"

"Depends on what she's teaching." One looked down, tapping his index finger on the table as he thought. "Can you prove this? Take us there. Let us see for ourselves."

Alex leaned back.

"I thought not. You're acting contrary to the interests of the Council you've been sworn to protect since childhood, and you have nothing with which to excuse your actions."

"Detain Jacob Brayer. Take the records from his possession. Let me see them. I'll find the camps. I'll get your proof."

One threw back his head and laughed. It was the most lively thing Alex had seen him do. Alex swallowed his bitterness. He'd risked everything giving this man the truth, and he'd gotten nothing for his trouble.

"Detain the grandson of Councilor Four, the man who makes our survival possible through favorable treaties and agreements, the man who leads the Council in its decisions to protect and guide us all to better lives?" He shook his head and looked at Alex with weighing eyes, his fingers gently tapping his lips. "By all rights and by your own admission, I should detain *you*, Agent Reyes."

"Then do it." Alex flicked a glance at the security man. He'd come more and more awake as their conversation progressed. He was primed to move. Alex allowed a tiny smile to play around his lips. If either of them thought local security could take Alejandro Reyes, they were sorely mistaken.

One leaned back in his seat. He rubbed a hand over the back of his head as he considered Alex sitting calmly before him. He shook his head. His watery eyes had somehow changed. They weren't defeated. They were sharp, considering. "Can you convince your radical to come to the Meet? Can you convince *her* to prove her sanity and her cause?"

Alex caught his breath. Was One offering him a chance? "Perhaps?"

One raised his brows.

Alex nodded. "I will."

One rose from his seat, shoulders still hunched, belying the steel in his eyes. "Understand, Agent Reyes, that my answer remains the same until I have proof. You have a very narrow window of time in which to supply it before the activities that you have admitted to here come under greater scrutiny. That scrutiny will include a hunt for any allies. Be very certain you want to continue down this path…that your new, young Councilor is willing to risk everything for you to do so."

Alex pushed back his chair and stood as well. "He is."

"Very well. The clock is ticking." One left him there, slipping out the door with his Security guard to go and join the traders.

How could one man be so defeated he'd refuse even a chance at a new way, a chance at prosperity and hope for his people? Alex shook his head and cursed as he strode down the narrow streets. How could he himself have risked so much? And for what? Zone One support?

Alex snorted at his own stupidity. A risk like the truth was worthy of a Councilor like Sloan, who was primed to be a power in her own right. But One? Bent, defeated, hopeless One? Yes, he ruled the zone that produced most of the strongest Sparks, and logically was the source of the greatest number of those strong girls. But he had little power of his own on the Council, and both his stature and his risk aversion was evidence of that. He wasn't willing to move against those with more power, even if he suspected it was right, as he clearly did. The man was ruled by fear.

Alex cursed him again. Perhaps it was time for another Councilor to be replaced?

His shoulder smacked into someone coming the other way. Alex grunted an apology and pulled himself out of his thoughts. He looked around. The grey, mostly empty streets weren't anymore. Where had all these people come from? He turned his head.

The square. He'd wandered into his former neighborhood. Across the street, people moved through the small, hand-made displays and booths of local and small, independent trader goods. Alex stared across at it. It seemed a pitiful shadow of the robust neighborhood markets that he'd experienced in both zones two and three. But what he saw now and what he remembered both told him the same thing. Though it was small, it was the life's blood of this neighborhood.

Alex crossed the street. He wandered among the booths, looking at what they had on display. At first, he kept his head down and didn't make eye contact. As soon as he became aware of what he was doing, however, he growled at himself. What was he afraid of? Running into someone he remembered? It wasn't like they'd ever make a connection between the agent moving among them now and the little neighborhood boy who'd been sent off to the Council so many years before. He was just one of many gone over the years in this zone—whether to the Council or to illness. People here worked hard to forget.

A familiar smell in the air turned his head. He tracked it through the growing darkness as night fell, a smile pulling at his lips. A woman was making candy, offering tiny, irregular pieces on a dish for sampling to entice purchases. Her face was wrinkled, her hair wrapped in an old cloth, and her eyes were tired. Others were already packing up their goods and abandoning trade for the night, but she was hanging on for any final shoppers. She gave him a wide, genuine smile when he approached.

"Sweets for your sweetie?" She chuckled and winked at him.

"That's what I'm hoping." Alex gave her a wide grin. He took a bit of candy from the dish, and his brows rose in surprise at the pure maple taste melting into his tongue. "That's *good.* Perfect. What sizes do you offer?"

She gestured over to her little hand-made cloth bags.

Alex shook his head. "I won't be coming back this way for a long time, if ever. I need something bigger. Can you have all of this delivered to Ace Coffey of Dragonfly House at trader's housing by tomorrow afternoon?"

The woman's eyes widened. "You want all of it?"

He laughed. "Can you do it?"

She nodded.

"How much?"

She named a figure and he nodded and scrawled his note without haggling. She'd cash it in with Ace or a representative of the house when she made delivery. Not dickering over the price took away some of the fun, but the money mattered more to her than it did to him. The pleasure Lena would get from this extravagance was worth every C-note.

When he finished, he turned away. He was on the edge of the far side of the square. Across the street from him was the faded lavender door. Just down from it was the Goose.

Alex's smile died. He stared at the door, and then the sign, and back again. Before he had a chance to second-guess himself, he stepped across the narrow street to the walk. He faced the door for a long moment, then turned to the right and strode down the street.

When he'd been small, he'd struggled to keep up with his father's long stride. He'd had to trot along beside him, clutching his father's fingers, telling him about his little-boy day. On a good day, he'd skipped beside his Dad.

Now his own long legs closed the distance to the corner of

the alley faster than he remembered. He glanced around self-consciously, then ducked his head and walked up it. The street was narrow and dark, but clean. The people here were poor and dealt with more spiritual blows than most, but they were proud. They hadn't given in to despair.

He almost walked past the bakery. If it hadn't been for the faint smell of yeasty heaven clinging to the building well after morning baking, he might have. The bakery was closed. He wasn't surprised. It was getting late. He should get back to the Council building and his temporary quarters. He had work he should be doing. The clock was ticking, after all.

But he didn't. He stood in the darkness, staring up at the narrow, shuttered windows above the bakery. He'd been born up there. He'd spent his first five years there, happy and loved. What would it have been like to be one of the mid-range children? What would his life have been if he'd stayed to be raised by his parents in this place? He'd have been a very different man, of that he was sure. Would he have been content?

A cold wind gusted down the narrow street, funneled by the walls to either side. Alex tugged his coat across his chest and began to button it against the cold. A sudden thought hit him and stalled his fingers.

The one thing his father had managed to pass on to him was a love of poetry. He'd achieved it through the book of verse and scrawled questions he'd shoved in young Alex's only bag. Would his father have felt the same compulsion to share it with his son if he'd stayed? Would Alex have felt the lessons carried the same weight?

In his mind, he could picture the familiar worn fabric cover of The Collected Poems of Stephen Crane. It wasn't the original cover. That had long since worn away. Someone along the line had hand-stitched and glued a new cover made of fabric sewed over thin, narrow slats of wood.

His thoughts jumped to a poem he'd struggled with again and again over the years.

Behold, the grave of a wicked man,
And near it, a stern spirit.

There came a drooping maid with violets,
But the spirit grasped her arm.
"No flowers for him," he said.
The maid wept:
"Ah, I loved him."
But the spirit, grim and frowning:
"No flowers for him."

Now, this is it —
If the spirit was just,
Why did the maid weep?

It was one he'd looked at again and again, wondering what his father's cryptic comments meant. He'd been able to figure out the rest, or he'd told himself he had, anyway. But one comment had always haunted him: *Justice is wickedness to those bearing violets. Be mindful of their grief. The spirit is righteous. The man is loved. Stern vs wicked. Look for the violets and find Perspective...* He'd always assumed that his father meant for him to be a stern spirit. He would be the bad man that made others quail but who kept order. That was the role that had been handed to him when he was five years old, after all.

Then he'd met Lena. She made him question everything.

What had his father, a man who loved deeply, meant? What had he wanted for his son, being sent away to become Justice?

So go inside. Go ask. He shook his head at himself. *Just like that? Hello...remember me? Hey, there's something that's been eating me all these years...*

A sound that was half-laugh and half-sob escaped from his throat. What would it be like to be able to simply...ask? What would his father think of the man he'd become, of what Alex had made of the lessons a father left for his son in the pages of a book of poetry?

Alex dragged his palm across his brow, using his wrist to swipe at the moisture gathering below his eyes. He glanced up one more time at the dark windows above.

Some things are better left alone.

Alex turned away. He raised his head to find his way back down the alley and stopped.

A small, round woman with short, curly white hair above sallow brown skin stood leaning, one hand on the wall beside her to support herself. She stared at him. A knit bag sagged heavily from her other arm, filled with small bags and folded boxes all covered by the brown, papery, rounded tops of onions—her groceries.

Tears ran down her cheeks and dripped from her sagging jawline. Her mouth opened and worked, but no sound came out. She tried again, and managed one word. “Mijo.”

My son.

Alex stared at her, though she blurred as his eyes filled. It felt as if something collapsed inside his chest then bloomed, a swirling pain that took his breath. He managed a single word, too, somehow infused with the accent of his childhood and not the clipped speech he’d been trained to.

“Mama?”

THIRTY-FOUR

Lena

Lena swam up from sleep to wakefulness, pulling herself through the dark, syrupy pleasure of a deep sleep. Her eyes fluttered open, and she blinked through the darkness. She was curled on her side, facing the wall. Something had woken her. Anxiety crawled through her.

She reached out for the Dust, making a quick check. No one had tried to enter their valley. There were no disturbing ripples from those who didn't belong.

It made sense. The day before, she'd settled in and reached up to fly with the Dust, intent on spying out any Scavenger or Neo-barb incursions. How close were they? From what direction would they come? What she'd discovered had shocked and worried them all.

No one was in their area. The Neo-barbs were sealed tight in Taos—not even a patrolling guard ventured out. The boys were there, alive and their energy signatures still strong. As for the Scavengers…Lena had searched hard for groups of human life signs. She'd had to range further and further out.

She'd found them in temporary huts clinging to the bottom of the inner cliffs of the Rio Grande Gorge and the tangled metal that used to span it as a bridge. Was this why she'd never noticed them before? She'd been looking at surface level? Or perhaps they had been further out, marauding, when she'd looked toward the gorge before?

She'd asked West about the presence of Scavengers at the gorge when he'd traveled through before they came to the valley. West had been the agent Thomas sent to recon the area, and he'd claimed to be thorough. He'd shaken his head. There had been no sign of the group before. She hadn't seen anything, either, that first time she'd looked up toward the gorge. But she hadn't been looking closely that night. Had West?

Whatever the reason, they were there now, and they weren't moving much or far from their camp. What were they waiting for?

Lena rolled over, still filled with unease but trying to comfort herself with the knowledge that her defensive net registered no intruders.

She jerked back. Leo stood next to her bed, eyes wide. He said nothing. He didn't move.

"Leo?" Lena sat up. "What's wrong?"

The little boy was silent.

She pushed the covers back and swung her legs over the side of the bed. She wanted to reach for him. There was something wrong. She sparked the candle across the room, telling the Dust to make the flame flare tall and bright.

In front of her, Leo's little fingers picked at the side of his sleep pants. There was a long stain along the inside of both legs. Mud coated the bottom of his pants and his knees. He wasn't this upset because he'd had an accident, was he?

"Leo. What happened?"

He shuddered when she touched him and leaned forward, burying his head in her chest. He was cold—too cold. His hands clenched her shirt. He mumbled something.

"He said? Who said what?"

Leo pulled away, but only slightly. "He saw me. When I went to go pee-pee. I hid from him so he couldn't get me, too. I didn't help her. I hid." The little boy whispered his confession.

"What?" Horror grew. Help her? Help who?

"He said he didn't have time for me. He said if I told anyone or if I moved or if I came out, he would cut my tongue out. I didn't want to come out. But I got cold."

"Who said, Leo?" She slid her hands from the child's back to his small, thin shoulders and gently pulled him away so she could see him. His body shook under her hands. "No one will hurt you. I promise. Who said that?"

"The man from the table, yesterday. The man that took Marissa."

Lena stared at Leo in horrified disbelief for a single beat of her heart before she swung him up into her arms and raced from the room and across the hall. She'd sparked the candles in the girls' room, all of them, in the time it took to step in and turn toward Marissa's bunk.

It was empty.

She screamed for Marissa, and for Jackson and Rose. Voices sounded behind her as she fled down the stairs and out the front door, still shouting for Marissa.

The stars and the moon were bright above. No clouds meant plenty of light from above, and plenty of cold, too. Her breath frosted in front of her in a near constant stream as she shouted and gasped for breath and ran.

"Where, Leo?" One hand swept up to his cheek to make the terrified child focus on her face. "Where did you see him? Where did he take Marissa?"

"Where did who take Marissa? What the Dust is going on?" Jackson swung her around.

"Marissa's gone! Thomas took Marissa!"

"Thomas did no such thing." Thomas's voice cracked out from behind Jackson. "What's going on?"

Lena gaped. He'd just woken, too. She hadn't even thought to check the room they were staying in. She'd been sure it would be empty.

She shook her head. "Marissa's gone. Leo said—Leo—" She looked down at the shivering child. "You said the man from the table."

Leo nodded. "The man from the table. The other man."

Thomas moved closer. He settled his hand on Leo's back. "Which man, Leo? Was he close to me?"

Leo shook his head. "Down the table. The angry man."

Thomas leaned away again. He turned to Patrick, who had appeared behind him in the night. "West or Carlo. Check their cots."

Patrick hurried away. Lena swung around again, her eyes searching the valley. Figures moved now, and voices called out. None was an agent carrying a little girl. Once she'd made a circle, scanning all the while, her gaze fell back on Thomas.

"We'll find her." He made a gesture for her to give him Leo. "He's wet, Lena. He'll freeze. So will you. Come inside."

"I have to find her."

"We will." He paused, shifting Leo into his arms as a thought occurred to him. "Can you not look for her? Like you did the Scavengers today—yesterday?"

Lena dragged a frigid gasp of air into her lungs and nodded. He was right. She should have thought of it. "I need to sit."

"Inside," Jackson said, taking her arm. "Let's go."

As they headed to the rancho house, Ghost appeared out of the night and stopped Patrick on his way back. The agent's face was grim as he conferred with the huge Neo-barb.

"Tell me," Thomas snapped as they drew close.

Patrick swung to face them. "West is gone." He jerked his head at an agent hovering in the doorway behind him. "Carlo didn't hear anything. He has no idea how long West's been gone. And Thomas—West handled that kid at the fort's final questioning. The kid collapsed after he left the room…"

"All of his contacts are suspect now." Thomas's voice was as furious as his face.

"But we can root them all out," Patrick said.

The cold inside Lena now rivaled the air seeping through her thin nightclothes. West was behind all of it? The plot against her? And now Marissa? Threatening Leo?

"No one heard anything," Lena said. Her voice sounded hollow in her ears. "If Leo hadn't gotten up to pee, we'd all still be sleeping and no one would know."

"How long ago, Leo?" Ghost leaned over the shivering boy in Thomas's arms. "How long ago did you see them?"

Leo shook his head. "I hid."

"West threatened him. So he hid. I'm guessing for a while." Lena nodded at the little boy's pants.

Ghost glanced down and his lips tightened. "We'll get him," he promised the little boy. He looked at Lena. "We'll get her back."

"I'm going to go inside and try to see them."

"Good idea."

Lena opened her mouth to tell Ghost it wasn't her idea, but he kept talking.

"I'm sending parties to check the routes out. I had men at every access point. We'll reinforce them. He shouldn't be able to get out of the valley."

"My men and I will go with you," Patrick said. "Jackson?"

"I'm staying with Lena. I need to make sure she doesn't overtax herself."

"I'll go." Rose stepped out of the rancho house, shrugging into a heavy wool coat.

"The girls?" Lena asked.

"Are shaken. Gabriela is up with them. Theo is stationed outside in the hall. I need to be out looking." Rose's eyes pleaded with Lena to agree.

Lena nodded and passed her, squeezing her hand on the way in. She went straight to the floor in front of the fireplace, settling herself before it and counting on another Spark in the room to get it blazing again for warmth. She needed everything she had now to find Marissa.

Thomas coaxed the fire into a merry crackling heat himself before he murmured about returning after he'd gotten Leo changed and delivered upstairs with the girls.

Lena and Jackson were alone in the room. She took a deep breath, preparing to immerse herself in the Dust-view. Jackson crouched in front of her. His face was worried, but when he spoke his voice was low.

"Did you really believe Thomas had taken Marissa?"

Lena swallowed. "Leo said the man at the table. I assumed—he's been obsessed with us for so long. And deprived of any involvement in the next generation." Her hand curved over the soft swell of her belly. "I guess I did."

Jackson said nothing in response, but he nodded, and his face was bleak. She knew he'd been tense since Thomas had confronted him over that same table. So much of what Jackson had been raised to believe—to be—had crumbled around him in the last few months. She was afraid it was too much.

"But I was wrong," she reminded him now. "It wasn't Thomas; it was West."

"Why don't we reserve judgment on anyone until you go up and see who it is—and where they are."

Instead of answering, she took her deep breath again and plunged into the twilight world of the Dust. It was becoming easier. It should be. She'd done it so much lately.

Lena soared up to the swarming bright Dust. For the time being, she ignored the brilliant, glowing energy of the Sparks below her surrounded by the less brilliant life forms of non-powered humans. She was looking for prey that might have made it further afield.

She sailed up and up until she had a panoramic view of the earth beneath her. There were bright bits and blobs everywhere, but she thought the Dust what she needed, and everything non-human faded from view. Below, it was human lights swarming in and around the little village they'd created in the valley. It was human groups moving together with a purpose to the few access points to the valley—the main one down the long orchard path, the two steep paths to the heights of the cliffs surrounding them, and the twisted secret route that wound around through the back of the valley.

She checked ahead of the groups for a single pair of bright Spark lights. It was all darkness. Her gaze from above moved from access point to access point, looking for the life shapes of those given guard duty on this cold night.

When she reached the curving secret path at the rear of the valley no human life registered at all. That was wrong. Ghost's men had been at every access. She descended to search again, rushing along it with the speed being one with the Dust afforded her.

She found the darkened, crumpled form of a young man tossed to the side of the path. The opaline glimmer of Dust oozed from his pores to return to the air and the earth around him. She couldn't tell which of Ghost's young warriors this had been, not in this form. She'd come to know them all, and now one of them was gone—tossed away into the brush as if he never mattered.

Grief and a wild rage clutched at her throat. She flowed up along the path and the trees now, flowing to the hidden end of the valley. Unsatisfied, she rose again, to see down the hidden, overgrown path that lead away down a sloping rocky slope on the other side.

She didn't find them on the path, nor at its base where it branched along two smaller game trails. They were well away on the trail leading to the crumbled remains of an old road that curved up and around through the northern mountain pass. He'd stolen a horse. He rode as fast as he dared along the narrow trail, the little girl clutched in front of him. Another, brighter form rode behind him, clinging to him.

How long had Leo crouched, terrified, in his hiding place that night? A very long time.

She rushed at them in her Dust form now, an avenging ghost they couldn't see. She wouldn't kill him—no, not yet—because she wouldn't risk Marissa being alone in the wilderness. She could weaken him. She could offer strength and comfort to her girl.

She flowed down and around them, unseen. The agent's Spark was strong, a bright light flowing through his veins and suffusing him with a glow. The light behind him was familiar…and frightening.

Had he taken Karina? Or had she followed him, not understanding, and the opportunist had decided to include another powered girl? Karina's glow wasn't disturbed. Had she gone with him willingly? Lena remembered their odd encounter, and the girl's fierce, feral smile. Now, if anything, she was content.

Marissa's own light was wrong. The Dust moved within her in a chaotic whirl, starting and stopping, turning back on itself through her body. The Dust was confused.

Lena pressed closer, keeping pace with the movements of the horse, swirling around them as she leaned in. The chaos originated from the region of Marissa's neck.

He'd collared her.

Rage erupted from the well of anger deep inside, pouring out. She sucked it back in with the Dust as she gathered herself for an attack. If Karina could attack in the Dust form, so could she.

He'd collared Marissa.

Lena stabbed at him, white hot and sharp.

The pain turned back and crawled over her own essence like stinging ants. He was one of Thomas's Originals. He'd been taught to defend himself, probably by Alex himself. He'd anticipated her coming after him, attacking him, perhaps even searching for him like this. After all, he'd been in the room yesterday when she went up to look for enemies.

She'd had no idea there was an enemy in the room with her.

A moment later, Lena was tossed back with the force of Karina's counter-attack, tumbling away, feeling as if she contorted in agony though her physical form was far away across the mountain. Karina had apparently decided she wanted freedom more than wellness. She was clinging to West willingly. She'd protected him, driving off Lena.

Lena and the Dust pushed through the pain and she reoriented herself, swimming back.

West slowed the horse. The man-shaped light twisted in the saddle, looking back. When he turned again, he craned his head, looking up into the night as if he was searching for her. He'd felt her attack. He knew she was out here. Karina hunched closer and whispered in his ear. Not even a breath later, he urged the horse onward, pushing the animal to widen the distance between them and Marissa's rescuers.

Lena pulsed with helpless rage. Marissa hadn't moved. She hadn't given any indication she was even conscious. There was nothing Lena could do. Not from here.

She rose up, staring down, marking the man and the trails that spread before him, trying to anticipate where he might be going. When she'd seen what she needed, she sent Marissa a silent promise and swept back along her own spectral trail zooming back to her body, and the rancho, and the people she would use to exact her vengeance.

She came back to herself with the psychic equivalent of a thump, opening her eyes and letting loose a shout of fury that made Thomas and Jackson leap to their feet in alarm. Lena speared Thomas with an accusing stare.

"Where would one of your agents have gotten a restraining collar?"

Thomas held her stare. "I have no idea. Presumably in the field. West had just come back in from his assignment."

"Patrick assured me that any men you brought here were personally vetted by the two of you. You're responsible for Marissa's kidnapping, for the collar around her neck, for anything that happens to her because of your failure." Lena pushed herself up from the floor.

Thomas opened his mouth to answer, but Jackson spoke up first. "She's collared? That's how he managed it?"

Lena nodded, once, hard. "Karina is with him—willingly. She attacked me when she became aware of me. He's either heading north through Nations territory, which I doubt, or he's headed for the Scavengers in the gorge. That's why they didn't come here. They didn't have to. They were waiting for one of us to be delivered to them." She took a deep breath and pushed her hair behind her ears with shaking hands. "Jackson, would you mind finding Ghost and Rose? We need to leave immediately."

Jackson left the room, almost smacking into Thomas with his shoulder.

She looked down at her arm to check how her ability to adapt to the new activity was holding up. She wasn't glowing. Not yet. She'd still have to ground before she left. More time lost, but there was nothing she could do about that. She had to be ready to tear him apart when the opportunity presented itself.

She lifted her head. Thomas watched her, eyes narrowed and lips pursed.

"Why are you blaming me for this? Why assume I'd taken Marissa?"

Lena cocked her head. "Really?" At his nod, she huffed an unamused laugh. "Because Thomas, every bit of significant danger we've experienced can be traced back to you. Not finding any decent intel on those prisons and the traders used to transport girls. Not acting on what Alex brought you after the Meet. Refusing to confront the traitors in your own midst. And now this—the men you've vetted and sworn as safe…aren't."

"One man."

"One is all it took." She stepped up close to him, refusing to lower her gaze. "And yet you are supremely capable of plotting a resistance and running both a zone and a school. It makes me wonder, Thomas. Are you stretched too thin? Are you prioritizing things as you see fit, and we don't rank? Or are you the source of the problem?"

His pale eyes went cold and angry. "And what conclusion have you reached?"

"I haven't yet. When I do, you'll be the second man to know."

"The second man?" He paused, eyes widening, then narrowing. He laughed softly. "I like you, Lena. I admire what you're capable of, and what you're building, in spite of what you might think. So does Alex. Please don't think to play us against each other. We've been brothers longer than you've been alive. You don't understand the experiences that bind us."

"And you don't understand the bond between *us*," she snapped. She shook her head. "But have no fear, I wasn't threatening you with Alex. I was acknowledging that if I decide to punish you—and I *will* punish you if anything happens to Marissa—I'll give Alex the courtesy of knowing first." She turned away from him and marched up the stairs. She had to gather whatever she might need and do the same for the girls. She didn't have time to engage in a pissing contest with Thomas, no matter how much she might enjoy demonstrating why he should fear her and not her relationship with Alex.

At the top of the stairs, she turned to look back. He stared up at her.

"You should go prep your men. I'll be damned if I'll leave a single one of you behind with my wards while I'm out hunting your agent. You're all going with me, and you'll do whatever I require to help bring down West. We're leaving as soon as Gabriela can have her people ready."

She stepped outside to a crowd of horses and people. Jackson had helped the older girls ready for the journey himself while she and Rose slipped away to the area they all used to ground. She was still muzzy-headed and aching from the grounding. She ran her hand over her belly and told herself again that pregnant Sparks did ground. Just because circumstances required her to do it more often, she wasn't damaging her child. Was she?

She shoved her hair behind her ears and blinked as she stepped into the milling people and animals. The sun was rising, and she was anxious to be gone. Every minute that passed was another minute of distance between them and Marissa.

Her little group of five warriors, wearing layers of wool and thick coats, was behind her. Rose followed them. Lena had misgivings about bringing Hania, but the girl was right—why train her if they refused to allow her to use what she'd learned better than some of the other girls?

They'd decided Jackson would remain behind. Whatever path he chose for himself now, he was a trained agent and a skilled healer. The children and the People knew and trusted him. He was capable of caring for and leading them. He wasn't happy about staying behind, but he understood the decision. Marin would be going, and she was an exceptional healer. Here at the rancho, Jackson could pull double duty.

Thomas and his men checked their horses and gear to her left. Ahead of her, Ghost towered above everyone, giving final instructions to those of his warriors staying to guard the valley. The burial of Jaime, the young fallen guard, would be done while he was away. When Lena had told them where he was hidden, they'd gone to retrieve the body. Ghost and his people were already committed to defending the rancho and pursuing the kidnapper. Now they rode in pursuit of justice, too.

Ghost caught her eye and swung his arm for them to join him. A line of horses waited. Charity and Constance would share a mount, and Hania would alternate riding with Lena and Rose. Lena took the head of the horse Ghost indicated was hers and checked him over to be sure his gear was strapped on tight.

Jackson appeared at her shoulder. He settled one hand on the horse's neck and took a deep breath.

She shook her head, already irritated. The speedy grounding hadn't helped her mood. "You won't change my mind about going." There was an edge to her voice. She was the only one who could check West's position.

"Both the cold and the route by horseback will be hard on everyone," Jackson began, "and with your condition—"

Ghost laughed brusquely behind Jackson as he came back from securing the girls on their mounts. "My wife traveled on horseback and worked the fields outside our village in Texas until the day she birthed our son."

"See?" Lena told Jackson. "And she ended up fine."

As soon as the words were out of her mouth, she wished she could snatch them back. Ghost's wife hadn't ended up fine, had she? Lena spun to Ghost.

His face rearranged itself into a mask of unconcern. He nodded agreement. "At that time, yes." He stepped away to his own mount.

She shook her head at her own stupidity. "Just keep everyone here safe, Jackson."

Jackson sighed and left her.

As she was about to awkwardly swing herself up into the saddle, Gabriela darted over. Her face was grim. She glanced at Ghost.

Lena groaned. "You heard?"

Gabriela nodded and leaned over, fingers interlaced to provide Lena a step up into the stirrup. Lena stepped in, and Gabriela boosted her up.

Before Gabriela could turn away, Lena leaned down to grip her shoulder. "What happened, Gab?"

Gabriela ducked her head. When she looked up, there was an

old grief and a deep, festering heart wound raw in her eyes. "They died."

"But what happened in Texas?"

"That part of it is his story to tell. He doesn't speak of it, and I respect that." The Neo-barb woman who ruled the People with him shook her head. "They're gone, as is my Corazon, and you should leave it. It was his choice, Lena. He made a decision for the good of the People and did not foresee what it would cost him. It cost us both. It is a pain we willingly bear, but it doesn't make it easier." She fell silent for a moment. When she spoke again, her voice was filled with heat. "All I will say is that he should have killed Damar then. Or let me."

She gave Lena a final long look before she turned away and went to find her own horse. She'd told Lena what she needed to get off her chest. Damar had been involved with the loss of Ghost's family and Gabriela's daughter. Had this been before or after whatever disaster had befallen the village itself? Or had it been all one event?

Ghost rode toward her. "Your instinct is to follow the same path north that the traitor took." It wasn't a question.

Lena nodded. What else could they do?

Ghost took a breath. "Do you trust me, Lena?"

She raised her brows. "I swore an oath binding our people together."

He nodded. "We need to ride south."

She frowned. "He's taking the old northern pass road."

Ghost nodded again. "And what are his choices of destination from that road? He can branch off anywhere along it, yes, but all of those paths lead into the heart of Nations territory. He's a Council agent. He wouldn't survive. He knows this."

"His only other choice is to follow the road around the mountains."

"And south again."

"To Taos. Or to the gorge."

Ghost watched as she weighed the routes. When she didn't speak, he added, "The route south is faster by a day, at least. We can catch him."

"*If* he's going to Taos or the gorge."

"Where else? You and I both know the Council has contacts with Scavengers. Why else would he risk this here, in the middle of nowhere, with no support? He's going to the gorge. We can beat him there or meet him there if we go south now."

She closed her eyes, offering a rare prayer to whichever spirit might be listening. When she opened them again, she nodded.

Ghost pulled his horse away and drove him toward the mouth of the valley. The rest of the herd followed, Lena in their midst.

We're coming, Marissa.

Please let us be coming the right way.

THIRTY-FIVE

Alex

He didn't run to his mother like a boy. He didn't embrace her. Perhaps it was shock? He did cry, unashamed, as she crossed to him and reached out to touch his chest and then his cheek. If there was ever a time for a man to weep, it was upon seeing his mother for the first time since he was five years old.

"You came home." Her voice, so familiar and unfamiliar, was husky.

Alex nodded. He cleared his throat, and then again, before he answered. "Not to stay."

She shook her head. "No. No, you're an agent of the Council. But you came back tonight." Another gust of cold swirled down the alley and around them, and she drew her coat closer. "Come inside."

He almost refused. Not because he didn't want to come in, but because a part of him wanted to go back to the square. He could wait for his father, who would be coming home soon. Would he recognize Alex as readily as she had? Would they have the chance to make the walk from the square to home again, one more time before Alex left?

That was just little-boy fantasy. He'd go in with his mother to wait for his father. There would be time enough to catch up, to ask him so many questions.

He followed her into the store and through the little bakery to the back. Every step brought memories, every smell and shadow was somehow as familiar to him as if he'd never left. They climbed the narrow wooden stairs at the back, and then went through the thin door and into the apartment at the top.

Alex stood in the living room and looked around. It was the same and yet…not. It all seemed so small and worn. He didn't fit in the space like he had. He forced himself to straighten shoulders that were rounding, as if he could pull himself in and down and somehow fit the memories he'd made here.

His mother crossed four steps into the tiny kitchen. As a Spark and a baker, she rated a rare full stove. There was sink and a small icebox to keep her perishables fresh. She unloaded the little bag of her few items.

A smile fluttered across Alex's face. He remembered a friend daring him to lick a fresh block of ice that had been delivered once. He remembered the painful aftermath.

He followed her a couple of steps and then stopped in the middle of the room. There was something more than memory pulling at him… He looked around, but other than the space itself, nothing was familiar. It had been over forty years. Of course, the furnishings were the same, but the little touches…a knitted throw, a woven cover on the chair…those were different.

After a moment, it came to him. He inhaled deeply. The smell of so many dinners, the rice and beans and meat cooked with garlic and the herbs in the adobo and sofrito, was layered in with the yeasty smell of the bread that rose up from below. It was the memory of the smell of home.

His throat closed, and his nostrils flared as he fought to contain the tears again. If he cried again, so would she, and then he'd be undone.

She glanced at him as she slid the onions across the counter and must have seen the battle on his face because a question slid across her face.

Before she could ask, he told her, "It's the smell of your cooking. I didn't realize that I remembered it."

"Oh." She glanced around her little kitchen. "And I haven't cooked yet. I can cook for tomorrow. If you come back, I can cook for you. Tonight, I have nothing to offer you—"

Alex shook his head. "It's fine. I didn't come to eat."

"Why did you come?" She took a quick breath. "Not that I'm not happy you did—I am. I just—I was so startled—"

"How did you know…?"

"That it was you standing in the street?" She smiled. "You always looked like your father." She ran her gaze over his face. "You have my chin, I think. You're a little taller, too. But your hair, your nose, your lips. Those eyes. Ai, those eyes." She laughed now, though the sound was tinged with tears. "It was those eyes that first turned my head! They are all your father." She brightened. "Plus, I have his drawings."

She gestured for him to follow her, and she led him into the small room off the kitchen. There was a little table with a chair on each side, an empty blue-glass, wide-brimmed bowl in the center of it, and a single mat on the tabletop in front of the closest chair.

But the table only garnered a quick glance from Alex. His eyes were drawn to the artwork that lined the walls. Centered on the wall opposite the chair with the mat set before it were two faded pencil drawings, one of a little boy and one of a little girl. It was obvious that they were siblings—their features were so similar except for her longer hair. He had a sister, then?

More drawings of each of them covered the wall. The pictures extended to the walls on either side.

Alex moved closer, his gaze moving over the simple black and white lines and shaded work. The original drawings were of a boy and girl at about the same age—five years, if Alex had to guess. The drawings that spread across three walls aged them. There were small changes from picture to picture, but the inexorable aging was clear. Alex stared at the drawings of himself. Except for little shifts in jawline, ears, and shading, the drawings managed to capture Alex through the years accurately. It was a little spooky.

"He did an amazing job, didn't he?"

"Papa did these?"

She nodded, her own gaze moving over the familiar pictures. "One every year, on your birthdays."

Alex reached up to tap the edge of the frame holding the face of the little girl at about eight or nine. "What's her name?"

"You don't remember?"

Alex turned back to her, startled. "Should I?"

"She was born a few months before you left to the school. We named her Maria, though you called her Mimi." She laughed and shook her head. "You were so jealous of her."

"Maria. Mimi." He tried to remember. Dimly, as if the thoughts were of someone else's life, he remembered a baby. Why had he thought it was a boy? He returned his focus to his mother.

She stared at him, and there were tears in her eyes.

"I'm sorry." She managed with a soft sniffle, "I don't mean to make you uncomfortable. I can't stop looking at you. It makes it easier somehow to be able to see you again, if only for a night, to bear the loss of all of you."

"All of us?" Alex glanced at the door, where he'd been expecting his father to enter any time.

Her fingers came up to her trembling lips. "I'm sorry. I forgot. Of course, you couldn't know. Your sister, and then your father…they're gone now. It's just me here with all of the memories. I'm all that's left of us."

Alex stared at her. He shook his head. His gaze went again to the door. "But—I—" He swallowed back the rising grief and disappointment. "How?"

"Your Papa?"

Alex nodded, not trusting himself to speak.

"An accident. The plant is old and poorly maintained. There was feedback, and it caught a younger man in it. Javier pushed him away and got caught. He was burned, over-powered. By the time they came to get me, he was already gone. His mind went first. Then a few days later, his body, too." She sighed. "It was four years ago, this Spring."

Four years? He'd missed seeing his father by four years? It sounded like a lot, until Alex factored in the fact that he had never anticipated coming back again ever, and that it had been more than forty years since he'd left. Then it sounded like so very little.

He'd come so close.

He ducked his head and lifted his hand to his eyes. A fluttering thing was caught in his chest and throat. When he raised his head several long moments later, his mother was still there, lost in her own memories and grief. Alex took the two steps to her and gingerly put his arms around her small, round shoulders. She leaned into him, burying her face in his chest.

She made no sound, but he knew from the movement of her shoulders that she wept. He made no sound, either, but his own tears dripped onto her silver curls. He didn't know how long they stayed like that, but his grief had time to wane to an ache, and his tears dried on his face. His mother leaned back, patting the damp spots on his chest.

He sighed. He was afraid to ask, but he already knew she was gone, so the facts couldn't make him feel any worse. "And Maria? Was that recent or…"

His mother lifted her face to him. She shook her head, giving him a small, sad smile. "No. It was long ago. We lost her at the same age we lost you." She nodded at the chair beside him. "Sit. Let's at least be comfortable while we talk."

She waited while he pulled out the chair and sat. She sat in front of the little placemat. Her fingers fiddled with the edge of it. "At least with you, we knew you were alive, with the Council. We could pray that you were happy, healthy. If something happened, we would get a letter. And each year went by, with no letter." Her eyes became distant. "With Maria…Papa had told her a story about you, about how you used to wait for him at the square in the evenings. Do you remember?"

Alex swallowed and nodded. "I remember," he answered, his voice still husky with tears.

"She begged me to do the same. 'I'm a big girl now, Mama.' And what could it hurt? This area of Macopany is such a tight community. She knew the way. She knew the people who worked the stalls." His mother stopped and shook her head. "But somewhere between here and there…Maria disappeared."

"Disappeared?"

Her head rose and fell in a slow nod. "We searched.

Everyone did. Councilor One even sent agents to help us, imagine? Council agents searching house to house, just to help us?"

Alex swallowed bile. His stomach sank, twisted. "Mama…was she strong?"

Her brows rose. "She was a little girl, Alejandro."

"No. I mean…you and Papa are both Sparks. She would have been, too." He leaned across the table, his hand reaching out across it to hold her wrist and still her hand crumpling the corner of the mat. "Was she strong?"

When she understood, she nodded. "Yes." She smiled. "She was almost as strong as you already. She had started her Testing Year that week—she hadn't even learned to ground yet. She shone so bright. She was so beautiful. So beautiful."

Alex sat back, his arm sliding across the table to fall into his lap. He stared at the table top.

They took my sister. Rage ticked one of his eyelids. How long had they been grabbing little girls? For how many years had they been locking them up, experimenting on them, tormenting them? Alex and Thomas had noticed the pattern of disappearing or dying five-year-old girls twenty or so years before and assumed that the biological shift had started in Lena's generation. Finding Lena, and then Rose, had seemed to confirm that. But his sister was only five years younger than he was.

They took my sister.

It had been going on for longer than they'd anticipated. Where had she been taken? Did he dare hope she was alive? Considering what the Council did to them, should he hope that she was, or that she wasn't?

He needed those records that Jacob was picking up. He would have them.

"Alejandro?"

He looked up.

His mother flinched.

Alex wiped his fury from his face, sighed and sat up, shaking his head. "I'm sorry. It was a shock. It was—I can't imagine." He looked into her dark eyes, holding her grief stricken gaze. "It wasn't your fault."

Her gaze skidded away.

"It wasn't your fault. It wasn't Papa's. It was…whoever took her."

Her chin wobbled, but she shook her head and took a ragged breath. "I still look. Every day I look. It was long ago. So hard, but so long ago." She turned back to him. "Now one child has come back to tell me he's well. Perhaps before I die, I'll see Maria again, as well."

Alex gave her what he hoped was a sympathetic smile. "Perhaps."

"I want to hear about your life, now. Can you tell me? Is an agent allowed to do that?"

Alex laughed. He nodded. "Yeah. I can do that. What do you want to know?"

"Where do you live? Are you happy? Are you married?" She gasped and sat up straight. "Am I an *abuelita*?"

Alex laughed. "I live in Zone Three. I am…happy. Yeah. I am, now." He smiled. "I am not married, and you are definitely not an *abuelita*. Though…there is someone."

She sighed and tilted her head. "Someone? And she is…?"

"Special." He laughed at himself. "Strong, like Maria was. Tough. Beautiful and bright. Her name is Magdalena. Lena." He laughed again, ducking his head. He hadn't said her name aloud in months to anyone but Ace. It felt odd in his mouth, and it made him miss her with a sudden, vicious ache. "My Lena. She's my home now. She makes me happy."

His mother smiled. She kissed her fingertips and then reached out to touch his cheek with them. "Then she makes me happy, too."

Alex kept his head down as he wandered back to the Council building. It was late. No one else was on the streets. He'd stayed much longer than he'd meant to, but sitting and talking with her warmed him. The evening he'd had with his mother after so long warmed him still, even as the now frigid wind blew hard enough to make his eyes tear.

The sound of a horse clopping along the road ahead made him lift his head and grimace into the wind. The horse and rider crossed and continued away off to his left. Alex squinted down the darkened road. There were covered torch lamps set twenty feet apart on each side of the road, but the wind made them sputter. The light they gave off was enough to affect his night vision but not enough to help him see.

His raised head heightened his focus. The scrape of a foot from behind him might have been missed when he was burrowed into his coat. He caught the murmur of sound and glanced back over his shoulder.

The road behind him was empty. He scanned both sides. As he was about to turn back, another gust of wind roared from the east. It came rushing down the alley to Alex's right, and down the alleys behind him, as well. A corner of dark material from a coat fluttered out from the side of an alley whose mouth was dimly illuminated by the light from one of the lamps.

It could be a stray bit of material. It could be a man, dressed in brown…

Like the kid from the forest?

Alex turned back and continued down the street, as if he'd not noticed the fluttering tell. He walked slowly as he passed each alley, and quickened his pace between them, waiting for the next gust of wind. When it came, he was ready.

The gust roared down the cross-streets again, rattling the metal hoods of the torch lamps. Alex reached out to the Dust of every lamp fire along the street and extinguished them with a thought. In the sudden pitch darkness of the street, he stepped up and slid sideways into the nearest alley.

He crouched, leaning back close to the wall, listening.

The man was slow in coming. Not bothering to relight the lamps, he followed Alex's lead in relying on night vision and starlight. As he came closer, Alex focused on each careful, quiet footfall. The man paused before crossing in front of the alley.

At the soft rustle from clothing, Alex crouched lower, readying himself, watching the dark, sharp corner of the building with the darker spread of night behind it. The man swung out, intending to stick close to the wall and slide in sideways to present as narrow a profile as possible. It didn't matter.

Alex unwound like a spring, powering forward but not up. He smashed into the man's lower legs, stealing his balance, and wrapped his arms around his thighs, then thrust up with his legs. He lifted up and out with his arms, releasing at the top. The man flew backward, impacting the pavement behind him with a dry wheezing grunt as the air in his lungs was forced out. It was followed a second later by the crack of skull on cobbles.

Alex pounced. He got in two quick blows, the shock of them vibrating up his arms. He reared back, strafing the man with a fast glare. Brown uniform, thin coat, no identifiers—clothing identical to that worn by the kid from the forest. On the edge of his vision, the man beneath him struggled to turn his outflung arm and swing it up.

Alex glanced over to check that it wasn't a gun.

Not a gun. The sudden flash of light was brilliant, blinding Alex. He instinctually reared back, saving his eyes as the man below him smashed a narrow glass tube against the side of Alex's face. Two balled fists thumped into his unprotected chest, knocking him back and freeing the man below.

Alex jumped up, blinking the bright spots in his vision away. He lifted his head to the sound of footsteps running away. The road was a long, dark tunnel with a bright orange and white spot in the middle of it, spinning with colors.

"Son of a bitch." Alex squinted against the afterglare. He took a few careful steps, speeding up as his vision cleared. It was too late. His predator and prey was long gone.

He reached the corner. A few bright spots still danced in his vision. In spite of them, he looked up and down the street. He was alone.

Alex looked behind him. The street was empty. He reached up, running his fingers up his cheek, slick with blood, until it encountered the glass still lodged in his flesh. There were two shards, one crossing the outer top corner of his eyelid and the other splitting his eyebrow, forming an inverted "T". He'd almost gotten an eyeful.

"Son of a bitch," Alex growled again, leaving the glass in place for now. It was already bleeding freely. He'd take it out when he stitched it up. Shaking his head in disgust, Alex continued back to the temporary trade house housing, all of his senses straining and on high alert.

He'd caught one. Then the bastard had weaseled away. All he had to do was wait for the next opportunity…and figure out who the Dust *they* were.

He pulled open the door and looked back over his shoulder, moving his pissed-off gaze over the empty street outside. The lamps flared and popped in the stiff breeze, leaving wavering circles of light that smeared the empty road.

He opened his mouth to curse again, but swallowed the words in disgust. He'd had him.

And then he hadn't.

Son of a bitch.

The knock at his door came as he pried the first shard from his eyelid. He set it on the side of the sink near the tap and placed the tweezers beside it, yanking up a towel and gingerly pressing up from below. The last thing he needed was to jam the other piece deeper.

The knock came again, harder and more insistent.

Either the mystery "they" had gotten bold, Councilor One had decided to go ahead and arrest him, or Ace really needed to see him. He was willing to bet it was the latter. From what he'd seen, the other two were happiest skulking in the background.

It wasn't an electronic lock, so he had to physically cross the room and turn the key to open the door. Ace's head was down. Alex turned and crossed the room to the little bathroom again, allowing Ace to close the door behind himself and follow Alex.

"Sorry for the late-night visit, but I've worked hard to get it out that we're forced to travel together at Councilor Three's request, and I wanted to keep up that appear—hey, man! What the Dust happened?"

Alex didn't pull the bathroom door closed behind himself. Ace had hovered outside the door, talking, until a stray glance up caught the blood smeared everywhere and the reflection of Alex's face in the mirror.

Ace leaned in, craning his head. "Damn. That looks like it hurts."

Alex sighed. He flicked Ace an "Oh, really?" look in the mirror and picked up the tweezers again. He ignored the blood running down his face and dripping in bright splotches onto the sink. Leaning in close to the mirror, he gripped the shard and tugged it free. It went down on the sink beside the other piece. Alex turned the tap and leaned in, splashing water over his face. He raised his head and leaned in again, using his fingers to spread the wounds and make sure there wasn't any more glass hiding in them.

Satisfied, he grabbed the towel and pressed it to his face. He looked up at the mirror again and grinned at the slightly green Ace.

"Dust," the big trader managed in disgust. "You and Lena. What a pair."

Alex tilted his head in question.

"She almost took a finger and a half off once while I was out there visiting. She'd been working on some bit of machinery and it started spinning before she could pull free." Ace shook his head. "She made me watch while she healed it. She'd just figured out how. She thought it was *neat*."

Alex snorted and smiled. "Little show-off." He could hear the fondness in his own voice. He shrugged. "Too bad I suck at healing. I've got to do it the old-fashioned way."

"You took care of that little girl back in the mountains."

"Yeah, well…" Alex shook his head and admitted the bitter truth. "That was one part desperation and two parts raw luck."

He used his free hand to rummage in the little kit he had opened on the top of the closed toilet. He pulled out a small packet of folded waxed paper that had thread in it and another that held a hooked needle.

"This is gonna suck. Go ahead and distract me with tales of

how you managed to distance yourself from me, and all of the marvelous things you accomplished because of it. And feel free to dazzle me, Ace. It's been a—" He'd been about to say a terrible night, but then he thought of the hours spent in his mother's company. He shook his head at himself. "It's been a night."

Ace crossed his arms and leaned in the jam, watching as Alex threaded the needle and leaned in. He winced when the needle entered Alex's skin and averted his eyes.

"Yeah, so…I figured it would be good if people believed I thought you were a dangerous, pain-in-the-ass tag-along we brought to curry favor with the Councilor."

Alex grunted. "That's different from how you really feel how…?" he gritted through a clenched jaw.

Ace chuckled. He wisely chose not to answer that question. "Told the story of some of your shenanigans back in Zone Two and how pissed Sloan was. Told the story of your *donation* at that Neo-barb village—that's the one that gets the other traders sympathetic, by the way. Made it sound like I could barely control you and I was worried about my new position—without saying any of that, of course."

"Of course." Alex exhaled and swallowed as he jabbed the needle in again and found a nerve.

"This evening over drinks after dinner, a certain Locust House trader approached me." Ace laughed in appreciation. "He approached me, Alex." Clearly, Ace expected acknowledgment for his coup.

Alex glanced at the man in the mirror and gave him a tight smile.

"He said he'd heard we'd be heading back via Zone Six. Told me that he'd heard I had a problem controlling you, and said he had a problem with security running back through Nations territory on the return to Zone Six. He wanted to know if I'd be interested in a one-time inter-House travel partnership. Safety in numbers, on both fronts."

Alex paused and turned his head, swinging his upper body to keep his hand and the needle in place. "The caravans are going back together?" He'd have access to all of it—caravan, cargo, manifests?

Ace flashed his broadest grin. "We're meeting to sign the travel agreement in the morning."

Alex stared at Ace. He couldn't believe their good fortune. It took less than a second for him to reject that it was fortune at all. "He's playing you."

"He's not playing me." Ace scowled his scorn at Alex. "I played him. When are you going to admit I'm good at what I do?"

Alex turned back, pulling up on the needle and flicking his wrist in a quick knotting motion that caught the thread. He tightened it down and forced the needle into his skin, across the wound, and up again. He flicked a glance back at Ace, who had his face turned down to the floor. Still, Alex could see the resentment and disappointment that washed across it.

He looked again at himself in the mirror. He'd been in Ace's shoes once—a quarter century old and shouldering responsibilities he wasn't ready for, no matter what he told himself. Alex had Thomas and the other Originals to share the setbacks and disappointments and fears. And none of them had a jaded older agent looking over their shoulders, critiquing everything they did. Oh, they'd had supervisors in the roles they hid in, but not a single one of them had been aware of what the young men were really after. Sam had known—but Sam had always preferred a gentler method of encouraging success than they'd been taught at the Ward School.

Alex sighed. He finished off the last stitch on the first wound and tied it off. Before he started the other, he blotted at the blood and pressed the towel to the wound to slow it again. Head down, he turned around to face Ace and leaned back against the sink.

"You did good, kid."

Ace raised his head and gave him a wary look.

"You did good. Doesn't matter what he thinks he has planned for us. We'll figure it out, and we'll be ready. You set the stage for him to approach you, and you did it on your own. We'll keep playing up the tension between us. One is—" Alex grimaced, then winced and pressed the towel a little harder. "One is ruled by fear and loss. He's not ready to commit, and what he wants from us to be ready…" Alex shook his head. "I'm not sure Lena's ready to give."

"Lena?" Ace cocked his head. "If you expect her to come out of hiding, or to show any of those girls…"

Alex shrugged. "He wants her at the Meet. He'll want an inspection of the school. He's not the only one. Sloan expects the same."

Ace shook his head.

Alex nodded and turned back. "I know. Just—let me handle her. We'll get through the next few days, then I'll start working on my strategy."

Ace held up a finger. "One day. We'll get through the next one day. You made quite an impression on One. Trade is done." Ace smiled and tapped himself on the chest. "And concluded favorably, thank you. He's got his roughnecks working overnight to get us loaded. Both caravans leave Zone One bright and early the morning after tomorrow." Ace rolled his eyes at the late hour. "Or after today. There's a gala dinner tonight."

Alex cursed.

"Thought you were in a hurry to get back to Lena?"

"I am, but I—" Alex shook his head. He was entitled to keep some things for himself. "I made alternate plans for dinner. I can't cancel them."

Ace's eyes were wide. "You're going to skip your final opportunity to work Councilor One?"

Alex shrugged. "There's no working that man. He's too scared of Four. Besides…" Alex dropped the towel in the sink and picked up the needle again. "This'll give you another chance to do your thing. You've proved you can handle yourself. Impress me again." He grinned at the man scowling behind him through the mirror.

THIRTY-SIX

Lena

The wall of the Neo-Barb holding rose ahead of them, but down on the road before it, only the sound of their own people and horses broke the silence. Lena exchanged a nervous glance with Ghost. "They're all in there. All of them."

The rough, crumbled road wound through the hills with the river off to their left. A cold, brisk wind blew. No one stirred outside the wall around Taos.

No one lurked outside of the town walls. No scouts stalked the hills. No workers roamed looking for meat or forage or supplies. No guards patrolled.

Ghost nodded, gaze roaming over the rough wall thrown up years before around the center of town. The collapsed ruins of buildings that hadn't been maintained surrounded them. When the Neo-Barbs had taken over the town who knew how many years before, they either hadn't bothered to maintain anything outside of their walled compound or they hadn't bothered to repair it.

The road went straight up to the gate before them, then all the way through in a straight shot to a gate on the other end. It was the only direct way, via this route, to get to the gorge.

"Then inside is where we'll go." He looked at her, calm. "Do we have a choice?"

They didn't. He'd been right. The agent had turned south. Depending on how things went here and how long it took, they'd either beat the man to the gorge or meet him there. It had taken them two and a half miserable days to close in on Taos. The physical discomfort was bad enough—Lena felt terrible every time she had to slow them down so that she could climb off the horse and find somewhere to scurry off and pee. Her worry for Marissa also grew increasingly sharp.

Every time Lena checked on them, Karina seemed content with the journey, and Marissa remained unconscious. Had he harmed her? Was the current of the collar too high? Could she recover?

Ghost glanced over his shoulder. "Are you going to talk to Thomas, or do you want me to?"

"Or you could let me." Gabriela's amused voice came from her other side. She and Rose had been talking softly as they approached the settlement ahead.

Rose snorted a laugh.

Gabriela made no secret of her distaste for Councilor Five. He'd never managed to make up for the initial insult on the day they'd met.

Lena sent Gabriela a flash of a smile. "I'm sure you'd enjoy it, but no. Thomas trusts me. He'll listen."

She glanced behind her. He watched her. He had been for the entire ride, measuring, weighing. She knew why. Once she'd calmed down, she'd been able to apologize and to discuss her fears for Marissa, for all of the girls, with him. Their fire-lit talks reminded her of the early days when she was still included in planning their revolution. The decision to bring him, made in anger, was the right one. She needed his experience. She wanted the agent's guidance and ability to reason with or outsmart West, and the additional fighting strength gave them another advantage. She just didn't know if he'd be on board with the plan she and Ghost had made.

Lena pulled on the reins and directed her horse closer to the Councilor. He anticipated her and met her halfway.

"Thomas." She took a breath, intending to launch into the request she and Ghost agreed would be best.

Thomas caught her off guard with his laughing greeting.

"Lena." He mimicked her grave tone, then chuckled again.

"I'm glad you're in a good mood. It'll make today easier." She glanced away. "I've made the decision that you need to move farther back. All the way back." She felt no satisfaction at the surprise on his face.

"That's a mistake." His voice was flat. His good humor vanished.

"This is our fight. It's our land. We have to live with whatever happens here, and with these people afterward. We have to do this for ourselves."

"Lena." Her name sounded like an admonishment. "Don't throw away my experience."

"I'm not."

"By banishing me to the rear, you are." He shook his head and pinned her with his gaze. "I don't want us to be at odds, not now that you understand a little better the difficulties of leading. But this is unacceptable. I won't do it."

His flat refusal took her back to the summer, and how often he'd refused to listen. The goodwill of the prior two days evaporated. She pulled her gaze from him and took a moment to look out over the landscape around them. When she did answer, she was proud of how even she kept her voice, all things considered. "What exactly is it you think I understand better?"

"That the costs of decisions aren't always paid by those making them. It's a huge lesson, and a painful one. I thought after Marissa's abduction, you'd understand. That's why I won't—"

"Excuse me? You brought your *vetted man* into my home, but you're saying I'm somehow to blame for his actions?"

Thomas made a more or less gesture with his hand. "You made the deal that allowed him in—the deal you made with me and then revised with Patrick because of your plan to use the girls as bait to draw out the Neo-Barbs and Scavengers." He held up his hand and raised his brows. "I'm not criticizing, but I would like to point out that you spent the summer unhappy with me for using the girls to lure out trouble. But when it came time to make the difficult decision, you made the same choice."

She stared at him in disbelief. "It was *not* the same choice."

Her voice sounded as heavy as it felt in her throat.

"It was."

"No. It wasn't. I didn't use them. I trained them. I showed them how to build defenses. I taught them to protect themselves. Those men were coming anyway. We were willing to wait them out, yes, but on our terms and no one else's. That's not the same!"

Heads turned at her raised voice. Ghost and Gabriela and Rose ahead of her had turned in their saddles to watch Lena and Thomas. Gabriela muttered something to Ghost.

Thomas sighed and shook his head. "My intent isn't to start an argument. I'm only pointing out that the things we balance and weigh to make decisions aren't always clear-cut. They're messy. They're difficult. Innocent people, like Marissa, sometimes get hurt. It doesn't make the decisions made any less valid. I hope you can find some comfort in that. You made the right choices. I'm proud of you."

She gave him a tight, furious little smile. "This is also the right choice. Whether the people ahead have issues with the Council or not, we won't risk you stepping in and complicating things for us. Despite your assurances to the contrary, I'm not sure you do respect me or my decisions. And I no longer give a damn if you're proud of me or not." She felt her savage satisfaction at the surprise on his face reflected in her grin. "We'll negotiate or not for ourselves, regardless of what you think of our decisions. You and your men *will* take a position in the rear and wait to make yourselves useful when it's time to hunt West. Is that clear?"

He searched her face. She didn't know what he saw there, but he nodded stiffly and turned his mount to ride down their line to the rear. She stared after him. Who was this condescending man? Had the camaraderie at the beginning, and again over the last two nights, been an act? Had Thomas been like this the whole time, and she hadn't noticed?

It didn't matter. Lena straightened her back and returned to her place with Ghost. He opened his mouth to say something, but she shook her head.

"Please don't. I need a minute."

She struggled to bring her racing thoughts under control as the gate ahead of them drew closer. By the time it rose before them, she gave Ghost a tight smile.

"Sorry," she whispered.

He shook his head. "No apology needed. You want me to hurt him? He looks tough, but he's little. It wouldn't be too much effort."

A laugh bubbled up. "No, but thank you for that image. I wish I knew why…" She shook her head.

"People change," Ghost said. He smiled and seemed to shake off his melancholy for a moment. "Even you."

"I think I'm pretty predictable."

Ghost gave a bark of laughter. He quickly swallowed it when the gate before them opened, and a tall, whipcord lean man, surrounded by four younger warriors, stepped through. She didn't recognize any from the confrontation in the valley. The gate closed behind them. The leader strode out, unafraid, his chin lifted as he faced all of them on their mounts.

His skin didn't have the deep burnished tone of Ace's, though it was more than sun-darkened. Springy white threaded through his short curly hair. He wasn't a young man. That made him even more formidable. Keeping hold of a Neo-Barb tribe with violent young people eager to take it wouldn't be easy.

He stopped short of joining them and eyed the four of them atop the horses.

"I know why you're here. You've come for the boys." He took a breath, his shoulders rising and falling. "I was away, negotiating with allies—" his lips twisted on the word "—when some of my more ambitious young warriors found and took your men and supplies. They've been punished. I would have returned the boys and the supplies, but—"

He shook his head. "I returned to sickness here. We'll return the boys, if they survive, when we have weathered this storm. Go back to your people now. You don't want what we're suffering."

"What proof do we have what you say is true?" Ghost challenged him.

The old man pointed at the wall behind him, drawing their

attention up. A man stood there, his face grim. He leaned down and picked up what looked to be rags.

Not rags. Blankets, wrapped around a small child. The man pulled the blankets back from the face of the child, freeing his head and shoulders to the cold and the sunlight, and turned him so that they could see.

A red rash covered the boy. Even from a distance, Lena could see eyes glazed with fever and pain.

Beside her, Gabriela gasped. She looked across Lena at Ghost and shook her head.

"We must go," Ghost told Lena softly. "I'm sorry. We should have taken the northern route."

Lena shushed him, weighing the old man's gaze. They held no deception, merely weariness.

"We require safe passage through your town," Lena told him.

"We cannot!" Gabriela whispered the words at her furiously.

Ghost leaned in more diplomatically. "Lena, you're Sparks. You can resist the infection. We cannot, and we don't dare carry this back to our children. We're barely recovered from our journey."

"Do you trust me?" She asked the same question he'd asked of her when they set out.

He nodded.

She turned back to the old man before her. "We can pay for our safe passage through your town. You may keep the supplies, though we insist on the return of the boys. If you let us pass, I'll return in three days and heal your sick. All of them. But today, you must let us through. We cannot afford the time it would take to go around."

He gave her a look of disbelief. "You cannot have medicine for this. It doesn't exist."

"I exist."

He shook his head and started to turn away.

"Bring the child down. I'll prove myself. Bring him down."

The old man turned back to her. She met his gaze without fear. This cost she could pay without question.

He must have seen her certainty because his lips parted and

he nodded. "Come in. If you dare to try, come in. Heal the boy, and you'll have safe passage."

They rode in slowly. Ghost and his people kept one hand on their reins and one hand on the end of a weapon. Lena glanced over at Gabriela. She refused to meet Lena's eyes.

She should know after weeks of living with Lena and the girls that Lena would keep her and her people safe. There was no threat. Even if any of the warriors carried the infection back, Lena and Jackson, Marin even, could heal them .

Lena shook her head. Rose caught her eye and raised her brows. She understood Gabriela's emotion. She wouldn't give Lena a pass on being offended. Lena scowled and focused ahead.

Once inside, Lena forgot her mood. She stared around, wondering how much of this reflected what Taos must have been in the past.

There were no ruined buildings inside the walls. No adobe walls had been allowed to collapse back into the earth.

The buildings here rose up from the single main road in earth-colored adobe that curved smooth and firm from the ground to the roofs of the buildings. Archways opened from the street, leading back into courtyards with many doors. Faces peered out from those doors—some healthy but curious through despair, others rashed or feverish.

Once she'd caught sight of them she glanced around again, noticing for the first time what she'd failed to see at first. The community was too quiet. No voices raised in chatter or argument. No children played. No adults worked. Only the echo of hooves off walls set close to the road came back to her. This was a community close to being devastated by the disease that ran through it.

It was a story, Lena knew, repeated all too often. She'd seen illness rage through the people of Santo Domingo by her old home. She'd helped them as best she could and had learned what she could do through it. Necessity made the best teacher.

Alex had told her of the first time he'd encountered a Neo-Barb village that had been emptied by disease. He'd been a young agent in training, and they'd stumbled upon the dead town during an exercise. New graves crowded in the small yard on the outskirts of the village. Newer graves dotted the town square as those left to bury the dead had weakened. The last of the bodies had been found in their beds, where they had withered. All except one. One man had died curled in the corner of the main house, alone. Alex told her that one man had haunted him—what would it have been like to be the last man? He'd asked himself what he would have done. Would he have left, abandoning his home and all of the dead, his only family and friends? Or would he have stayed to die, curled in despair, to be with his people, too?

Alex had looked at her then and given her a small smile. He'd leaned in close and whispered, "I think my answer has changed since I was a boy," before kissing her on her temple, tucking her hair behind her ear, and changing the subject.

Lena blinked back tears at the memory and sucked in a deep breath. Alex wasn't here. This town would not disappear into memory like that other one. She would make sure of that.

The chieftain waited ahead of them in an arch that opened onto a smaller courtyard. A fire pit inside glowed with coals. A young man carried the bundle of rags from the wall into the courtyard and sat before the fire pit, waiting.

Lena turned to Ghost. "If you'd rather wait out here, so you're not exposed, I'll understand."

He frowned at her and swung down from his horse.

She followed suit, ducking under her horse's neck to grab Ghost's arm. "I mean it. You don't have to be there for this."

"We're a unit, each of us leading half of our people. We both go, or neither of us does."

Lena released his arm and turned back, telling Rose, "Everyone else stays out here. This shouldn't take long."

Rose nodded.

Lena risked a glance at Gabriela. The woman tilted her head and gave her a tiny nod. She understood. It didn't mean she wasn't unhappy with the risk that she perceived, but she understood. Lena turned away.

She hadn't made it to where Ghost stood with the chieftain before the sound of a horse trotting up the road caught her attention. Thomas made his way to her at speed, his face grim.

Lena groaned. Why couldn't the man do as he was told? She'd made her position clear. If it had been his command, he'd expect nothing less than obedience.

Before Thomas could make his way to the three leaders looking back at him, though, Gabriela kneed her horse forward and cut him off. He yanked hard on the reins to slow and turn his horse.

Thomas glowered at Gabriela, his mouth open to snap at her, but she cut him off before he could say a word.

"Be still. I won't allow you to undermine them now." By her face, she meant business. She'd had enough of the Councilor. He presented a target she'd enjoy taking her temper out on.

He stared at her in disbelief.

Gabriela ignored him for the moment, looking over her shoulder to toss her head at Lena. "Go on, Lena. Do what needs doing. This one isn't going anywhere."

"Is that so?" His words were dangerously soft.

"Yes. It is so. I'm not afraid of you, Council Man." At his narrowed blue eyes, she laughed and tapped her waist where the knife she always carried rode sideways, handle out. "Unless you'd like to find out who's faster?"

"I wouldn't take that invitation," Lena warned him. "I've seen her in action."

Gabriela nodded. "You have, and on the day it was baptized in a Council agent's blood, too."

Lena's lips parted in shock. Surely it wasn't the same knife Gabriela had taken from the Scavenger six years before? Lena peered at Gabriela's waist, trying to tell from the handle.

Gabriela gave her a small, knowing smile. "I made a promise to myself to never be taken again. I made Ghost train me, and train me well." She raised her gaze from Lena to Thomas again, meeting his stare with a challenge. "I named my blade after the agent I killed with it, so I'd never forget: Marreau."

Thomas started, his eyes widening. "What did you say?"

"Marreau." She stared at him defiantly. "Did you know him?"

Thomas laughed. "I did. I almost killed him once myself." He flashed her a smile. "True story. I'm happy to know he's dead. You did the world a service."

Gabriela's brows dipped lower for a moment as she weighed whether to believe him before her face cleared. She nudged her horse closer to talk to him. She still held her body stiff. She didn't trust the man, but she'd listen to him.

Lena sighed and turned back to the men waiting for her. As long as Thomas stayed away and let her do what she needed to do, she didn't care what they bonded over.

She and Ghost followed the leader through the adobe arch. At the far end of the courtyard, two doors exited. A thick wooden barrier probably led into a home. The other was more of a wooden gate. She could see through it to the hallway that led away to more rooms. The cracked, worn tiles in the courtyard floor had been re-filled with grout.

Before the fire pit the young man from the wall cradled the small child. She looked at the chieftain for permission, and at his nod, she crossed to them. Before she could raise her hands and reach for the Dust, a clatter of footsteps came from the hallway toward the back of the courtyard. Ghost tensed behind her.

"What is this?" Damar demanded from the back hallway. "Why did you let them in?"

The leader's eyes narrowed. "You forget yourself…and the lesson you watched when I returned and discovered the deception of my own. The only reason I did not punish you, too, was because…"

The old man stopped to glance at Lena. "The things he said. He showed his friend's hand as proof. He had information that I could use to negotiate with others."

"With the Scavengers, you mean." Lena kept her voice even. "He told you about us and urged you to sell us to the Scavengers, just as your young men had planned."

The chief was still for a long moment. The he dipped his head, acknowledging what she said was true.

Damar began to speak again, but the leader slashed his hand through the air. After the earlier warning, it was enough. Damar silenced himself. He came into the courtyard and dropped down to the floor to sit behind the old man, intent on bearing witness to this meeting. The disrespect was breathtaking.

"What's waiting for us at the gorge, Chief?"

"Ruthless men who have connections and resources that would have made our lives easier through this long winter." He cleared his throat. "And a Spark."

"So the Spark seen here by the boys and men—he wasn't yours?" Ghost asked.

"Mine?" The old man's face was startled, then he laughed. "No. We have no Sparks here, other than the boys that belong with you. We have talks several times a year. Formal discussions about the state of the area." He paused.

The state of the area? Or how best to divvy it up?

"The talks can be lengthy. We exchange a man each—someone we would not want to lose—as a show of faith. The Spark was their man. Our temporary guest."

A show of faith? Or of mistrust? Lena peeked at Ghost under her lashes. He seemed unimpressed. If you have that little faith, Lena thought, you probably shouldn't be negotiating with someone.

The minute she'd had the thought, she glanced around the room and realized she was doing the same. Oh, they'd not be leaving anyone behind. But they didn't trust this man or his people. Not yet. She gave this demonstration because she wanted him to have a vested interest in their safe return. Enough so, that if he held back any information about the Scavs waiting for them, he would volunteer it before they left.

She turned back to the child and knelt before the man holding him across his lap. The old man and Ghost took positions on either side behind her. The chieftain craned to see what she did.

She unwrapped the child. She wasn't an expert in children, but he couldn't be more than two years old. An angry, lacy rash covered his head and torso. His features were swollen beneath dry, hot skin. His breathing was shallow. She took a deep breath, settling her hands over him as she always did to help her focus. She closed her eyes and reached out to the Dust.

Since she'd started traveling with the Dust, everything she did was so much more…vivid. She saw the Dust coursing through the boy, opalescent and shining. It didn't appear molten, as did the bodies of Sparks, saturated with the Dust. It was still brilliant and beautiful.

She told the Dust what she needed. First, she focused on removing the virus that had invaded, and she strengthened his little body. Then she began work on removing the outward signs of illness. They'd have faded on their own in a few days anyway. She needed them gone now. She needed their leader to know the child was well again.

She knew the moment she'd achieved that point. There was a gasp behind her from the chieftain. Damar cursed behind him.

She gave a final instruction and withdrew back into herself. The little boy smiled up at her and sat up.

His wide-eyed father ran his hands over the child's head and face and down his back, then he lifted the boy to his chest and held him tight. "Thank you," he managed before his throat closed with gratitude.

Lena ducked her head. "You're welcome." She never knew what to say after healing someone. She didn't need their gratitude. She smiled at the child as his father carried him away. Little fingers wiggled in a farewell wave over the man's shaking shoulders. Lena pulled herself to her knees, awkwardly turning to face the men behind her.

The chieftain stared at her in wonder, his mouth agape. Before she could reassure him, he turned on Damar. "You told me they were monsters! You told me there was no question we should sell them to the Scavengers."

"They are! You saw what they did to Hildario!"

Lena smiled and extended her head, willing to admit to that. "We did, yes. He attacked us. We're permitted to defend ourselves."

The Neo-Barb's eyes narrowed, but Lena didn't think it was displeasure with her anymore. "He said you intervened in his People's business and marked them to send away."

Beside her, Ghost snorted. "He probably said many things, all of them untrue."

"I believe you can judge them for yourself now." Lena watched emotion wash over the man's face. He wasn't sure which way to go, but she thought he wanted to err on the side of his people. She could help him with that choice. "Did he tell you that he owes me—the woman he would see you attack for him, the woman he would have you give to the Scavengers to sell as slave—he owes me a life debt?"

The chief in front of her blanched.

To Neo-barbs, there was no greater debt, no oath more binding, than that owed to another who saved a life.

"That debt was paid by my brother with the rancho." Damar's voice was a hoarse growl of rage.

"No. Your brother paid *his debt*. He asked my help in getting you back from the Scavengers who'd killed your people. I helped *him*. I *saved* you."

The chief turned to Damar, face mottled. "No other can pay that debt for you. No other can release you."

"I never asked her to save me!"

The leader recoiled.

It was done. She'd made her point. Ghost sealed the deal.

"Now you know," he said heavily, his voice full of grief, "why I sent my brother, the last of my blood, away from us. He has no honor. He deserves no People."

Damar spat in rage. "Are you going to believe them over—"

"Enough! One word more, and I'll cut your throat myself!"

From the look in his eyes, Damar considered testing the man. But he subsided. His anger still simmered. Lena hoped the chieftain had the sense to end him. She couldn't do it. She wouldn't be able to look at Ghost again if she did.

The old man closed his eyes. He saw the truth now, and it pained him as much as it would Lena.

He'd been used. He'd been fed lies, and he'd led his people, already weakened by sickness, into more danger. He thought he'd earn medicine for his people with information about Lena and her girls, monsters who deserved no better than to be carted away for the safety of the entire area. He thought he'd made the right choice for his people.

Oh, she had no illusions that he was an imperfect man. He'd seen an opportunity with the boys and the supplies taken from the Council, and he snatched at it with both hands. He dealt with Scavengers even before the Scavs forced the weakened tribe to bow to their will, no doubt. As long as he'd not crossed a final line, she could forgive. She could work with him in the future.

"Look at me." Her voice was very quiet, but she infused it with every bit of authority she'd learned at the Ward School. She filled it with the power of the Dust. "Tell me now, and tell me true: have you ever given humans over to the Scavengers as slaves?"

He met her gaze. The fear cleared from his eyes, and she saw the truth before he spoke it.

"No. We've done much to bring us shame, but not that. Not until—"

Not until Damar had taken advantage of the illness of his people and coaxed him into it.

She nodded. "The Scavengers will be gone today. For our passage, we'll return and heal your sick. While you're waiting, I suggest you consider who best to approach to fill the void the loss of the Scavs will leave in your very short list of allies."

He swallowed and nodded. He rose with her. As she turned to leave, he thrust his hand out to stop her. Ghost's hand shot out to grab the chieftain's wrist.

"Stop." The man directed the word at her, not at Ghost who squeezed his arm painfully. That he endured. "You cannot move against them. They are too many. Too strong. I'm sorry about our role in the danger to you, but you must listen to me. You cannot win that battle. And my people—" He took a ragged breath.

Lena filled the silence. "We will win," she told him.

"But if you don't? Can you not heal them first?" He looked out across the road that opened through the arch behind her. Those of his people well enough to be up and about waited. They'd seen. They wanted the Dust medicine for themselves.

Lena shook her head. "If we don't succeed, then watching your people wither will be the price you pay for choosing not to fight in the beginning, when they first came. When you were strong."

Yes, she'd scored a wound. Her guess was true, she could see it in his eyes. She let him absorb that possibility for a moment before she reassured him.

"But we *will* succeed, and we will return." She nodded at Damar. "Before you punish him, have Damar tell you what happened to the last Scavengers who threatened those I'd sworn myself to. Have him tell you the truth."

The chieftain glanced back.

"She burned them all," Damar snarled, his voice low and throbbing. "She burned the entire camp."

"That was me alone." She cast a meaningful look back at the young women behind her. "We are not monsters. But we protect what's ours as well as we heal the damage."

"Just you," Damar mumbled. "Like the head of a snake." He raised burning eyes to her.

Lena didn't know what Ghost heard when his brother said those words, but he shifted protectively, twisting the old man's arm with him. In one step, he moved between Lena and Damar.

Damar uncoiled like a snake himself, arm flashing down for his knife and then up again, reaching. He launched himself at her, already slashing. He didn't care which of the three before him he damaged. His leap was a final, desperate move.

Lena threw up her hands to ward against the blade. *Go!* A brilliant flare of electricity arced from her hands toward Damar, the same bolt of energy she'd taught her girls.

Except it wasn't a rock in front of her. It wasn't Damar alone, either.

The bolt caught Damar on the head. It branched out and struck the chieftain on the back of his shoulder. Horrified, Lena watched the crackling energy course along his arm to pass into Ghost before it wisped away. All three men collapsed.

The men lining the walls, who'd been frozen by fear in various poses as they reached for their weapons to come to their leader's aid, gaped at her. Behind her, she could hear raised voices and the sound of people trying to control panicked horses.

"I'm fine!" She gasped out the shout to Thomas before he and the others did something stupid. *Like you did?* She dropped to her knees. She had to help the men here with her.

Ghost already woke, his left arm lifting shakily to hover over his right, hidden from her.

Please. Not like Hildario. Not his whole arm.

She turned her attention to the chieftain. He had fallen face down. A charred hole in his jacket over his shoulder blade revealed a livid, purplish red mark on his skin. The same mark branched in the jagged pattern of lightning across the back of his wrist and hand down to his fingertips. His shoulder blade, where he'd caught the brunt of the bolt, had a charred mark in the center.

She reached out to his Dust. His heart still beat, irregular at first, but she strengthened it, gave it power. The Dust worked with her to close his wound, healing the burn, easing the pain. As she was about to begin correcting the long, brilliant scar, a gasping croak came from her right.

"Stop." Ghost managed to push himself up with his left arm. The same lightning mark coursed the flesh of his right hand and wrist. "He's one of the People. He's made by his scars. If he's out of danger, leave him."

Lena stared at Ghost. She withdrew her hands. "He's out of danger," she said clearly, so the shocked witnesses would be reassured, as well. "I've healed the worst of the damage."

"Check Damar," he whispered, his face lowered as if ashamed of the request. "Please."

Lena rose and stepped over the old man, now stirring. Damar had been thrown back across the room. When she saw the ruin of his face, she gulped back a sob.

"Don't come over," she warned Ghost, her voice breaking.

She sank down beside Damar. "Stupid boy. Stupid boy! I didn't save you for this!"

Almost as an afterthought, she reached out to the Dust.

Damar lived. His heartbeat had steadied on its own, though his breathing remained ragged and shallow. Raw burns wrapped around his face to the right side of his head and down his neck.

"He's alive!" She leaned over, intent on fixing the damage.

A hand fell on her shoulder. Ghost pulled her back.

"Leave him." His voice was stronger—no less grief-stricken, but determined.

"Ghost, I can't leave him like this. Look at him."

His nostrils flared and his throat spasmed against the smell of burnt skin and hair. "You have to."

"It's inhumane. I won't. I'll put him out of his misery before I—"

"You must." The chieftain struggled to his knees, assisted by two of his men. He waved them off before sitting back on his feet to stare at Lena through hooded eyes. "You held his life debt, and he attacked you. It was one thing to try to arrange your capture using us. This—it is worse than murder. There can be no mercy for him. Not in death, and not in healing."

"If he survives, Lena, it will be because his will is stronger than his dishonor." Ghost's words were soft but implacable.

Lena looked between them and then back down at Damar. What life would the young man have? Failing that, how painful and prolonged would his death be?

"I *can't*. Ghost—"

"You must." He echoed the old leader. "It is our way."

She shook her head. "I'm not one of you."

Ghost took a breath, then raised his undamaged left hand. He turned it to face her, palm out. The scar from his knife was still vivid across the full flesh below his thumb. "You are," he said softly. "And when it comes to *our* People, there are few decisions I will challenge you on. But this one…I insist. Leave him, Lena."

He turned his hand to hold it out to her. Before she took it, she glanced back down at Damar. What she'd done to him was a punishment more terrible than death. She stumbled up.

The chieftain climbed to his feet. He wasn't steady, but he stood tall.

"We will care for him while he lives. If he heals and he's unable to survive on his own, we will keep him. This is the price we'll pay for our role. You can ask after him each time you return."

She stared at the man. Each time she returned? He no longer

questioned that she'd be back to heal his people. Presumably, he no longer harbored illusions of over-powering any of them, either.

She nodded. "Free passage for us, in exchange for healing. And a lifetime of care for him, in exchange for forbearance of your crimes."

The man nodded. He raised a hand to one of his men, snapping his fingers. "Bring me ink and a skin. I need to draw a map."

Lena didn't dare to smile.

The chieftain nodded deeply, as if reinforcing his decision. Behind him, Thomas stood in the arch, watching. She didn't know if he'd come after the lightning strike or if he'd always been there. It didn't matter. He'd seen what she was capable of, too.

THIRTY-SEVEN

Alex

Alex leaned into the little protection offered by the thin wall of the warehouse, trying to shield himself from the brutal wind sweeping in through the wide-open double tall doors. As each was inspected for final load, the caravan train cars were pushed out through the doors into position outside along the inner walls. Both the natives of the zone and the Zone Three and Six caravaners moved as quickly as they could.

The wind of the night before had blown out the wisped remains of rainclouds. As the day dawned, it was clear the wind ran before a weather system from the north. The sky was flat and grey, with that peculiar heaviness that signaled snow. The wind battered them with cold and the occasional hint of ice crystals.

They'd be pulling out into shit weather. Ace and Oscar Hende, the Locust House trader, were snugged in tight in the office of the warehouse, sorting through maps and trying to plot a route they could agree on. The men had to balance speed against probable weather conditions and account for the complication of increasingly hostile Nations interactions with Zone Six and her representatives.

It gave Alex an opportunity to huddle at the back. He ran his gaze along each of the cars as they were inspected for integrity and contents. He sought out access points and weak spots, listening hard for the called out lists of cargo and passengers that each would hold. He picked a single detail of each that stood out to his eye as a mnemonic to help him remember.

They were finishing up the final two cars of the Zone Six caravan. It had fewer cars, so they'd pushed it through first. They were starting to line up the Zone Three cars behind it. The team dragged them into place one by one. It was arduous work, but it kept them warm.

He shifted his own frozen feet, but kept the movement as inconspicuous as possible. As a Zone Three security officer and Council agent, he had a right to be there, sure. But it didn't mean that Linus and his minions wouldn't find it suspicious.

The contents of the final Zone Six car were called out, and the inspector jumped free of the raised doorway. He shouted for the team to take a break after they'd moved it into position outside, then hurried himself into the warmer office at the rear of the building. The door, helped by the wind, slammed behind him.

Alex smiled. The men would no doubt head straight for the two smoldering braziers over here by the narrow side exit door. It was time for him to slip away. He walked along the wall, head down. The sound of the door slamming again made him glance back.

A woman, heavily bundled against the cold, walked across to the wide exit. All Alex could see of her was her blond hair shining above the thick collar of her fur coat. It was all he needed to see to know it was Erika.

She must have felt his attention, because she glanced around. When she saw him making his way to the side door, she flicked a look to it, blinked three times, then ducked her head again and kept going. Her pace never slowed.

She wanted a meeting, though. It was important.

He slipped out the door, controlling the swing behind him as the wind tried to slam it, too. He walked to the main road and crossed.

Erika was a block ahead of him. She hugged the walls of the buildings to avoid the wind. After a few steps, she glanced over shoulder to him. She widened her eyes, as if in alarm, and turned away, speeding up her pace.

Alex felt his lips turn up grimly. It was a game he'd taught her. It meant someone was watching—either him, her, or both. Based on her use of the "evil man harassing me" gambit, he guessed the likelihood was that he was the one being watched. She was trying to keep her association with him covered.

He glanced over his shoulder and checked up and down the street. He didn't see anyone, but that didn't mean anything. He wondered how many of them there were, and how many different people they represented. Councilor Four? Councilor One? Councilor Two, even? He closed in on Erika. It was time to give them a show. He hated it, but it was always effective. Men who didn't value women never questioned when someone else treated them poorly.

He reached out and grabbed her elbow, turning her to face him and pushing her back into an alley. The angle of the roof above and the walls to either side meant they'd have an easier time hiding their conversation from anyone with skill at lip-reading without being obvious about it. It made the subterfuge that much stronger.

She struggled against him, and he leaned in threateningly. "What's so important?"

She shook her head, as if telling him no, but when she caught sight of the stitches and swollen bruising on his face, her eyes widened. She blurted, "What the Dust happened to your face?"

Not even a second later, she'd remembered she might be seen. She angled her face down as if she was intimidated by him. Her low words were quick and controlled, meant to convey maximum information in minimal time. "You cannot come on the caravan to Zone Six. Find another way home. You're in danger—you, very specifically. And Alex, this is coming from—"

"I can handle danger," he interrupted, pushing at her shoulder as if unhappy at her words. He didn't need to know who'd made the order. If she'd discovered the information, it meant Four and Six. Possibly One.

She stumbled back as if trying to circle around to the street again. It hid her face from view. She shook her head. "You don't understand. We're going to arrest you."

He swiped at his mouth, covering his words. "On what charges?"

"On any charges. It doesn't matter. You'll be in Six's custody. Your new Councilor Three won't be able to help you until the Meet, months of interrogation away. You can't risk it." She stepped in now, as if taunting him. "Trust me to do my damn job—all of it, not just the bits you used to enjoy."

Yeah, she was still pissed about his rejection and her orders. He hadn't asked of her anything he wouldn't ask of one of his men. He swallowed hard and didn't bother to hide his mouth or face. "Things change. People change. I changed. We'll talk about it—"

"We'll talk about it?" Her gaze moved over his face. A look like disbelief faded into disgusted anger. "I can't believe I missed it. You've fallen for someone. Really fallen. Who? That little revolutionary everyone is buzzing about? Have you forgotten what you told me when you sent me away? We can't afford that. It makes us stupid."

He started to speak, but she held up her hand and stepped away again. She was almost to the street.

"Don't. I've given you the warning. What you do with it is up to you." She glowered at him, and he knew she wasn't acting anymore. "One more thing—Jacob asked me to ply you with drink and seduce you at the dinner tonight. Turns out you're not the only one who expects me to whore myself out for his cause. Just so we're clear that my behavior is work-related and not personal."

"I won't be there, so you're safe from his demands."

"His demands, but not his bed," she snapped.

Alex sighed. If it was that much of a damn issue… "Fine. If you can figure out another way—if you can get the job done your way—do it. I trust your instincts."

She stopped, staring at him. After a full minute, her lips twisted. "Good to know." She rolled her eyes. "I'll use sex if I have to, I just don't like being ordered to. I know how to get what I need."

She shook her head and stepped back. When she spoke again,

it wasn't with her head or voice down. It was for any watching audience. "Stay away from me. Everyone thinks you're so dangerous, but you're clueless. You should be more careful who you piss off."

Alex stared after her as she whirled away. Warning him off made sense. To anyone watching, he'd followed her out here. She was wielding the hammer she had—the threat of Jacob Brayer.

But how much of it was for show? And why did he have a feeling she wasn't talking about Councilor Four's grandson?

Alex stalked back to his room after his brief meeting with Erika to focus his attention and energy on the agents who lived and worked in the zone. He'd met with two of them his first night here. Their reports led him to expect much of what he'd experienced himself—Councilor One knew more than he was letting on but was so paralyzed by fear of deprivation for his people that he had become little more than a yes-man at the end of a very long supply chain.

After the meeting, he'd postponed meeting the other three young men actively involved in the Spark Rising work. He'd been set to meet them this afternoon, but he'd send coded messages out through Ace's people instead.

It was bad enough that he'd been followed since he'd been in Zone Two. He wasn't risking the identities of any more of his men.

Their reports sat on the corner of the little makeshift desk, opened, read, and waiting to be burned. There hadn't been much that surprised Alex in them, with one exception. One intrepid young man had discovered that Zone One had its own holding area for girls. He hadn't specifically stated "girls," but on his single foray into the empty cells that summer he'd noted that the cots, tables, chairs, and physical components of the oldest basement area were all child-sized.

He'd also noted that the single ledger sheet that had been mistakenly delivered to him instead of the Councilor's Security Chief indicating supplies delivered and "product" shipped out seemed to indicate two separate receivers.

Alex wished he'd had that information before he set out from the Ward School months before. With travel distances and Alex's first stop in Zone Two, the original message home must have arrived after he'd left. Alex hoped Thom had been able to put the worrying pieces together without the benefit of Alex's experiences on the road.

Alex bowed his head over his packaged responses now, fingers tapping on the uppermost one. With his recent experiences in the forest on the road and then again here in the city, with Councilor Four's sudden reclaiming of personal trade documents, with Leng Sloan's consolidation of power and supplies, even with the mystery old man in Sloan's basement, Alex figured theirs wasn't the only revolution being plotted. Unless Alex had more time to debrief Erika, he had no way of confirming if Four was a player or if his power made him a target twice-over. Sloan, as Two, was no doubt a player. Whoever controlled the young mystery agents in brown was a force to contend with, as well. Alex felt sure there was at least one more. His intuition hummed whenever he took everything out to mentally examine it. Who?

If Councilor One split his deliveries of young, powered girls, who was getting the other shipment? If there were other players involved, how many worked together, and how many were at odds?

Alex needed the answers. He had no doubt that he'd come up with a strategy that would pit them against each other and allow him to work those weaknesses. He had to know them first. He needed all eyes, in every zone, and he needed them looking for very specific things. With a final hard tap on the pile of intricately folded and wax-sealed notes, Alex leaned back and dragged the candle across the desk. He lit it with a thought and reached out for the first of the read, discarded messages on the corner of the desk.

After a moment, he laughed at himself.

Do you expect to get better if you never use those skills?

He extinguished the flame on the candle as easily as he'd lit it, then grabbed the incoming messages and walked over to the sink in the bathroom. He threw the messages in the sink and focused his thoughts—not a big, flashy fire and not something that would have him standing here forever. He needed it to burn to ash, but he wanted the Dust to do it exactly as he asked.

Black spots appeared across the sheets. They grew, spreading together like a disease on leaves but at speeds nature hadn't intended. As the black became solid, the spots where they'd started crumbled to grey ash. Soon, all of the sheets were ash. Alex sifted it through his fingertips. There were no solid pieces. He scooped most of it and threw it away, then rinsed the rest down the drain.

He returned to collect the notes and the small gifts he'd gotten for his mother. It was getting late. He wanted to have plenty of time to take the long way to his childhood home. He shrugged into his coat, and on the way out, he tapped on the door of the young caravaner he'd recruited to run his messages. He'd be down at the warehouses helping with the final prep, but he had a young wife who travelled with him and helped the cooks.

She opened the door, stepping back to allow him in, but Alex shook his head. He handed off the small stack. "These are for Michael. Last ones out."

She took them and nodded. "I'll run them to him now. They'll be finishing soon."

"Wait a few minutes and then go." He smiled at her and pulled a C-note from his pocket. "Stop and pick up something for the two of you on the way."

She took the money and stepped back, sliding the notes into her pocket and closing the door. When she went, she'd appear to be nothing more than an eager young wife wanting to enjoy her final night in the city with her man.

Alex turned and left the building.

He felt his skin tighten as soon as he was in the fading sunshine again. He shrugged deeper into his coat but left his hands to swing free at his sides. Instead of moving to the right and then straight, he turned left and walked past the Council building. What should have been a brisk twenty-minute walk was about to turn into an hour-long ordeal.

THIRTY-EIGHT

Lena

Lena wobbled back to the others after relieving herself for the last time before they rode down on the Rio Grande Gorge. The land was flat and open here with the mountains rising up behind them. She'd asked Ghost to stop at a cluster of ruins so far gone by the harsh weather of the northern desert that it was hard to tell what they'd been. The only thing they were good for now was a bit of privacy screen.

The People stood together, stretching their legs, joking, and laughing, though their faces were grim. Thomas and his agents stood off to the side, still livid at being excluded at Taos. The four boys that had come with them from Taos were in their midst.

Lena's gaze moved from the agents to the other Sparks on the field. Rose spoke to the girls, arms moving as she explained something, pointing toward the gorge. The last minute reminders would be good for them. They'd gain plenty of experience today.

Lena fought back the pang that came with the thought. She looked at Hania, tracing her form, stuck somewhere between a girl and a young woman. Yes, they were all young, but they were survivors. These were the skills the girls would need to ensure they never experienced the trauma of their early years again.

Ghost noticed her and peeled away from his People to come speak with her. Gabriela watched at first, then wandered over to join them.

Ghost flashed Lena a smile. "Are you ready?"

Lena arched her brow at him. "Are you?"

Gabriela laughed behind him. "Always."

Ghost glanced over at the girls. "Are you sure? When the People race into battle, it's to fight, not to peel away at the last minute."

Lena reached out to take his right hand in hers. She held it up, tracing the livid lightning scar on his skin. She suspected it went all the way up his arm to his shoulder, but she hadn't asked, and Ghost hadn't volunteered the information.

"I'm trying to avoid more of *this*. We discussed the plan, and everyone agreed. It was Gab's idea, not mine." Lena glanced at Gabriela, who nodded.

"It's a good one. It'll work."

"It will," Lena agreed. "But those men have got to get out of the way or they will end up as damaged as the Scavs. All of you will see plenty of action after the first strike." She rubbed her teeth over her lip. She wished she didn't have to risk any of them.

Ghost nodded. "After the initial attack by lightning, we'll climb over in the lull. Then we can chase them down."

"There you go, bloodthirsty ghost."

He laughed.

Lena wanted to join him, but she needed to clear up one more bit before they finished their journey. Something had been pricking at her, and she wanted to know if she might be right.

"Ghost—wait." She took a deep breath. "I've been thinking."

"Uh oh," Gabriela murmured.

"Ha." Lena gave the woman a joking, narrowed-eyed gaze. "The Native Nations people above us are so close, and so insistent on not trading with another group who might cause them troubles because of the Scavengers."

"We're not taking on the Nations next." Ghost's voice was flat.

Lena laughed. "I'd never be so stupid. But can't we use this somehow? Is there anything that I might do—some way to prove to them—to show them that we want to trade so much that we took care of this problem for them. I mean, if we're going to do this, we may as well turn it to every advantage, right? Can we take them Scavenger goods on the way home?"

Ghost and Gabriela exchanged a look.

"You can't take them goods," Gabriela said, her voice soft. "They'll assume you trade with the enemy, then, and they'll never deal with you. Ever."

Ghost nodded. He searched Lena's face. "Are you sure this is what you want? We can manage on our own—"

"We can't. The Council sent one man this time, sneaking. Next time they may come in force. It isn't just trade anymore. We need *allies*." She'd been thinking about it all wrong before. It wasn't food and supplies they needed. It was friends. It was security.

"Then we take them heads. It's a custom of the People, but one the Nations are familiar with. We've been doing it a long time." Ghost held her gaze. "We take them the heads of their enemies to prove we're strong and we wish to please them. We ask for nothing at that time—tell them we did this to honor them and to create peace between our people. They'll come to us in the Spring, and they'll have gifts for us. They'll ask for nothing in return."

"No weakness," Lena guessed.

He nodded. "That's how the People build relationships. It's our custom. Ask Rose."

"It starts with heads." Lena looked at Ghost and Gabriela. "No offense, but that's disgusting."

Ghost laughed. "You want to build a relationship?"

"How do we—I mean, what are the logistics of—they'll *rot*." Her stomach heaved at the thought.

Gabriela patted Lena's shoulder. "Let us worry about that. You and your girls can take them out. Just be sure to leave enough of them that there are heads to take."

Lena blinked. "Okay."

"Ready?" Ghost asked her again.

"As I'll ever be."

Gabriela laughed as the two of them left her. Lena glanced back over her shoulder. The Neo-Barb woman had a bounce in her step now.

Lena turned back to join her girls. Rose was still talking to Charity and Constance. Hania stood close by Phoebe and Marin. She and Phoebe were talking now, twin grim smiles lighting their faces. The Neo-Barbs weren't the only ones hungry for blood.

What are you doing? You have no idea if this is what they need, or if you're about to damage them even more! Lena swallowed and shook her head. They had to be taught to defend themselves. The Council had taken Marissa. It had put a collar on her again.

Lena's heart hardened.

They *had* to be ready to defend themselves. The Scavengers ahead of them weren't simply vile slavers and marauding murderers, though that would have earned them death anyway. They had colluded with the Council for years. The Council offered them bounties. For West to be headed to them, now, with Marissa—there had to be a deeper relationship.

Lena and her girls would end this part of the Council's reach into their territory. She smiled grimly. The Council might be a many-limbed beast, but today they'd cut one of those arms off—and it would serve them well. It would serve them all.

"Lena."

She started and jumped back, heart racing. "Thomas!" She hadn't even heard him approaching. "Don't do that!"

His brows rose. "I called out to you twice as I walked up."

"Oh. I was—going over everything. I want this to go off without any problems."

His lips curved up in a smile, but there was worry on his face. "Then expect the unexpected. It always happens."

"I am the unexpected."

He snorted. "Truer words…" He stood facing her for a moment before speaking again, finally broaching what had led him over to her. "You're not going to like what I ask…"

"Then don't ask it."

"Hear me out. Please." He waited.

Lena looked away at the distant horizon. Her battle waited out there, but only if she could get through the next few minutes with Alex's best friend.

She looked back at him. Patrick had joined them. He hovered behind Thomas. As support for Thomas or for her? "Say your piece, Thom."

"I need West back. Alive."

She burst into laughter, but it was not a joyful sound. "You can't be serious."

"I am. We were so close to figuring it all out. So close."

"We thought we were close," Patrick amended from behind Thomas.

"And then this. West. He's one of us, Lena. One of the Originals. We need him back. We need to question him. We need to get answers—how? Why?" There was heat in his voice.

But those eyes. They were still so pale and so cold.

"This is about more than you and the girls," he added. "This is about all of it—the entire Spark Rising movement."

"No, this is very specifically about the girls. It isn't one of your wards out there with a collar around his neck. It's one of mine. Right now, all I care about are those girls."

He made an impatient noise. "That's both foolish and short-sighted. I expected better of you." When she said nothing, he leaned in. "What if West has compromised Alex? You don't care about that?"

His words were sharp and pierced her heart, a searing tear that took her breath away.

He swung his arm in an angry, wide gesture at her belly. "What's another fatherless super-powered little girl? She won't need Alex. She'll have you. You're all they need, right? After all, growing up like that worked so well for you. You're not damaged at all. I guess Alex doesn't matter anymore after all."

She took two quick steps and raised her hand to slap him, not thinking. It wasn't until Patrick's big body was suddenly between them, one arm around her to pick her up and physically move her back from Thomas and one hand holding back her forearm, that she was even aware of the crackling ball of electricity that had enveloped her hand.

"Okay," Patrick said. "Okay. Take a breath." His voice was

steady and calm. He held her gaze. She could see the alarm behind his eyes. She could see the awareness that his intervention could cost him. He'd done it anyway. She didn't know if it was for her or for Thomas. Not for the first time, Patrick reminded her very much of Alex.

That thought had the emotion thickening her voice. "He matters," she managed.

Patrick nodded, glancing up at her still crackling hand.

Lena gulped and called the Dust back.

"You need—" Thomas's voice intruded, still implacable.

"You need to go back to the men." Patrick snapped. He tried to reclaim her gaze, but she'd already looked over his shoulder at Thomas again.

"Shut up, Patrick." Thomas cocked his head to the side to hold her attention. "This is bigger than you, Lena. You need us. You're a weapon, and weapons need direction. We can't give effective direction without West. Bring him to us."

Thomas stepped away and turned his back on them, moving away to his men.

"I have no idea why he pushed you like that. I do know that we all need each other." Patrick moved his head so that he filled her view instead of Thomas. "We do need you, but you also need us. We are what you've needed for so long."

"Go with him," Lena told Patrick.

"Are you—"

She pulled herself out of his grasp. "I'm fine. Go with him, and make sure he stays out of my way, Patrick." She didn't give him a chance to say anything else. She walked away.

A few breaths later, she heard him again. He must have caught up with Thomas. "That wasn't smart." Patrick's words were curt and still angry with his superior.

"No, but it was necessary. I need to know, Patrick. I need to know—"

Angry buzzing filled her ears and angrier tears welled in her eyes. She blinked them away. She didn't need the rage or the grief right now.

"Are you ready?" she asked the girls when she reached them.

She could hear the huskiness of those threatening tears in her voice. She cleared her throat.

Charity's gaze jumped to her. "What's wrong?"

Lena shook her head. "Nothing."

"We can do this," Constance told her.

"You trained us. We're ready." Phoebe's eyes were clear. There was no irrational bloodlust. There was no terror. There was determination tempered by anxiety.

Hania wrapped her hand in her horse's mane for a moment as she peered up at Lena. "Do you think we can do it?"

Lena smiled at them. This time when she spoke, there were no tears in her voice. "Absolutely. We're going to do it together. Let's go get started."

She and the girls rode back onto the dark gravel of the road, leading the way. The rest of them would follow. Lena would ride at the fore, reaching out with the Dust. When they were close enough, or if danger rode to greet them, she would stop the line. Then they would begin.

The land was flat and spread out before them. Because she was watching with more than merely her eyes, she was aware of the gorge looming before them well before the girls. Their first sense of it was the faint roar of the river echoing off its walls, heard above the sound of the wind in their ears. It was so subtle that even though the sound grew as they drew closer, they adapted to hearing it. Their gasps told her when they'd seen the first hints of it.

The Rio Grande Gorge was a jagged slash carved deep into the land. One moment the land appeared straight and unending to the horizon. The next, the first inkling of a gap in the land was realized. Not even a quarter hour of riding later, the true sense of it became clear.

The closer they came, the clearer the images in her head. She'd never done this before. She wasn't using only her eyesight, but she wasn't floating above with the Dust, either. She was somewhere in between, seeing and *seeing* in shapes and heat and movement.

"Stop!" She pulled her horse in, staring ahead with her Dust-vision alone now. She'd caught a hint of motion…

A horse wandered alone away from the rim.

Not any horse, she was sure. West's stolen horse. There was no crossing here for a horse. There wasn't one for several days in either direction. West had released the horse to scramble away without it. How long ago?

She focused again on the gorge, sweeping her vision up over the lip and down with the Dust, flowing with the air currents, swarming down the rocky slope toward the muted glow of people.

Forms scrambled below on the narrow strip of ground between the river and the wall of the gorge. They dismantled their tents and packed everything in a line of boats pulled up on the shore. This was how they came and went without anyone in the area being aware of them.

More of them climbed the cliff. She followed their glow up as they scaled the twisted wreckage of the former bridge, using it as a ladder to climb toward the edge of the cliff. They paused below it, taking up positions to wait. It seemed some of them were meant to be seen, a distraction to attack, while others were hidden behind cold tangles of metal, waiting to begin the counter-attack.

Her gaze skipped across the gorge to the raised span that still hovered in the air halfway across before twisting and diving into the gorge. The muted glow of human beings crouched within tangled metal cradles. She had no doubt that the hands that curved around colder materials held missile weapons—bows or spear-throwers. She had them marked. She knew how she'd deal with them.

She still hadn't found Marissa.

Her vision rode the currents back down again and curved off on an eddy, over the foaming water. It was the chaotic, jittery movement of Marissa's bound energy that caught Lena's eye. She was flanked by not one, but two sets of looming bright Spark bodies leaning over her.

West and the Scavengers' Spark loaded her into some kind of long box. Behind them, over the cold, terrifying motion of grey that was the river, a large black shape waited half in the water. The brilliant glow of Karina waited for them in it, perched on a seat and, by the signature of her energy, pleased to be there. Karina was happy to be going, either completely controlled now by her twisted match or lost in some fantasy her broken mind had created. But Marissa…

They were preparing Marissa to be loaded into the boat like cargo.

Lena swarmed back up to herself and the girls, the dismounted Neo-Barbs spread out like a cup in front of them now, and Thomas and his agents forming a disgruntled line behind them. She blinked, and the normal landscape spread out before her.

"Did you find her?" Rose watched Lena, waiting for permission to go in after their youngest student.

Lena nodded, then gave a gesture to Ghost and Gabriela. They were ready.

Lena and the girls dismounted and approached the back of the Neo-Barbs on foot as the line moved toward the edge. They wanted to be close enough to be seen, close enough for the Scavengers to think they knew what was coming. But she had to keep them far enough away that they could accomplish the first strike without risk to the girls flanking Lena and Rose.

The agents behind them dismounted too, and swept out to the sides. One group held back, leading all of the horses away.

Lena spread her arms, and all the Sparks by her side linked hands, forming a chain of power. Rose was on her right, with Charity and Constance linked to her. Hania was on her left, and Marin and Phoebe held on to her end. When their hands dropped again, Ghost would give the signal. She hoped the people in front of her moved quickly. She hoped it would work.

Closing her eyes, she drew on the power coursing through her from their linked hands. She had one chance to get this right, one chance to strike before the bravest of the warriors hovering below the ledge boiled up to strike at the girls. She could make one strike using the combined force of all of them, and then they would each be on their own.

The energy built within her, the Dust pulsing as it released its stored energy. The same energy traveled to her through Rose and

Hania's hands, and through them from the other girls—all of it moving through and then being pushed into her small body. Electricity crackled along their linked bodies.

She heard voices to the side and behind her—Patrick and Thomas.

"Dust…" The single word infused with Patrick's awe.

"This is a mistake. We cannot lose them all." Worry and fear filled Thomas's voice.

Lena opened her eyes. From the corners of her eyes and radiating up from the bridge of her nose, she saw her own glow, magnified. The energy was more than she'd ever contained. She couldn't release their hands.

"Let me go," she gasped. "Let me go."

The moment first Rose's hands then Hania's fell away from her own, she swung her arms in an arc before her, urging the energy out that way instead of through her feet. Dust poured down her arms, coating her from the inside out, protecting. She showed the Dust where to discharge as the bodies in front of her peeled away, creating an opening.

The bright bolts discharged from each arm with a boom that threw her backward. The sound rolled through the air, a crack that deafened her. Dazed, she lifted her head to see—she had to see what she'd done—but it was already over.

The lightning she'd released forked, and forked again and again until it reached the spots she'd sent it arrowing toward. It released, spectacularly, on the men and women lying in wait within the upper levels of the twisted metal framework of the old suspension bridge. Bodies sagged, then fell hundreds of feet to the water below. Some slumped forward, skin charred to the beams around them. It was horrifying.

It was exactly as she'd planned.

THIRTY-NINE

Lena

The charred bodies remained seared to the beams. Lena swallowed bile and looked away, dragging her eyes to the girls to either side. Rose was already on her feet, directing them, pointing to the Scavengers scrambling over the edge. Ghost and Gabriela ran forward, leading the People and agents in a swarm to overcome those in hiding below. Hania stood frozen, staring at the bodies out on the span. Her body turned, her head moving with it, and she looked back at Lena, eyes wide.

"It's okay," Lena whispered. "It's okay." She couldn't hear her own voice over the ringing in her ears and shouting and gunfire from Thomas's agents. She could see the terror on the girl's face.

She scrambled to her knees, lifting her arms and gesturing with her hands. *Come here. It's okay.*

Hania stumbled to her and buried her face in Lena's shoulder. Lena awkwardly rose, holding tight to the girl who was almost as tall as she was. She watched over Hania's shoulder.

Phoebe, the one who'd bonded tightest with Hania in a shared hunger for vengeance, experienced no crisis of conscience. She walked close to the edge, striking out at Scavengers who pulled themselves over it, sending them reeling back to fall. Many of them were dead before they began the fall, hearts stopped by electrical current and will.

Marin stayed close to Phoebe. She mimicked her match's movements, though she felt none of the rage. She was controlled and efficient, almost more terrifying than her match.

Charity and Constance held back, choosing targets from a distance like the agents to their sides. They worked in tandem, one striking while the other rested. Rose stood with them, her face contorted as she shouted at Phoebe and Marin. They were too close to the edge, both physically and emotionally, and in the way of Ghost and Gabriela's forces poised to swing down over the edge. They'd take the places of fallen Scavengers, beating back any others they encountered on their mad, racing climb down to the river shore below to find the boat. They'd dispose of any resistance below, yes, but she'd been explicit. Their mission was to find Marissa and bring her to Lena to get that damned collar off.

Lena wanted to go with them. She needed to be out there on the edge with Marin and Phoebe. But Hania needed her here. She stepped back several paces, dragging the girl with her, trying to figure out where to leave the terrified child—

She never should have been out here in the first place, you fool!

"Give her to me." Patrick leaned down from a horse. Its eyes rolled wildly at the discharges coming from the edge and it danced sideways. "Come on! Now!"

"Keep her safe." She lifted Hania, the burden almost too much for her until Patrick reached down and easily took Hania from her.

"I'm sorry, Lena. I'm sorry I wasn't enough—" Tears soaked the girl's face as she was passed up to the agent.

"No. Don't say that. Don't think it." She cupped the little face in her hands. "You are enough. You are the light and the heat and the force, the same as all of us. You're going to use it differently. You have everything you need to be the perfect Hania inside of you already. Do you hear me?"

Hania's face crumpled as she fought more tears.

"We have to get back." One of Patrick's hands held the reins low and tight as the horse fought him. The other pushed a belt into

Lena's hands. He was giving her his gun? "You're overloaded. Alex taught you—this takes less to fire. Take it—just in case."

Lena took it and stepped away, letting them go. The minute she did, Patrick wheeled the horse about and it leapt away, throwing back clods of earth at her as it raced off to join the others.

She'll be okay. He'll keep her safe. Marissa needs you now!

Lena whirled, slinging the belt around herself and awkwardly tightening it. Rose and Charity and Constance still fought, well back from the edge, sweeping stragglers off and over the edge. More than half of Ghost and Gabriela's mixed forces of Neo-Barbs and agents had already gone over the edge after them, but in a controlled descent down the twisting girders clinging to the inside of the cliff.

Lena scanned to the left, searching through their own combatants as they swarmed the edge and over.

Marin stumbled back, head shaking, eyes wide. Her skin had the sheen of a glow. She fell backward, and the man before her grinned. She'd overextended herself. She had nothing more to give. Phoebe leaned in to help the fallen Marin.

Lena reached out to freeze the man's muscles—stop everything—as she struggled to pull Patrick's gun. The man froze. The large rock he'd held double-handed smashed down on the side of Phoebe's head. She fell.

Lena raised Patrick's gun and fired at the center of the man. His body collapsed backward and fell over the edge.

She ran to Marin and Phoebe. Marin had already rolled over to Phoebe, her hands hovering over Phoebe's head. Her hands shook and she gasped with effort.

"Marin, let me." Lena pushed her hands in under Marin's and lifted Phoebe's hair back from the side of her head. It was sticky with free-flowing blood. Lena reached deep. The damage was surface, she thought. It was scalp and skull, that's all. She sent the Dust swarming to heal and knit bone and flesh together.

"Help me." Phoebe was still woozy, but she had to be moved away to safety to recover. Lena took one of Phoebe's arms and wrapped it around her shoulder, ducking her head under the larger girl's arm. Marin slipped under Phoebe's other arm and they dragged her back together, grunting under the weight. Both she and Marin were small. Phoebe was solid muscle.

She settled Phoebe on the ground, looking up to see what she'd hoped for—another of Thomas's agents from the rear, swooping forward to take the injured girl to safety.

"Go with them, Marin. Keep her safe." Lena tucked Phoebe's arm across her chest. She looked back up at Marin and noted the exhaustion in the girl's eyes, so similar to the stunned slowness in Phoebe's. "I'll be back to check on you both soon, okay? Go with them, and rest. You were amazing."

Marin nodded, the barest of movements. She wasn't a warrior. She was a healer. They all knew it, but she'd insisted on coming to the front with her match. She'd done well, too.

"It was my fault," she whispered now.

Lena leaned back down. "No. It was *their* fault for taking Marissa. For being willing to trade in humans. For fighting us. It's their fault. Don't forget it."

Phoebe reached out and grabbed Marin's hand, squeezing it reassuringly.

Something flickered behind Marin's eyes. She didn't nod this time, but Lena could see she understood.

She left them as the agent pulled the horse up short and hopped down to help Marin with Phoebe. She could see as soon as she turned, it was all but over—at least for them, here on the surface, it was over.

No one else came up over the edge. Almost all of the Neo-barbs had gone over the edge. Those few who remained were no longer in a hurry to go down. A few of Thomas's agents stood on the edge, watching. Every so often, one would lift his gun and take careful aim, sighting in the direction of the water, and then fire. Based on the satisfaction of the agents sighting and firing, the Scavs weren't successful in using their boats to escape.

Rose, Charity, and Constance were off to one side, crouched at the edge, peering down. She hurried to them.

Rose turned to her, face tense. "They haven't reached her yet. The Scavs are fighting hard."

Constance took her sister's hand. Was it because of the fierce expression Lena felt twisting her face?

Charity wiped a line of tears tracking through dust on her cheeks. "We're so close to overload. We can't do anything else."

Lena stared at them. All three of them had the sheen of a glow. Rose's was brighter. They were right. They couldn't do anything else.

She could. Not only did she have Patrick's gun, but she was used to working with larger amounts of energy. She was used to channeling the Dust in dangerous quantities.

But the baby...?

Lena swallowed back the flare of panic, and peered over the edge. Far below, Scavs fought their People and the agents. Blades and bows were as effective at eliciting war cries and screams of pain and fury as the gunfire that echoed off the steep cliff sides. In the river itself, boats floated freely, twisting in the current. None were controlled. Either the people trying to use them had been gunned down at the shore as they pushed them out, or their bodies lay unmoving within them.

Up the river below, the one boat Lena searched for was tended by a Scav and two Sparks—West and a young man in a brown uniform. The long box Marissa had been stored in like cargo was already aboard. Karina sat serenely, watching the men throwing supplies onto the boat.

None of the People were around the boat. Ghost and Gabriela were working toward it, but delayed by battle. West and his collaborator were going to get away. They'd take Marissa and Karina to the Council.

Never. The thought repeated in her head, accompanied by the throb of her heartbeat. *Never, never, never...*

She leaned out, checking that the twisted frame below them was cleared of Scavs. It was. She'd have a rapid descent, and there was a shelf where she could cut across about twenty feet up from the bottom of the gorge to avoid the battle raging. It was risky, but it was clear.

Rose would never let her go. It wasn't only the danger of the descent. Lena knew how close she was to overload. Rose could see it. She could feel it.

Lena leaned back and poured her rage and frustration and fear for her unborn child into her voice. “You’re right. There’s nothing else we can do. Not without killing ourselves.” She hugged herself and raised her gaze to Rose. “Take the girls back. I’m going to watch. I have to at least stay here and watch…”

Rose’s head tilted and her voice held a warning. “Lena. You can’t—”

“Take them, Rose. I’ll follow. I owe her staying to witness.” It wasn’t a lie. She would follow, but she’d do what she had to first.

Rose stood still for a long moment. She didn’t trust Lena not to do something stupid. Of course she didn’t. She knew Lena too well.

Constance took Rose’s hand. “Please, can we go back? I’m so tired. And I—I can’t watch.” She threw an ashamed, apologetic glance at Lena.

“Go.” Lena whispered the command to Rose.

Her friend led the twins away. As soon as they’d moved through the opening the agents made for them in the line of horses and were hidden again on the other side, Lena whirled around and dropped to the edge.

She knelt and turned, feet searching out the topmost bar of corroded metal that had been part of the collapsed bridge. The rocky edge bit into her round belly as she scooted down.

*The baby…*she savagely shut down the terrified internal voice. She would bring Marissa home. She had to save the little girl she’d promised to keep safe.

Her feet found the bar and she began her descent, working as fast as she could. She thought she heard her name shouted. From above or below? Her heart pounded in her ears. She couldn’t be sure, and she wouldn’t look around to see. She focused on the next bar, the next grip. She focused on the ground moving up from below.

When she reached the shelf that cut off to the right, she spiderwalked to the edge of the tangled metal and hopped off. Her ankle turned under her, but she ignored the pain. As soon as she righted herself, she ran.

She refused to look anywhere but ahead. The box. The boat. The men.

Those men had defensive training, she reminded herself as she ran. Alex did it himself. She wouldn't be able to affect them with the Dust, but she had the gun.

Her breath sawed in her ears. The way was rocky and steep and she slowed. She flicked her gaze between the ground in front of her and the boat ahead. The men were almost done loading. West was still ashore, but the other man waded along the side of the boat, leaning into it, pushing.

No. No, no, no!

In the boat, Karina watched her come. She didn't warn them, but she didn't move against them, either. She seemed placid and almost pleased. Lena's stare jogged down as she slipped.

Karina was stroking Marissa's box.

It didn't bother Karina that Marissa was imprisoned within it. In fact, she rubbed the wood with the fingers of one hand as if it was a treasure.

Lena swallowed bile and tore her gaze from the broken young woman to focus again on West. As long as he was still on the river's bank, she had a chance.

"Lena!" Ghost's roar, shocked and furious, echoed off the cliff side behind her.

She refused to look to find him. She refused to turn away from Marissa.

West dropped the box he carried on the beach and whipped around. He'd heard. His eyes searched for Lena.

When he saw her, halfway to him on the raised shelf, he smiled. His gun was in his hand impossibly fast. He raised it. The smile never left his face.

She couldn't freeze his muscles. She'd never pull Patrick's weapon fast enough. She couldn't stop him.

Lena reached, and power thrummed through her as the Dust responded. She was so close to overload. The power throbbed in her forehead, deep and painful.

Protect this baby. The thought was a flash of desperation.

Dust, please, protect her.

She told the Dust what she needed at the same moment his finger flexed on the trigger.

The gun exploded. Black smoke and red mist flared out and away to the sky and the earth in an arcing spray.

West shrieked, staring at the ruin of his hand.

Lena couldn't control his body, no. But the Dust was in everything.

West stared in horror before he was tackled from the side by Ghost. They rolled, fighting. West managed to land a blow that rocked Ghost's head back, but the warrior retaliated with vicious efficiency. He grabbed the agent's bloody hand and pressed in, working his fingers into West's wounds.

West cried out, an inarticulate howl of defeat. The injured agent, struggling to pull himself out of shock, was no match for the Neo-barb.

Lena climbed down from the shelf and ran for the water's edge. The boat bobbed in the water now. The young agent in brown had managed to push it free. He gave it a final push, then hauled himself out of the water over the side and rolled into the boat.

Could she shoot him? Not without risking Marissa or Karina.

"No!" Lena didn't think. She ran after them, slowed by the pull of the frigid, rough water on her legs. She stumbled, reaching out as the agent shoved an oar beneath the water, using it to push the boat further into the water. It spun away from her, out of reach.

You'll kill you both! You can't swim! Helpless rage at herself beat in time with the feedback headache. If she died, she'd take her baby with her. Months of ambivalence about the life within her burned away with sudden clarity. In order to save the baby, Lena had to survive.

Somehow, she had to save them all. Marissa was on the boat. The water wasn't even at her waist. Surely she could reach them. Lena had to get her back.

She waded three steps further. The river bottom beneath her already numb legs fell away and Lena sank, choking on water.

Her head went under. The cold of the water was absolute, needle sharp, all around. Panicked, Lena tried to draw a breath. She choked, and choked again as more water flooded in.

A sharp pull on her scalp hauled her backward, freeing her from the water. She vomited water. Between wet coughs and gags, she desperately dragged air into her lungs.

"Take her!" Ghost turned her around in front of him, his fingers still tangled in her hair, and passed her to someone behind her on the shore.

She clung to him, terrified of the water. Hands pulled at her from under her arms.

"Lena, let me go. There's another boat. Let me catch them!"

"I've got her." Gabriela's voice was rough with emotion. "Go!"

"Marissa." Lena wheezed the name, forcing it out. "In a box. Boat cargo."

Ghost splashed away through the rough water along the shore. Lena stared after him, pushing with her legs to help Gabriela drag her from the water. A moment later, he gripped the edges of the only other boat still ashore. He pushed it out into the water and clambered over the side.

"I can't swim." Lena's choked words were more despairing self-recrimination than explanation.

Gabriela pulled Lena closer in comfort, but her eyes never left Ghost. "Neither can he."

Lena caught the whites of his wide eyes as he flashed a look at the water all around him before he shook his head and oriented himself to find the agent's boat. Lifting the oar, he fumbled with it. A moment later, he'd caught the rhythm from watching the frantic younger man ahead of him and struck out for it with clean, strong strokes that cut through the chop of the river.

His greater strength brought him close to the edge of the other boat. The agent tried to batter him with the oar, striking out at Ghost. The Neo-Barb dodged back, his movement shaking his craft and sending him stumbling, arms and oar pinwheeling for balance. He fell, his back cracking against the edge and his shoulders slapping the water as the boat tipped. Only the length of his legs kept it from overturning. He looked at the dark water behind him and Lena caught the sense of his terror warring with determination.

He scrambled to his feet, leaving the oar and extending his arms for balance. The agent leaned out, poised to strike with the oar above his head.

The moment stretched on as the boats rocked. The men stared at each other across the moving water as the far end of their boats slowly moved closer.

Ghost's arm suddenly flashed out—relying on his longer reach. His fingers brushed the front of the agent's shirt. Still gripping the oar, the agent struck out.

Ghost caught the wooden oar. He ripped it away, throwing it into the water behind him. His long arm shot out and dragged the agent to him, thumping their boats together. Both rocked, splashing water over their edges. Ghost landed three heavy blows on the young man before the agent managed to kick out and push Ghost off of him. The second oar swung out and caught Ghost on the head.

He fell back, hands scrabbling at the wooden edge to keep momentum from tossing him over. The force of his fall sent the boat sliding back. The agent smacked the edge of his oar against the side of Ghost's boat and shoved, sending it spinning away.

The agent spun and dipped down. He rose with something small clutched in his hand, and his lips twisted up in an ugly curve. He lightly tossed it into the closest end of Ghost's boat.

Lena felt the agent reaching and caught the bright flare of his energy bloom as he worked with the Dust. She shoved herself up, hands splashing into the frigid water. What was he—?

The end of Ghost's boat exploded. Bits of wood shot away, heavier than the smoke that hid Ghost.

"What was that?" Gabriela's shout seemed to echo in her ears.

Lena shook her head, eyes straining. She didn't know. She willed him up. "Ghost…" The smoke cleared and Lena could see the curved end of the boat, still intact.

Ghost rose to his feet, roaring with rage. Blood ran from his face and chest. He shouted words Lena couldn't hear at Karina who still watched from her bench. She watched, head tilted as if mildly curious, one hand still on Marissa's box. The agent dipped his single oar into the water and pushed, carrying them away.

Lena saw the frustration and desperate anger on Ghost's face. He turned to look around, likely searching for his own oar to pursue them again. Then he froze. He stared into the boat. The far end listed now, its edge sinking deeper into the river.

It was filling with water. Ghost stared, and his rage flickered over to terror. He lifted his face to them on the shore, eyes wide. He scrambled back as the end ahead of him dipped into the water, sliding deeper, and his end rose into the air.

It was breathtaking how fast it happened. Lena watched, frozen, as the lithe Neo-Barb gripped the turned end and slid around it. He went into the water. His weight made the boat dip to the side, then twist under the water. The end popped back up, upside down and somehow still buoyant. Ghost clung to it, gasping and sputtering.

It wasn't sinking anymore. It spun away down river, dragging Ghost with it.

How long could Ghost cling to it in the cold water?

Gabriela spun her around. "You have power! Do something!"

Lena gaped at her. She shook as she stared into Gabriela's desperate face and then looked back at the river—both Ghost and Marissa being swept away from her. What could she do? There was nothing. It was water. What could she do to it?

Panic set in as she realized she had no idea. "I don't know—I can't—"

Gabriela snarled her frustration and pushed Lena away from her to spin and shout for the young People near by.

"*Sigueme rio abajo*!" Vicente, one of the younger People, shouted at the rest. "*Vamanos*!"

They ran now, racing Ghost downstream to a narrower portion of the river. When they reached it, the men and women climbed the rocks and waded into the water, linking extended arms, making a chain. Ghost and the partially submerged boat swept toward them. As he spun, Ghost saw them. He reached out, linked hands with Vicente, and was pulled in to them, pushed along to the next, held up as they dragged each other in.

The boat spun below water, its end above the surface pulled by the force of the water. The end of it smacked into the side of Vicente's head. The others, focused now on passing Ghost along and dragging themselves free, didn't notice as his grip loosened.

Lena ran, though her legs were numb and her whole body shook with uncontrollable tremors. She shouted to the others as she stumbled down the shore to meet Ghost where he crawled onto the rocks.

Vicente, at the end of the chain, slipped back, tried to catch himself again, failed. His reaching hand splashed on the surface as he went under. The river swept him away.

At her shouts of warning, the others turned, splashing and trying to unfurl again to catch him. It was too late. He was gone.

A silence fell. It was broken only by the sound of Ghost's ragged breathing and splashing as they each made it back ashore. She wrapped fingers she couldn't feel around Ghost's shoulder and helped him roll over on the rocks of the shore. Water poured from his clothes and hair.

"I'm sorry," he gasped. "I couldn't—I'm sorry." He tried to sit up, but she pushed him back down.

"Let me help you."

"No. I need to find another boat. I can go after her."

"There aren't any more on shore." Gabriela sank down on his other side and helped Lena press him back.

"You're hurt." Lena's head still throbbed, and the tense, uncontrollable shivering didn't help. But she had to help him. He'd tried so hard…

Please. Just give me this one thing.

She raised her shaking hands to hover above him and focused, allowing the Dust to do as it would so long as it healed him. She was pushing too far. She might already have built up too much power within her for the daughter that she desperately wanted to survive. The sacrifice had to be worth it. *Make him strong and whole. Please.*

The Dust complied. The pain in Lena's head blossomed into

a deadly, spreading vine that tightened around her skull, writhed within her brain. It spread down her neck and between her shoulder blades.

Gabriela brushed her hands over him, wiping away the pieces of wood that had lodged in his skin as the Dust expelled them and closed the wounds.

Lena leaned away, pushing herself up and staggering back. Two young People stood at the top of the pile of rocks that jutted into the water, looking downstream. She climbed up to join them, slipping on the wet stone and tearing her fingers. She reached the top, jerking free Patrick's gun in a final bid to strike at the young man. It didn't matter. She stared down the river with the man and woman beside her and slid the gun back into its holster.

They were gone. Vicente, the brave, quick-thinking young warrior, had never resurfaced. The boat carrying the agent and Karina and their helpless cargo was gone, too, swept around a curve ahead by the current and his victory.

There were no more boats. There was no way to track them along the rough sides of the river, lined with steep cliffs. There was no more anger to mine like jewels for one final push. She had nothing left, and the weight of how far past capacity she'd pushed herself to get to this brutal moment of helplessness tightened around her brain like a vise.

She'd failed Marissa. The woman who could do anything…hadn't. How would she tell the others? How could she face them, or herself, knowing what the future held for the girl whose smile lit their lives?

"I'll come for you, Marissa." She whispered the promise into the wind. "I'll track you. I'll find you, and I will come."

If I haven't already burned myself out. And if she had? What about her daughter?

What price would both girls have to pay for Lena's failure? Lena's head bowed. Her hands, tremoring with cold that was as much fear as temperature, wrapped around her belly.

You don't know. She tried to whisper the reassurance to herself, but the words stuck in her tight throat. *You don't know. Leave the fear. Focus on the next step.*

She'd failed Marissa.

But she had West. And she'd burn him to ash to get Marissa back.

FORTY

Alex

Alex arrived at his mother's bakery from the other direction. He'd traveled almost the full circuit of that side of the city and had drifted in from close to the outer walls. He stood outside for a moment, looking up. Then he looked down at his hands.

In one hand, he had a trio of seasoning sauces in tiny bottles that he'd gotten from Ace's private stash. In the other, he had a small bag of some special salts he'd managed to con out of the caravan cook's supply. He hoped they'd make her happy.

With a final long look up and down the narrow alley, Alex opened the door to the bakery and closed it behind him.

"Alejandro?" His mother's voice floated down the narrow staircase.

"It's me," he called back in answer.

"Lock the door. I left it open for you." He'd figured as much, and he'd already turned the lock. Now he traipsed through the back of the store and up the stairs. Halfway up, he closed his eyes and moved by smell.

He'd forgotten he knew that aroma—the special mix of spices that his people had brought with them to the north from Puerto Rico a hundred years before the Cataclysm. It was rich and filled his nose. He smiled as he pushed open the door she'd left ajar for him.

His mother looked up from the kitchen, drying her hands and

giving him a wide smile in return. Her smile froze. "What happened to your beautiful face?"

"Oh." Alex paused in the doorway. He reached up and felt the stitches with the edge of fingers clutched around miniature bottles. "It's nothing. Just…work."

She nodded and looked away. She patted her hands on her hips and bustled around the tiny kitchen again, rechecking the food.

Alex felt a surge of tenderness. She was as nervous as he was. This dinner—what would likely be the last time they saw each other—meant as much to her as it did to him. He swallowed away a lump in his throat as he moved into the room.

"It smells amazing in here. I'd forgotten that smell. Now I'll never forget it."

She laughed nervously, and looked down. "I hope not."

Was she trying to hide the sad smile?

Alex crossed the room and held out his gifts. "I, um, wasn't sure what you might like. But I thought something for cooking…?"

She took the sauces and salt from him with a little exclamation of appreciation. "I've wanted to try these, but they were so expensive." She gave him a look that said he shouldn't have spent the C-Notes.

"It was my pleasure." He grinned at her, unrepentant. "I thought about making you a hand-made card like I used to, but I figured it'd be much less charming at this age."

She shook her head as she put the sauces away. "You might be surprised."

When she turned around, they both fell silent. A long, awkward moment passed. Alex felt panic begin to stir inside of him.

It was as he feared: what if they ran out of things to talk about? What if there was no real connection? He'd been gone so long, it was almost as if he wasn't even her son anymore—

She cocked her head and smiled at him. "I hope you're hungry. I made your favorites. Well, they were your favorites. I hope you still like them. I'd like to talk while we eat. I'd love to hear more about your life. About how you came to be—" She gestured at him, indicating all of him.

How he came to be…an agent? Whatever he was now?

He wasn't sure, but he found himself nodding. "Sure." He leaned against the wall and inhaled deep. "What were my favorites?"

She took a plate down and went to each pot in turn, removing the lid and scooping a generous portion of each food as she added it to his plate. "*Arroz con gandules.* Your favorite beans. *Pollo en fricassee.* And then this…" She set the plate on the counter to pick up something from behind her. She wore a wide, mischievous smile. "A treasure. So rare. And you, greedy boy, used to sneak off with them. We had to hide them when we could get them." She pulled her hand around and showed him a small, dark-skinned fruit. "You called them abogados." She laughed now.

"I still like avocados. And I still snatch them up on the rare occasions I can find them."

She turned and took up a long, sharp knife, slicing through the avocado and around the pit, then pulling the two halves apart. She settled one half on his plate and turned to hand it to him.

"Thanks," he nodded at the other plate on the counter. "You're eating, too?"

"Yes, of course." She gestured him to the little table, joining him a few moments later. She watched him.

Alex scooped up a bite that took a bit of each food. The moment it was in his mouth, his eyes closed. Memories flooded in—voices, laughter, the sound of a baby fussing—and his chest clenched. He chewed and swallowed, savoring the flavor of the food even as the memories rose inside on a tide of grief and nostalgia.

He opened his eyes to his mother's still, calm face.

"It's the best I've ever had."

A grin crinkled her eyes. "Of course it is." She waved her fork in the air. "This food is the reason you're so tall and strong." She nodded. "Your first five years you ate this food. It fed your body better than anything."

He laughed and scooped another heaping helping into his

mouth. "That may be."

"It is."

She launched into a teasing story of a night he'd tried to arm wrestle his father to see who would get the biggest serving of *pernil*, the roast pork shoulder they both loved. Alex and his mother were both so focused on each other and the food and the laughter, that neither of them noticed the front door swing open.

It wasn't until the young man took a step into his mother's home that Alex's head whipped around.

"Alex? Is this one of your—"

"No, Mama." He held up his hand, finger and thumb up for silence. It was heavy-handed, but Alex didn't want her drawn into whatever was about to happen. Because something was about to happen.

The young man was not quite as tall as Alex, but had the same rangy, lean build. His black hair was cut close to his head, and his bone structure spoke of Native Nations blood. He was dressed in a tight, mottled brown coat belted over brown pants tucked into dark leather boots. His glance moved over Alex's mother with disinterest and dismissed her.

The clothing he'd noted on the dead kid in the forest and the shithead who'd tried to ambush him the night before weren't merely similar, they were a uniform. It was similar to that issued to new young agents. The differences—markings at the shoulder and wrist, the fit of the pants, the color—were subtle.

Alex narrowed his eyes. There was no aura of Spark energy around him, though that didn't mean he wasn't a Spark. It simply meant he'd not used the power recently. There were no bruises on the young man's face, either. Not the man from the night before, then. But one of them.

Alex slid his chair back and stood, turning his body to slide out from between the chair and the table and positioning himself in front of his mother.

"Finally." The young man spoke in a voice filled with laughter. "You and me."

Alex said nothing. He watched the young man, noting that he moved forward with his right foot first, that his right shoulder was slightly higher than the left as he moved, readied for attack.

"I've waited for this. They don't think it's time." The kid cocked his head, and a smile flickered over his face. "But if you want something done right, you let your best man do it his way. Isn't that right? It's what they did with you, until you weren't the best anymore."

Alex moved forward a step, hoping to put enough distance between himself and his mother that she'd be able to slip out of the tight confines of the dining area and escape. Now he cocked his own head, mimicking the hostile young man in front of him. "I'm sorry," he drawled, "should I know who you are?"

The smile fluttered away. "I'm you." He bounced on his toes and shrugged. "Well, not exactly you. And not yet. But given enough time to win over a certain Councilor, I will be the younger, faster, better version of you. They've trained me for this. I'm particularly looking forward to taking over your special duties in Zone Three." The bouncing stopped, and a slow smile full of promised menace spread. "All of your duties. She's not my type, but I'll make an exception…"

Alex blinked and exhaled. *No. You won't.*

He needed to be free of the confines of the small, narrow room. The kid tracked the movement as Alex moved forward, leaving the dining area behind him. The kid took two slow steps to the left.

"The idea of fathering a new breed of Spark is a great aphrodisiac, isn't it?" He continued. "Of course, I'll have to kill your spawn first…"

There was a gasp from behind him, but Alex laughed at the attempt to rattle him. He shook his head. "Sloppy, kid. If you're going to taunt someone into attacking, you should be sure the scenario you're using is accurate. Or possible."

The kid stopped moving. His eyes widened as he searched Alex's face. "You didn't know yet?" He threw his head back and laughed.

The humor was short lived, but it was effective.

Alex swallowed. The laughter hit like a kick in the gut. All of those little touches, those moments before waking or sleep when he'd felt her—he'd been right. His gut had told him it wasn't just homesickness. It had been her. The changes in her body had been a reflection of reality, not his subconscious playing with him.

That weight of yearning and importance hadn't been his imagination. She'd been trying to reach him, because it *was* important.

No. It was impossible.

Had it been her? Could it have been?

"That's funny." The kid stopped laughing and bounced again, eager. "*I* knew before *you*. You're losing your touch. What are you, 49? 50? You're getting too old for this game."

Alex's eyes narrowed. He slid forward another step, his fingers curling into his palms.

"Ooo, are you sure, old man? I'm younger, and I'm faster. You can't handle this."

"Try me, asshole."

They launched at each other at the same time. Alex lunged forward, his left arm moving up to block the right-handed blow the kid had already telegraphed. They smashed together, and Alex knocked the descending fist away and got in two hard, fast blows of his own before the kid yanked away, twisting his body and kicking Alex as he spun.

Alex whirled, his heart pounding as he caught a flash of movement. His mother darted from the dining area into the little kitchen. The glimpse was all he had time for. The kid was coming at him again, using the back of a thick, padded chair to launch himself. Alex crouched at the knees, arms up, and braced to absorb the impact. Alex wasn't knocked to the ground. Instead, he threw the kid back again.

His descending fist managed to connect with the side of Alex's head. Alex shook it off and moved in, pouncing as the kid tried to push himself away from the wall again.

The kid landed as many blows as Alex did. They pummeled each other, punching, grasping, fingers slipping as they each tried to wring an advantage from the other. Inarticulate shouts burst out as freely as the blood from their noses and lips.

Evenly matched. The realization was fueled by fury. One of them had to get the upper hand soon. He pulled away enough to get a knee up and slammed it into the kid's groin.

He missed his target, but the kid flailed. His knuckles grazed Alex's right brow, but the force was enough to rip away the stitches.

Blood poured from the re-opened gash, blinding Alex in that eye. He pulled away and shook his head, attempting to clear his vision.

It was the opening the kid needed.

He dropped his arms to plow his doubled fists into Alex's crotch. He didn't miss.

Alex dropped, breathless.

The kid barreled forward, smashing his fists into the right side of Alex's face.

Alex fell back, raising his arms to block blows that didn't come. He lowered his arms.

The kid backed away, chest heaving. Blood flowed freely from his nose and mouth. He swiped at them with torn knuckles, then almost fell as he backed into the chair Alex's mother had pushed out as she fled the dining room behind him. Instead, he turned and grabbed it. He lifted it over his head and surged forward those few steps.

Alex managed to half-rise and turn. The chair smashed into his side and back. Pain exploded in his side, leaving him breathless. He fell to his other side, struggling to regain his breath. The kid's feet came into his field of vision. A long, splintered leg of the chair dragged along the floor beside his feet. Alex ignored the wood, now being lifted. He focused on the feet.

But he couldn't breathe. *Focus.* He visualized what he wanted, tried to communicate it.

The kid's breath came in pained pants, too. "Like I said, old man—"

Push.

In a flash of heat and brilliant light, the kid flew back.

Alex heard his impact with the table. Their plates and cups smashed beneath him or against the walls. Alex rolled to his knees. All he needed was a minute. One minute to overcome the pain from his ribs that stole his breath and his focus. He pushed himself to rock back onto his feet, aware of the sounds of movement behind him—the sliding of fabric on wood and crunching of glassware. There were hisses of pain and spat curses, too.

Alex pulled himself upright and turned.

The kid had crawled out of the dining area and regained his own feet, swaying at the entrance to the kitchen. He glanced behind himself and managed to move to the side, aware of Alex's mother cowering in the kitchen behind him. He'd give her no opportunity to help her son.

Alex didn't need her help. He intended to finish this. He managed a wheeze of laughter. "Younger and faster, huh? I think someone underestimated the damage I'm capable of dealing."

The kid nodded. "I thought we'd do this straight-up, but if you want to play like that—" He reached into his coat pocket and removed a small, flat disk. With a muttered word, he flung it at Alex and spun away into the kitchen.

Alex threw himself to the side. Pain clawed across his chest from his ribs, and he barely caught hold of the top edge of the heavy, upholstered chair to support himself. They both tipped over.

The floor where he'd been standing erupted in a flash of light and noise. Wood chips and upholstery rained down.

What the—?

Alex choked on the acrid stench of gunpowder.

"She's not the only one capable of teaching us how to be weapons. And you're not the only one learning." The taunting growl came from the kitchen.

It was meant for Alex, and there was no doubt the kid was talking about Lena. His mother's frightened, angry gasps and grunts as she tried to fight off the kid told Alex that he'd turned his attention to her, though. A spasm of coughing left him gasping in pain again. He managed to push away the chair that had been between himself and the explosion.

Blinking against stinging smoke, Alex looked for the kid.

He eased out of the kitchen, Alex's mother in front of him.

The long knife she'd left on the counter was at her throat. "You knock me back again and I take her head with me."

"Let her go." Alex didn't look at his mother's eyes. He couldn't meet her gaze.

The kid dragged Alex's mother with him around the periphery of the room. "You, Agent Reyes, have greatly underestimated the damage we're capable of."

Alex shook his head, holding his arm tight against his side. "You're not getting away."

The kid laughed. "I'm you, remember? I always get away, just like you, you bastard."

"Not this time. I'll be right behind you."

"Coming after me, are you?" He laughed again, the sound a little breathless. He lifted the knife, pressing it tighter against her throat. "Do you think you can catch me before she bleeds out? Or maybe you can catch up to me after you heal her up…if you can." An ugly, knowing smile twisted the kid's face. "Isn't that another of the things you're too old to handle?"

He reached back with his free hand and pulled open the door to the stairs. He raised his gaze and held Alex's stare for a moment before reaching back around and pulling Alex's mother's head back by the hair. He slid the knife deep across her throat.

Blood spurted, pumping in time with her panicked heart. Her hands went up, desperate to stop the rush of blood.

Alex roared his rage and rushed forward, the pain in his side forgotten.

The kid danced back, shoving his mother at him.

Alex caught her, pulling her in and staring at the back of the man as he fled down the stairs. He turned his face down to his mother. Her knees buckled. Her weight sagged in his arms, and he collapsed to the floor with her.

Her eyes were wide. Terror filled them, but it faded with the light in them.

"Don't die." He knew he said the words out loud, but he didn't hear them. He couldn't hear anything over the ringing in his ears and the sound of his own breath. His vision had narrowed to her face, her neck. Blood filled her mouth and nostrils. It bubbled and popped as she choked.

Beneath her fingers, the wound gaped. Blood spurted, filling her hands, running over her chest and pooling under her head. He tried to pull her hands away, but she fought him.

"Don't fight. Let me help. I can help."

Can I?

He pulled at her fingers, replacing them with his own even as her blood spattered the front of his shirt and his face. He pressed down, reaching beyond the capacity of his fingers, feeling for the Dust within her.

Hear me. Please hear me.

Her fingers, weakly picking at his wrists and hands, stilled. The bubbles between his fingers slowed.

Please. She matters. A memory flared: the smell of dust and debris and electric ozone in a dark room, a voice he knew now, a voice he loved, sounding so broken, "Reyes, my mother…" and his own voice, "You can't fix this."

He told himself the same thing Lena had told him then. *I can.*

But she'd been wrong.

He closed his eyes. A sob of frustration broke from him. He bore down harder, reaching out to the Dust, focusing so hard lights flared before his eyes. "I need help. Give me a little help."

Give me a life.

FORTY-ONE

Lena

The fight was all but over. Warriors chased the remaining, fleeing Scavengers down through the gorge, but the main area was cleared. Lena stood back, still shaking in her blanket, as one of Ghost's men slipped a wounded young man into a rope harness rigged across the chest and waist of another. As soon as he was secure, the man began climbing. She watched their progress, her heart in her throat.

A hand on her shoulder pulled her attention from them. She traded tired looks with Ghost. She looked back across the strip of land they'd fought on, keeping her eyes away from the river.

"How many did we lose?"

He took a deep breath. "We haven't made a final count. At least four that I saw myself."

She closed her eyes. She'd brought them here. "Including Vicente?"

"Five, then."

"And the wounded? Have they all been taken up already?"

"The worst of them. The rest will follow us. We'll care for them until you all have rested and can heal them."

Lena swallowed and nodded. "I have to check on the girls. Phoebe and Hania need me." *Marissa needs me. Oh, Marissa...*

"We all need each other."

The gentle correction was a reminder that she wasn't in it

alone, no matter that she felt she was drowning in pain with responsibility and failure as weights holding her down. She was grateful for it.

"Are you ready?" Ghost continued.

She noticed for the first time that he wore a harness similar to the young warrior who'd taken the wounded man up.

She shook her head. "You're not carrying me up."

"I am." His words were implacable. "Because otherwise you'll fall. You're frozen."

"You were in the water longer, and I just healed you."

"You did a good job. I'm not tiny. Nor am I pregnant. This is how we go up, Lena. If you want to tend to our people above tonight, if you want us all to figure out how we get her back, then cooperate."

He was fighting dirty, and they both knew it. She stood in front of him, chin raised.

He tried a different tack. "I won't risk you, and I know you won't risk your child. So, please…" He held out his arms.

I know you won't risk your child. His words reverberated in her head, an echo even more painful than the pressure and heat.

She felt her face collapse into tears. "But I already did. I risked everything, and I failed. I chose it." She gasped a breath out. "What am I supposed to do? If the baby's gone, how do I tell him I lost them both?"

In one quick step, Ghost was there, his arms around her. She buried her face in his chest. She couldn't have anyone else see. No one else would understand the grief.

"I know," Ghost said softly. The breath he drew in was ragged, and his voice was hoarse. "You'll tell him. And you will bear it. And you will go on." He pulled away from her. "You will. I promise."

He had tears in his eyes, but they were for her. She knew without question that he didn't weep for himself but for the potential pain and loss that terrified her.

How could the thought of losing something she hadn't even admitted to herself she wanted bring such searing pain? How could she bear this on top of losing Marissa?

He glanced up behind her, and she felt a hand curl around her shoulder.

Gabriela leaned in, resting her forehead against Lena's. "He's right," she told Lena. She reached down and pressed the flat of her palm against the round of Lena's belly. "But let's not mourn yet. She's not gone." Gabriela shook her head and gave Lena a small smile. "She's used to this, I bet. You've been training her, too, with all those groundings. Let's wait to panic—over the baby and Marissa. We'll figure them both out, okay?"

Lena stared at her. After a moment, she sniffed back the tears and nodded. Gabriela was so good at mothering, murmuring and gently moving Lena with comforting touches, that Lena wasn't even aware that Gabriela had been getting her into the harness until Ghost stepped away from Gabriela and moved to the face of the cliff, reaching up for the first bent bar of the former span's skeleton.

Lena shook her head. "Carried like a child."

Ghost rumbled beneath her. "Or a wise woman who knows her limits."

"Limits? What are those?"

He smiled down into her face. "Child it is, then."

She rolled her eyes.

"Wait!" Gabriela called out. "I almost forgot."

Ghost swung his head around but remained in position so Lena could look over his shoulder to Gabriela.

The Neo-barb woman gestured over her shoulder. "What do you want me to do with him?"

Behind her, West knelt on the ground waiting to be carried up. His hand was wrapped in bloody cloths, but they were bound. His head was down. As she watched, the Neo-barb watching him reached down and grabbed the agent by the hair and twisted his head up and around. West's eyes rolled briefly, and then cleared. They focused on her. The malevolent rage in them pulsed at her.

Close by, several of Ghost's warriors swarmed over a heap of bodies off to the side. A growing pool of viscous blood stained the rocks around them. The Scavenger corpses were headless. One of Ghost's men shoved something rounded and bloody into a bag and slung it around to his back.

Several of the People stood near West. They waited. Waiting for her to tell them the man's fate?

She stared at West. Thomas wanted him. For questioning, he said, so he could get to the bottom of the mutiny in his camp. West was one of his Originals—one of the boys who'd grown up with Alex and Thomas and plotted along with them the whole way. Was that the real reason he wanted him back?

Lena didn't care. She didn't care what relationships this man had, what his role had been, what his intentions had been. She wanted him dead. She also wanted the information in his head, but he'd never give it up to Thomas, of that she was sure. He knew what to expect from them as far as torture—he'd had the exact same training. He knew how to resist their techniques.

Their techniques. If she wanted Marissa back, she'd have to make sure she got the information she needed herself.

"Make the decision, Lena." Ghost's voice was soft and sympathetic, but he still left the burden on her, where it belonged.

Lena looked down. It should be harder than this to send a man to his death, shouldn't it? She should feel something more. Her gaze wandered to the side as she remembered Marissa's laughter.

Lena did feel something. Satisfaction.

Tears pricked in her eyes—memories of the first time she pulled one of those damned collars from Marissa and the other girls, of what it had been like to have one put on herself. No matter what Thomas thought of what she'd done, she'd keep her promise to Alex. She'd kill the man who'd dared to put a collar on one of her girls again. And she'd do it again and again until they learned not to come or she'd killed everyone the Council had to send against them.

West *would* die by her hand. First, though, he would help her get Marissa back.

She lifted her chin and met West's furious gaze. "Keep him alive. Keep him hidden. Distract any agents still working down here. Have several of the strongest warriors take him south, the long way around to Taos. He'll answer to me, and when he has nothing left to tell me, he'll die." She looked up at Ghost. "I can handle Thomas."

West grunted out an ugly laugh. "You can handle Thomas? Where do you think I got the collar from? You think he's on your side?" His lips twisted in an ugly smile as he struck deeper. "Did you really think Fort Nevada could be infiltrated by a group that big without his knowledge—without his approval? He wanted you gone."

A stab of betrayed fury twisted with the grief inside. She raised her hand, ready to call the Dust. It only took a minute before she realized that's what the man wanted. Either she'd die in a spectacular flare-out, or he'd die at her hand and avoid whatever she had planned. She lowered her arm and laughed back at him. "If that were true, you'd never tell me. You have no reason to warn me."

"Warn you?" He tried to shake his head, but Ghost's warrior held it fast. "I'm not. I'm taunting you. Where that little girl is going now? You'll need allies to get her free. You'll need people you can trust, in strength and numbers. And you can't trust the man who started scheming against you as soon as he figured out he can't control you."

"You're a liar." She swallowed back bile and tried to tell herself that it was disgust and not betrayal.

He grinned. "Don't believe me? Check his saddlebag. Look for a box. Your partnership is the lie."

Ghost said something over his shoulder to Gabriela. Lena was inches away, bound to his chest, but she still didn't hear his words over the roaring in her head.

Gabriela turned around to walk over behind West. She picked up one of the rough squares of blanket they'd been making into sacks and wrapped it around his head, tying it off in the back. Another of Ghost's men, who'd been swinging a hatchet in anticipation, tossed it lightly at a piece of driftwood. It wedged there, waiting his need again. He stepped forward and dragged West to his feet.

Ghost began climbing. He carried her up to the surface above, away from the carnage below. Lena turned her gaze to the opposite cliff. *He's lying. He'd say anything to make you doubt.* She didn't look back down to the floor of the gorge. If she did, she might be sick. Her head pounded and her heart hurt nearly as much. She didn't know what to believe, but she *would* get Marissa back. Whatever it took.

When Ghost reached the top, he pulled himself up, one hand reaching out to take an offered hand and the other cradling Lena's head so it wouldn't smack against the edge of the cliff. Hands helped Lena out of the cradle of the harness, and she backed away. Ghost turned away, pulling off the harness and sending it back down. When he turned to her, there was fire in his eyes. "I'd like to be there when you kill him."

West? Or Thomas?

They both looked up at the sound of hoofbeats on the ground. Patrick slowed his mount and slid off, coming over to them. Lena had to resist the urge to push him away. Yes, he was Council, and Thomas's soldier. But he, like Alex, had her trust. West was a liar. Doubt was his final weapon. What he'd said couldn't be true. Could it?

Patrick looked around. "Marissa?"

Lena shook her head, not trusting herself to talk.

He digested that as he took in Lena's condition. "Let me take you to camp. You both need warmth and rest. Then we'll figure out the next step."

Ghost nodded his agreement.

Lena scrubbed sudden overwhelmed tears from her eyes with her fingertips. *See? They're in it for the long haul. West is trying to destroy you with doubt.*

"We'll figure it out. Then we'll go get her." She looked up at Ghost. "It's okay to rest?"

Ghost smiled his answer. "They're all gone. For good."

"Or until the Council sends more in to replace them," Lena answered bitterly as she looked back over the edge. The fight was over…for now. She paused. "Can you have one of your men find a light-colored blanket in their things? I want bodies left on the metalwork. And a sign, big. 'No more Scavengers.' Write it in English and Spanish. I want it clear. We won't have this anymore.

No more slavers. No more Council interference. I don't want anyone moving back in while we're off getting Marissa."

Ghost smiled, a savage expression. "I'll do it myself. Gabriela will be happy with this." He turned and lowered himself over the edge, climbing away to deliver the assignment.

Lena followed Patrick to his mount. When they reached the horse, he helped Lena up. As soon as she was seated, he swung himself behind her.

"West?" From his expression, even asking about the man was distasteful.

Should she tell Patrick she was keeping West? Would he keep it from Thomas? She already knew Thomas wouldn't rest until he had his Original back in his custody. He'd made that much clear. She didn't think she had the energy to fight him anymore, and she needed them to get back Marissa.

"Dead." Lena answered. "In the fight." The lie felt heavy in her mouth. She didn't want to lie to Patrick, but he wouldn't keep the truth from Thomas. She lessened the weight of the lie with a truth. "But his young protege got away with Karina and Marissa, down the river."

Patrick said nothing. He urged the horse forward.

Lena sighed. The elation she'd anticipated at getting Marissa back and rooting out the evil here was instead a mountain of exhaustion and guilt. She'd failed. She couldn't afford to mess up anymore. None of them could afford it.

When they made it across the plain to the staging area where her girls were gathered around a small fire, she slid free of the horse. The girls looked up at her, and there was more than weariness reflected back at her. Somehow, they knew Marissa wasn't coming back up the cliff. Lena stepped across the little circle to check first Phoebe, then Hania. Phoebe's eyes were tired, but aware. Hania tried to avoid Lena's gaze. She couldn't avoid the small hug Lena gave her to reassure her.

She dimly heard raised voices behind her and looked back. Patrick pushed Thomas away, pointing his leader back to the fire where the other agents gathered.

"Not. Now." Patrick's voice was firm.

You can't believe West. It was a last, desperate lie.

Lena turned away. Rose tapped the ground beside her, and Lena settled in, keeping a watchful eye on the rest of them. They were quiet and sat in a ring, tuning out everyone else around them. She should reassure them somehow, promise to get Marissa back.

All of them had varying degrees of a glow coming off their skin.

We need to ground. We need to purge this.

A frisson of fear worked through her. It was an odd thing, thinking about grounding after what they'd done. Lena thought the massive discharge should count as a grounding. But it had been different. Different use. Different intention. She didn't care what the men said about the Dust being robots, she knew such things mattered to the Dust.

She soothed them, and herself, in the back of her mind now, thanking them for helping. She apologized for asking for more, but did anyway. She needed more help.

The Dust wanted to help more than anything.

Lena assured them they could. All they had to do was make her baby strong enough to survive no matter what came.

She sat with the girls, breathing, recovering. She wasn't even aware of the Neo-barbs filtering back in until there was a soft *thunk* on the sand behind her. She craned around. A young woman had deposited one of the bags used to collect a Scav head in the sand. She made a gesture, fingers moving in the air as her head dipped before walking away.

A young man was next. He left his bag and made the same honorific in the air and continued to join his people by the horses. They'd set up a fire to tend to the wounded. Everyone would have to eat soon, too. Lena needed to go to them. She'd brought them here. It was her responsibility.

Frozen, Lena stared down at the rounded bags before her, nausea rising. Another fell beside the others. And another. She wanted to turn away, face back to her girls, but she felt she'd be dishonoring the Neo-barbs. She'd asked them to do this. It didn't matter that she felt like a failure. They'd fought for her. Some of them had died for her. The least she could do was look at what they'd done in her name.

Finally, she raised her eyes and it was Ghost standing before her. He settled the bag he carried on the pile with the others. "It's done," he said softly. "Your guest is away, and Gabriela is still below, supervising the…placement of the warnings."

"You said she'd like that," Lena answered. And then, though she didn't understand why, she said, "I'm sorry."

"Why?"

She lifted her hands, gesturing in general. She was sorry she'd failed to recover Marissa. She was sorry for the loss of life—she dreaded learning which of their People were lost. She was sorry for the physical and emotional pain to come. She was sorry there would likely be more fighting, more losses to come because they had to get Marissa back. She was sorry for all of it. And she was sorry for none of it. It had been necessary. What came next would be, too. She and Ghost would have to talk about that soon, she knew, along with plans to heal the wounded and honor the lost. Her gaze wandered to Hania, sitting curled around her knees, her face turned away. She looked at Phoebe, leaning into Marin and watching Lena and Ghost with eyes still a little hollow after the attack.

"All of it. It wasn't—it was what I expected. But it wasn't. I brought us here. I thought we'd get her back. I caused all of this, and she's still—" She gestured behind her to the gory bags, indicating all of the violence and losses together.

Ghost crouched beside her and waited until she looked at him. "No doubting what's done. It changes nothing. You did—we all did—what needed doing. If we'd let some go…the Scavengers would have come back harder and stronger. If we hadn't taken their heads, we'd have no way to prove to the Natives the threat is gone, and we lose that opportunity, too. If we'd done as Thomas wanted, the girls would grow up under constant threat. We'd never know peace. And we may not have Marissa back yet," he swallowed, and she knew he felt that failure as keenly as she did, "but we *will*."

Lena looked away. He was right. He *was* right. When she

glanced back up to tell him so, though, he'd turned his attention away from her.

"Are you okay?" he asked Phoebe. He rose and crossed to her. He used one finger to tilt her head so he could see the drying, matted blood in her hair better.

"I'm okay," she told him. She gazed up for a moment, then veered her eyes. "It looks messy, but Lena already healed it."

Ghost nodded. "Of course." He took a breath and settled back, pulling his hand away. "Well, if you have headaches at all, we have tea. It can help. Just ask." He stood up then, and looked around him with a bemused smile. "You did well. All of you. Definitely worthy of your teacher. We're not done, no, but now you all know what you can do." He nodded at Lena and crossed to leave them, moving on to join his People by their crackling fire.

"We should get up and go over there," Lena mumbled.

"We should," Rose agreed.

Lena looked over at Charity and Constance. "You both did so well today. I'm proud of you."

The girls exchanged a glance. "You're not going to let the man who took Marissa get away with it, are you? We're not just going home?" Constance's question was tinged with dismay.

Lena shook her head. "Nope. There will be no mercy for him. And as soon as we're ready, I'll be tracking her. We're getting her back."

Appeased, they leaned into each other. Phoebe allowed a smile to curve her lips. Even Marin was giving Lena a small, approving smile.

Lena looked at Rose. "They were amazing. So were you, match."

Rose allowed a smile to flit across her face. "We had a hell of an example to follow."

Lena grimaced. "You missed all of my mistakes at the bottom of the gorge."

Rose shrugged. "We all did what we had to. And now you have one more thing." She gestured with her head.

The sun was mostly below the horizon on the other side of the gorge. Darkness grew around them. Someone stepped between

Lena and the fire, blocking the light and heat. She looked up.

Thomas and Patrick stood above her. Lena found herself barely able to look at Alex's best friend. The weight of all that had happened and the lie to come—and all of her fears for Marissa and the baby—crashed back down on her. And what about West's lie? She didn't know what to think anymore. Anger curled inside. Did they have to do this now?

"Patrick tells me West is dead." Thomas's voice was quiet. His lips were thin.

Lena looked away. She let the anxiety and pain turn to anger, allowing it to flare brighter still. He wouldn't even ask about Marissa?

"I thought I made it clear he was to be brought to me?"

"Things happen in battle. In case you hadn't heard, a lot went wrong down there."

"That's unfortunate. But West was mine."

Unfortunate? The word swept through her, and it brought fire with it. The cold was suddenly not so oppressive as it gathered in the night. Rage pushed it away. "And so he will be," she snapped at Thomas. "His body will be burned with the others. His head is here." She gestured at the bags. "You may have it back when it's served its purpose."

When she looked back, she could see a shadow playing with light on the side of his face as the muscle jumped in his jaw. His eyes were lost in darkness, but there were waves of emotion—fury, disappointment, disgust—washing over his face. Unless she misjudged him, some of it was directed at himself.

A vision of another time those emotions had washed over his face flashed into her mind—a day when he'd been talking privately to *West*. A day when he'd been plotting with West for all she knew. Had her initial suspicions been valid? Had he been behind all of the plots against her and the girls? Had West told her the truth down in the gorge?

Now, like that day back in his office, he mastered his face. Voice clipped, he said, "I see. Taking heads as trophies like a Neo-barb, are we?"

That wasn't why they'd taken the heads. She'd be damned if

she'd explain her decision to him now. She stared up at him defiantly, silent. She wasn't explaining anything to the man who'd promised her again and again that *his* decisions didn't put her or her girls at risk, only to be wrong every single time. Even if he wasn't a traitor, he hadn't inspired her confidence. The mere fact that he clearly didn't care about Marissa's loss damned him in her eyes.

Thomas stared her down. He dropped to crouch beside her, still holding her gaze. She could see his eyes now, and the contempt in them made her swallow. She refused to look away. She wasn't sorry, no matter how he felt about her.

When he spoke, it was so soft she could barely hear him, and his voice was icy cold. "Be careful, Lena, that you don't become the thing that you most fear."

Lena felt a grim, ugly smile spread across her face. "I could say the same to you, *Councilor Five*."

Thomas blanched. A flash of something like self-loathing joined the rage in his eyes. He didn't say another word. He rose and walked away.

Lena watched him, well aware of Patrick's measuring gaze on her face. He stayed there until Thomas called for him. Thomas called for all of his agents to gather around him.

Patrick shook his head at Thomas now, raising his voice to override whatever Thomas told him. "A mama bear will rush a hunter to protect a cub. It's not reasonable. It's instinct. Don't set us up against that."

Thomas answered, but she couldn't hear him with his face turned away. She did hear Patrick's response as he defended her again.

"You're wrong. She thinks she's doing what's right."

Thomas rounded on him. She could hear him now. "It doesn't matter what she thinks is right. I've worked too hard—we've all worked too hard—to have it all undone because some twenty-five-year-old, emotionally stunted little girl thinks she can make decisions as well as I can. She can't. She's making mistakes!"

"I'm not arguing. I'm saying your reaction is out of line. Like we weren't emotionally stunted twenty-five-year-olds once? Like we never fucked up?"

"The stakes are higher now, Patrick. We don't have the luxury of giving her time to grow up. We never did." He shook his head. His raised voice had a tight, desperate quality to it. "There is no one—not one of you—who knows what I've had to do, what I've had to *risk*, for us to win in the end. I'm not going to watch everything I've built be destroyed. We're pulling out. Everything. Let her fail on her own. When she does, then we'll come back to salvage the rest."

A new way to get rid of me and gain access to the girls?

"What?" Patrick stared at him, shocked. "Are you kidding me? They need us to get Marissa back. No…we're not abandoning them out here. I won't do it. Think about what you're—think about what'll happen when Alex—"

"This isn't about Alex. This about control."

Control.

Patrick shook his head back and forth, over and over.

Lena had heard enough. She pushed herself to her feet and ran through the gloom to their horses. Which was Thomas's? *That one.* She dipped her head below its neck, watching them, then stood on her toes to work at the leather thongs and flip the heavy sack open.

"Yes!" Thomas held up a finger in Patrick's face. "Alex understands that sacrifices have to be made in order to push forward an agenda. If he didn't, he'd be here with her now. I'm not worried about Alex—What are you doing?"

She stepped back, pulling free the long box. It matched West's description. He wasn't the liar. Whatever else he was, he had told her the truth about Thomas. She stepped out from the horses now, holding the box awkwardly.

"Give that to me."

She shook her head, not trusting herself to speak to him. Patrick was staring at each of them, his brows knit. He had no idea what was in the box. She held it out to Patrick. "Open it."

He took it, looking at Thomas.

"Give it to me, Patrick."

Patrick looked down at the box in his arms. It was locked, a heavy padlock securing it. But the wood itself wasn't thick. He dropped it at his feet. His heel smashed into the top of it. Again.

"Patrick!"

The third time, his foot splintered the wood. Another solid kick had it open. It flipped onto its side and three collars spilled out of the hole, scattering around it in the sand. They were inert. No red lights glowed on them, but the firelight reflected off the smooth metal. There was no mistaking them for anything other than what they were—Thomas's insurance. West had been telling the truth.

"What were you going to do? Wait until we fell asleep, like you had West do with Marissa?" Rage beat in Lena's head with the pulse of her heartbeat and the feedback looping within her. "Why did you even play along with us leaving Fort Nevada when you had no intention of ever letting us out of your grasp?"

"I had nothing to do with Marissa." Thomas's voice was quiet. "And I certainly never would have allowed anyone to hurt you."

That's not a real denial.

Lena held her chin high and her shoulders back—and then there was the glow. He wouldn't intimidate her now. She pushed past her exhaustion. "The only thing I care about is getting her back. What do you expect me to do? Walk away? Pretend? *Forget?*"

"I expect you to have the intelligence to *reason*. There's more at stake than your revenge. There's more we needed from West than *your* why. Whether you believe it or not, he betrayed our trust, too. We needed answers. After what you've done, I'm not certain you deserve my protection anymore."

Patrick sucked in a breath and held it, his jaw pulsing.

Lena held up her hand to keep him from diving in. She shook her head as the rage withdrew. No…it coiled within, waiting. "You think I didn't reason? I made a choice. Look at those girls." She pointed back at her little circle. "They don't need your so-called protection. Protection?! Everything we've been through...because of *you*. The only reason you're still breathing right now is Alex. You want to cut your losses and go? So *go*.

Take your boys back to your half-assed training and don't come back. Don't you dare come back—not ever—because I will never trust you again. And don't even think about collaring any of us. I will kill any man—every man—who tries."

Thomas's chin dropped to his chest and he glowered at her, but said nothing.

Patrick shifted his alarmed gaze between the two of them. "We'll destroy the collars, Lena. We need to focus on working together. That's how we'll get her back. This isn't what any of us needs or wants." He appealed to them both, trying to appease.

"Yes. It is." Thomas bit out the words.

Lena shoved her hair behind her ears, took two steps closer, and leaned in to make her final point. "You're wrong about everything. You think control is the way. Control the revolution. Control the girls. Collar us if we challenge you." Her voice shook with emotion, but she smiled. "That's the Council's way. Your role as Councilor Five is controlling you instead of the other way around, or you wouldn't be willing to sacrifice and alienate the people you claim to be fighting for. Jackson sees it. Patrick sees it. I think you do, too. You're too emotionally stunted yourself to admit it. You're too human."

Too human? The words both puzzled her and felt perfect. She wasn't angry anymore. The coiled thing inside was content. The throbbing in her head and spine eased, an unexpected gift from the Dust.

Thomas shook his head in a tiny arc. His stare was cold. "You forget yourself. You're overpowered. Exhausted. And you're pushing me too far." He glanced down at the collars in the sand, a quick, threatening motion. "You're playing with fire, little girl."

From the corner of her eye, Lena caught the movement as Rose and the girls stood. They joined hands, waiting. Lena looked at them. Thomas's head turned too, noting their posture, no doubt remembering how it had been used shortly before. She laughed. She stepped closer, then closer still until she and Thomas stood chest to chest. The glow radiating from her skin and eyes lit his face. The light and shadows playing over the lines and angles of his face made the twitch as he swallowed obvious.

"For such a smart man, I'm surprised you haven't figured it out yet." She tilted her head and held his gaze without fear. She wasn't in a pissing contest with him over power anymore. There was no contest. "We *are* the fire."

She scooped up the collars and the box and threw them all into the flames nearby, urging the flames to burn hotter, higher. The agents around the circle were silent. She walked away from them, returning to her girls. By the time she'd reached them, she could see around the fury and frustration. She stepped over the closest of the bagged heads and swooped her hands at the circle staring at her. "Come on, it's time for us to join our People, get some food in us, rest. You can ground, and we'll heal our warriors. Then—then we'll go get our girl back."

Her smile for the girls was genuine. Her voice was light. That indefinable something settled within her, finding its place. And in that moment, her daughter woke, too, moving again for the first time since Lena had overtaxed herself.

Her heart swelled, and she curled her fingers around her belly, treasuring that brief, fluttering wave within her.

As if the world wanted to reflect the sudden shift within Lena, a gust of wind swept down like a sigh and moved over them. Lena blinked without thinking into Dust sight and watched the Dust swirling around them all, drawn like moths to their very bright flames. The bright opaline flows moved in and around them. The Dust may have started as death machines, but it was more now. It was life. It had transformed itself, and it wanted to help them do the same.

Tears flooded her eyes, and she let them spill. Sam was right.

He'd been right about it all.

She returned to the regular view of the world and the people in it. The wind didn't glow with promise or pulse with life and the promise of justice. But she knew the truth.

As she followed the girls toward the People waiting to welcome them around the fire, she looked back over at Thomas and Patrick. They stared at each other, grim-faced.

Lena flashed them a soft smile. "Thank you," she said softly in the same happy voice. She meant it. If they'd heard her, they'd probably think the sudden shift was another sign of madness, but she didn't care. Thomas and his betrayal had a role in this discovery, too, even if it had been to push her to the breaking point, into rage, and beyond it. Now that she knew the truth, she could lay the fears that had risen at Fort Nevada to rest. Thomas knew what waited for him if he ever tried again.

Their gazes followed her, one troubled, as he gathered his things and stalked away from his brothers, and one furious. That was fine, too. Eventually Thomas would figure out what had just occurred to her. There was no way to have a revolution without evolution.

The rage that had grown and threatened to explode from the moment Marissa had been taken had been tempered by the mistakes she'd made, by fear and acceptance, and by the kindness of friends. It had burned away the doubt and now waited—colder, darker, ripe with possibility. It had evolved to be more like the Dust, dark energy newly awakened and waiting.

She was fire and force. She was ready. Like the man running scared with one of her girls, all who threatened those she loved would face a reckoning.

If the world tried to come for them, the world would burn again.

FORTY-TWO

Alex

Alex leaned against the cool tiles of the bathroom wall. He'd managed to seat himself on the closed toilet and lean stiffly to the side, holding his abdomen tight, to rest his forehead against the wall. He hoped the pressure would help stop the bleeding.

He'd bled all the way back from his mother's house. If anyone wanted to track him, it was there in bright drops. He should have taken precautions. He was too busy carrying her too-light body away from the wreckage of her home. He'd managed to get her back to his rooms, settled her peacefully on his bed. Then what?

Instead of figuring it out, he'd turned and left the room. After stumbling in here from the bedroom, he didn't have the energy to get up and get the medical kit he'd shoved under the sink He didn't have it in him to do more than wait for the sound of Ace's return to his room.

He'd never felt so tired, so empty, in his life. His eyelids drooped, but they merely sent his gaze down to his hands, curled in his lap. They were dark with blood, as was his shirt and pants and shoes. He was coated in blood, and only half of it was his own. He'd never be able to wash it all away.

Was this how Lena had felt, coated in dust and wearing her dead mother's dress? He remembered her, small and defiant in the hallway of Ace's home, telling both of them to shut-up. Even then, she'd been vital, sharp. Even then, she hadn't stopped.

Oh, Dust, Lena, is it true? Was it something she'd decided on her own? Was it a moment of inattention—forgetting once to tell the Dust to protect her? Or was it a cruel lie, told to get the reaction it had provoked, to unfold the disaster that had followed like a sheet of paper with a carefully written plan upon it?

He needed to know. He needed her.

Every morning and night, as he'd hovered on the brink of consciousness thinking of her, he'd felt her, so close. Close enough to touch, to taste, to feel. That hadn't been dream. It had been real.

He needed it now.

Where are you, Lena?

Beneath his ear, there was a rumble of a deep voice. Ace talked to himself. Alex had been counting on the habit to let him know when the big guy had returned from the farewell dinner. The distant sound of water rushing through pipes followed.

Ace was back.

Alex lifted his hand, curled it, and banged on the wall, three slow knocks. A moment later, he did it again. He lifted it to bang again, but instead noted the blood—his mother's blood— he'd left smeared on the wall. He stared at it, his hand frozen in mid-air.

Pull yourself together.

He heard the sound of his door handle. He'd locked it behind him. Of course he had. It wasn't electric. He'd have to manually open it. Unless…

His lids fluttered down again and he reached out, across the room, and moved the tumbler within with the Dust. It was so easy.

Necessity is the mother of invention.

His eyes opened. He stared at the smeared blood.

Ace knocked three taps. The handle rattled again, but this time, it opened.

"Alex?"

"Back here. In the bathroom."

"I assume you're the reason some guy's mopping up blood in the hall."

Someone's cleaning the floors. How efficient.

He waited.

Ace's voice came closer. "You better not be operating on yourself this time. Or playing with yourself."

Alex turned his head and managed a smile.

Ace flinched. He'd frozen in the doorway. "Please tell me that's not all your blood."

Alex swallowed pain. "It's not all my blood."

Ace edged into the bathroom. "Dust. What happened?"

Alex shrugged his shoulder in a tiny movement. "Would you believe I fell down some stairs?"

"A couple flights of stairs, yeah. And whose ass were you kicking at the time?"

Alex smiled. "Help me up? Then help me put myself back together?"

Ace reached out and took Alex's hand, grimacing at what Alex knew was the tacky feel of the blood. He shook his head as he helped Alex to his feet. "Do I even want to know what the other guy looks like?"

"Very much like this, I expect."

"He's still alive? Damn. You must be slipping."

Alex gave him a look that should have turned him to ash where he stood.

Is that another of the things you're too old to handle?

"He hurt my mother," Alex offered by way of explanation. "I couldn't follow him. I had to stop. I had to try…"

Ace went still. "Yeah? How'd that turn out?"

Alex sniffed, but couldn't get good air flow. He had a large clot blocking one nostril. "Can you help me pull myself back together so I can go after him? Please?"

"Do you know where he went?"

"I have an idea, yeah." It was a lie, but Alex figured there weren't that many interested parties that could be behind this. Not that were desperate enough, and funded enough, to train young men the same way Alex and Thomas trained their agents.

Not the same way. They're further along with offensive use of the Spark.

Councilor One. Councilor Two. Councilor Four. He had

ready access to one of them, and to the beloved grandson of another.

Ace nodded. "Okay. We can talk about this some more after you're cleaned up."

Alex smiled. He'd figured Ace wouldn't just let him take off and do his thing. "The medical kit's under the sink. Grab that and we'll get this show started."

"Good idea. You're bleeding all over the damn place."

"You gonna give me shit the entire time we do this?"

"Pretty much, yeah."

He did, too. Alex had to talk him through the grisly parts. Ace was an excellent trader and could handle anything you threw at him intellectually. It turned out he wasn't a fan of blood and gore.

And he hated needles. Re-stitching Alex's brow and lid took longer than it would have if Alex had been flexible enough to handle it himself. But, he told himself, it didn't take as long as it would have if he'd had to do it alone this time.

They'd managed to figure out together that it was only Alex's ribs that were broken. Ace ran the fabric bandage tight around Alex's lower chest.

"Good thing Sparks heal fast," Alex managed.

"I can't believe you broke your ribs again." Ace shook his head.

"Yeah, well, it beats the hell out of having what they're protecting broken."

He meant his lungs, but Ace snorted.

"If I was going to bet on you having a heart—and I'm not sure I'd put any C-notes on that bet—I'm pretty sure there's only one person who could break it."

Lena. Her best friend was more right than he knew. Alex lowered his eyes for minute. When he looked up, he made sure his face reflected the seriousness of the request he was about to make.

"Ace, this summer, when you helped me…when you volunteered to keep helping. You said it was for family."

"Yeah." Ace's face was serious, and his joking tone disappeared. His voice was wary now. "Because family comes first."

"Right." Alex knew the family Ace had been referring to in their conversation that summer had been his chosen family—Jimmy. The man he loved. He was betting Ace extended the term to cover others. He needed Ace to step even further out of his comfort zone to protect them.

Alex eased himself away from Ace, maneuvering himself out of the bathroom. He walked to the sleeping area of his quarters and pushed open the door. He glanced through, then back at Ace.

He nodded through the opening for Ace as the big man approached. He saw the surprise register on Ace's face as he took in the woman stretched out on Alex's bed.

"My mother."

Ace nodded. "I figured."

Alex watched as Ace's eyes moved over her, making careful note of details. He knew the savvy trader would miss nothing. He wasn't disappointed.

"That scar—damn. Looks recent."

The scar across his mother's throat was a raised, purplish ridge of flesh.

"It is."

"You healed it. You finally got it right."

Alex swallowed, looked down and fiddled with the edge of the wrap around his chest. "Not quite."

Ace turned to look back into the bedroom. He tilted his head to look at the scar. "It's not pretty, but I'm sure that should have been fatal. She's alive."

"She's alive, but she can't talk. I couldn't fix it all. There's nerve damage. I couldn't..." Alex's throat closed on the words. The failure ate at him. If Lena had been there...Dust, if *Jackson* had been there, his mother would be in perfect health. She wouldn't have a scar. She wouldn't be sleeping off the trauma of the attack.

Ace turned back and held Alex's gaze. "She's alive."

"Yeah." Alex looked away. He rubbed his hand across his face, then winced as his fingers came close to the fresh stitches. "I've got to get her out of here. Get her safe."

She's not the only one in danger. Alex blinked himself back into focus. "So when you were talking about family, did you just mean Jimmy? Or were you talking about Lena, too?"

"You damn well know I meant Lena, too."

Alex nodded. "Good. I need you to do something for me. For Lena. There's a new player. Someone I don't know anything about, and that's dangerous."

"'Cause he knows about her?"

"Yep." He pulled the door closed again and made his slow way to the closest seat. "There's a woman embedded in the Zone Four trade delegation. Locust House trader."

"I remember."

"She has information about a prison. She has maps, communications, possibly information about who's behind this unknown group. It's in a lock box. I need you to get it from her, and I need you to give her someone you trust to go with her to Zone Four. Someone you trust with everything you've got."

"Alex, that list is really short."

"Can you do it? Without anyone knowing—even your own people. Especially your own people. Maybe even the person you send. Can you?"

Ace thought about it long enough that Alex started to worry. Finally, he nodded. "What are you going to be doing?"

"Going home."

"Going home?" Ace laughed incredulously. "And I'm supposed to do your job? Why?"

"Because the guy who did this to me?" Alex glanced down over himself, appreciating the damage the little bastard had managed to inflict. "He's good. He had way more information than he should have, and he mentioned Lena. He knows she's in Zone Three."

"Lucky guess."

Alex shook his head. "Not him. He knows. I've got to go back, because you were right. There's the revolution, and then there's family. A smart man doesn't place bets with the lives of those he loves. Family comes first."

A slow, approving smile spread across Ace's face. Alex was

surprised at how much that approval meant.

"Always. That's why I'll do it for you."

Alex didn't have time to share much with Ace. He intended to be on his way south with whichever independent caravan was leaving in the morning, whether they were willing or not. He was in bad shape now, sure, but Sparks healed fast. By the morning he'd be in pain but much more mobile. By the end of the week, he'd be able to leave the caravan behind and strike out on his own.

He eased into the fresh shirt Ace brought him and bent over the little map he'd sketched with locations of several secure camps. If anything went wrong along the way, Ace was to get his mother out and sit tight. Someone would cycle through the camps to check them. Someone would get them safely home.

Alex hoped it wasn't necessary, but at this point he would take no more chances.

He eased back, breathing in small pants against the pain.

Ace winced in sympathy. "You sure about this? Those independents—some of them travel rough. You'll be lucky to have a wagon to rest in. It'll be a bumpy ride."

Alex managed to grit his teeth together and pull his lips back in what must be a grim parody of a grin. "I'll have a wagon. I can deal with a little pain. It'll be better tomorrow. You know."

Ace and Jimmy had been together long enough that Ace must be familiar with the more rapid healing of Sparks. Even a mid-range like Jimmy would be hardier and heal better than most.

Ace nodded. "I know." His gaze flicked over Alex and the nod became a shake. "This is bad. This guy *roughed* you up. Is he going to come after your Mom again?"

Alex shook his head. "That was about me. With me gone, she'll be safe. So will you. Just get her back to Zone Three. I'll come for her, and by the time I do, there won't be a danger anymore."

"What if she doesn't want to go?"

Alex took a breath and let it ease out, expecting the pain. He almost welcomed it. If there was one thing Lena had taught him, it was that he needed to go easier on the heavy-handed, life-altering decisions for others. But this one wasn't negotiable.

"She'll go."

Ace raised a brow, but before he could respond, a trio of heavy knocks shook Alex's door. The two men froze. The knocks repeated themselves.

"Agent Alejandro Reyes? This is Council Security. Please open the door."

The Councilor making good on his threat? Little coward.

Alex raised his arm and pointed silently at the bedroom.

Ace whispered fiercely, "But they'll—"

"I'll handle it. Go." Alex's voice was low, even, and brooked no argument. "Leave the door ajar, like I just came out of it. They can't see in at that angle."

Ace rose and crossed the room, following Alex's instructions without question.

There was no way Alex would allow anyone to take the two of them into custody. Ace and Alex's mother would stay safe, regardless of what happened to himself.

Alex lifted himself from the chair, wincing and breathing through his teeth.

Yeah. You're in perfect shape to fight them off, Reyes.

"I'm coming." He managed to raise his voice and went to the door.

He eased it open to find four agents glowering back at him. One of them he knew. He'd been meeting with the young man in secret, learning about the zone. He moved his eyes from face to face as if they were all strangers. He said nothing, just let them take in his wounds.

The man who spoke, an older agent Alex didn't know, looked him up and down first. "Agent Alejandro Reyes?"

Alex leaned against the jamb of the door as if it pained him to stand straight. It wasn't much of an act. "Yes?"

"Are you alone, sir?"

Alex stared at the man in feigned confusion. He widened the door slightly, looking back over his shoulder. When he turned back, he was still under inspection. "Yeah?" Then he nodded. He gestured at himself. "This isn't from here."

"Where is it from? Where have you been tonight, Agent?"

Alex focused on the mouthpiece. "I was accosted on the streets of this fine relo-city. And right now I was in bed, trying to rest. This hurts worse than it looks, gentlemen. Is there something I can help you with?"

They exchanged a glance. "We need you to come with us."

"Come with you?" Alex glared at them. "What's this about?"

"We can discuss that next door."

They were going to take him into the Council building. Councilor One was going to do this? Erika had warned him. He just hadn't believed.

Alex cut to the chase. "I'd like to go back to bed. Are you telling me I'm being detained?"

The older agent leaned in. "I'm telling you you're being arrested." He lifted the hand he'd held behind his back. There was a restraint collar in it. "Professional courtesy is why this isn't already on you. Don't make me use it."

Alex stared at the collar. He opened his mouth, then thought better of it. Instead he stared hard at the senior agent. The man clearly didn't like this any more than Alex did. Alex gave him a curt nod and straightened to step through the door, leaving it open behind him as if he had nothing to hide. "You can put that away. I'll come. But I want to know the bullshit charges. And I expect to be released in time to make my ride home on the caravan tomorrow."

One of the younger agents shook his head. It was a small movement, but telling. Alex stepped out into the hall and they fell in around him. He glanced back. The youngest of them—*his* agent—stepped across the hall and quietly closed the door. They led him away down the hall. All of them followed.

Alex allowed himself a small, internal sigh of relief. Unless they had a fifth man somewhere watching his room, Ace would be clear to get his mother out of the room. Ace would be smart enough to get them both out as soon as it was safe. Once they were gone, Alex didn't care if these men went back to search his rooms. They wouldn't find anything. He'd already sent out all his correspondence.

Not that they could make sense of it anyway. His brief personal notes were all coded.

The trip downstairs and across the street to the Council building took longer than it should have. They were allowing for his injuries. It was a silent journey. They didn't speak. They didn't harass their prisoner. They let him be.

It told him everything he needed to know about the charges against him and the agents taking him in. The charges were bullshit. They were also probably as serious as Councilor One could come up with. The agents, even those not aware of Alex's true role, were good men who weren't happy about it.

That meant when he did get free, they'd do their jobs. They'd search. They just wouldn't look overly hard.

He'd be long gone.

And a Council fugitive.

He sighed. That would complicate the Dust out of his life.

The senior agent looked back. "Hurts, huh?"

The men had stopped before a locked and sealed door. One of the men reached out and triggered the electric lock.

"Yeah. It hurts."

"Care to give us any more detail than, 'I was mugged'?"

Alex looked at the man. No doubt he was a good agent, but Alex was tired and in pain and they both knew he'd been dragged over here on bullshit charges. He wasn't giving them anything more than he had to. If they knew about his mother's house, fine. If not, it'd make it easier for Ace to get her out of the city if Alex said nothing. "Yeah. He was young and stupid. I think he said something about kicking an old man's ass right before I started fighting back."

The senior looked him up and down. "Looks like he managed to do it."

Alex bared his teeth. "You haven't seen *him*." Let them think it was bravado.

The man laughed. "Actually, I think I have." He gestured into an interrogation room as they passed it. The door was open and two agents were inside with a third man seated at the table before them. Alex couldn't see his face, but his body was canted in his chair, shackles held his arms on the table, and a restraining collar wrapped around his neck.

The agents shifted, glancing over as Alex and his escort passed. The movement was enough for Alex to see past them.

He felt a surge of fury and fierce pleasure. Except for the ribs, the little bastard was in worse shape than Alex. And he was collared.

"Recognize him?"

Alex turned away and shook his head. "It was dark. Should I?"

They were good agents, but Alex was better. They frowned at the lie, but not because it was obvious. "He's beat to Dust. Maybe he's your attacker?"

"Or another victim. How often does this happen around here? You have a population unhappy with Sparks?"

There was always a population unhappy with Sparks. Leeching energy off of them to live a comfortable life wasn't enough. They had to resent the fact that Sparks had an ability the unpowered could leech off, too. If Councilors Six and Four had any kind of presence here in the form of workers or regular trade, that population would have grown. Sparks were strictly controlled in Zone Six. They were treated as subhuman in Zone Four. That particular brand of intolerance spread all too easily.

There was nothing a beaten-down, demoralized population liked more than to have their leaders provide them with a scapegoat. Sanctioned hatred made for easier governing.

The agents exchanged another uncomfortable glance.

The senior stood by while another agent unlocked an interrogation room. "I'll go and get my S.O.," he told Alex. "He's running this show tonight. Wait here."

The junior agent ushered him in. Before he could get settled, though, a voice rang out.

"I don't want him in an interrogation room. He goes down in a cell until they're ready for transport. I don't care what he has to say. He's not my problem. He's Zone Four's problem." There was a long beat. Alex strained to hear a response, but couldn't. Perhaps the response wasn't verbal.

A moment later, the booming voice had an edge to it. "Did you hear me? Cell. Now."

Alex didn't bother sitting. He waited by the table for the return of the agent. Outside the door, he heard their opinion.

"This is bullshit," one of them muttered.

The older agent appeared in the doorway. He gestured for Alex to follow him out of the interrogation room.

He followed along. He assumed transport to Zone Four would be achieved in a cell car. He'd be sent with the caravan in the morning. They'd collar him for sure. That didn't give him much time to work his way around this. Being cooperative and working the agents' discontent was in his favor.

The cell level had electric and traditional tumbler locks, and there were multiple agents moving around. He'd have to finesse his way out.

He walked into the cell, trying not to be bothered by the sound of it closing behind him. The agents turned to go.

Alex sighed. "Can I get some water?"

The man didn't respond, but as he went out through the closest security point, he gave the order to the youngest of the agents. Alex had counted on that.

A few minutes later, the youngest agent returned. He approached the cell with a small wooden cup of water. His partner remained at the door, but he chatted with the agents in the outer room with more interest than he gave the cell with the innocent, beat-to-shit agent in it.

Alex drank the water and lifted the cup to return it through the bars. He made his way to the cot in the corner and eased down on it. His breath hissed out.

"We'll get medical in here to look at you soon."

"All I need," he told the young agent in a low voice, "is to be put in a box with that punk in the interrogation room upstairs. Don't care when, but we need to be alone, and you need to give me some quality time with him before you get me out of here. Since transport is in the morning, you should figure that out pretty quick."

The younger agent stared down at him. Alex watched dread play across his face. "That could be difficult." His head started to shake negatively, but he stopped and swallowed instead. "This order—the charges against you—it could be next to impossible." The junior agent gripped the bars with one hand and finally did shake his head.

Alex didn't know if the kid meant getting Alex in a cell with the young punk who'd sliced his mother's throat, or if he meant getting Alex free.

Either way, it didn't matter. He eased back on the cot and raised his legs to take some of the pressure off his ribs and rested his battered arms on the cot beside him. He was so tired. As soon as the kid understood Alex wasn't giving him any other options, he'd rest.

"Make it happen."

The kid cleared his throat. "You're going to Zone Four, sir. The order didn't come from Councilor One. It came—" He sighed heavily. "It came from Councilor Five."

Councilor Five? Wait. What? Thomas?

Alex frowned. "You mean Four." Alex kept talking, even when the kid started shaking his head, even when the ice of betrayal began to creep down his spine. "One is doing Four's dirty work. That's hardly surprising."

The ice stole his voice. He clenched his hands into fists at his sides until they shook. The regret and grief on the kid's face was unacceptable. Unacceptable.

"No, sir. I mean Five. It came from us. It came from Fort Nevada. There's nothing I can do."

FORTY-THREE

Lena

Jackson reached down from the ridge just outside the wall above Taos and offered his hand. Lena gratefully took it. She used her other hand for balance, but let him pull her to the top. Rose followed behind. He'd arrived that afternoon with Gabriela. They planned to leave the walled village again in the morning. There was only one thing waiting to be done, and Lena had refused without Jackson present. Gabriela had volunteered to race back to retrieve him.

When the three of them reached the top, they were careful where they stepped. The earth here was rocky and scorched. The areas that had been sand were glassed. It was where Patrick, Rose, and the girls had been grounding these past five days as they healed the people of Taos. It made for treacherous walking.

Lena's glow made the way safer. The night was held at bay by the unnatural gleam of the Dust beneath Lena's skin, tracing her veins in bright branches. The path at their feet was clear.

Lena was exhausted but still defiant. She leaned against a blackened boulder, not caring if her clothing was smudged dark in the back. Her hands curled around the small, hard ball of her belly.

She would have been exhausted anyway, even if she had dared to ground. But there was no way she would discharge that much energy without having Jackson check her and the baby first.

Every roll and kick reassured her. But not enough to risk this level of discharge without Jackson there to help if something went wrong afterward. She'd been adamant, no matter how difficult it made things. The other Sparks would ground. She would not. Period.

The glow had worked to their advantage. When Lena had escorted the girls back into Taos, the Neo-Barbs had been shocked and awed by her appearance. Even when she'd told them the girls alone would be healing them, the People of Taos had agreed. She was aware of the murmurs behind her as she passed, that she was touched by spirits, that she was the daughter of the Moon. She had exchanged a look with Ghost, whose name now had taken on special significance by association. She wasn't sure what to make of it. He was so amused he fought to maintain his composure.

They had certainly managed to secure their alliance. She doubted the Neo-Barbs would ever be tempted to betray them now. She told herself that was what mattered.

They'd had much the same reception from the Nations people to the north, even if it was more muted. They'd been drawn down by the thick column of smoke from the burning of the bodies. A small party had been sent to investigate. Lena and Ghost had ridden out to meet them. There was no murmuring at her appearance, but they watched her closely and accepted the gift of the heads.

It was a good thing, since they no longer had or wanted an alliance with Fort Nevada. Patrick had remained. He left unspoken that his presence had caused a rift between him and Thomas.

Was revenge worth it?

It was. She wasn't done quite yet, either. Once she'd grounded, she'd be visiting West in his improvised cell. He hadn't spoken the entire time they'd been at Taos. She wasn't surprised. He'd talk soon. She'd have answers, and she'd use them to hunt the bastard who had Marissa.

That he still had Marissa was her only regret. Her head bowed, and she ran her hands over the swelling of belly and baby. The connection she felt to the life inside her was another new surprise. Those moments between making a conscious decision to save the child she did know and realizing how much she'd endangered her baby—and how much it terrified her—were lightning quick. But it was as if the entire world had tilted somehow. She wanted this child. She wanted her with a ferocity that was overwhelming.

Did I hurt her?

Was it her imagination, or did her belly glow even more brightly than the rest of her? The light seemed to move in waves, as if in time to an inner pulse. Hers? Or the baby's?

"Please," she repeated the question she'd asked of Jackson at the base of the trail. "Will you check first?"

His face was drawn and tired, too. He'd been shocked when he arrived to find her both brilliantly lit and wanly pale-skinned from exhaustion, but still defiant. He'd been more shocked when she and Patrick told him Thomas had been the source of the plot at Fort Nevada, and that she'd renounced him. Jackson promised Alex would intervene when he returned. He'd tried to tell her all would be well.

She already knew that. All would be well, or the world outside of her new family would regret it.

"Lena—" He shook his head at her. "You *have* to ground. I've never seen you like this. It's been too long."

In the days after the battle, the glow of over-extending herself hadn't faded, though the pain had receded until it was barely noticeable. Rose had tried to convince her to share it, but until she knew that using the Dust at all in any way wouldn't be a danger, Lena had refused. Yes, she was being unreasonable. She didn't care.

The refusal cost her more than exhaustion. It meant she couldn't track Marissa yet. It meant she could only wait and plan. It meant the fear grew bigger every day.

It also meant she no longer had the comfort of her dream reunions with Alex. She understood now it was part of her gift and their connection. Perhaps it was a different kind of match. Those moments had been real. Her acceptance was a part of the new confidence the experiences after the gorge had seared into her.

It was real, and as soon as she had grounded, she would find Alex. Overloaded, her brain couldn't reach out to him. She'd lost that comfort and joy. She would get it back. And once she had, she'd use it to fuel the search for Marissa.

"I have to know, Jackson." When she told Alex about their child, as she intended to do, she needed to be able to assure him all was well.

He pursed his lips and shook his head. "Afterward, Lena. I'll check you afterward. You need to ground now. Discharge all this energy, and I'll check the baby while you recover. I promise."

She sighed and looked at Rose.

Her friend gave her a tired smile, made eerie by Lena's reflected light on her. "He's right this time. Get rid of the energy first and make it easier to see."

"He can already see." She turned to look at Jackson. "I know you can already see. You're that good. Tell me." It wasn't a request any more. "Is something wrong?"

Jackson stared at her. He exchanged a long look with Rose before shaking his head. "Not wrong." His voice was soft, but it held an unspoken question in it.

"Don't hold back. Don't you start lying to me now, Jackson Lee."

He tipped his head at her in acknowledgment that he'd been waiting to finish. "Not wrong…but the baby is surrounded by Dust. A lot of Dust. There's a…glow around her. I don't know if it's her or some kind of protective layer, but she's there, Lena. She's alive and well."

She'd known that. She'd reveled in the movement inside of her. "But we don't know what this grounding…what discharging this much energy through me, through her, will do, do we?"

Jackson shook his head. "No one else has ever done it."

Another reminder that she was different.

Lena turned back to Rose, who took her hand. Her touch was gentle and she ran her fingers over Lena's in a soothing, circular motion.

"Come on. It's late, and you're exhausted. Let's do this. You can't delay any more." Rose tugged Lena away from the rock she leaned on. She helped Lena undress, leaving her clothes behind with Jackson, and then moved away, trudging over earth that crunched beneath their feet as they ground glass and rocks together. The cold clawed at her skin like a living thing, stealing her warmth. She'd be warm enough soon.

When they reached the farthest edge of the grounding field, Rose turned back to her and they faced each other. "Ready?" She asked the question in a light voice, trying to pretend she wasn't worried.

Lena wasn't embarrassed by the tears that flowed down to drip off her jaw. She'd earned the right. She swiped at them anyway and took a deep, shuddering breath. "Ready," she answered firmly. "Now go back to Jackson. I don't want you caught in the field."

She took a deep breath, setting herself as Rose retreated. Lena could feel the Dust swarming, moving to protect her tissues from the discharge. She could feel the charge pulse within, moving eagerly to release. What would a release of this magnitude do to the delicate life within her?

Protect her. It wasn't the begging request she'd made of the Dust back at the gorge when she'd been lost and devastated. It was an expectation. *Protect her.*

She'd had a plan…

Alex. Without thinking, she reached with her mind. She wanted him. Not because he could change anything for her or protect her from what she'd done, but because he was her comfort. Having him, knowing he was in the world with her, made bearing the burden of her failures easier.

Alex. She would have that comfort now, whenever she needed it. She knew she could. She believed it. She tried again, pushing further.

She couldn't think about the danger of pushing now, before she grounded. The Dust would protect their daughter. She needed a touch of him before taking the risk of discharging so much energy. She wanted a moment to feel him. She needed to know he was still in the world with her.

"Alex." She strained against the limits of her mind and the pain the dust had been holding back stirred, rose again as black tendrils unfurling into her mind. They stabbed deep. Where was he? How far?

Then it was there, a bright awareness, tinged with pain, but unmistakably Alex. It was a fleeting glimpse, like a gasp of air dragged into starving lungs. He was slipping away. The cold rage stirred in her heart.

Enough! Enough? Yes, it was. Enough grief, enough doubt. She knew he was there. She knew she could reach him. He was right there. *Help me.* She demanded it of the Dust and the dark, curled energy within her. The Dust wanted to help? Let it help now. She pushed harder, holding her breath now, bearing down and not caring that the charge within her had grown to pulsing white light like a beacon in the night as her body prepared for the discharge that could devastate her. She ignored the distant voices urging her to let go. She only wanted to hear one.

"Alex!"

He was right there.

"Lena?"

She let her head fall back and let go. The Dust discharged with a flash unlike any other. There was noise, and pain, and then darkness.

ACKNOWLEDGMENTS

They say raising a child takes the dedication of an entire community. A book baby is no different. This book had a group of beta readers to whom I will always be grateful. You'll notice this final version of *Spark Awakening* is a bit different from what you all originally read. Those changes are due to your diligence and thoughtful comments. To Penny Bencomo, Jenn Call, Tim Call, Jennifer Cruz, Genesis Davies, Amy Riddle DeClerck, Caroline Gill, Crystin Goodwin, Emily Haney-Caron, Lisa Hilgenberg, Rebecca Norman, Alicia Porter, Trisha Rohal Tunis, and Ann Marie Walsh: you each touched this book in countless ways and I am eternally grateful for your time and friendship.

My family also had more than a little influence on the making of the book. Whether it is through cheers of support, challenges to characters and plotlines, or babysitting, you have all always been there. Thank you!

My editors at Finish the Story are amazing and patient. Thank you Bryan Thomas Schmidt and Claire Ashgrove for your work and your friendship. I'd be lost without you!

My cover design is original photography and design by Regina Wamba at Mae I Design. She is amazing and always an inspiration. Thank you forever!

And my readers--oh, my readers! I really do read the notes and emails that you send, and they always seem to arrive just when I am struggling through a life or writing crisis. You keep me going. Thank you.

I'm sure I've missed someone. I'll probably wake in the middle of the night soon, sit bolt upright, and shriek your name in dismay! I'll let you know when it happens!

I am more grateful than I can express for the dedication you all put into this "little" book. I could go on...but there are a couple of cliffhangers to be resolved, so I'll get back to it. Much love to all!

ABOUT THE AUTHOR

Kate Corcino is a reformed shy girl who found her voice (and uses it...a lot). She believes in magic, Starburst candies, genre fiction, descriptive profanity, and laughter over a long meal with friends. She is a firm believer in the transformative power of second (and third...) chances. Cheers to works-in-progress of the literary and lifelong variety!

She currently lives in her beloved southwestern US desert with her family, three dogs, two cats, and a rotating cast of invisible friends. For more information, or to keep up-to-date on releases, free offerings, and general news, feel free to follow the author on her Facebook author page or her web page at www.KateCorcino.com